Crown
of
Beauty
and
Anarchy

A Retelling Of

SNOW WHITE
&
QUEEN MATILDA (12TH CENTURY)

CROWN
of
BEAUTY
and
ANARCHY

AURORA BELLE

AURORA BELLE

Finding history in a fairytale

To my Heavenly Father. I am nothing without You. May this book bring You honor and searching hearts closer to You!

To my sweet daughter. When I prayed to God for you, I was so humbled that He answered me. He gave me everything I asked for—"Beautiful on the inside, as well as the out"—and, wow, did He ever do a good job. I couldn't be prouder of you.

~ The Harmony to my Melody!
I love you.

To the one who feels unloved. May these words illuminate hope that you're truly loved by the One who has known you since the beginning.

Sometimes the echoes of our past try to define us, but it is our future that shapes how we are remembered!

"A tranquil heart gives life to the flesh, but envy makes the bones rot."
-Proverbs 14:30 ESV, Crossway Bible

One

EIRA

Whiteshire, England
1137 AD

TODAY WAS SUPPOSED TO BE DIFFERENT.

Instead of a party and enjoying a celebration, Eira pushed the feeling of dread down with the last gulp of her fermented juice. She savored the tangy, tart currents lingering on her tongue. Licking her lips, she gazed at the jewel-encrusted goblet, noticing her bright red lips in the reflection. Whether bright red from the rubies casting their color back onto her, or red from her own skin, she couldn't tell. Her plump lips puckered, and she admired the curves they formed. She lifted them into a smile.

Her stomach clenched again, and she watched the corners of her lips fall. It didn't matter if she thought she was pretty, the queen made it very clear she wasn't. She placed the goblet gently down on the small round table beside her.

Eira tried to take in the great hall. A gentleman bumped Eira's right shoulder. Instantly, she was thankful her now-empty cup was secure on the table. She brushed off her shoulder with her fingertips, making sure to smooth down the delicate lace. It wasn't what she imagined her dress to be, but it was her best dress, and she didn't want it to get creased in the kerfuffle.

The man swiveled to say something. Eira hoped for an apology. Instead, he vanished, engulfed by the swarm of people surrounding her.

Her brows fell and Eira blinked. Twice. Forcing a smile, Eira tried to ignore his carelessness. How could he know who she was? That was why today was so important. The announcement that she would be officially brought to court as the regal Princess of Whiteshire. Perchance then people would give her the respect she was due or simply notice her.

Eira skimmed the crowd and wondered how her mother would have handled getting bumped by her subjects with no apology or recognition. She tsked herself. There was no doubt her mother would have captivated the room with boldness, grace, humility, and poise. The whispers of servants in the halls told her so. The memory of her mother's kindness lived in the memories around her. It was in the echoes of the Great Hall itself. She longed for those memories to be her own. Her muse was cut short.

Eira felt another whoosh of a servant breeze by on her shoulder. She sighed. Her eyes wandered the room, looking for anyone she could recognize. It fell on servants, merchants, members of the royal guard, and the townsfolk mingling about. She drank in the scene, following the movement of the guests' heads. Like bobbing apples in a wooden bucket, Eira watched as they mingled about. There were noble men and women, members of the church, servants, laborers, animal care takers, and others too. None that she recognized though. They were all strangers.

Eira was usually confined to her room and knew little to no one.

But not tonight! Tonight was going to be different. Her eyes eagerly ran along the large stone wall and found the head table where the queen sat. Her father was notably absent. Another more obvious absence was Eira's place at the head table. Typically, she never ate with her family at the table, but tonight she was to be honored there. Had her stepmother not known what today was to set her a place?

Eira's shoulders sank a little. Her gaze fell onto her family's crested banner hanging directly above the center of the table—conveniently above the queen. Eria frowned. Its vibrant and royal-blue color demanded the room. It stood at attention against the stark contrast of the cold stone wall around it, radiating strength.

She followed the stones' jagged path to the grand fireplace, which only added to the room's drama. She breathed in the smoky air. With each flicker of light the flames expelled, the embellishments of pure gold fibers seemed to dance on command in the image of her family's crest. The six lions seemed to roar their bravery, valor, and dominance all in a row, representing all the traits her family's legacy earned over the years. All the traits Eira seemed to lack.

Was she ready to be brought into society, into her father's court? Would she be able to face her people as the promise to lead her father's empire? After all, wasn't she 'nothing but a pale and weak girl' according to the queen? The pain of repeating those words shot through Eira's chest, tightening its grip on her already shallow breath.

She inhaled quickly, regaining her composure. Eira turned to move toward the small hallway leading out of the Great Hall. A booming voice rose above the crowd, and a throaty question stopped Eira dead in her tracks. Its icy sound froze the smoky room.

"What are you doing out of your chambers, child?"

Eira's eyes widened. She knew who the question was aimed at. Hushed whispers fell around the room, and suddenly, Eira felt even more alone. She scorned herself for thinking today would be different.

Swiveling toward the head table, Eira avoided eye contact and dipped into a low bow, acknowledging Queen Amara.

"Forgive me, m'lady. I was merely seeking my father. I assumed he would be with—"

The queen stomped on the floor with her heel, demanding the attention of the hall. A moment went by when Eira finally asked, "Shall I seek him elsewhere, Queen Mother?"

There were subtle gasps throughout the room. Eira kept her eyes as low as possible, but her brows forbade her and sinched together in arched defiance. Eira tsked herself a second time. She should be meek, humble—like her mother. Why then did she feel such a resentment coiling in her stomach?

Eira rolled her shoulders slightly to ease the tension building in them. Whether her stepmother liked it or not, today Eira was to be presented to court as Whiteshire's only princess and heir. Princess of Whiteshire, daughter of King Geoffrey V. Sucking in a deep breath, Eira closed her eyes and eased her question out slowly and controlled.

"Milady, shall I seek my father elsewhere?" Eira let the question hang dead in the air, as lifeless as one who dared question the queen in such a manner.

The clank of a few chalices on wooden table slabs echoed in the large room, and the smell of freshly baked goods wafted toward her, taunting her empty stomach.

The queen cleared her throat and Eira stiffened.

"Your father wishes not to sup today." Queen Amara paused, bringing the eyes of the entire room to them. "Seems he has nothing to celebrate," the queen continued. A deep, throaty laugh ricocheted off the stones, seeming to close in on Eira. "Actually, he was in quite the sullen mood, as I recall." The evil cackling laugh bit at Eira's bowed posture, threatening her to stand and face the queen square in her eyes.

Bile rose from Eira's stomach. She gulped it back down. Despite it being her birthday, Eira couldn't stand the way Queen Amara talked about her papa. What hurt even more was the deafening silence of her father's people.

Would the people of Whiteshire allow the queen to speak of their king with such ill-regard and disrespect? Did they fear her that much? Not one person volunteered to be the 'hue and cry' from the mung that surrounded her. *How could that be?*

Clearly, the king wasn't here to defend himself or Eira. Why should they defend Eira, a stranger? Her clothing was not extravagant like a real princess's should be. In the eyes of the people, the queen was speaking to a peasant, and the queen knew it. Or perhaps they did know and were ashamed. She could not tell.

Queen Amara hissed. "Be gone with you! Go back to where you belong."

Eira stood a little higher and puffed out her chest as best as she could. This is where she belonged! If Papa wasn't here to stand up for her, Eira would have to do it alone. Eira lifted her eyes and met the queen's gaze dead-on. This was a forbidden move. One that could result in immediate death. The room gasped, but Eira didn't care. She was determined to let her people know she was Whiteshire's princess, worthy of being respected, just as much as Queen Amara.

Eira grinned. "As you wish, Your Majesty."

Holding her head up high, she squeezed her shoulders together and turned her back on the queen, leaving Queen Amara to fume and sputter like a hot kettle over fire. Eira did not return to her chambers as commanded. Instead, she veered down the corridor adjacent to the Great Hall, determined to find her Papa.

Two

IT WASN'T LONG BEFORE SHE HEARD HIS FAMILIAR VOICE.

"Eira." Her papa snatched her arm and tucked it in the crook of his own.

"There you are, Papa!"

Eira quickened her step to fall in line with her papa, who, she noted, was walking rather quickly.

"The queen is quite upset. I dare say, I've left her in quite a disarray. She'll be even more upset to find me speaking with you." Eira giggled. "But how could she expect me to be alone and stuffed in my chambers on such a fine day? Besides, you promised, Papa!"

She glanced up at his rugged features and hoped to catch a glimmer of laughter in his eyes. Alas, there was none. He was stoic and his expression as still as the creek she'd seen weaving through the forest near the castle. *Strange.*

Eira lovingly patted her Papa's arm. She smiled. Even though the queen made it difficult for her to spend time with him, she knew Papa would make time for her today, regardless of his duties.

Her thoughts sprang back to what the queen said. Was there any truth to it? Did Papa not want to be with her after all? She stole a glance at him. His stoic look had deepened to a scowl. Perhaps something else was troubling him?

He gave a slight tug on her arm, which brought her back to the present. Lit by candlelight, the hallways had a warm, golden hue, though the cold stones sapped the mood. The juxtaposition brought her senses back to when she was young. She would sneak out to play in the cold corridors, bringing along a dark wool shawl, the color of her inky hair. It served two purposes: One, not to be seen when blending into the shadows. And two, warmth when hiding in a cove or nook until someone passed her by.

Her thoughts were interrupted by Papa's voice echoing off the stone walls.

"Where were you?" Before she could give an answer, he continued with a grunt. "It doesn't matter now. I have everything in order, and we need to hurry. We don't have much time." His words came out low, quick, and husky.

"Time for what, pray-tell?" Eira whispered in a playful way. "Are you planning something special? For a special *grown* girl of yours?"

She couldn't help but lift her face into a grandiose smile. Turning down the corridor, Papa's face was immediately illuminated by the nearest candle. There was no smile matching hers. Pain was etched into his features, like dried mud between crevices of bricks. She almost tripped from what she saw pass through his eyes. *Was that terror?*

"Something's terribly wrong. Isn't it?" Her voice hitched as she slowed her pace.

"Eira." He leaned into her. Their steps becoming one as he whispered in her ear. "Yes, there has been some news." He paused. "King Henry has died."

Eira gasped. "How tragic, Papa." Her left hand fluttered to her chest. "I feel bad now. I was terribly rude and challenged Queen Amara in her deepest misery. Her father. Dead. I couldn't imagine the hurt. I am so ashamed. She must feel awful that her father has died. We should go back to comfort her and celebrate the new king." Eira paused. "Wait. Who would be the new king since Prince William died at sea?"

Tugging on Papa's arm, Eira pondered who could be the next successor to England now. She attempted to swing him back toward the Great Hall, but his strong arms didn't budge. His stride never ceased.

"I don't mean to alarm you," Papa said. "You need to be quiet. Don't say another word until I tell you. Follow me in silence. Do you understand?"

Eira's concerned eyes turned to meet his and jumped from one of Papa's irises to another. *Had he gone mad?*

Papa's index finger went to his lips. "Shhh," he whispered.

Instantly Eira's mind started to race, but she calmed herself. If it was one thing she knew, it was to trust her papa's lead. Trying to relax, she bobbed her head in a nod.

With a whoosh of dirty hems, she followed him. The sound of their feet shuffled along the walkway, echoing down the corridor with rhythmic precision. With every beat, or swoosh of her skirt, another silent word was left unspoken between the two of them until Eira's step faltered on the edge of a marble slab that was slightly lifted. It jolted her. Papa caught her and before she could say thank you, he lifted his eyebrows and fingers to his lips. "Shh," he silently motioned.

She gave a curt, unspoken nod.

So many questions swirled in her mind. This was not a game like she was young. This was much more serious. Eira snuck another glance at Papa's profile as he continued to propel them forward.

There was a reason why the kingdom called him 'Le Bel'. He was undoubtedly handsome. Time had not been nice to her beloved papa. His admirable and sturdy features had permanent lines of weariness in them now, yet his clothing was still arrayed in regal elegance. Such a sad contrast.

Eira dropped her gaze and stared at the floor tiles disappearing under her dress. A nagging thought caused a pinch in her heart. *I'm to blame for him being in so much pain. If only I had died with my mother, then he wouldn't have had to marry that miserable queen. He would be happier without me.*

Perspiration started to soak through her garments. Eira slipped her left hand out from holding Papa's arm. She reached into her bubble-bow and patted her prayer book. She sighed. It was still in her pocket where she put it. This was one of the best gifts her papa had given her for her birthday last year. She watched her footing as they wound up the narrow staircase. This was the last ascent until his bedchambers.

Her father led the way, but as they approached, Papa kept looking back at Eira to make sure she was close behind him. Light flickered in the slight breeze they created. It sent shivers down her arms. Her eyes caught hold of each candle nestled in a sunken space along the curved walls. They were getting closer.

Nearly running into her papa, they came to an abrupt stop. She peered around him, seeing his bedchamber doors. They had indeed arrived. Before she could smooth down her dress, Papa quickly pulled her into his room. Then, with his shaky fingers, he grabbed a key dangling by a leather cord near his chest and locked the door behind them both.

The turn of the key startled her, bringing back horrible memories of her crying, locked in her room for days, as punishment by the queen. She shook them away but gasped as Papa snatched her wrists up in one firm grasp.

"Prithee, Papa, why such haste? I have been good and quiet as you asked." Breathless, she searched his eyes for answers to such strange behavior. Was she in trouble? "What is it, Papa? What have I done? Is this a jest?"

Eira's eyebrows seemed to hug themselves when he didn't answer. Instead, he pulled her to his trunk by the far wall of the room, near the long window. Eira could feel his skin laced in sweat. Was he having another fit of fever? She eyed him closely and noticed sweat beading on his forehead.

"Papa? Are you alright?" she whispered.

Without even a glance in her direction, Papa released her wrists as he worked the trunk with the key he used to lock his door. It, too, clicked open. He flipped the heavy lid, and dust danced in the light near Eira's nostrils. Wriggling her nose, she suppressed a sudden onset to sneeze.

Her lips begged to form questions like, *Why the intense urgency? What is so important in the chest that made him act so strangely? And why must I stay silent?* She knew her coming out into society as the royal Princess of Whiteshire and only heir was a unique experience, one she had never witnessed. But this ... this was not how she imagined the day to go.

A gentle pull and soft rattle of the door handle made the hair on the back of Eira's neck stand straight in response. They both paused, motionless. Eira's eyes widened as she suddenly realized her papa had never locked his bedchamber door before today.

Perhaps someone followed us. Perhaps I must stay silent because Papa doesn't want anyone to know where we are going. She shook those thoughts from her mind—but they persisted with each rattle. Eira's throat went dry. She gulped, but her tongue stuck to the roof of her mouth.

Papa was too busy rummaging in the chest again to pay attention to the fact that she was losing color in her skin. Her eyes fixed on the door handle attempting to open again. If someone was following them, perhaps *she* was in some kind of danger too.

The room dimmed, and Eira's vision tunneled. Suddenly, Eira could feel the nervous fear exuding from her papa. Invading thoughts screamed through Eira's silent eyes as she finally was able to lock onto Papa's. *What do you fear, Papa? What is happening?*

Her questions were replaced by the sound of the rattling door handle growing louder. Clearly, there was no time for answers.

Tears welled as speechless words flowed through the two of them. She followed Papa's gaze to his hands. There, in his palm, were coins, a crumpled looking piece of paper, dried food, and his dagger. Taking a piece of thick wool from the trunk, he quickly wrapped the items, tying them off with a linen string. He placed the small package into her hands.

The rattle at the door ceased, and she let out a breath in time for Papa to wrap her in his arms, engulfing her. Silent questions swirled in her mind as his musky scent whirled around her. *How long has he been planning this for? Did Papa know all along this was how my birthday would go?*

The sharp hair of his beard scratched the soft skin on her cheek and brought comfort to her. The smell of garlic and leather tightly wrapping around her with each squeeze of Papa's arms made her feel at home. Dropping her chin into the crease of his shoulder, she sucked in his smell, his strength, his love. This was her loving, protective, beautiful Papa.

A muffled whimper escaped his lips and almost undid Eira entirely. Tears spilled from her eyes. She loved these big hugs as a child. Why, then, did this one feel like a ball of chains wrapping around her?

Was this—

She pulled away from him.

"Is this goodbye, Papa?" She sniffed. Her brows creased with confusion and disbelief. Eira had never really seen her father carry such intense emotions before. Tears of joy, yes. But this was devastation. This was deep sadness. This was serious indeed. Before she could utter the questions filling her mind, Papa spoke.

"Eira. You must leave." He looked down and started to twist something off his finger. "I don't have much time. I'm getting increasingly ill as you know. Aye, and you're—" He almost choked on his words before continuing. "You are so beautiful." He cupped her chin with his hands for a moment. Then he went back to working something off them again.

She noticed the red under his eyes and the gauntness in his face. She hated to admit how ill he had looked the past month.

"I understand you are getting ill Papa. But you are still strong. You have many years ahead of you." Eira attempted an assuring smile which went unnoticed.

"You're like your mother, you know." He sputtered something between a curse and regret. "Which means, you are no longer safe here. I've recently gotten word—"

A bang on the door cut him off.

"I—I don't understand. Why am I not safe? And why today of all days are we in danger?" Her throat squeezed, burning like an uncontrollable forest. She rubbed her eyes to stop the tears.

Papa lifted Eira's hands in his and kissed her knuckles. "My sweet little Eira. You have been kept from so much evil and dangers of the world. I thought by keeping you hidden, that would keep you safe, so I went along with the queen to keep you unknown to the kingdom. But I see her plan now. Oh, how I was so wrong." Papa shook his head. "Alas, you are old enough to know the queen's envy for power is beyond my control anymore. She is in line to become Queen in King Henry's stead."

"But that is not our kingdom Papa. Why should it matter to us."

"It is much worse than I originally feared. Especially now that King Henry has died. I fear there will be a war coming..." Papa voice trailed, and he had a faraway look in his eyes before saying, "Though the world will tempt your heart to become black as ebony—"

A louder bang caught both their breaths. She had a feeling he wanted to say more, but he squeezed her hand and looked up toward the ceiling as if asking for help from God himself. His eyes pinched together, releasing his own tears. An ugly form of desperation tucked his eyebrows up toward heaven, then dropped when he caught Eira's questioning gaze.

"Eira." He smiled, pointing at her heart and still holding her hands. "You must remember. Remember what your mother told you. It will guide you and help you." He kissed her knuckles once more.

Eira looked at her hands in his. She once knew this story. She got him to tell it to her every night until one day, he stopped. But the story had faded over the years, and Eira didn't have the heart to tell him she'd forgotten what her mother had told her.

"I will try, Papa." Her voice sounded small as she nodded like his good little girl—as if this day were happy and full of laughter. A day she imagined having today.

Not this. She did not want this.

Eira swept her eyes to his white knuckles wrapped around her tiny fingers and held back more tears. What if she couldn't remember? Would a tale from her mother really matter now? What if this was goodbye, what then? Why was she getting the feeling she would never see her papa again?

An icy chill ran down her spine as more voices rumbled and footsteps padded by the door. She could hear commotion not far from the bedchamber. Eira's legs began to shake. No doubt, she was paler than her sickly-looking papa now. He peeled her fingers back, opening her palm and forcing her fingers to spread.

"Here." His royal signet ring fell into the center of her hand. "A birthday gift for my special girl. My sweet little Eira White."

His smile filled her heart. It was the kind that crinkled his eyes and stayed with her for years.

"Don't forget what I said..." Papa whispered. "Never forget the words of your mother!"

He pressed her fingers, folding them around the cold curve of the ring. His warning rang through her like a convent bell, and her gaze dropped to her hand holding his ring—the King's signet and seal. The most important piece of jewelry over any other royal jewels.

She was not worthy, and certainly not ready for it to be hers. She was seventeen, and nowhere near prepared for the kingdom to be placed in her hands. The ring felt heavy, like lead pulling her down.

"Papa?" She searched his eyes.

Both of their faces shot toward the sound of a man's loud, muffled voice on the other side of the door.

"Quick, Eira." He grabbed her wrist and pulled her toward a servant's door hidden behind one of the thick tapestry curtains. "Take these and go." He pushed the items from earlier into her chest. "Don't look back," he demanded.

She tore her eyes away from her papa and looked at the door leading her away from him. "I can't leave you, Papa. I'm—I'm not ready."

"I will send for you when it is safe. Head to the eastern kingdom. I will try and send men I trust to meet you there. Don't look back ... and remember the words of your mother. Promise me, Eira!"

She nodded.

Pulling Eira back into one more embrace, he whispered, "I love you, Eira. I will always love you. Now go!" He shoved her into the passage.

"Wait—"

Eira watched as Papa's-stained tunic from her salty tears vanished, and the door swung shut. Separating her from him. Leaving her alone in complete darkness with only her questions to keep her comfort.

Everything's happening too fast. What is all this about? How am I going to an Eastern Kingdom when I have never been there before? How will I know who to meet once there? Who am I running from? Is the threat the Queen or King Henry's kingdom? Or worse, her own people and her own kingdom? How long shall I be gone for? How will Papa reach me when I am to return? What are they going to do to Papa once I'm gone?

Thoughts spun her dizzy. But Papa told her to go, and she would obey. Reaching up with her left hand in the pitch black, she touched the cold, damp stones around her to get her bearings. She took a step, then another.

All she wanted was to be with him for her birthday. A dreadful feeling of loneliness swept over her, and her legs became leaden. Feeling the hard ring in her right palm, she took another step, then another, and then another.

The thought of turning back suddenly took her captive. She stopped and faced where she came from. She blinked into the dark space and scratched her hand. Her papa—the king—decided to throw her out of his kingdom. He thought she was unsafe and gave her the signet in secret. Perhaps he didn't trust his kingdom or his guards any longer?

Swinging herself back, Eira faced forward and cautiously took more steps. Even if she wanted to push the door open, she was too weak to do it on her own. She pressed both palms into the cold stone wall as she walked on to balance her foothold. It seemed to calm her. Or at least make her feel a bit more in control of the situation. She started to pray that her papa would feel the warmth of her love through the stones. She took another step, then another. She continued to press into the blackness before her.

"I love you, Eira. I will always love you."

His last words brought a melody to her mind and illuminated her heart, directing her unknown path. The sound of her papa's voice played repeatedly in her head. Foot over foot, she continued to walk the passage toward safety.

Or perhaps, danger.

She couldn't tell…

All she knew was that her life would never be the same.

Three

OWEN

PRINCE OWEN WILLIAMUS OF GWYNEDD FROM THE TERRITORY
of Wealas noticed the scent of a wood fire burning through the thick
trees. His gaze followed a billow of smoke dancing on the treetops,
mingling with the woolly clouds, each slowly turning into pink-and-
gray hues.

Owen heaved a deep sigh of relief. The map marked his way
perfectly to the final stop before entering the city of St. Swithun's
shrine at the Winchester Cathedral. He tucked the worn piece of
parchment back into his brown leather bag.

From what he could see, the trek to the cosh wasn't too far. He
would be content to finally rest in the quaint home. This had been
such a long journey, and no doubt his horse needed a break too.
Perhaps a good rub down and some water. He patted Absalom's mane.

"We're almost there, ol' boy." Owen clucked his tongue, then
kicked his horse into a gallop.

Drawn away from the cosh to the canopy of trees to the sky, his
eyes observed each brush stroke, each shape and puff of white cloud
suspended high above him. *Aye. It is beautiful here.*

To Owen, the heavens were a slender piece of glass separating man from God. Such remarkable beauty transpired when the sun rose or set on this prism of glass. This 'prism', as he called it, produced a splendid array of colors for every eye to behold. It was breathtaking. Owen often pondered on how it was a nightly gift from his Maker.

Approaching the cosh, the sky changed, becoming darker and deepening in tone. A shiver ran through his body. The blue suddenly turned green. The pink turned purple. It was creating a stunning sunset. At least he knew that with a sunset, a sunrise was soon on the horizon. His eyes glistened.

'God, you are the same yesterday as you are today. I thank thee for your steadfast love and faithfulness. I Thank thee for this beautiful sunset as a reminder of Your goodness. What a marvelous spectacle to commence my journey!' Owen mused.

Owen hesitated and then tried to correct his last few words to God. This wasn't completely the end, of course. He still needed to visit the Holy place and receive his miracle. Originally, he wanted to go all the way to Jerusalem. But with his father's health, he couldn't tempt fate with how long his journey had already taken him. He had been away for months. More than he anticipated.

Thinking of his father made Owen suddenly sit up straighter. Pulling up on his reins, he slowed Absalom. His mind turned to his sister again. Focusing on the path swaying ahead of him, he felt the colors around him begin to fade. This time, words refused to stay within the walls of his mind and spilled into the chilly air surrounding him.

"God, I don't know what I have done to deserve what happened to my sister, but prithee, bring me peace. Give me assurance. Provide for me deeper understanding, healing, and—" His voice became exasperated as he slowed his horse almost to a stop. Absalom's head pulled at the reins in protest. "Perchance, you may provide for me a miracle. Relieve me of my guilt if anything, Heavenly Father. But above all, please help me find my sister. I need to know if … if—"

A thought, like a dagger pierced at his heart.

…it's my fault she's gone.

She was just a wee young lass when his sister left—or was taken—*God forbid*. No one really knew what happened. Upon searching, Owen noticed there were some signs of an intruder. But then there was a letter left saying she had gone to fetch some berries but never returned. Some say the letter was forged, others say that it was real.

But the guilt of him being the reason she was gone held on with vengeance. Leading up to the moment she went missing mirrored fog, blurring the lines of reality and the unknown—even potential danger lurking in front of oneself. It stung to know the last words out of his mouth to his sister was that he hated her and wished she was never born. How could he know what truly happened or why she was gone? Only God knew. And the only way to know what happened is to cautiously move forward into the unknown. Regardless of what could be revealed in the fog ahead of him. That is why he was here—to know the truth and find his sister.

Absalom nudged his head to the side, and Owen adjusted the reins, giving him some slack. Owen stared at the small home ahead. He tucked his heels gently into Absalom's sides. The view of the cosh became more vivid with each trot.

Perchance the answers and salvation he longed for were mere steps away … or the miracle of his sister being found alive and unharmed after all these years was about to reach his ears. How could he ever know the plans of God?

Breath, as loud as Absalom's pants, heaved out of Owen. Was his sister in trouble before she left? He could have helped her! But if she were in trouble, why didn't she say anything? And why not allow Owen to help her? Was his sister taken against her will? Or did she willingly leave behind her father, brother, and kingdom for good, not wanting to be a part of it any longer? If so, why?

Ugh! Owen scratched his head.

Nothing made sense, and he was running out of time. Father was dying, and before his death, he had to find out what happened to his sister. Otherwise, his father would force Owen to find himself a wife to be fit to rule in his sister's place.

Aye.

He would find answers about his missing sister first or die trying!

Letting out a grunt, he gripped the reins and pulled them back. "Woahhh, boy!"

Absalom slowed to a stop. Owen was finally at the evening's destination. The small cottage now before him looked peaceful.

He leaned and whispered for Absalom's ears only, "Lord willing, the people of this small home are friendly and just as peaceful."

Many had done this pilgrimage before him, which concluded in miracles, answers, and tales of great victories. Would this journey be the same for him? He supposed only the Lord could know.

Clenching his fists around the reins and swinging his leg over Absalom's back, Owen dismounted. For better or worse, he was eager to find out.

Four

QUEEN AMARA

Q<small>UEEN</small> M<small>ATILDA</small> A<small>MARA WENT INTO A ROOM OFF HER PRIVATE</small> bed chambers, typically used as a personal prayer closet. While Whiteshire Castle was designed for such a place, this was no prayer closet for her. Queen Amara's lip curled with disgust. This small room was designated as her inquiry chamber, and that was all. No God deserved her pleas or the beggings of a queen.

She lifted her gloved hand and dusted the cobwebs running along the wainscotting. Only one person in Whiteshire was privileged to have an invite to her private chambers, and that was Herrick, her chamberlain. She preferred his title of personal spy over private secretary, but that was too obvious. A useless, disposable henchman, except for one matter, one dear to her heart:

Her beauty.

Running her fingers over the silver curls framing the crystal-clear mirror before her, she mused. This was finery her old kingdom couldn't render, nor could her previous, even more useless husband offer either.

Memories of being a mere child and married off to a stranger stole her breath. Her left eye twitched, and her nose suddenly felt itchy. She supposed she did eventually grow to appreciate her young husband. But those thoughts were minimal in the grand scheme of things.

She shook her head and flicked the dust off her finger. It was all in the past now. No sense dwelling on something that was not worthy of her time. She was here. This was her moment. Her father was finally dead, and she would be empress. With the sworn oaths her father made, it was already assured and in motion. The only thing getting in her way was her husband and his pesky heir.

Queen Amara picked up the parchment paper with the wax seal broken and read the letter again from off the side table.

"...we regret to inform you that your father, King Henry I, has died..."

Queen Amara smiled. Her destiny was being fulfilled. She had built one kingdom with her own wits and kingdom connections, but never got the recognition owed. He got the crown; he stole the accolades of all her conquests when he was really a coward and hid behind her. She faced battles on the home front while he fled. But not her! She made his kingdom great and faced enemies just for him to leave her in death.

"Your Majesty..." Herrick stood at the door.

"What, Herrick, can't you see I am busy!"

"My apologies, My Queen. I wanted to merely see how you faired with the news of your father."

"Oh, that. It is terrible and wonderful news, as I am sure you'll agree." She awaited his proper response with eager ears, but he never spoke. "Is that your response? Muteness. Are you an idiot? Or just wish to die?" she hissed.

"I—I don't know what to say at this news, Your Majesty."

"You say, 'Long live Empress Amara'," she yelled.

Startled, Herrick ran in the room to her and lay on the floor prostrate before her feet, groveling, pitifully spilling the words 'Long live Empress Amara' over and over again.

"That's better."

Queen Amara soaked in the moment. She was determined more than ever to never live behind the crown of a *king* again. She would, again, build a marvelous kingdom on her own. But this time, she would get the recognition, she would rule and be known as the true conqueror. Queen Amara smiled. She would now officially hold the title of empress, and rule alone. Not even her husband could say that.

It was made for HER.

The side of her lip lifted. The English kingdom and all the realms surrounding it, including Whiteshire Castle, would be hers and hers alone from now on. Her father's death sealed that!

The beaded pearls, laden with silver, suddenly caught Queen Amara's eye. It was the finest in French designs that her husband owned. But she had plans for those to be hers alone too.

She skimmed the room. This was the best room in the castle, besides her throne room. Being one of the richest women in the realm, she deserved no less. She reminded Herrick of that often. How fortunate he was for the queen to allow him to sit in her presence at all.

She moved over to the side of the room, leaving Herrick still lying on the floor. She bent closer to the Looking Glass, admiring her red-painted lips. Queen Amara made a mental note to thank Gertrude, her healer, for the newest concoction of red ochre, carmine, and swine fat. She touched her cheek. Maybe she would tell Gertrude that the queen had considered her newest coloring made of saffron flowers and rouge. If it was the deepest red possible, she'd be willing to pay a hefty price for it.

Queen Amara studied herself in the mirror again. She gasped. The pasty flour mixture covering her cheeks had somehow been wiped off. She licked her fingertips and tried to rub the spot where her pure white skin had vanished.

Dragon's breath! It is too spotty now.

She sighed and lifted her chin. Her skin was still whiter than Eira's, and that was all that mattered. Now ready, Queen Amara was able to play her little game for the day. She eyed the door as if to summon Herrick's assistance.

"Ready, Herrick?"

"Yes, Your Grace." Herrick stood, wiping the dirt off his garments, and drew near to the mirror.

"Looking Glass, Looking Glass on the wall, who in this land is the fairest of all?"

No answer came, only silence.

Queen Amara cleared her throat.

"Herrick?" She swooned. "You know this is our little game. Come now. Play along. Answer your queen." A wide and even smile spread across her face, revealing her white teeth.

Herrick held his tongue, fidgeting with the hem of his tunic. Whipping her head around like an owl, Queen Amara faced him.

"Herrick." Her voice snapped like the jaw of a dragon. "This is where you say, '*You, My Queen, are fairest of all*.'"

Herrick coughed.

She stalked three steps toward him. Wrapping her long, painted nails around the front of his tunic, Queen Amara lifted Herrick off the ground, clenching the plain, stiff fabric deeper into her skin. His face was now only inches from the queen's.

"Answer your queen, Herrick." She paused. "And be honest. I can see you are holding back." A peculiar smile gradually parted her cacked lips, separating her pale features again. It was a warning, but his eyes stayed on the ground.

As she squeezed harder, Herrick began to choke, spitting out the words, "You, my beautiful queen, are fair. It is true."

"Yeeesss," she purred, wanting more.

"But Eira White is—" Herrick gulped. The clicking sound of his throat was like claws down her spine.

"Eira White is what, Herrick?" She dropped Herrick into the chair beside her.

He avoided eye contact while spilling out words foreign to her ears. "...Is a thousand times fairer than you."

Queen Amara's hands instantly fluttered to her throat as if someone were choking her. Sweat beaded on her forehead. She gasped for air. When she finally caught her breath, her eyes pinned on Herrick's, burrowing in as if she could stab him to death with each iris. Stab him until the words she desperately needed to hear bled out from his mouth.

Words she *must* hear.

Queen Amara pulled her shoulders back, rigid and tall. She breathed in once, then out. She felt the corset digging into her ribs, the strain on her diaphragm and crackle of her spine as she elongated herself even more.

Her hands fell elegantly in front of her. Queen Amara tactfully evened out her breaths like she'd been taught as a child—repeatedly. Gathering her wits, her father's words were the rhythm of air in her lungs.

"It is never a king or queen in rage you should fear, for they are showing you the only cards they must play. But it is the quiet ones you must fear. They are the deadliest."

"Herrick, my dear. Are you ill?" She swallowed.

His head stayed bowed. "No, m'lady."

"I see."

Like gangrene weeding through her veins, a green envy began to fester in her blood. She wished she could rid her veins of the disease it carried, the poisoned anger like hot molten lava through her heart. And the focus of that anger was not on her wretched servant, but on that of *Eira White*. She could spit out her name. Spit it in the dirt. Why did she insist on always getting in Queen Amara's way!

Queen Amara blew out a huff and put her hands on her hips, pacing the old wooden floors.

Eira was heir to the throne, and the only thing in the way of Queen Amara gaining the official title of empress. Plans were in place to rid her of the menace. But now she must take her title as fairest?!

"How dare Eira be more beautiful than me, Herrick? She's had the king's heart this whole time—is that not enough? She's had no toil, no pain, no regret, no incredible hurt to her name. She is not worthy of this kingdom. And now, she claims my beauty too—MY beauty. Never! It's not fair."

Her eyes shifted over the glass, seeing her reflection out of her peripheral vision, but she darted them away and narrowed them on Herrick once more. Queen Amara's jaw muscles pulsed to the rapid beating of her heart. She had to make this go away. There was no way she would let some petty, sniveling, little rat live any longer.

"Well, Herrick. I will have to move my plans up a little sooner than expected." She placed her fingers on her chin and pinched its tip. "I could maim the pesky girl."

Her eyebrows cinched further together, and she pursed her lips, letting ideas fill her mind.

"People might wonder who the poorly disfigured child was, m'lady. They might show her pity and ask why she was deformed, who she was, how they could help and aid her?" Herrick's voice was almost a whisper.

Though Herrick was right. Those questions would do her no good.

She shook her head. "Yes. There would be too many questions. Too many questions mean a possibility I could be exposed for having some part in it. That would certainly not do. You are right for once."

Think, Amara! Think. What can be done with Eira?

Queen Amara flung her hands, gesturing with each pace along the wood-lined floor. "Keeping her in obscurity, hoping the measly girl would be forgotten, has clearly not worked. She must be put away for good. Did you see her today, Herrick? The girl had some audacity to defy me in front of everyone. What is it to say she will not do it again, and perhaps win over the court with confidence? We must act quickly!"

Herrick nodded in response.

Banishing her away from the kingdom will not be enough, Queen Amara thought. Her fingers found her chin again, and she pinched harder. Queen Amara's eyebrows inched together even more until they bounced with excitement. Something clever came to her mind.

"Perhaps a more drastic plan needs to happen in order for the girl to be completely forgotten..."

"Oh, My Queen. What plan is that?" Herrick feigned interest.

"Yes. *Yes.*" A grin formed on her lips. Quite the plan was forming... "Eira White will be forgotten, Herrick. Simply forgotten!"

Completely vanished, she dared say. *As if she never existed.*

Her left eyebrow lifted, and the grin formed into a full smile. Queen Amara's heart raced and thumped hard with her thoughts.

Eira.

Little Eira White.

Must die.

Queen Amara stopped pacing. Her eyes found her reflection in the mirror again. Glued to the mirror, she barely turned her face toward Herrick. She continued, "Find your best huntsman and bring him to me."

Herrick fidgeted.

Queen Amara craned her neck carefully. Then, she tilted it, her eyes challenging Herrick's to reject her proposal.

"Herrick?" Queen Amara's question of obedience hung in the air between them, simple and sweet. Sweet like poison hidden in fragile fruit.

"Yes, Your Majesty."

"You have my permission to leave now."

Herrick hesitated. Instantly, Queen Amara's fake smile crashed like a castle gate being charged in. A rumble roared from her throat, and she screamed, "NOW!"

Queen Amara rushed Herrick out of her chambers and slammed the door. Her breathing was rapid and difficult as she pushed herself off the door.

"*Little Eira White*"—she mimicked the king's affectionate term for his daughter— "will not get in the way of me becoming empress."

Queen Amara tsked at the air. She allowed the girl to be present in their lives for far too long. She hadn't expected the girl to become so beautiful upon the day she was to be presented as heir. Something she could almost allow and seemingly live with, but now with her father's death, things have drastically changed. Having the crown of Whiteshire and England would ensure her claim to being Empress. Not simply the Queen of England alone. She would not fail at this conquest and there was no time to waste. A roaring siege of anger burst within her, spouting out in the form of a venomous promise.

"I will become an Empress. Not the bishop, not the king, and not even Eira White will stop me! You've overstayed your welcome, little girl, and I've worked too hard for you to take all that is mine. It's either you or me. And when you are dead—well, it will only be me left, won't it?" She cackled to herself.

Blinking back a stinging sensation in her eyes, she stood to her full height and squared her shoulders toward the mirror.

"So help me, I will do everything in my power not to let that weak girl steal all I have left."

Her hands began to shake, and the queen's lips threatened to quiver. She tried to purse them together as she approached the mirror. But all she could see was the image of her as a little girl standing before her.

Small.

Weak.

Fragile.

Her father loomed over her childish image in the background. His angry face threatened her.

"You're going to be a failure like your mother." His gnarly voice echoed in her mind. *"You're so ugly. How did I get such a leech of a daughter? A good-for-nothing piece of stale bread is all you are! Good enough to be thrown at the dogs! You hear me? I should throw you to the dogs!"*

Queen Amara quivered. She knew what was coming next. His large frame came into view closer to her small frame. With his heavy hand, he would soon smack down hard, beating her. And beating her.

She blinked and clenched her jaw. Her hands were up over her head to protect herself from the imaginary blows. Immediately, Queen Amara sucked in a breath and went to strike the Looking Glass before her. But midair, it stopped. Lowering slowly, as if on its own accord. She could feel her hands trembling. She gently touched the mirror, stroking the fine features staring back at her. Her father's image was gone now; it was only her left in the room again.

She bit her lip and did her best to push out his brutal remarks. Lips quivering again, she stroked the young girl in the image once more. The glass was cold on her fingertips.

"I am the most beautiful." She examined herself in the glass. *"I am."*

Hearing her miserable voice made her memories freeze in time. Queen Amara watched her reflection as a single tear slid down her cheek. It loosened the pasty white cream covering her face, covering her scars. It carved out a single line of old, weathered-looking skin as it slid down.

"There's no need to be angry. I can fix it," Queen Amara said to her young self.

An image of her mother's sad face suddenly appeared like a ghost in her mind. After the regular beatings from her father, her mother would somehow find her and pick Queen Amara off the ground. Smoothing Amara's hair out of her face, she would help her sit on a chair in front of the vanity where she could see the damage her father had done to her little body. She remembered her mother would say, *"That's okay, darling. I can fix it."*

Though her mother's measly attempts at 'fixing' her father's mess all over her body never worked, Amara was happy about one thing. She grew familiar with her mother's tonics and concoctions to cover up the bruises and scars left on both of their bodies. Something she still held dear to this day. Their mending was a time they somehow grew to cherish. A time when they could relate and feel the same. It was all they shared.

"Soon, I'll be the only one beautiful, and the ruler over every man as Empress of all. No one can tell me otherwise."

She picked up a tiny, intricate container from off the dresser. With her fingertips, she dabbed the white concoction onto her face. Each swipe smoothed out where the insecurities had been exposed. The single line streaking her face would never be seen again. She closed the metal container with a snap and smiled at herself.

There, all fixed.

Queen Amara was now perfect. Completely covered, with not a single flaw remaining. Truth could no longer be exposed, and soon her future would be just as flawless. Lifting her arms up, she straightened the fabric dangling from her dress. Like inky rivers cascading down her shoulders toward her back, she smoothed her dress down and every detail down.

Queen Amara positioned her hands regally in front of her once again. Turning into a semicircle, she positioned herself toward the door. She was now ready to handle anything else the day had to throw at her.

Five

MASON

ARMS STEADY.

Aim, at ready.

"Who goes there?" Mason's voice demanded, halting the silent hush of the wind.

Perking his ears up like his hunting hound, a rustle in the bushes caught Mason's attention again. Positioning his bow toward the noise, he pulled his index finger and focused on the bush near an opening to a small path. Mason's arms pulled the recurve bow taut. He wanted every pound to count when he plunged his arrow into the unwelcome intruder.

"I come in the name of the queen." A weak, shrill of a voice bounced off the bark.

Mason could bet his horse on who that was.

"Weapons down, men." Hooves padded lightly through the bush as Herrick emerged and advanced onto the path. Mason noticed the fine linen clothing first. Pools of thick wool and linen with details of gold and flecks of silver were interlaced in the man's showy attire. The weight alone made Mason squirm. No fast movements would be obtained in that garment, which served Mason well if Herrick decided something sinister.

"If it isn't Sir Herrick Langston of Whiteshire. To what do I owe this great honor?" He tried not to laugh.

"I am the queen's advisor. Please. Weapons down."

Despite himself, Mason did as the queen's adviser said and lowered his weapon, releasing the tension in his bow. He remembered Herrick well. How could anyone not? A man who looked like a weasel, with a pointy nose, long, gnarly fingers, and messy hair was hard to forget.

Herrick was a backstabbing, sniveling whiner, and the queen's own pet. Everybody knew the slimy rat who shrank at the sight of the queen. It was hard to respect a man with no courage in him whatsoever.

Mason avoided going to the king's court, as most of the shop-keepers did. The chance to avoid the luxury of speaking to men like Herrick was all but forfeited. Often, they were only seeking to exhort taxes from Mason or his men. He growled under his breath.

Mason's lip lifted into a side grin at the thought of releasing his arrow and giving the man a startle—even to take out a small line of fabric enough to make the man shiver—but he refrained.

"Are you trying to get yourself killed?" Mason questioned. Squinting his eyes up at Herrick, Mason let out a dry shot. Then, lowered his bow.

"NO! I am most certainly not trying to get killed," he scoffed, then sat up higher on his horse. "Mason Barnett, is it?"

"That is I."

Mason watched as the fragile man's legs wobbled when Herrick dismounted from his horse.

"I've been searching for you most of the day. I believe you are the fur trader and tanner we've been looking for. It's been said to me that one of your men is the finest huntsman in all Whiteshire, despite the official title of course." He smirked before asking, "Do I hear correctly?"

Considering the man would be dead within seconds if the bow was still in Mason's hands, he would imagine the simpleton to be correct.

"Not bad, I suppose. We"—he waved one hand at his men— "can bring in fine quality hart for the queen, and she knows it." He almost let out his own smirk and snort but stopped. He was positive the queen had spies stationed in the realms of Whiteshire. She knew everyone and everything.

"It's perhaps the most sought-after meat in all of England and"— Mason stared hard at Herrick— "I can assure you; we only hunt on land that is permissible. We've not done anything illegal."

Mason, however, could hunt anywhere. He was untraceable, and had to hunt where the deer roamed, legal land or not. But he would not let that slip.

"Sir, in all due respect, 'tis a serious matter that the queen wishes to speak with you in direct confidence," Herrick said, craning his neck.

His shady gaze landed on Charles—Mason's apprentice and falcon trainer—who stood gripping his own bow. It was still locked on Herrick as his target, ready and waiting for Mason's cue to shoot.

"Which of you is the finest in your group?" Herrick's shaky voice let out a squeak before continuing. "I only need one and he must be the best."

All faces in his group of men spun to Mason. Mason licked his lips. He didn't want Herrick to know *he* was the best hunter without knowledge of what the queen's sudden interest in his talents was. Knowing the queen's character, it probably wasn't good news.

Before Mason could respond, Branson suddenly interjected, "That would be me, fine sir!"

Taking a step forward, Branson lowered his arrow. Mason's clenched fist flung to his mouth, and with his teeth, he bit down on his knuckles, suppressing a bout of laughter. *Foolish Branson.* Mason dropped his gaze to the dirt floor. *Silly boy.* Always looking to 'best' Mason in every opportunity without thinking first. A wee man of security, but big on competition.

However, if Branson wanted to get involved with the queen's men, Mason wasn't about to stop him.

Mason dropped his clenched fist and looked up with a smile. Perhaps this might be the perfect opportunity for Mason to get some much-needed respite. He relaxed his shoulders and watched Branson saunter his way toward Herrick.

As Mason eyed their interaction, he noticed something off about Herrick. Mason cocked his head. Something wasn't sitting right about this situation. He would let Branson pretend to be the best huntsman all he wanted—but something was about Herrick was off. As if sensing the fear in the eyes of the hunted elk, Herrick squinted and took a step forward.

There was a sneer and a glint in Herrick's eyes. Mason's gut twisted. *Indeed.* Something about this mission of Herrick's had a bad target on it, and it was his job to protect his men. So, in some way, he would have to figure out a plan to keep an eye out for Branson.

He twisted the leather in his belt with his finger and looped his thumb to secure it. He leaned on his back leg for support and watched the men carefully. *Yes, something was off.* Why wouldn't Herrick get a huntsman of the court to kill game for the queen? Why come all the way out to seek expert services like his? Perhaps sinister motives were in fact the nature in which he came to them. Mason's eyes furrowed. *That must be it.*

"He will not go alone!" Mason announced loudly. "I will attend if he's to assist you. We men never hunt alone."

And they didn't ... technically.

Herrick cleared his throat. "I beg your pardon, but this is a private matter."

Herrick leaned closer. "'Tis urgent. We only need one man! And your little interruption is wasting my time."

Mason calmly stood taller but clenched his fists by his sides. "I am Branson's boss, and you'll have both of us or none at all. If he leaves, I go!"

He could hear Branson try to intervene, but Mason ignored him. Herrick met his challenge and stared back at Mason. There was a beat of silence. A challenge of wills was exchanged.

Herrick curled his lip and spat. "Fine!" The stubby man stuttered toward Mason. The tip of his finger poked into Mason's chest. "You must come and return to the castle post-haste! Now!" The sour scent of vinegar from Herrick's mouth grew like a cloud of smoke, stinging Mason's eyes. "And stop wasting my time with your nonsense."

Mason avoided the response he wanted to make.

"Yes, sir." He blinked. "We shall close camp by nightfall, and on the morrow, Branson and I shall make ready to see to the queen's inquiry. You have my word."

"I am afraid 'tis not possible. At the queen's request, I must return with you now. Make haste and get your horse and gear ready." Herrick's eyes suddenly turned murky. "I will wait on the path and lead you there myself."

Six

EIRA

WHERE DO THESE OLD SERVANT HALLS LEAD?

With all the cobwebs Eira kept breaking, she was certain the corridor had not been used in a century, and that was probably why no one had noticed she was in there yet. Dust forced its way into her lungs. She coughed. Quickly, she looked back. Could they hear her?

Her head spun. The darkness made her dizzy. How long had she been walking? Blackness was before her and behind her. She wouldn't even know if she was going the right way. The path veered again, it seemed. Disorientated, she held still as a scream followed her, echoing from down the corridor. Had that come from her papa's bedchamber?

Papa?

The ceiling above her made the sound of cracking, followed by a crumbling sound, as if someone was walking above her. Dirt fell on her head and shoulders. Eira forced herself to move faster, away from the noise. No doubt her dried tears were now marks of black dirt caked onto her skin. Her limbs were heavy with weariness, and she stumbled on a stone sticking out from the dirt floor. Catching herself from the fall, she grunted. Eira felt hopeless. She was lost and confused, running from … what?

Stopping, she dropped to her knees. The back of her hand swiped her nose. No longer able to hold back the sniffles, she sneezed. Twice. Three times. She took the ring still digging into her palm and put it onto her index finger.

"I love you too, Papa." Her whisper seemed to swirl around her, unanswered. The echoes created a hollowness in her soul.

Sobs vibrated softly out of her. Her legs, her head, her lungs—and especially her heart—hurt. Deeply. She pressed the back of her hand against her lips to stop the sound of her pain from escaping. She had to stay quiet. She had to press on.

Standing, she pictured her papa when she was young, smiling and encouraging her to get up after she'd fallen into the garden. The rose bushes had scraped her knees badly, and she was bleeding. It didn't take long for her papa to convince her to get up and make her laugh. He could always make her laugh and somehow seemed to make everything better.

But not this time. It was his hands that pushed her out of the kingdom. Her papa's own hands. How can he help her now?

Tasting dirt in her mouth, she licked her lips. She was so thirsty. The path felt like a dusty tomb. She leaned her right side into the stone wall. Was she even strong enough for this journey?

She remembered overhearing servants talking about traders and merchants who were thieves coming to Whiteshire. The memory made her uneasy. Would she encounter them when she escaped? Perhaps she would be safer if she stayed within these dark walls?

No. Do not give up, Eira! Don't give in and let your heart turn dark.

Pushing herself off the wall, she kept moving. Stretching forth her shaky fingers, she cautiously patted the damp, frigid walls ahead of her. She shivered. She could feel a slight breeze. Perhaps she was close to the end of the hallway. She pressed on. Knowing night was coming and feeling the cool wisps of air, she wished for her wool shawl. Had she known she would be escaping, she would have prepared better. She could feel the cold seeping into her bones.

Bit by bit, Eira's steps carried her forward. The whole day flashed before her eyes. The only image that haunted her was of the queen. Truly the queen was the only one at the heart of all this. She had to be. Nothing else made any sense. No one else knew her in court to render her such evil. And with how the queen had ostracized Eira from the beginning and the frigid relationship she had growing up with the queen, she wouldn't put it past her.

Thinking back on her papa, she remembered that he had said someone wanted her dead. How could they want her dead? And the few who did know Eira—the few servants tasked to her—only showed love and kindness. But not the queen. If Eira were honest with herself, the only person she could imagine wanting her to be dead was the queen. But why? And why now?

Eira wasn't very good at the politics of royalty, seeing as she was forbidden from that education, but if she had to guess why she suddenly became a threat to the queen she would render it was due to Eira coming of age and being presented as heir to Whiteshire. But something still didn't fit. The queen could have easily killed Eira as a child if she so wished. So, why now? Did it have something to do with the queen's father dying? But what exactly?

I have always tried to be kind to her. What could I have done to warrant such hatred?

She held fast to the wool sack with the small dagger. Eira shook her head, as if to shake some very bad dreams away. At least Papa had given her a weapon. Too bad she didn't know how to use it.

She stopped and pinched the bridge of her nose, holding back another sneeze. The faint voice of her papa filled the dead air, calming her. *"Remember, Eira. Remember what your mother told you..."*

Her mother loved her, but what she said, Eira could not remember. And why does that matter now? She had no idea what lay ahead of her beyond the dark path, finally reaching the end and escaping Whiteshire Castle. It was the only home she'd ever known. Never allowed to leave, except now. Now, she was thrust out into obscurity. But perhaps Eira was made for such a time as this. The story of Queen Esther came to mind. But Eira was no queen like Esther. She was merely a forgotten princess.

She sniffed back more tears that threatened to well up, stinging her eyes. Regardless, her papa told Eira to escape and not look back. And that is what Eira intended to do.

She mustered enough strength to take another step. Pressing her way through the corridor, simple words of faith consoled her mind, sparking a little light into Eira's darkness.

"I love you, Eira. I will always love you."

Seven

QUEEN AMARA

WHERE IS HERRICK?

Scanning the crowd once more, the queen didn't see any sign of him. She clenched her teeth. *He should be back now.* She wanted Eira to go by nightfall. Releasing her jaw, she resumed a regal position.

With one long, pointed nail, she picked a piece of pig flesh from her teeth and ran the tip of her tongue along the front, licking them clean. Pig's heart was her guilty pleasure. She grinned, casting her eyes out into the crowd once more.

Movement from the corner of her eye caught her attention. Seilda approached the head table and quickly curtsied. She flicked her hand for Sielda to draw near. Queen Amara's eyes greedily followed her healer's new concoction of mixed fucus. Seilda placed the container in the queen's hand. Queen Amara couldn't contain how pleased she was.

"What has my healer delighted me with today?" She cracked open the container. "Yes..." Queen Amara sniffed the familiar scent of fishy oil but stopped abruptly and narrowed her eyes. Queen Amara huffed. "Will this be red enough?"

"Try it, Your Majesty, and see for yourself. It's the purest and deepest red I've found."

She dipped her pinky finger into the thick red coloring and lifted it to her lips, admiring how vibrantly red it appeared against her skin. "Yes, yes—this is perfect. Well done." She snapped the container shut and lifted a few gold chinkers from her purse. "Here. This is for your troubles."

"Of course, Your Majesty. No trouble at all." Seilda tucked the coins into her bubble-bow, dipped in a low curtsy, and like a slithering snake, weaved through the people back to where she had come. All without turning her back to the queen.

Queen Amara's eyes twinkled. Now she would have the reddest, most vibrant lips in all Whiteshire. As if a scream demanding attention, a thought pierced her ears: *It will be the reddest in all the kingdom, until precious Eira is dead. Then, I will smear her blood on my lips, and it will be the deepest red of all!*

"Where is Herrick?!" She slammed her fist onto the table, shocking those around her.

Queen Amara stood. Pinching her fingers together, she slid them tightly to make a sharp snap, signaling the minstrels to stop the music. Everyone halted their movements.

"I demand to know where Herrick is at once!" Her foot slammed into the floor at the head table as if to accentuate her demand.

A voice shrieked near the back of the great hall, and a small woman burst through the throng so the queen could see her.

"It's the king!" the women squealed. "Someone has attacked the king!"

Voices rose all around, filling the tall ceiling.

"I saw it with my own eyes!" the woman kept crying.

Ignoring the woman's pleas, Queen Amara stepped down from the head table and marched through the throng of people in the Great

Hall, out of the Bailey, and toward the corridor. Two guards followed closely behind her.

She would have to feign illness if the king had died already. Though he was gradually dying—thanks to Sielda's potions—he was showing more and more ill of late, as was their plan. Had the concoction been too strong in his morning tea?

His ultimate death now wasn't what she was expecting. *But doable,* she thought. Things could still work in her favor for timing. Pursing her lips, Queen Amara swung her head back and caught the eyes of Selida, who had already begun following. *Good.* The guards did not see the exchange, and she was pleased.

The poison that Seilda had given the king wasn't supposed to be strong enough to kill him so quickly. Had it done its job already? She peered back when they rounded a corner. Seilda smirked slightly, dipping her head in a nod, and the side of Queen Amara's lip responded with a curl.

"Tsk, tsk," Queen Amara mused.

Had their initial plan not fully worked and Whiteshire's beloved king and heir apparent were both found dead in one night, it would indeed be sad. *Such tragedy...*

Queen Amara suppressed the crackle rising from the pit of her heart. But her eyes glittered, revealing the deep green hiding within them. Maybe the crown would be hers sooner than planned. She pressed her ruby lips into a firm line. *No time to rejoice just yet,* she thought. She must appear in despair at the sight of the fallen king. After all, her beloved husband was dead.

The queen bit at the inside of her lips to keep from smiling, producing enough pain for her eyes to tear up. *Perfect,* she purred to herself.

Queen Amara burst into the king's bedchamber. She went to throw herself on the floor beside her dead husband in a theatrical scene of sadness but stopped abruptly. Then blinked.

Was he still *alive?*

Is he not dead?

Disgusted and barely able to breathe, she put her hand to her stomach in shock. Holding back the temptation to look at Seilda, she inwardly growled. Anger flared through her veins.

"What on earth is the meaning of this?" Queen Amara shrieked.

She threw her arms out and pointed first at her husband—alive—and *not* dead. King George was sitting on the bed, his hand on his head, most likely where a wound had been made.

She switched tactics and pointed at the wretched fool she noticed, writhing and lying on the ground, and wounded. "Who is this? I'll have you know, this ruckus has interrupted the Great Hall and *my* meal. What do you have to say for yourselves?" Queen Amara paused for theatrics. "And you?" Her eyes darted back and glared at her husband as more men and onlookers pressed in behind them. "What have you done to this poor man?"

"Me?!" The king laughed and shook his head. "To you, a king needs to have an explanation for a man wounded in his bedchambers. He attacked me. But you—*you* question *me?*"

The king glanced at his guards, still holding one hand to his head. "Do you not see that he broke in." He pointed to the chamber doors leading to his private room. There were shards and splinters of wood where the man clearly broke in. "This man deserves execution at once! Why do you stand as spectators?"

He waved his free hand around the room. "While you were all enjoying yourself on the food I provided, your king was getting thwarted by a menace. Clearly a peasant with no regard for his king." He continued, pointing down to the man. "Fools! All of you! What do you have to say for yourselves?"

The room went silent. The king rose from his bed. A deep sadness settled into his countenance. Queen Amara shrugged it off. She watched him carefully as he stared at the people crowding the room.

"This is how you protect your king?"

The room stayed quiet. Queen Amara followed the king's gaze to the guard closest to him.

"Get this whiffling away from me," the king blurted, waving his one hand. "His execution will be for the entire kingdom to witness—a testimony of what happens to those who try to kill their king." He directed himself towards another of his guards. "Question the man on his occupation and family so they can be advised and present, if they so wish."

Queen Amara's eyes narrowed as the king walked past the man lying on the ground and sneered at him with disgust, kicking him in the ribs. When the king stopped beside her, Queen Amara felt the heat of his eyes on her profile. She kept her chin high and jutted toward the wall in front of her.

His whisper was low and accusing. "Glad to see you would take this man's side over your king's. More so..."—he paused. Queen Amara felt more than saw his eyes grow cold on her face as he continued— "over your husband's, the man you are to love and honor. Surely, by your actions here today, you have proven that I am not any of those things to you anymore. Am I, Matilda?"

She clenched her hands into a fist, keeping her eyes forward, not breaking her stare from the wall in front of her. Queen Amara would not give in to his will. She licked her lips. He won't be king, nor her husband for much longer. Therefore, technically, he was accurate. Whether aware of it or not, death and subjection to her was his fate.

So, a fool had tried to kill him tonight. She wasn't in a checkmate yet. Soon, *the king* would be in checkmate, and the queen would win the game of Kingdom Whiteshire. She dipped her chin, feigning obedience, but gave him a side wurp.

"I will always defend the king." Her words were like velvet, as if wrapping around him.

If only she could tighten them around his neck. Queen Amara's eyes lowered in submission as the king stormed out. Soon, she would never be second to the king. She, Queen Amara, would be king ... or better yet—empress! Plans only a few knew lingered like the grin on her face.

Queen Amara approached the bed while others filed one by one out of the room behind the king. Sielda inched her way near to where the queen stood and they shared a quizzical look between the two of them. Queen Amara's curiosity compelled her towards the man. She had not been the one to order this attack. So, then who? One of the guards pulled the man who thwarted the king off the floor.

Queen Amara held up her palm to him. "Wait." She stepped toward the man who was held up by the guard. "What is your name?"

The man laughed, and blood sputtered out onto the floor. "Wouldn't you love to know."

"Tell me your name." She looked at the guard holding him up. "Strike him hard if he doesn't."

"Uh, uh—Jason." He smiled wide. "Your Highness." He stared at the queen, eyes swollen, blood dripping from his lips.

"How did you get into the castle. It was heavily guarded, was it not?"

He laughed and blood splattered near her. "I have my ways. While you were all eating in the Great Hall, I snuck in and followed the king to his bedchambers. It wasn't hard actually."

"And why did you want to harm the king?"

"Let's just say, I have my reasons." Anger flitted across the man's face.

Queen Amara crossed her arms. "Did you act on your own accord, or were you hired to do this attack?"

The man jutted out his chin. "T'was on my own that I acted. And I would have done it again if given the chance."

Queen Amara's gaze flicked to the guard clutching his tunic. "Place him in the dungeon and fetch Herrick for me."

"Your Majesty, the king wanted his execution."

There once was a time when she would obey the command of her husband. An obedience born of respect, not true love. Respect for his position alone. He was a means to an end. A strategic marriage built on mutual convenience. But respect was no longer there and if any ounce of feeling had developed, it was obsolete. She spoke slowly, "And your queen said to place him in the dungeon. Unless I am mistaken, your king did not give a time as to when this execution would take place. Did he?"

"No, Your Majesty. I suppose he did not. I will place him there right away until the king decides."

"Exactly. Now go."

Once alone, she gently rubbed her chin, planning her next move.

I think Jason will be of great use to me.

Eight

EIRA

EIRA WHITE COVERED HER HEAD WITH HER GRAY HOOD, ducking through the small opening hidden by vines and brambles. She emerged into more darkness. Night was a little less dark than the corridor. Her eyes didn't need any time to adjust. She aimed east toward the forest on the edge of Whiteshire Castle and began to move forward.

The gate would be drawn soon, ending the day of trading. However, she knew there would be stragglers along this road hoping to get in a few chinkers or lodging before the moon set in the night sky. She could only hope there weren't any thieves out tonight. Large hedges ran along the road, keeping her hidden as she grazed along the edges.

A few small makeshift markets sprang up along the road. Darting in and out of the hedges, she thought she had avoided any living soul until she bumped into something. Looking down, she caught the bright whites of two beady little eyes peering up at her.

It was a child.

The child stood there almost in as much shock as Eira upon running into her. Eira looked around for an adult. Perchance a caretaker or servant was milling about, but there was no one. The little girl had torn and tattered clothing. There was a smear of dirt on her cheeks that blended into what looked like freckles along the bridge of her nose. She must be a beggar from another village looking for food. Or stealing it. Eira looked over at the girl once more and then scanned the outside courtyard again.

The girl's eyes glazed, getting misty, and she started to say something. Lifting her index finger to her lips, Eira puckered them in the form of the sound "Shh." Then, smiled.

The girl returned the smile, her teeth white in the moonlight. The poor thing looked so ragged. A twinge caught in Eira's chest and threatened to squeeze her from the inside out. Eira wished she could pull this wee little girl into a warm embrace. But she had a better idea, one that would suit them both.

Eira leaned down and spoke softly. "If you promise not to tell anyone I was here, I will give you this." Eira pulled out a coin from the package her papa gave her.

The little girl's eyes grew big and round as she fixated on the coin. The girl placed her palms out and nodded wildly. Once the coin fell into the wee girl's hands, she took off running. The only sound Eira could hear was the girl's soft feet padding through the grass in the opposite direction of Eira. She hoped the girl would honor her request and not say a word.

The moon caught Eira's eye. Looking ahead to the unknown path before her, she was glad for its dim light. Sucking in a deep breath, Eira squared her shoulders. She had no idea what lay ahead, or the encounters she would face. But she was thankful—thankful to be out of the horrible, dark, and dirty corridor. Thankful for the clear sky above her. A sigh of relief escaped her. Eira was finally able to do something. All she could do was walk openly under the night sky... But it was still something. For once, Eira felt a little less helpless and a little more hopeful in the situation she was in.

Following the gravel path that led to the forest, she kept east and prayed for God's hand of protection. Her fingers held onto the prayer book in her bubble-bow, bringing her a sense of comfort. As the path grew and the light from the castle dimmed, fatigue set in, and doubt plagued her mind with horrible questions.

Maybe Papa doesn't want me in his kingdom any longer. Maybe he knows I'm not fit to be his heir apparent. Perhaps it was another way of getting rid of me before I put the kingdom to shame.

Overhearing more than enough conversations from the queen about not having the proper dowry made her question if she would ever be presented in court. Perhaps Whiteshire was in dire need financially. It wouldn't matter now, anyway. Thrust from her kingdom with only her father's signet ring could mean a handful of things—

The sound of horse hooves clicking along the dirt path interrupted her thoughts. Veering to the darkness surrounding her, Eira tried to hide. A black carriage with what appeared to be four men was approaching her. Two figures were riding in the carriage itself, and two were walking alongside it. If Eira had to take a guess, she would think these men were traders for the market. But with little experience, it was just that—a guess. And wasn't the market closed now?

Eira ducked her head down, avoiding any eye contact as they started to pass by.

Their carriage slowed to a halt.

"What is a fine lady like you doing on such a dark night as tonight?"

Eira scolded herself for not hiding well enough and tried to ignore the men. She continued walking at a steady pace. But they repeated themselves, even more loudly than before.

Keeping her head down, she replied, "Good eve, gentlemen. Merely visiting the poor and needy."

Technically it wasn't a lie. She had seen the girl who was indeed poor and in need.

The men laughed, two of them left the carriage's side and started to come nearer to her.

"Perhaps..." The tall man's teeth appeared green in the moonlight. "...you're just wandering about and willing to do some trade this fine eve?" His eyes lingered on her skirt, and his brows seemed to dance mischievously. "I detect a faint bit of nobility in this one, boys!"

She turned and peeked up at another man, nearly the height of a lance, drawing near to her left side, as if they were pinning her in.

"Did I hear a young noblewoman is walking alone, seeking to trade? How lovely..." The lance-man purred.

Eira heard the carriage door crack open. She peered back, and a short man with an evil grin eyed her. He stepped down from the carriage, and Eira shivered. She gripped her prayer book and whispered a desperate plea for God's mercy.

One girl against two—her eyes shot to each man, numbering them —*three, four, five men.* What were the odds? Her eyes darted all around, looking for a way to escape, a way to run.

Fastening her focus on the forest, she released the grip of her prayer book, slipped her hand from her bubble-bow, picked up her skirt, and propelled herself forward, pulsing her legs on the ground as fast as her heart was beating. The burn was intense while the men hollered from behind. Faint steps were closing in on her. She ducked under a large limb and picked up speed as the forest began to narrow. The moonlight faded fast as thick branches started to cover her in blackness.

She continued to beat her feet on the ground until her skirt caught on a fallen log. The rip was loud and ricocheted abruptly in the silence of the forest. She could hear the heavy huffs of one of the men getting closer and closer.

"Come here. We only want to talk with you!" He laughed, wheezing, and then coughed out language she had never heard before.

She tugged her skirt hard and ripped it loose from the snag. A hand snatched her arm.

"Got her boys!" Lance-man hollered.

"Let go of me in the name of the king!" Eira screeched.

"Oooo. The king," he scoffed. "The dead king, ya mean?"

"What?" Eira's words seemed to bounce in her mouth, not quite making sense as they came out. "You don't mean the King of Whiteshire? He is not de—dead?"

The pewter image of the tall man swam in front of her as she was being flung back and forth.

No. No. No. This can't be. He's lying!

Were the screams in the secret passageway of the corridor from her father? Had they killed him after he thrust her out of the kingdom? Was that what he was protecting her from?

She blinked back the terror burning in her eyes. "Unhand me this instant!" she yelled.

Her voice sounded small and weak to her ears. Like a tiny bird chirping in the large and deep forest.

Dull thuds and more footsteps muffled around them. The other men were coming. She couldn't be sure how many now, because the thudding of feet and her beating heart all sounded the same.

Her shoulder jerked up as Lance-man pulled her over the fallen tree she had been snagged on.

"We are going to market, boys!" He laughed. "Some will pay a pretty price for you, my dear. And lucky for me, it looks like no one will know you're gone." He pulled Eira in close before continuing, "Seeing as you're all alone."

The word 'alone' cut deeper than he probably anticipated. Rotting fish mixed with dirt from his breath hit her in the face. Her mind tried to shut out the smell, but her nose could not. Her hand swung out, smacking him in the face.

"I demand you to let go of me!" She squirmed in his grasp.

A growl came out of Lance-man, and his large fingers wrapped around Eira's bicep. His grip grew tighter and tighter until she couldn't feel her hands any longer.

"You aren't going anywhere. I should tie you up and make you walk. But I can't do that, you see … you're a pretty penny. But—" He laughed again. "A pretty penny can be tarnished, if you know what I mean." He roughed Eira up a little to make his point, and she whimpered in pain. "You owe me for the trouble it's taken to get you. You little whiffling! And I always get what I'm owed!" Another growl left his fishy lips as the warmth of his breath hovered over Eira's face.

"In one foul breath, you say I am worth something, and in the same, you call me a whiffling? How can someone so insignificant be of any value to you?" Eira hissed, trying to stomp on his feet. "LET. ME. GO!"

"Hush," Lance-man snapped. "Before I make you worth nothing at all."

Eira puffed at a piece of hair that fell in front of her face. The rough pull of her arm again made her wince in pain. She squinted, eyes tearing up. *God. Please help me.*

A large snap cracked from behind them. A branch, perhaps?

Lance-man stopped. "Larimus, what took you so long?"

Silence.

Lance-man stopped moving. Tiny hairs sprang up on Eira's skin. Someone else must be in the forest. Someone that didn't belong to the band of thieves. She wasn't the only one who could sense it either. Lance-man's grip tightened, and Eira cried out in reaction. Another splinter of wood snapped. This time, closer.

"Keep moving." A pain shot in her arm as he tugged her again. This time, he made her walk, but more like dragged her behind him.

"You're hurting me!"

"Be quiet, woman!" Lance-man hissed.

"I believe the woman asked for you to unhand her." A voice came from the black trees ahead.

Fishy fingers smothered her mouth, covering her nose. She couldn't breathe even if she wanted to. She stayed still. The grip loosened on her arm, but something sharp pressed into her back. *Wait.* Was that a dagger?

She let out a whimper.

His deathly breath was on her neck again. "I said be quiet, featherhead." He poked at her to move forward. She did.

"I wouldn't do that, if I were you," the same mysterious voice spoke from the dark woods in front of her.

Lance-man halted. The vibrations from his hand shook down her arm. *Was he scared?*

"Surely you're a crier!" Lance-man yelled into nothing but the black night. "Blutter and show yourself, you fool!"

"I would say *you* are the fool today, sir."

A thrum and a wisp of air flipped the hair close to Eira's neck. The hand on her mouth fell away. Then a thud came from the ground behind her. Like a bag full of barley, the man who once held Eira as a prisoner fell with a thud behind her. She waited to hear something. Movement, anything. But there was nothing. Lance-man lay completely still like a solid brick. She didn't dare move for fear of whatever hit him would strike her.

Is Lance-man dead? Or just stunned?

With the back of her hand, Eira smeared her mouth free of Lance-man's filth. Her threat was no longer making a sound. Not even a moan came from his stiffening lips. He was indeed dead, she thought.

Turing back, she locked eyes on the arrows feathers as it protruded out from the man's eye socket. Eira's hand flung to her neck. She rubbed where the air had whisked her hair away, the very path the arrow made to claim its victim. An incredibly close-range shot—too close. Her neck was right beside it! Whoever shot the arrow was either insane or very skilled.

She choked back a sob. She could have been the victim. She could have died with Lance-man.

"Come," a deep voice demanded.

She spun around to face the mystery man. Eira gasped as a hand grabbed her right arm in the darkness. She couldn't quite make out his features.

"I will lead you to safety."

Something in his voice brought her a sense of comfort. Eira looked back at the body lying on the ground. The dead body whom the man now grabbing her arm had shot down and killed. Would he be as quick to kill her? Should she fight him?

Eira recalled his voice, and it reassured her. *No ... she'd better not fight back. At least not right now. He promised safety yet* knew how to kill. So, where exactly was he taking her? And could he be trusted? Though she was happy to be rid of one monster, had she now encountered another?

Eira flinched remembering how blood pooled around the arrow sticking out of Lance-man's eye. She had never seen a person die. Her mind went back to the screams in the corridor, where she had been only mere moments before she escaped. Was Lance-man speaking the truth about her papa? Was he dead? Her stomach felt sick. Though saved from one horrible man, she still felt like a prisoner being tugged along through the brush and trees.

Oh God in Heaven, help me...

She looked through the darkness toward the hooded man still clenching her arm. Pinching her eyes shut, she breathed in deep. The smell of cedar trees brought clarity to the pain invading her mind. Freedom from the forest she once dreamed of playing in. Now that freedom was starting to take shape into a nightmare she hoped to wake up from.

Following the new stranger deeper into the eerie forest, she suddenly became highly aware of her surroundings. Picking up every small creak, snap, or crunch of their feet hitting the earth, every squeal of night animals until it became a cadence and rhythm of her steps. She clenched the bag she still carried and remembered the knife Papa placed in the bag.

Eira scolded herself. Why had she not thought of it until now? The thought of using it to escape zipped through her mind. Tilting her chin up, she matched the pace of her stranger and put more confidence in her stride. With a little help, she might as well see if what the man's offer for safety held true. If the man's intentions were evil, she would at least have a weapon to fight her way out of the situation. Regardless of whether she knew how to use it, she had it, and it was a gift from Papa. Knowing it was with her brought some kind of comfort and a faint sense of protection.

Besides, one thing was certain. Despite being scared, confused, and unsure of everything happening in her life, she wasn't completely alone anymore. And somehow, that brought her some ease as she stared ahead into the eerie night before her.

Nine

OWEN

PRINCE OWEN SLID OFF HIS HORSE AND FLIPPED HIS LONG white hood down to get a better panoramic view of his new lodging. He tied the reins near the front step of the small, humble abode, and gently rapped on the door.

From behind the door, a voice cracked like bark peeling off the trunk of a tree.

"Who goes there?"

Prince Owen cleared his throat, taking a moment to steady his voice. Though a prince in Wealas, he was a pilgrim in England. Having encountered some friends and foes—or rather, sheep in wolves' clothing, who cared more for the gold he brought than spiritual well-being, he was natural cautious. He needed to be vigilant and kind. Composed and assured.

"Yes, Alo. I come in peace on my travels for pilgrimage to see the place of Saint Swithun and be granted a miracle of my own. Might I ask for your hospitality, sir? May I come—"

The door swung wide.

A man of good stature and height stood before him. He was

drowning in brown, rough wool, with a brim of hair along the edges above his ears. There was an opening of bald flesh on the top of his head, as if a human halo. He greeted Prince Owen with a beaming smile. An instant connection was made.

Prince Owen sighed.

A friend.

"Greetings, traveler. I welcome you to my home. Come in. Come in!" The monk gestured with his weathered hands and stepped back to give Prince Owen room to walk in.

"Thank you, kind sir." Prince Owen looked behind him. "But first, do you also have room for my horse somewhere? Perchance some oats or hay? Water?"

The monk laughed. "A man who is concerned more for his animal's well-being than his own is a good man, the Lord says."

The monk stared at him for a long moment. His eyes were grayish. His veins, curvy and old, protruding slightly. It was as if his wise eyes held stories within them, stories that ran like streams through them. Perhaps some wisdom and stories were in them for Owen too.

The monk smiled. "Yes, indeed. A good man." He nodded as if agreeing with Owen's thoughts.

Owen followed the monk back into the evening air. The distinct glow of a lantern and the halo of brown hair breezed past him as they both moved toward Owen's horse.

"Have you been traveling long?"

"Aye." Owen's words rushed out as he tried to keep up with the monk. "For almost a day. I do recall a few beautiful stops along the way. A quiet stream. A waterfall and a view at the top of a large hill that could take your breath away."

Of course, he didn't mention the looters he had to thwart with his sword and dagger in the last two villages. "Do you have many pilgrims coming through here?"

The monk followed a small path ahead of Prince Owen, which led to a shack in the thicket of large cedar trees. It was getting dark out, and Owen had to keep close to the lantern in the monk's hands.

"I do," the monk replied.

Prince Owen shuffled closer as the monk's voice carried ahead of him.

"I've not had some visitors in some time, however. It will be nice to have some company." His face turned, and the man looked at Prince Owen again with the same smile as earlier. "Winchester Cathedral is not too far from here. For many, we are their last stop before the monastery." He turned away from Owen and faced the small path ahead. "Are you thirsty?" The monk's words wafted back toward Owen, slightly muffled. His lips seem to crack in response. He was thirsty.

"For Adam's ale, yes indeed, kind sir! Do you happen to have a well nearby where I can fetch some?"

Just outside the small stable made of wood, the monk picked up a pail and pumped water from the well into it. Once the monk was finished, Prince Owen cupped his hands under the water and drank. He noticed the monk placing his horse into a small stall near the back of the stable, appearing to house another horse. The monk's, perhaps?

"You are very gentle with animals yourself, dear friend. I am surprised you don't house more fair creatures here. Any chickens, perhaps?" With the back of his hand, Owen wiped water droplets from his mouth and chin, imagining some nice chicken meat to sup on.

"I have three or four. But at the monastery we have plenty to keep us busy. Here, I tend to other duties the Lord has me working on." The monk paused and studied the horse closely. Almost as if dissecting every inch of Absolam. A sudden urge to protect his faithful animal swam through his gut, but he put the storm at ease.

"Your horse will be well until morning. And you, what of your hunger?"

"Bread would be nice," Prince Owen said.

"I will tend to it when we get back to the cosh." He laughed. "But

I was speaking of your soul, pilgrim. No need to look at me like that."
He paused, staring at Prince Owen. "Everyone comes here hungry for
something. What is it that you are hungry for? What does your soul
crave?"

A javelin of guilt and shame hit him so hard, the wind sucked out
of his lungs, knocking him completely off his high horse—in layman's
terms—and he stood speechless. Desperate.

Was Owen's pain that obvious? Had this monk heard of his family's history? Or did this monk know his family somehow? No one had
asked him why he was on his journey, only offered prayers. Was it the
monk's divine nature that made him different from others? Or something else?

Owen realized he'd stopped walking, but the monk kept moving.

"I—I crave..." His words stumbled like his feet on the trail. His
hands gripped tighter to his staff as he quick-stepped to catch up to
the monk. "Rather, I mean to say, thirst—I thirst for answers ...
mostly."

"You spoke of a miracle. What do you wish God to do?"

A deep-seated wound slithered out of his heart. Trying not to
pound the walking rod into the ground with each step, Owen's fingers
squeezed around his staff, relieving tension. Could he trust this man
with certain pains of his heart? His family?

No.

"Prithee, dear brother. Don't be offended. But I prefer to keep the
unanswered for God's ears only."

"I admire your wish, sir—"

"Owen. Please call me Owen."

"All right, Owen. As I was saying, I admire your request. Your
silence too. There's no shame in that. I will assist you in any way I can,
and help you find what you are looking for. Even if your only desire is
for hope."

Owen let silence fill the space between them and didn't offer any more conversation either. He worked his jaw. Owen had believed words from trusted lips once before, only to be ruined and dashed into pieces soon after. How foolish he was to believe the words of his beloved sister.

Weaving along the tiny dirt path toward the stone house, Owen noticed how peaceful it was. Despite the past creeping into his conscience, peace was something he could learn to appreciate. Even perhaps live with.

The gentle breeze carrying the wood-burning smell from the cosh reminded him of a few years back. His sister would play her harp near the fire each night and bring almost the same sense of tranquility as the scene before him. A beautiful memory. One that he wished he could experience again and again. He kicked the dirt ahead of him. Fire seared behind his eyes, and he pinched them shut. He would not cry in front of this man.

No... He must stay strong and find his sister. Hope wasn't lost completely. He had to continue forward. Following the man who promised to help Owen find hope until they reached the little cottage door. He let the monk's words simmer in his mind like a warm pot of stew. Perhaps hope was all he needed after all?

"And you, dear friend," Owen said, "what is your name?"

The monk smiled as they entered together. "You may call me Brother Obadiah."

Inside, Brother Obadiah served him a warm bowl of chicken stew with one dry barley loaf. As the night drew near, Obadiah retired to his own room, and Owen lay on the cot near the fire, completely content.

The door to Obadiah's bedchamber closed, and not long after, melodic notes ascended and descended, as if climbing up and down heaven's ladder, reaching Owen's heart. How majestic was the sound of Brother Obadiah's prayers. Prince Owen listened eagerly to the soft

Gregorian chant. Each note lifted his soul a little closer to heaven. He took in a deep breath and leaned back, closing his eyes.

The familiar crackle of wood and the sizzling sap hissed now and again, reminding him of the harp his sister once played. Not quite as elegant and smooth, but the sound of her memory and the prayers mingled together in a kind of harmony that made music in his heart.

Is this what hope feels like?

Without knowing it, and within a few moments, Owen had let the walls of his heart and mind down enough for the monk to wiggle through—just a bit. Of course, anyone who deserved a place there had to be tested. Especially a man of God. This was without question.

Owen would have to test the fruit of him to see if he were made of honor, had true beliefs of Christian morals and values. Time would tell him if this man was a fake.

"Thank you, God, for bringing me here," Owen whispered.

Reaching his arms up, Prince Owen tucked his palms under his head and stared at the ceiling. Eyes too heavy to stay open, he closed them and sighed. Drifting to sleep, a nagging thought stayed with him, causing him to awaken.

What did he really want God to do as his miracle?

If God found his sister buried, would he want Him to bring her back from the dead like Lazarus? If she were poor or rich now, would he want God to lead him to her whereabouts? If she didn't want to be found, would he want God to change her mind? Or was this pilgrimage not about God doing a miracle to find and rescue his sister? Perhaps Owen was the one who needed to be rescued?

He ran his hand down his face and turned onto his side, pinching his eyes together to make the question go away. But it wouldn't. The countdown was on for his father's death. Once gone, his sister was supposed to rule. Not him! If she was nowhere to be found, he would have to rule. Which meant he would have to find a wife. He shuddered and pinched his eyes again.

Without his sister taking the throne, Owen would have to wed or bring shame to his father and all he'd worked for in his kingdom. His thoughts fluttered like ashes from the fire to his father—the one who *didn't* bless him on this journey—saying Owen was running away from his responsibilities. Which may have been true. However, Prince Owen tried to convince his father that he only wanted a miracle for his sister, insisting Owen would find her and return the rightful heir to the throne.

But what if he couldn't find her?

What if this was just another failed attempt?

What if—

Owen pinched the bridge of his nose.

What if there was no time left, and he had to wed? The ladies he had previously courted wouldn't object. Nor, of course, would his father. But his heart didn't want those women. He knew they were only wanting to marry him for status—for convenience—for family. He wanted something real. He wanted to be loved for who he was, not what his privilege could offer them.

Forcing him to find a wife now meant he would have to settle for less than his soul longed for. And what honor would that truly give his sister? She deserved the kingdom. She deserved the throne of their family, and he didn't want to be the one to take that away from her. Not when he was to blame for her being gone in the first place. He wouldn't be responsible for taking everything she had left before she had a chance to claim it

Peace suddenly left the room, and a deep agony tore through Owen until he finally fell asleep.

Ten

EIRA

A WARM HARMONY OF BEAUTIFUL AMBER COLORS LIT THE SKY. Dawn had begun. The trees were awake now, showing off their evergreen vibrance, displaying leaves of red, yellow, and brushed gold.

A smell took Eira's senses back to where she was—in the forest with a stranger.

"Did you rest enough?" His low voice was still groggy.

"Yes." She tried to smile, but it felt awkward. She sat up. "I did." Yawning, Eira stretched out her arms. "Thank you."

"Where are we?"

Eira heard the rustle of wind dancing through the trees overhead. She glanced around. There were trees, shrubs, and an open clearing where they camped. Yet, there was nothing in particular she noticed that could gain a sense of exactly where she was. Were they closer to the East like her father prompted her to go? She felt a peculiar sense of hesitancy suddenly being in a vast open field, full of freedom, discovering something completely new to her, while being alone with a stranger doing it. An abrupt longing for her Papa pulled her back to the present.

"We have traveled North mostly. We are still on Whiteshire lands. They reach quite a distance."

"I see. That it does."

'*Well,*' Eira thought, *that answers that.*' She was not going in the direction her father wanted.

Eira's mysterious protector was cooking something on an open fire, and her stomach grumbled in satisfaction. Her belly being the deciding factor that she would go with the man a little way further for food and protection. But soon, despite not knowing where she was or how to get there, she would plan to follow the direction of her Papa and go to the Eastern Kingdom.

Prodding it with a stick, the man lifted his eyes to hers. This was the first time she had seen him in full light. It had been so dark in the forest when he came to her aid, guiding her away from her assailants with his strong arms. She let her eyes follow his features. They were chiseled and defined. His jaw protruded to the sides slightly, and his nose was crooked with thin, tight lips. His eyes were dark, and his clothes were fine, but rugged with fur and leather.

"Don't mention it." His shoulders stiffened suddenly, as if uncomfortable with her stare. Embarrassed, she looked away quickly. "Eat up." He grunted. "I'm sure you're hungry."

Eira's tongue instantly watered in reply. "I am hungry."

She was in fact starving. She hadn't eaten since early yesterday. When he went to hand her a piece, her fingers suddenly faltered. An unnerving fear sprang up. Could he be trusted? Was he safe? Her stomach grumbled, as if arguing with her hesitation. Pushing down the fear with a gulp, she cautiously reached out and took the food. Nibbling the hot meat from the edge of the stick he gave her; she couldn't help but exude her thankfulness with a moan.

"Mmmm. This is wonderful. Almost as good—" Her words died mid-sentence.

Don't look back, she reprimanded herself before quickly changing the subject.

"Has anyone ever told you you're a great cook?" She swallowed and spoke again before he could answer. "If I may ask, who taught you?"

Taking a slice of meat, along with a small pot of something she figured was some kind of sauce, he said nothing. Eira changed the conversation again, attempting to evoke some kind of conversation out of this stranger. He was beginning to make her feel a bit uncomfortable.

"Do you feed every damsel you capture, or am I an exception to the rule?"

He looked at her and squinted, as if scrutinizing her, or perhaps hiding something. Fear? Anger? She tilted her head while she ate, staring back at him. *What is this person about?*

The stranger dropped his eyes to the meat on his fingers. With his left hand, he lifted another small container and sprinkled something over the rest of the meat. She watched as he snapped the metal lid of the container tight and pressed the raw meat onto the wood. After washing his hands in a basin, he finally lifted his gaze back to hers. And though not captivated by his gaze, as she would have thought a man as handsome as he would have taken her, he had a sense of curiosity about him. An intrigue that made her want to know him more. A sense of mystery hung about him.

He grunted. "You are not captured," he finally said. His focus swung from her nose to her lips, then swiftly over her body before he continued. "But in these woods, m'lady, if you are not careful, you may be hunted."

She shivered, wanting to wrap herself up in something, anything.

"Is that a threat, sir?" she managed to squeak out.

"Nay. But those men were looking to trade you like this here piece of meat." He wiggled the meat between his fingertips back and forth. "I am sure you realize you were in great danger."

The sound of sizzling meat from the fire seared her ears with his words. Eira was aware of the potential dangers of those men. She wished she could clean her face repeatedly from the fishy smell of the man's hands that held her hostage. Then she remembered who killed him. Her eyes snatched up to the stranger. Her fingers fluttered to her neck, where the arrow had almost grazed her very own neck. Her eyes widened. The question hung in the air. If the man could kill oner person, would he be just as quick to kill a maiden? Even her?

"That brings me to another question," he said, while he was perking up his left eyebrow, his gaze steadfast on the fire between them.

Swallowing a piece of meat that seemed to be stuck in Eira's throat, she said, "Go ahead."

"What is a young and, might I add, beautiful maiden doing out in the woods?" He shot her with a direct look. His face was cold like a carved stone, with his arched eyebrow seeming to point right at her, before adding, "Alone?"

The beat of her heart sounded in her ears like waves crashing. She was alone, wasn't she? One of the men that attacked her said the same thing. And now, she was alone again with a stranger. If she went with her gut instinct, he couldn't be trusted either. Or could he?

Eira watched the stick in his hand rotate, allowing juices from the meat to fall onto the coals and sizzle with a salty aroma.

"I—" Her once-strong voice wavered before him. "I was told to travel this way…" She let her voice trail off.

Should she lie? Her eyes darted all around the forest, trying to find a suitable answer. She noticed the cross symbol on the stranger's water flask. Pilgrims must follow this path all the time. Even nobles, she assumed. She could say she was on pilgrimage, which wouldn't be such a lie. She truly needed answers and prayers. Especially now.

She took another bite, avoiding the question, like he previously had, to gather her thoughts. Swallowing, she lifted her chin and spoke slowly. "I am not sure why it is of concern to you. But since you have been so kind to save me from those men and feed me, I shall answer you." She cleared her throat. "If you must know. I am on a pilgrimage. But have lost my way."

Keeping her view on her skirt, she twirled the wood in her fingertips and followed the spin of the meat on its tip. Her cheeks burned and she was tempted to lift her fingertips to them and put them at ease. Could he see right through her? *The liar. The royal outcast, who hadn't lost her way at all, only cast out with her own father's hands.*

Her eyes burned from the tears wanting to burst forth. She rubbed her nose to distract herself and would have feigned it was the fire smoke that made her teary-eyed, if asked.

"I see," he said, taking his stick out of the fire and blowing off the flame. The smoke went up, and he leaned in to take a bite, smiling for the first time. Eira watched as he chewed. "I know of a place." He swallowed. "If you like, I can take you there. They allow lodging for pilgrims. Peculiar at times, but kind. I think you'll like them."

"That is kind of you. Prithee, what is your name? I shall mention you during my prayers for blessings to be returned."

He snorted. "I am not worthy of your prayers. Or your blessings." He finished his meat in one bite. "Come." He rose to his feet. "We'd better hurry to get there before nightfall."

He kicked the dirt over the fire, and she blew the dust away from her face, then stood. She had not been in the presence of many men or held conversations with anyone besides her papa, but she grew up watching people from her window. She could tell in only a few moments what kind of person they were, and from what class they came from based on their mannerisms. So, who was this man who rescued her? And why was he so angry and rigid, yet kind toward her? If this man were a nobleman, he wouldn't be so careless and abrupt with a lady present. No, he must be something else. But what?

Obviously, he was familiar with the forest. He navigated it as if he owned the entire countryside. If he were a traveler, he wouldn't know these woods so well. Being crafted in archery would make him useful with this skill, and the locals would demand he hunt for them. Or perhaps that skill was why he was leaving Whiteshire. Was he running from something? Or someone like her?? If so, where was he going … and why help her?

Thoughts muddled together as she pulled her hooded cloak to cover her eyes from the sun inching its way above them. The man hopped onto his horse.

"My apologies…" the stranger said, grabbing at his horse's reins, a half grin on his face, "…there is only one horse."

Eira's eyes widened, then narrowed. "I am not daft, sir. I can surely see there is only one horse."

"Then, you understand my predicament." He grinned again as he veered the horse away from Eira and onto a narrow path using its reins.

"Ah, yes indeed. I do see," Eira said flatly. Sighing heavily, she focused on following behind the man on foot. *Nay. Not a nobleman,* she thought to herself.

She continued to keep up with the horse. Eira concentrated on matching her feet to the clip clop of the horse's hooves, and the swoosh of her arms to the tempo of its tail flipping from side to side.

As the horse in front of her dropped excrement on the trail, she carefully maneuvered around it and thought, *"Things could be worse."* She could be dead or traded for less than a peasant's worth in chinkers.

Her heart almost stopped just thinking about it. Such disgust. Such indecency for any living creature to endure from those men if they had done what they intended. And yet, going by her experience in the woods, she could imagine others having fallen to the likes of those men. Her stomach flipped. How could that be happening in her father's kingdom?

She forced herself to be grateful for the non-nobleman. She

glanced up. He was strutting proudly, perched on his horse, almost making her regret the thought of gratitude. But he had protected her from that man, and for that, she would repay him. Moments like these, she wished Papa had taught her to wield the sword, or even how to use a bow. He never let her participate in any hunts either. Papa said she was too weak, and perhaps she was.

Spinning Papa's signet ring around her frail finger in her pocket, a temptation rose to look back at Whiteshire. Pushing away the urge to run back home, she looked up again at the horse's tail and followed its swaying rhythm.

The man turned to face Eira with another faint smile, as if aware of her eyes on his back. The man's smile didn't reach his eyes and she did not return it. He quickly spun back around. Veering his steed southeast, he stated.

"There is one stop we must make before we head to the safe place."

"Pardon?" He never answered, so Eira spoke up. "Dear sir, I fear I did not hear you correctly. We are to make another stop?"

He swiveled in his saddle, finding her eyes this time. "Aye, we have to pick up another for the journey."

"Another?"

He only nodded and turned, facing ahead.

Who could that be? Another damsel in distress, perhaps? Was Eira kidnapped after all, and he planned to do it again? *No.* A nervous laughter slipped out of her catching the attention of the man, but she brushed it off as a memory, and he continued forward at the pace of a slow trot. It was probably another friendly person to pick up. Hopefully someone a little chattier than this man. She wouldn't let his demeanor get the best of her. Instead, she giggled to herself and mused, *Goodness knows, I can barely keep up with his conversations as it is. A new distraction would be advantageous.*

She laughed to herself again, bringing a kind of comfort to her nerves and eased the thought of this unexpected addition to an already unclear plan. Eira's smile dissipated as time went on. Dust from the horse's hooves left a bad taste in her mouth and Eira was getting tired. Her legs were beginning to grow heavy, and her soul a little weary. All she had gained after leaving her father was more unknown answers to her ever-growing questions.

A memory of her and Papa embracing one another flashed before her eyes. She looked down and remembered there was a piece of paper in it with the money and items he gave her. Perhaps it was a map to help her get to the Eastern Kingdom? When she had a moment, she would look to see if it was in the satchel and if it was indeed a map.

Her hand fluttered to her heart where an aching sensation grew. Why did her papa thrust her out of the kingdom now? Was he dead? Or were they just rumors? Who was the man leading her through the forest, and who helped rescue her to be trusted? And where were they going now? Would she be safe?

Eira blinked away dust kicking up at her as Whiteshire faded in the distance, and the unknown continued to grow before her.

Eleven

HER MYSTERY PROTECTOR FLUNG THE CALF SKIN FULL OF ADAM'S ale toward her. Eira caught the water and raised it toward him in a toast-like gesture.

"I thank thee."

Eira quickly tipped the container to her lips, allowing the cool liquid to slip down her parched throat. Instantly it refreshed her body and replenished her spirit. They traveled quite a distance before finally taking a break. She didn't realize how exhausted she was.

Was this really happening?

She took in the wilderness around her. Hearing the breeze rustling through the leaves, birds chirping in the distance, and the faint smell of earth and sweat. Was she truly out of the kingdom walls? It seems like such a long time ago she was there, imagining when she would be allowed in court, trying to get a glimpse of the people in their great hall, sneaking out of her chambers to find Papa when she knew he was home. How could she be out in the world with no one to tell her what to do, how to do it? It was as if it were a dream.

But this was no dream. It was more like a nightmare.

Her mind couldn't stop thinking of her father. Eira pinched back tears as she took another swig of chilled water, cooling her emotions. Eira knew her freedom was fragile. Hairs on her arm stood at attention, and she felt a tingle down her spine. She glanced up and noticed her mystery protector out of the corner of her eye. He was looking at her. Watching her. Perhaps she wasn't so free after all. She tried to smile at him, but it was forced.

Avoiding his stare, she looked around and tried to get her bearings. She remembered they were to meet up with someone else, and imagined this would be the place. Perhaps that was why they had stopped.

As she lowered the calf skin from another swig, her eyes caught a man approaching them. He was not very tall, but had wide shoulders that swung like a wobbly gate as he sauntered over to where she was.

"May I call you Beauty?" he asked, bowing in a grand gesture toward her.

She raised her brows at him, cheeks streaking with warmth. Eira ignored this new man's outright charm and threw the leather container back at the man who rescued her. Her rescuer caught it in one single swoop of his hand. She darted her eyes at the newcomer.

"And what, pray-tell shall I call you, sir?" Her eyes dropped ever so slightly in acceptance of his bow.

His voice grunted out. "Forgive me. I see you are a true lady. I should not be so unmannered. My name is Mason. Master Huntsman, here to assist you on your journey."

Interesting. Eira caught something strange in the so-called huntsman's eyes. Was his confidence perhaps arrogance or something else entirely?

"And what journey would that be?" Eira questioned the new man while secretly wishing she had more experience for all these new encounters with strangers. Perhaps she would be better equipped to understand if they were true in the actions, honorable friends, or conniving foes if she were trained by her papa or allowed out of her bedchambers and in court more often. So far, she has had plenty of reasons to *not* trust strange men, and very little to trust. Yet, what choice did she have in this situation?

Mason's wide shoulders perched a little higher, and he gave her rescuer a quick glance before barely looking back at Eira.

"To assist you, of course, to wherever you need to be. That is what gentlemen do, do they not?" This time, Mason's eyes met hers.

Eira felt a funny twinge in her gut, and her hands and feet were suddenly cold and numb. "I would not know." Her voice was weak and constrained. "I've not had the acquaintance of many gentlemen to say whether that be true or not."

The raw honesty that trembled out of her snaked around her heart, stopping it for a moment. Immediately she wished she could take them back her words. Papa never shied from vulnerability. Yet somehow, this honesty felt too vulnerable, as if she had shared too much.

Eira crossed her arms over her body and kept her eyes lowered.

"Well, I should say, we shall have to change that." Eira glanced up as Mason whipped his awkward stare at her rescuer.

"Right, Branson?" he continued with an overly jolly gesture toward her. "She should learn what a true gentleman is like."

Branson. Finally, a name to her rescuer's face. *What a nice Christian name. Why did he not say it himself?* she pondered. Was he hiding it on purpose?

"Get settled, Mason, and eat something," Branson ordered. "We need to continue the journey."

There was annoyance in Mason's demeanor and eyes. Whether the irritation was for her or Branson, she couldn't tell. But it was clear to her who was the chief of the two—Branson—and Mason did not seem to like that one bit.

Mason waved his arm in a half salute, then swiveled toward the direction of the brush where he had popped out from only minutes ago. Eira watched as Mason retrieved his beautiful horse from the forest. A cream-colored mare with speckles of rich brown dots trotted out toward them.

Eira walked up to the gorgeous mare and began brushing her soft, velvety nose. The mare's eyes watched her carefully, and he nestled into her touch. She was a gentle animal. Eira whispered to her, and the horse responded with a sweet upward head nod.

Eira sighed deeply, relaxing into the animal. Finally, she didn't feel alone. There was another female in the mix of these unknown men. A friend.

"Here." Mason rummaged into a sack and pulled out a handful of oats. He motioned with his fist. "For my horse. You can feed her if you want."

Cupping out her hands to receive the oats, Eira smiled. "Thank you. I would enjoy that very much."

She held her hands out to the mare and let her nibble at the grain with her soft, velvety mouth. When the mare finished eating, Mason tied his horse to a thin tree. Mason's back was now turned to Eira, but she couldn't take her eyes off the beautiful mare. How she wished she could see her father's horses again. She loved to sneak out of the palace and go to the horses at night.

Something caught the corner of Eira's eye, breaking her fond memory. Branson reached into his quiver, pulling out two arrows. He took out what looked like a knife and started to sharpen the tip of his arrowhead.

He would probably be hunting for tonight's dinner soon. Perhaps he would find grouse. She loved eating grouse. Or perhaps wild turkey or peacock—wouldn't that be splendid? Her stomach grumbled in delight. It would almost be as if she were home again.

Her mouth watered, and she licked her lips. *Very delightful indeed.* Eira, not knowing what to do or when they would be moving again, went to sit down on a log to rest. A drop of something cold landed on her nose. It melted. A shiver ran up her spine.

Snow.

Already?

Her eyes looked up into the canopy of branches. Small flakes wove their way through the arms and fingers of the treetops, dropping down on her. Sweat clung to her from their journey and brought a chill to her bones. Subtle memories of her mother fluttered down with each flake.

Mason swept a small blanket over Eira's shoulders.

"That is kind of you. I thank thee." She smiled at him, and he gave her a kind side smile back. "So, do you know the king and queen, then? Being the huntsman and all, you must."

She noticed his broad shoulders jump and then stiffen like a ton of bricks.

"No!" he said with such flare and pomp. "Why on earth would you suggest such a thing?"

"I merely thought—" Eira fumbled over her words. The feel of Mason's eyes on her again made her cheeks warm. Good thing she did not mention she was the princess. How foolish she was.

Placing her hands into her bubble-bow to keep warm, she felt the ring and her book of psalms snuggled against her. She wished she could read it. She only knew a few words, but not enough to read the book itself. At least it brought her comfort.

"Sir?" Expecting at least a grunt, he said nothing and kept his back to her. She continued regardless. "I've been thinking. You may call me Snow if you wish, but I would like to call you Mercy. I don't particularly think Branson would be suitable enough for you. It was by the mercy of God that He brought you both to me when I needed your help in the forest."

"Why would you ask such a thing?"

"Don't mind him." Mason gestured toward Branson. "He is a grumpy old man at times."

Eira caught a slight glare from Mason to Branson. She fiddled with her dirt-stained skirt, and wrapped her arms around her shoulders, pulling the blanket closer. She could feel the cold deepen into her now. "I think it only fitting that one of you be called Mercy, Branson. I believe that it would be best suited to you, do you not? You are the very act of God's mercy on my life."

"I told you." Mason laughed a little.

"Well…" she probed. "Is it not the perfect name for such a time?"

Eira examined Branson's tight jaw as he turned around. She caught a slight stiffness in his gait when he swayed into his widened stance.

Facing the ground, Branson avoided her gaze and her question while crossing his arms. "You should go find some wood scraps to build a fire. I'll watch from here. When you have enough, I'll leave to find food. I am the huntsman, after all."

His words left a sinister feeling in her gut, but she waved it off as ill practice with men. Perhaps he wasn't in favor of the name she chose for him. She would think of another. He deserved something for his efforts.

Happy to be of use finally, Eira popped off the log. She turned away from Branson and gave Mason back his blanket. Eira bounced toward a group of fallen trees while singing the name 'Mercy' and picking up nearby sticks along her way.

"Don't call me that." Branson's voice pierced through the silent forest.

She twirled back to look at him, her hand covering her mouth and quiver running through her.

"I beg your pardon?" Eira's brows rippled. "I didn't realize that name would upset you so. Forgive me."

"Don't call me anything. Just go and get the wood." Branson's voice was as sharp as the arrowhead in his hand. So sharp it almost penetrated her heart.

"Branson." The tone in Mason's voice halted them both. Mason marched over and slapped Branson on the shoulder, harder than necessary. "You said you wanted to show this young lady what a gentleman is." His eyebrows wagged, animatedly lifting and dropping back down, while gripping Branson's shoulders in a very hard grasp. "Well! Show the lady how to be treated." His head tilted toward Eira, and his smile toward Branson was more of a threat. "Go get the wood yourself!" he grunted.

As much as Eira appreciated the kind gesture of Mason, she wanted to prove herself useful. "I thank thee, dear sir." Her eyes slid from Mason's to Branson's pointedly. "But I am quite capable of handling this task. I will be of use to you and fetch the wood."

Mason's arm fell from Branson's shoulder, and he gently touched Eira's arm. With the voice of honey, he said, "You don't have to. Please sit back down. You've walked a great distance and need your rest."

She glared at Branson, remembering how he didn't let her have his horse. She pulled her arm easily from Mason's grasp. "I insist." Her chin jutted, and her lip curled slightly.

She moved toward fallen leaves and started to dig through them. After grabbing a bundle, she noticed a small squirrel darting about. Laughing at how adorable the creature was, she forgot her anger and remembered the kindness Branson gave her when he truly didn't have to. She fought the urge to look back. Her stomach growled, and the squirrel scurried away.

Wanting to see if Branson had caught any food, she quickly looked back toward Branson—but he was gone. *Perhaps he had the call of nature.* Shrugging her shoulders, she walked a little farther. Looking at the ground, picking up random scattered twigs of dried wood, Eira hummed to keep her mind off her stomach. She had to get enough wood to build the fire so they could eat whatever the men caught.

Once satisfied with the amount of wood in her arms, she stood and turned. Then, she froze.

She could see Branson peeking out from a large cedar tree, angling himself into the discreet view of his prey. Which, if Eira wasn't mistaken, appeared to be her. Arms weak, she fought the urge to let go and let the wood fall to the ground. Her body shook. She glanced slightly around her right and left sides. There was a deer just a short distance behind her. Branson would let the arrow fly, hitting the target behind her, just like he had done to Lance-man, right?

Then why did this feel so different? She thought back on how angry he was with her calling him Mercy. She hadn't been around men a lot, she had to admit. Yet, had he not shown kindness towards her by saving her and feeding her, promising to bring her safety? Surely, he wouldn't hurt her. An uneasiness settled into her gut.

If she were to admit it, she had seen a difference between the gruff manners Branson had with her and his hot and cold way, in contrast to the kindness and assurance Mason brought her. If she had been as careless with the queen regarding her own attitude, she wouldn't have been able to sit for a week. Had she been so easily persuaded by a man's feigned kindness? Was Branson's intention to truly help her? And what about Mason? Was he to be trusted if they were, in fact, friends?

Eira wanted to look behind her again to see if the deer was still there. But she didn't dare move. Her stomach did a flip. Then, another. The image of Lance-man and his soulless body lying on the ground raced across her mind. Lifting her head up a little straighter, she swallowed, but the saliva got stuck in her dry throat.

If she wasn't mistaken, it appeared as though Branson's arrow wasn't going to fly *past* her neck this time. If she was mistaken, the arrow was meant for her. Her eyes began to widen. Was it aiming at her?

From the distance, she could make out his forehead wrinkling with concentration. He was blinking and then blinking again, repositioning himself and calculating his target carefully. Her fingers twitched and she sucked in her breath hoping she didn't scare off the venison. She wanted to move—badly. A part of her screamed, "run!" But how could she prove useful to them if she scared off their only dinner for the night? It would be all her fault she couldn't risk that.

She held her breath and stood still. This stranger had made the perfect shot before and saved her life. She hoped he would do it again. It was all she could think of holding on to.

She shut her eyes tight, waiting for the blow.

Twelve

LEAVES RUSTLED, AND A WHOOSHING SOUND SOARED THROUGH the space between them. Suddenly, a piercing smack ripped through the side of Eira's body. She saw rather than felt herself begin to fall. Had she been hit? She was too numb to know for sure. Everything around her appeared to be moving as if at a snail's pace. Then, as rapidly she had felt the blow, her world sped up.

Falling backward, Eira bumped her head on a stump with a cracking thud. Wincing in pain, Eira kept her eyes and mouth closed. She was afraid to look, to even move. Had dinner been acquired after all? She tried to laugh at the irony of it all but couldn't.

Eira's hand reached up and touched the back of her head. She winced and sucked a breath through her teeth. Suddenly, an excruciating sound came from the arrow's direction. But that sound was not of any animal. Squinting ever so slightly, Eira finally opened her eyes.

There on the ground was Branson, blood oozing and flowing over his leg. Eyes wide, he groaned again. Strong hands picked her up off the ground and carried her over to Branson's horse.

"Here," a ragged and gruff voice said. She looked up to see Mason's profile. "Are you well enough to ride? You look like you hit your head. Have you been hurt badly, m'lady?"

Her limbs were shaking. She felt sick to her stomach. She couldn't tell where the pain was coming from within her body, if at all, but she knew she wasn't well, and that she had fallen on her head, hard.

"I—I am not sure. But I believe I hit my head. And perhaps, I was hit. I just can't feel where."

"You might be in a fit of fear." He patted her knee. "Stay calm."

"Branson," she whispered. Peering over Mason's shoulder and seeing the poor man reeling in pain, arrow down. The fear of death rushed through her veins like a flow of water. Why was Branson hurt and she in pain? Her limbs began to tremble, and her teeth chattered.

"I am afraid there will be no dinner tonight." Mason's eyes had a chill to them that made her shiver even more. "We must leave. Branson will be fine."

Eira shook her head.

"I don't understand. The deer..." She pinched her eyes closed, remembering the point of Branson's arrow directly aimed at her. "How did Branson get hurt?"

Mason's eyes pinched up in what seemed to her like regret as he guided her wobbly arms to the reins of Branson's horse.

"Sit here and hold on to the reigns. They will steady you. You are not well enough to get on the horse yourself. I will be right back to assist you."

Eira tried to nod but pinched her eyes closed with intense dizziness. The warmth of his hands slipped from hers. She opened her eyes in time to see him dip his head with a slight bow and dart back toward Branson.

What was happening? How could a single moment change the course of history so much? They were meant to be getting dinner ready, eating, and being merry. So, how on earth did Branson get shot? And how did Eira seem to get wounded in the process?

Eira caught the long bow slung over Mason's shoulders. Her eyes widened. Had Mason shot Branson? She observed Mason as he approached Branson and landed a quick blow to his cheek. Eira closed her eyes and let go of the lead to feel her jaw. Why had she felt that he hit her? She rolled her jaw and knew it was fine, so she placed one hand back on the reins. Remembering she had been hit somewhere else on her body, she used her other hand to feel around. When she got to her side, she winced. She couldn't see any arrows. Perchance it was only a flesh wound but she couldn't tell with her clothing.

The men yelled back and forth, but Eira could not hear what they were saying. Only the low guttural grunts that seeped from Branson's body, like blood slowly oozing from his wound. She had to do something. Eira shifted and tried to stand. But her limbs wouldn't cooperate, and she realized she was uncontrollably shaking. She licked her lips and tried to keep a grip on the reins.

Searching the forest again for the two strangers, Eira instantly spotted them. She wanted to pity Branson. After all, he appeared badly injured, but something felt off. She scanned behind her where the deer would have been and saw nothing. Had the deer fled out of fear? Would she not have heard it?

She glanced back at Mason. He was snapping the arrow from Branson's wound. Then, she watched Mason pull the wooden weapon out from the hole it created in Branson's leg. A sharp cry followed. It echoed through the forest.

Eira grimaced, feeling his pain. Her vision fell back onto Mason. Their eyes met. Compassion and sympathy reached her, but also a distinct concern. Branson must be greatly injured. She watched him kneel to the ground in front of Branson, then rip a piece of his tunic off into a long strip. Mason wrapped Branson's leg in the cloth. She could feel the rumbling snarl from where she was, and the horse whinnied, then sidestepped, propping her regal head up in discontent.

Eira shushed the horse and tried to brush her mane with shaky

81

fingers. "Be still, girl. All will be well." She kept brushing the horse until she seemed to settle her nerves along with Eira's.

Eira's eyes caught the light glinting off a small metallic object near the men. She squinted. It was a knife. It looked like the blade was in the hand of Branson. Suddenly, it flashed again. It was done so swiftly, she wasn't sure she'd seen it.

Mason yelped and jumped away from Branson. Branson advanced onto Mason with a fury she had never seen in him before. Eira, wanting to help, yelled for them to stop fighting, but only managed to startle the horse again. The mare neighed and circled until Eira calmed her.

A low rumbling scream rang to the left of Eira. Before she moved toward it, something charged toward her. She swiveled to see Branson. He was incredibly close to her, and his eyes were filled with so much anger, it took Eira's breath away.

Mason came up behind Branson and jumped on him. The mare Eira was holding on to scurried backward from the commotion, and Eira hugged her reins tight. Mason's right arm quickly hooked around Branson's thick neck. Branson started to fight back, his blade slashing wildly in the air. His eyes fixed on Eira.

"You don't understand. I have to do it!" Branson growled.

"Over my dead body." Mason grunted back.

Mason managed to smack the knife out of Branson's hand and continued choking him. Branson groaned and swung wildly, advancing closer toward Eira. His dreadful eyes were on Eira like she was his next hunt. What if Mason couldn't hold him any longer?

Her stomach jumped, and her hands grew cold. Suddenly, she saw Branson's eyes roll back into his head and slowly grow limp in Mason's arms.

"Did you kill him? Is he—" Eira didn't want to finish her question and allowed it to hang in the air.

"Nay. I merely just made him sleep for a bit, is all."

"We need to hurry. It won't be long before he wakes up and seeks to harm you again."

"Me—" Eira covered her mouth with her left hand. "But why?"

"I have no idea. I am as shocked as you must be." He came to her side. "Are you too hurt to ride?"

"Honestly, I would feel safer riding. My head is hurting, because of that I am still slightly dizzy, and my side is painful. But I don't see an arrow protruding out of where I got hit or anything. I think I am fit enough, yes..."

Lightly, his sturdy hands lifted her foot and delicately placed it in the leather strap dangling near the belly of the gentle creature.

"Hold tight," Mason said. As he helped her grip the thick leather straps, the tough of his hand brought a sense of stillness seeping up her into her arms. His words sounded reassuring, but his creased brows told her otherwise. "Alas, we must leave immediately. I will speak with you in a moment." Mason was on his horse and beside her in one sweep of a motion. After a few moments of awkward readjustments to Eira and her horse, they finally made a steady pace. "My best guess as to why Branson would try and harm you...I don't know why, but perhaps, this is the queen's doing."

"The queen?" Her voice shook. "She wishes me dead. But why?"

Mason glanced down at Eira's hand.

"Perchance, you may know why she would want you dead?"

Eira followed his gaze to where her father's signet ring laid on her hand. In prominence, it reflected the light of the day back to her. She quickly tried to cover it with her other hand but couldn't hold the reins well enough.

"You weren't supposed to see that."

"Did you steal it?"

"No." Tears started to well up in Eira's eyes, blurring her vision. "It was given to me by my Papa."

"Your Papa—" His horse must have felt the shock from his master and scuttled to the left. "Whoaa" He soothed the horse and continued to veer it beside Eira's.

"Does that make you," Mason's eyebrows perched, "the illusive Whiteshire Princess no one has seen?"

"Yes." Her voice whimpered. "I knew queen mother hated me, but to have me killed—royal blood—murdered? How could she possibly —" Her gaze intensified. "If Branson *was* going to kill me in the woods when I was attacked, why did he save me? I don't understand."

He reached over and put his hand on hers. "There was a man who came to us and requested our help. He didn't tell me all the details— clearly, they were devious in nature—I would have put a stop to this earlier had I known what Branson's plan was"

Tears ran down her face. "My own mother … wants me dead. You must be lying."

"I am sorry. I will do what I can to protect you." He shook his head and looked around them. "I don't think we have been followed, but you are not safe here. I don't imagine bringing the news you are still alive will be well for Branson. They will soon be after us."

"It seems I am not safe anywhere," Eira whispered. Then winced in pain.

"Hush now. Reserve your energy. We have a long way to travel yet."

Her body was shivering. Silence seemed to stretch between them as he led the way out of the forest. So many questions ran through her mind. What had just happened? Why had Branson suddenly attacked her in such a way? Why did Mason protect her? And why did he assume it was her stepmother that wanted her dead? If she wanted Eira dead, she could have done it years ago. Why now?

They continued in silence for some time.

"We were never properly introduced." He sighed. "I am Mason Barnett, Master Hunstman of Whiteshire, and—" He licked his lips. "I am sure you have some questions. Knowing a bit more of who I am might help put you at ease." He glanced toward her with a lopsided grin.

"I Thank thee," she replied meekly. "It does. It is very nice to meet you." She nodded her head toward him. Eira knew the most appropriate thing to do now was to introduce herself properly, but she didn't know what to say—was she princess Eira? Was she now a lost, deserted maidan with a signet ring and no future? She quickly changed the topic.

"I do have a few questions," Eira exclaimed. "How did you come to know Branson?"

"He is my apprentice. A mighty fine one at that. I will be sad to see him go. But I will not have a traitor among my men."

"A traitor? How so?"

Mason cleared his throat and slowed his horse to walk more side by side with hers. "Ahh. Are you—are you not Eira White, Princess of Whiteshire?"

Eira's eyes widened, and her throat went dry, but when she looked at him, Mason's eyes were kind. "I have already admitted as such." She confirmed.

"I have only ever heard rumors of you," Mason continued, turning his face away so she couldn't hear him murmur the rest under his breath. "But the rumors are true. You are truly beautiful. I can see why the queen could be envious enough to request your death."

"How do you know who I am? We have not met before. Nobody has ever seen me, besides a few servants. Especially outside of the kingdom."

"Ahh, yes. I am aware of how you have been hidden from your people. Unfortunately, I only know of you because of Branson and what he was tasked to do."

"Pray-tell, what was that? I am still hazy on what happened." Eira knew what he was about to say. But somehow, by asking the question, she had hoped it would be something different.

"The queen's henchman came to my men, requesting a Master Huntsman. Branson offered his services to the queen. Sadly, it was a deceitful request, but Branson kept silent and would not allow me to know the mission. I told him I would meet him in the forest where you and Branson found me. But Branson did not know I had followed him and watched closely." Mason slung his head in disgust and then continued. "When I saw him aim his arrow towards you and not the deer, I instantly realized he was attempting to kill—"

Mason averted her eyes. "I was too far away. So, I pulled my own arrow and struck him before he could strike you." Mason swallowed. "When I approached him after seeing to you, he confessed what he was going to do."

The shock of being someone's target ran through Eira's veins.

"There was no deer behind me, was there?" Her voice felt weak. She must have seen an illusion to convince herself there was a deer there. How could she be so naïve?

"There was a deer. But I have trained my men well and could tell he was not aiming at the deer." Mason shook his head. "It is not your fault that this happened." Mason tried to reassure her, obviously seeing her despondency.

"What of Branson? Will he die?"

"I am afraid I had to strike him before he hit you with his arrow. But it was not fatal, I promise."

Eira studied him. She wasn't sure if she could trust this man or anyone. Could Branson really have known it was her leaving the forest? Only her father knew, she was certain. What if what Mason said were lies?

"Perhaps he wanted to hit you instead and not me? Perhaps he is truly the protector and you the villain. If what you said is true, why then did you not save me in the forest from those horrible men?"

"I was watching from a distance and would not have let them hurt you had Branson failed at his job."

It did little to help her feel safe, but Eira was satisfied enough with his answer.

"Still. I would have much rather have not gone through that horrible moment. I would have had you step in sooner."

"My apologies m'lady. I didn't know who you were at that moment. I should have stepped in sooner. I am sorry." He pointed down to her side. "Does it hurt?"

She peered down to where he was pointing and saw blood on her dress. Instantly, she felt the sting of her side. Her right hand let go of the rein and she pressed her side.

"You will be fine. I think it is only a flesh wound. Otherwise, there would have been more blood." He slowed his horse, examined the back of her head, and then sped back to his position beside her. "And where you hit your head is not enough to harm you."

Eira tightened her grip on the horses' reins. "I still don't understand why they wished me dead. Can mere beauty be enough to harm me? Does that not sound ridiculous to you?"

"Envy is an evil all on its own. And who but the devil, and those who follow him, know what harms it can yield."

"'Tis' true. My Papa did say it was not safe for me any longer in the castle. He mentioned the death of my queen mother's own father. Perhaps that is the cause?"

"I cannot say for certain, but when I confronted Branson, he confessed his conversation with the queen's henchman. Branson was ordered directly from the queen to kill you and provide your heart on a platter."

"Did you say the queen wanted my heart on a platter?" She studied him. How could she have been so blind? Had the queen always hated her? Was there no love in her stepmother for her?

Mason's cheeks went red. Whether from shame or perhaps anger, Eira wasn't quite sure. "Aye, m'lady. 'Tis what she said."

"I will reward you Mason—fully. I am unsure of how or when, but rest assured, I will tell my father, and he will avenge me and honor you for your bravery and for your kindness toward me." She dipped her head as if in a slight bow of acknowledgment. "You know, if I could, I would dub you Mason Barnett, *Knight* of Whiteshire, from henceforth. You would forever be known as The Merciful. A Noble Keeper of Justice for doing what was right and not seeking your own good, but honoring truth."

This time, she was certain his cheeks blushed from humility and pride.

"I don't deserve anything, m'lady. However, if you could, I would humbly accept that honor. I thank thee." He bowed to her and trotted forward, leading the way.

"To me, you do."

But it was all just words. Eira was not as strong, or even smart, like he was. She had no idea if the man who saved her meant to hurt her himself. She was unable to do anything to save her own life besides spooking the horse. And even now, Mason was in the lead, guiding them toward the unknown.

She slipped her left hand into her pocket and touched her father's signet ring. What is he had passed away like Lance-man said? What if she were now queen? Queen Amara would try and become regent, or worse, queen, if others thought Eira dead.

A sick feeling made her stomach tighten. Oh, how she wished she could seek her papa out for his wisdom, or remember what her mother had told her, or know how to be strong for either of them. Instead, all she could do was lift the ring out, kiss it, pray for a miracle, and place it back into her pocket.

Thirteen

EIRA COULD HEAR THE SINGING BEFORE MASON DISMOUNTED and offered his hand. Sliding off the horse with ease, Mason held her waist and gently lowered her to the ground. Grimacing, she thanked him and started toward the plain home. Stopping suddenly, she grabbed Mason's arm. "Wait. Who are we to meet here?"

"No need to fret, m'lady. These men are gentle—you have my word. They took me in when I was ill after being shut out in the rain and the cold during one of my hunts. Since, we have stayed in touch and built a kindred friendship."

"Are you sure?"

"They'd barely hurt a fly. Hugo is a bit of a killbuck, but harmless, I can assure you of that. We call him 'Wee Prince Hugo,' which he secretly likes." Mason laughed, then whispered, "Prithee, don't tell him that, or he'll deny it to your face." The smile that spread on Mason's face was encouraging.

"Fredrick is known for griping, but I think he means well. Laurentius—" His eyebrows shrugged with his shoulders. "I'll admit, you'll have to excuse some of his behaviors from time to time. But—" He searched for something on his person and then pulled out a sheathed item. "Here's something to hopefully bring you ease. It's a dagger."

"I can see that. Do I need it here?" she said, receiving the dagger and wondering where she would put it. There was nowhere on her person that she could carry it and her bag was already full.

"Heaven's, no! It's for protection." He laughed again. "Should you ever feel in danger when I'm gone."

"Gone? You're leaving me! Where are you going? When?"

Before Mason could respond, the singing stopped abruptly, and the door in front of them swung open. From behind the wooden door, Eira could hear rustling and murmuring. She looked at Mason with a question mark eyebrow.

"Who goes there?" a deep voice rumbled out.

Her eyes dropped to the sound where a short man, about the size of a child, stood, his arms crossed.

"Ahh, it's only Mason," the small man hollered into the cosh.

Eira had never seen such a little person, but remembered a story once told of a mighty man of valor, though short in stature. In the story, they had called the man a dwarf. Eira squinted. The dwarf's round face soured when he looked up at Eira.

"And he's brought a lady-friend with him. I don't think we should let them in!"

"Good day to you too, Fredrick," Mason said, looking back at Eira and winking. "Is Doc in?"

Fredrick growled and opened the door. "Take off your shoes, Mathew just swept."

"Thank you," Eira said as both she and Mason slipped off their slippers and walked in.

Mason ducked down with every wooden beam that lined the ceiling. The smell of dew and sweet pudding met them—it was everything a home should be and brought further comfort to her.

Passing through the narrow hall, they entered a large open room with many rocking chairs surrounding a stone fire pit, ascending the wall up to the ceiling.

She noticed there was more than one dwarfed man. Holding back her shock, she bit her cheek to keep a smile from creeping up her face. All of them were *adorable*. Many of them were bearded with wide shoulders and strongly built, but only met her height, waist high.

Surveying the room, she observed two men rocking in the chairs close to the fire. One held a recorder and the other a harp. Two red-haired men were sitting in the corner playing a game of Tric-tac.

Fredrick moved toward the opposite wall of the fireplace, joining the youngest of the bunch and helping him clean up from the dinner they must have recently eaten. Eira's tummy rumbled, and she licked her lips. They still hadn't eaten anything, and she was feeling weak.

The last man she noticed in the room was already standing and coming toward them. Hmm. *Seven men altogether.* She looked around. *And, just what I suspected, no women.*

"Doc!" Mason embraced the man nearest them. He was the oldest, with kind, crinkly eyes and gray hair. "It is so good to see you again." Mason turned to Eira with his one hand out. "This is Princess Eira White of Whiteshire."

A thud came from the two men cleaning. They must have dropped a dish. Suddenly, each small man stood in one accord.

"Your Majesty," they said, bowing to one knee.

Doc stood again and held out his hand. "On behalf of the *Men-Of-Ore*, we welcome you into our home and are honored by your visit this evening."

Reaching for his hand, Eira dipped with the same courtesy and respect. "Thank you for opening your door to us. I am very pleased to have met you, Doc."

"Oh, m'lady, please call me by my Christian name. Duncamus," he said.

"All right, Doc. I'll call you Duncamus. May we sit and sup with you? We are very hungry from our journey." She smiled at Fredrick, who only glowered at her in return.

"Why, of course! Please sit." Doc directed her to the fire and placed a chair for her there. Doc gasped. "You are hurt, m'lady!"

"It is alright. I don't believe it is that bad." Eira's hand fluttered to her side. She pressed into her small wound to prove that she was fine. Eira winced a little.

Doc sucked in his breath. "Do you need me to tend to it? I have all the fixin's to get you right and new."

Eira stole a look at Mason. He nodded.

"That would be kind of you. I thank thee, Doc—I mean Duncamus. I see why they call you Doc." Eira smiled at him, and his eyes glinted in response.

"I'll get right to it, m'lady."

He escorted her into a small, quiet room where there was more privacy, and tended carefully to her wound.

On their way back to the group, Eira said, "The music I heard was lovely. Do you sing every evening?"

Eira watched as Doc brought a large pillow for Mason to sit near the fire. She squeezed herself into a chair. Clearly, he would not be able to fit in the small men's chairs, as she had barely been able to do.

"Yes. Every evening, we sing," Doc replied, beaming with pride. "Each of us takes a turn playing while the others work cleaning or prepping the food. On this fine eve, Laurentius"—Doc pointed to the man with the recorder. He was much smaller than the others and had a distinctively dark mole on his right cheek. Doc's finger continued to sweep the room and landed on another man playing the harp who had broad shoulders, holding his instrument with reverence— "and this dear fella, Christopher..."

She noticed Christopher's hair was dark, like ore. Though his eyes appeared green from the amber fire, they were truly blue in color. Doc's fingertips clasped together with his other hand as he continued. "...they got to play the music tonight while the others work."

"Ha!" Laurentius scoffed. "Those fopdoodles wouldn't be able to hold a note with one of these." He wiggled the recorder in the air. "If I had it my way, I would play every night. It's a good thing you came when you did, m'lady."

"Don't mind Laurentius." Doc laughed. "He's not as refined as one would hope."

"No need to apologize." Eira looked at Mason. "I was forewarned."

Just then, a younger man tripped carrying a bowl of fine-smelling soup, almost spilling all its contents on her.

"Careful, Benjamin!" Fredrick yelled. "You don't want to burn the poor lass." He threw his towel on the wooden table in protest. Then he picked up Mason's portion and walked with emphasis toward Benjamin. Exaggerating each movement to emphasize how it should have been done. Fredrick placed the bowl in Mason's hands. "Here."

Fredrick turned to Doc. "I'm off to bed before Benjamin makes more of a mess that I must clean up. And don't you dare think I will clean up the princess if he spills all over her." Fredrick pivoted toward Eira. "Good night, Your Majesty," he growled.

Fredrick stomped out of the large room, mumbling as he went on his way down a small hallway. "...so much for trying to serve soup to a princess, only for it to end up all over her lap..." His murmurings continued to follow him down the hallway about a "clumsy something-or-other fool."

Looking at the floor, the young man slowly came up beside Eira. "Miss—m'lady—I am terribly sorry. Only mean to do good—I do. But I'm clumsy, you see. I really hope you like the soup." His face lifted into a smile when she met his eyes.

Eira breathed in the aroma, and instantly her mouth watered. "It smells delicious, and I am grateful for it. Thank you." As he was about to turn around, she caught his arm. "What was your name again?"

"It's Benjamin. But you can call me Ben." His eyes widened even more, and his cheeks reddened to the color of strawberries.

"Well." She laughed. "Benjamin. I am also thankful to Fredrick too. I'll be sure to tell him in the morning. And just so you know, I am not afraid of a little clumsiness." She put the bowl to her lips and sipped the savory broth with delight.

Ben scurried over to the wooden table and started cleaning up again. Bowls clattered while the two small men in the corner that she hadn't met yet sat playing Tric, and the fire crackled away for a few moments. The soup and the peace these men and this house brought to her was a nice present, despite everything she had experienced on her birthday.

"Doc, I have a favor to ask you," Mason piped up from the floor to her left.

"I supposed that was the reason for your visit. What can I do for you?"

"The princess is being hunted by the Queen of Whiteshire. She has escaped but needs refuge and a safe place to live for a while. Can you help us?" He got up and walked to Ben, handing him his dirty soup bowl. "Thank you, Benjamin. It was delicious." He returned to the pillow by the fire.

"We will," Doc assured. "But I am confused. Why would the queen want to kill the princess? She seems harmless." Doc gave Eira a once-over.

Mason put his hands closer to the fire to warm them. "She is harmless. I have word that the queen has plans far greater than killing only Princess Eira here, but I will need to go and find out. She will need protection and safety while I investigate the matter."

Laurentius was about to blow on his recorder when it shrilled. Eira turned to face him. He must have realized what Doc and Mason were discussing, as his jaw dropped before stating, "Aye, I daresay, it is nithe and hudder-mudder. The queen won't be mildful on the fairhead. I know it. She is full of vileness and nithe, if you ask me!"

"Now, now. How can you say that? We must be wise with our words, Laurentius," Christopher, the moral leader of the bunch, said while strumming his harp. "The Good Lord would not want us to be foolish to speak of the queen with such mannerism. You know that. Saying she is evil and has ill intent for the girl is not good. It could be treason." Christopher looked sheepishly toward the princess. "Don't mind him, m'lady..." He tossed his head in the direction of Laurentius. "He is often full of nonsense."

"Thank you." Eira giggled, then sobered. "However, in this case, Laurentius may be right." Eira's eyes dimmed. "And I can say with certainty now that her heart is as black as the coals in this fire."

"I'm sure Mason will see to the matter," Doc said, sitting next to her and patting her arm. "In the meantime, you are safe with us. I promise. Though we must tend to our work in the mountains during the day."

"You are so kind," Eira said, mid-yawn.

"Thank you, Doc." Mason reached up and patted Doc's knee. "I knew you would help." Standing up, Mason continued, "You need your rest, m'lady, and I should be leaving now."

"Must you be leaving so soon? I thought you would keep watch at least one night."

Mason's shoulders slumped, and he heaved a heavy sigh. "I wish I could. I overheard Branson say the queen demanded your heart on a platter this very night. I must bring something back to her by morning, or she will come looking for you and me. Besides, I need to discover all I can about her intentions."

Eira walked with Mason to the small wooden door while Doc followed close behind. "Please be safe, Mason. I am forever grateful for what you've done for me. Thank you."

"I will send word for you as quick as I can. I don't want to lead anyone here with letters or horse tracks. So, I will keep my distance until it is safe and will send word by a monk. He resides near the Men-of-Ore." Mason reached for her hands and kissed her knuckles. "M'lady, if anything were to happen to me as a consequence, it was an honor to serve you." His eyes held hers with such intensity, she almost couldn't bear it. He dropped her hands and smiled. "I've some hunting to do!"

Eira turned toward Doc as he shut the wooden door behind Mason. "He is a good man, Doc. Full of honor and valor."

"Indeed, he is, m'lady. Indeed, he is." Doc nodded.

"Duncamus?" she whispered. "Prithee, I wish you would call me by my Christian name also. Eira is all I've ever known, and I feel more comfortable with that name than princess or m'lady."

He paused and looked at her. He must have seen the sadness in her eyes. "I will honor your request on one condition." He smiled. "You may call me Doc!"

As small as he was, his kind eyes reached all the way up to hers and rested her troubled heart for one more evening. Maybe this place would bring a feeling of belonging, a feeling of safety, a feeling of home.

She would hold onto the feeling tonight. If the queen found out she was still alive and Mason's plan didn't work, tomorrow could bring her worst nightmares and fears. Only God could know.

Eira sighed even deeper as she walked back to the fireplace. The men began to play their instruments again, and Eira let the music release the tension in her shoulders. She would enjoy the moment, for as long as it was meant to last.

Fourteen

QUEEN AMARA

"SEILDA?"

Queen Amara dipped her pinky finger into the healer's concoction of fucus and applied it to her lips. She pulled out the small Looking Glass from her bubble-bow and eyed the ruby lips before her.

Perfect. As they should be.

"Yes, m'lady." Seilda crept forward, her shoulders hunched while her gray and blue shawl dragged on the floor.

"Our new friend Justin has brought good news from the king's trip to Normandy." Her smile widened in the Looking Glass. "It appears my poor husband has fallen ill and died on his long trek. It took some time, but all is well. His weak plans to build a home without me are foiled, I daresay."

"He is indeed dead. I have seen to the burial plans myself."

"Yes, yes." Putting the small, cracked glass back into her bubble-bow, Queen Amara stood and placed her fingers on Seilda's shoulder. She bent to whisper in her ear. "Now, all we need to do is get rid of his firstborn heir."

"Firstborn, m'lady?" Seilda's gray, bushy eyebrows quickly pulsed.

She was an ugly old woman, but a quick-witted one, and that's exactly why Queen Amara found her useful.

"Yes, tis' true. I am with child."

"But how can that be? The king has been away."

The queen scowled. "Just because I hate my husband doesn't mean I do not perform congenital duties as his queen. I can keep up with the duties of a wife, so long as it benefits me. And a child of my own would indeed do just that."

"But how far along are you?" She could see Seilda's eyes scrutinizing her body.

"I suppose to be further than a month long now. Perhaps a bit more." Queen Amara swept her hand unconsciously over growing belly. "It appears I have terrible news. The wretched little princess has gone missing. But of course, we knew that could happen, didn't we, Sielda?"

Seilda bobbed her head, gray wisps of hair flinging with each nod as Queen Amara continued. "Herrick found men outside the gates, and after some heavy persuasion, discovered she had run into the forest. It'll only be a matter of time before Branson hunts her down. Time is truly of the essence now, as I have even more unexpected and, sad to say, terrible news to share."

The queen dropped her hand from Seilda's shoulder and picked under her nails, flicking encrusted dirt onto the wood floor. She held Seilda's gaze.

"The news I shared earlier is one I was not expecting, of course, but one of perhaps good fortune."

"I always liked a good fortune." Seilda smirked.

"It will come as a shock to the entire kingdom if they were to find out that their king is dead. But given this unexpected news, perhaps they will be pleased. Because I have a plan."

"I do not understand. What news and what plan, m'lady?" Seilda's crooked fingers intertwined with anticipation.

"I am with child." The queen pursed her lips. Queen Amara's insides churned like sour milk at the bottom of a cauldron, making her feel even more sick than she already was. "Not fair news, I admit, and dreadfully unfortunate for one's beauty. Alas, we will have to prepare for that. However, it will be worth the troubles if it is a male child. He will be my future security, and the rite of the throne. Now, more than ever, it is imperative that the girl be found dead to secure my empire. So, you must keep this a secret and my radiance as beautiful as ever. I will bring news to the kingdom once Branson has brought word of Eira's demise." She paused and smiled. "With her and the king's death acquired, the throne and empire are mine."

Queen Amara's eyes locked onto Seilda's, who had a devilish grin matching her own, inching up her wrinkled cheeks. The old woman laughed.

"This will work out perfectly, Your Majesty. You are brilliant, My Queen."

Perfectly?

Yes, it's a perfect plan...

Queen Amara smiled from ear to ear. *It will be! Once Eira's unbeating heart is brought to me on a silver platter.* Until then, she had one imperfection needing to change at once—her title.

With a cold, hard glare, Queen Amara leaned into Seilda and hissed, "I will be your *empress*, Seilda, not your queen!"

"Where have you been all day? I have been waiting all morning for our rituals!" The queen's voice caused the mirror against the wall to vibrate.

"I—I have been seeing to your business, My Queen. I was following up on reports of the king's death and confirming it with letters and such, preparing his funeral and where his bones may lay, and seeing about the business of Princess Eira." He paused and then pointed to a side table.

"You also received a gift."

Queen Amara glanced over at the table. "What is it?"

"I am unaware of what it could be."

Queen Amara advanced near the table. She eyed the piece of jewelry. "Who is it from?"

"I believe it was made for you, but I cannot say by whom. Of course, I will investigate further, m'lady."

Queen Amara lifted the piece from its container. It was a thick, but small cross made of gold. It had an intricately made, swirling design covering its surface, while embedded with delicate round pearls, a large oval-shaped ruby at the top, and a hefty rectangle emerald at the base of the cross, along with other oblong gems along its sides. It was stunning. Truly jaw-dropping.

"Why a cross?"

"M'lady? I—I am unaware of the origins or its maker."

"It's *maker*?" She glared at him. "Do you intend to mock me, Herrick? You know how I feel about religion and…" Must she say it? "…*God*."

"Yes, Your Majesty. I will take it away this instant!"

"No. You will not." She eyed the design carefully. She was mesmerized by the elaborate details of the encrusted jewels. "No. I shall keep it."

"It is beautiful, as much as you are, My Queen."

"Indeed." She placed it back down and ignored the desire to look at it again. Another nudge pulled at her, a push to ponder the meaning of the cross a little longer. But she shoved the nudge down.

"Sit and speak. Give me your reports, and we shall continue with our little game." *The game was a must.* Noticing Herrick squirm in his chair made her instantly irritated. "Don't disappoint me, Herrick."

There was no time to waste. Court was almost in session. Of

course, they would all have to wait for her presence before commencing. And she would make them wait as long as it took to commence their game.

"Spit it out!"

"Yes—yes, Your Majesty." He folded his hands in front of him. "It is confirmed with witnesses that the king is dead."

"That was obvious. Move on." Queen Amara flicked her wrist.

"Yes, well. There was some discussion of who will be taking over the throne as regent or when the coronation should take place." Herrick cleared his throat. "None of which mentioned you, m'lady. Only the princess, Eira White."

"I have worked all her miserable life to keep her hidden. Why would they mention her now?"

"Some of the men remember her and were asking about her whereabouts. It appears she's made more of an impression than we assumed. Somehow, they even knew her birthday recently commenced, and she was of age to reign on her own." He pulled at his tunic and looked away from her. "Without a regent, as she is of age."

"Well, little do they know she's dead. Or will be, once Branson has completed his task, will it not?"

After swiveling his legs to one side, Herrick continued. "If Branson has completed his task, you are quite right, My Queen."

Queen Amara stepped forward. She had enough of him licking his lips and darting his eyes. "You do not believe the huntsman has completed his task." Anger filled her eyes. "Well?"

A noise startled them both. The door to her bedchamber burst open, and one of her knights knelt before them. "My Queen, the Master Huntsman is here to see you."

"Just in the nick of time. I was beginning to worry. Rise, and bring him to me." She turned to Herrick. "We shall see if your suspicions are correct."

"M'lady, they aren't suspic—"

"Your Majesty." Mason strode in.

A finely decorated silver platter was covered in his one hand. A cup with what appeared to be blood on the edges was in the other. He lowered himself into a bow, hands offering up the platter and drink.

The queen clapped her hands together. "The favored huntsman has caught his finest prey yet!" She walked toward him and smelled blood. "Fresh, I hope?"

"Last night, m'lady." He grinned, and she matched his smile.

"Herrick, do you see what our huntsman has brought me?" Her voice was young and high-pitched, like when she was a child asking her father to eat more of his kissing comfits.

Herrick moved slowly and stood by Mason, inspecting everything about him. "This is not the Master Hunstman. Where is her heart?" he demanded.

Mason handed Herrick the cup of blood and took off the lid of the platter. "The heart, lungs, and liver, My Queen." Mason's eyes slid to Herricks. "This is more than you requested, m'lady."

"You have outdone yourself." She spun on Herrick. "But you say this is not the man you sent?"

"No, your Majesty! Tis' not." Herrick glared at Mason. "He is an apprentice to the Master."

Slowly walking up to Mason, she asked. "Tell me. Does the dead girl have a sliver of blue in her eyes or specks of gold?"

"Neither. She has a faint sliver of green in her eye. But it is faint, my Queen."

"And which eye is that?"

"Her right."

"I am satisfied." Queen Amara spun to face Herrick. "He acquired what I needed. Fetch the cook. I am famished!" Her little game and the court could wait for this.

"You in—intend to eat it, m'lady?" Mason looked as if he were going to lose the contents of his midday meal.

"Tsk. Tsk. Mason. You wouldn't want to spoil the queen's appetite, would you?"

The glower from Herrick's gaze made Queen Amara's insides swim with excitement.

"Be off with you, Herrick. Fetch the cook. Make sure they add some strawberries. They have been increasingly appealing to me of late. Have it delivered to my bedchambers immediately."

As Herrick walked past and retrieved the platter from Mason's hand, Queen Amara could faintly hear uncivil words exchanged between the two men. Normally she would be intent on listening. Today, she couldn't be bothered.

Eira was finally dead!

She was so excited she nearly forgot to pay the man.

"Mason. I will reward you with a bulse full of gold. Or would you prefer diamonds?"

"If it is not too much trouble, gold is my preference, Your Majesty." Mason bowed.

"Very well. Gold it is. You won't run off on me with all your gold, will you?" She lifted her cap, laughing, and walked toward the window.

Mason didn't speak.

"I see." She smirked. "One last thing before you go, Mason."

He stopped. "Yes, My Queen."

"You are not the only huntsman I have that is willing to do whatever it takes for prestige and position. There are plenty of men who would die for your place of honor. To have the freedom of my lands to roam, hunt, and eat. Let it be known that whoever betrays their queen will end up with the same result as the little girl whom you have killed." She smiled and waved him off.

"I have no doubt that is the truth."

Leisurely, out of the corner of her eye, she watched as Mason stiffly bowed. Slowly, he backed up, and when far enough away, he completely turned his back on her.

Yes, this day is turning out very well.

QUEEN AMARA WAS STILL at the window when Herrick brought the cooked flesh. He placed it on a small table near her mirror. Then, he picked up a gold chair and positioned it for her to sit. Without a word, the queen walked over and sat. Picking up her knife, she began to carve away at Eira's heart. After a few mouthfuls, she pointed the tip of the knife at Herrick.

"Sit."

She watched as his wobbly legs moved forward, and he sat in his chair. *Pathetic.*

"Let us play, shall we?"

"My Queen, do you not wish to finish your meal first?" His fingers twisted in his lap.

"Why do you test me, Herrick? Can I not enjoy this celebration by playing my favorite game of all?" The knife clanked on her plate, and she stood chewing. Swallowing the tough muscle and gristle, she stood in front of her mirror. "Or shall you prolong my suffering?"

"As you wish, My Queen. But I—"

"Looking Glass, Looking Glass on the wall, who in this land is the fairest of all?" She beamed at herself in the mirror while Herrick hesitated.

Noticing meat stuck in her teeth, she swiped at it with her tongue. Waiting for Herrick's response, she slowly prompted, "You, My Queen, are fairest..." Her wrist and hand twirled, rotating in a circle, as if to allow him to continue.

Herrick picked up where she left off. "—are fairest. It is true." He paused. "Though Eira White is a—" Queen Amara's face swung toward Herrick's as if to stop him, but he continued with his hateful words even still. "—a thousand times fairer than you."

Eyes like hot lava bore into his soul. "How dare you!" She marched over to the table, picked up Eira's lifeless lung, and threw it in Herrick's face. "Does her lung breathe in air as if she were alive?"

She picked up the knife she used to cut through Eira's heart and paced the floor. *I should kill him now.*

"Did you not see what the huntsman brought me? Eira's heart on a platter! I've eaten it before you, and would you deny me this pleasure? Having the audacity to speak her wretched name to me! Why do you torment me?"

"I do not believe the huntsman. It was not the man I sent. I do not believe she is dead, My Queen! I swear it!" Herrick shrieked with fear.

A sudden fear crept up Queen Amara's back.

"You are not worthy to live. But I'll spare your life if you can prove your statement. Leave me and come back with proof. I cannot believe another word until I see proof." Queen Amara stabbed the knife into the liver. "Eira must be dead!"

Fifteen

OWEN

Prince Owen pulled his white tunic, which bore the iconic red cross, over his shoulders and grabbed the wooden staff by the front door. He was ready for his journey once again. The respite had proved to be well worth an extra day's rest.

"It has truly been marvelous these past few days with you. I cannot express all my gratitude for your hospitality. I wish I could repay you somehow," Owen said, knowing his offer would be rejected.

Brother Obadiah shook his hand firmly. "You are most welcome, my dear brother, and no need to fret! God repays. He will tend to my needs accordingly. I will walk with you partway down the path and pray for you there." His eyes crinkled.

"I will get my horse ready." Owen started toward the barn. Once Absalom was saddled and ready, he walked his horse to the cosh. Brother Obadiah Owen continued toward the forest trail.

"One day, I would like to see the work you speak about at the Abbey. You are an artist of some kind, I gather. It must be important, and I hate the fact that I've prevented you from it."

"You didn't prevent me. I simply took a break. I've enjoyed the last few days as well. Besides, it's best that I work alone. Too many distractions can lead to mistakes. Come, you must be off to tend to your own work, pilgrim." Obadiah didn't release his eyes from the path ahead as he spoke.

The morning dew rested on the forest floor. Being in his care, Owen couldn't help but notice how still and unmoving Obadiah was. He admired the monk's tranquility, honesty, and kindness, traits Owen often neglected in himself. One day, he hoped to be as confident as the monk.

Obadiah stopped beside him, and Owen stilled.

"This is far enough. You are on your own now." Obadiah smiled. "May the Lord be with you, shine upon you, and guide you in knowledge, my brother. Knowledge and wisdom to help you in the days to come." He spoke as if the future had been laid out and Obadiah knew the secrets of what was to come.

Obadiah laid his hands on Owen's forehead. Obadiah's Latin words transformed into prayers, releasing into the air around them as dew ascending into mist. Confidence filled Owen's veins for the journey ahead to St. Swithun. He would find his miracle there and—Lord willing—his sister.

"Thank you, Obadiah. If you should have need of anything, please send for me in Wealas. I will return instantly."

"Who's to say you will ever return home to Wealas? Life following a miracle can lead you anywhere. A life following the narrow path is much harder, yet it leads to life. Both are your choice." For an instant, concern rippled over the monk's face, then it was gone as if it had never happened in the first place.

"I thank you, dear brother, for your company and your gracious offer. Your intentions are meaningful and well received. However, God is my provider, as you well know. I would only ask of you one small thing—"

"Name it, and it is done," Owen interrupted as he mounted Absolam's back.

"Be sure to come visit this old man and see that I'm still at my father's work." Obadiah smiled with his eyes.

"That I'd be honored to do, dear friend!"

Owen kicked Absolam into a gallop and was off for his miracle.

St. Swithun's Cathedral was full of wonder and magnificence. Much more than Owen could have ever imagined. Seeing it with his own eyes was well worth the travels. The moment Prince Owen's vision landed on the towering structure carved in brilliance; he knew divine power lay beneath it. Power that, perhaps, could see his miracle come to life.

Finding a small boy about the age of eleven in monk's clothing, he dismounted from his horse. "Where's a safe place to keep my horse, Absolam, while visiting the cathedral?"

The boy led him to a nearby manger, where he paid a small fee to house him for the day. Finally, he was where he was supposed to be. The area around him was grassy and led to the steps and large doors. Once he stood near the entrance, his gaze naturally wandered up. *Such fine workmanship.* The castles at home in Wales had edges that were clean cut and square, but these were round with windows pointing to the heavens. *The design must bear some meaning,* he thought.

His eyes ran along pristine stonework, only made to look better by wind, rain, and the weathering of life. Not like the dull bricks of his home that crumbled to the tempest of storms and the scorching sun. Truly, it was breathtaking and the pivotal place to mark the beginning of miraculous change for the good.

"Are you wanting to view the relics of St. Swithun, or just admiring its beauty from a distance?" A voice laughed behind him.

Prince Owen swung around to see a brown-haired man in fine clothing walking up beside him. "As a matter of fact, yes, to both of your questions." Turning back to the door, ready to go in, Owen smiled. "One can't help but be spellbound by its sheer magnetism and beauty. Where I come from, cathedrals aren't quite as refined. One must take note of the detailed craftsmanship etched into this building." Glancing back at the man, he said, "Why would anyone else come here but to worship and be in awe of the Lord's business? That is what we are here for, is it not?"

"Well, some say people find refuge in places like these. Some say miracles. I am looking to find someone I've lost." The man turned to Owen. "What are you looking for?"

"Perchance a miracle. If the Lord is gracious to me. And I, too, am looking to find someone I've lost."

Standing side by side, Owen could feel the man's scrutiny. Staring at the building, he scanned it once more.

"You're looking for someone?" The man perked up. "A young maiden, I'd wager?"

The hair on Owen's arms sprang to life. Did this man know his sister? Could she be here?

"Yes," Owen said, eyes and hands steady. "As a matter of fact, a young maiden who has been lost to our family for some time."

"Does this maiden have black hair and lips as red as blood?" the man was quick to ask. He had parched lips that he continued licking as if he were a snake in the desert.

Owen's muscles instantly became taught.

A pilgrim entering made Owen move to give room. Then, another. He let out a sigh. How could he think his miracle would be as easy as finding his sister here of all places? And after all these years? The maiden whom the man described was not his sister.

"No." Owen sighed again. "She is fair with red hair and pink lips."

"She sounds beautiful, but it appears we are searching for two different people." The man's greedy eyebrows eased.

"Yes, it does appear that way." Owen's left brow rose instinctively.

Owen stepped forward, entering the building. The man followed eagerly behind. In the hush of prayers and bare feet on marble, Owen glided to where he had seen others with the pilgrim attire go—toward the relic behind the high altar. As he passed by people standing, he would quietly inquire if they had seen a woman, describing his sister. Each time he was met with a head shaking 'no.' They would quickly go back to seeking their own answers before God, ignoring Prince Owen. A few times he knelt to get a better look at a few women he thought may be his sister, but was met with more apologies, regrets, and refusals.

Defeated, Owen glanced about the room trying to find his place. The busy space thrummed and buzzed with a hum he'd never heard before. It was both terrifying and lovely. He observed the room fill with all kinds of people, from the highest of classes to the lowest. They seemed to be and flow as one. All bore gifts to be offered and laid before the St. Swithun's relic. Monks came in and out of the area like worker bees collecting the nectar for their queen. Owen padded his tunic for the sac of gold he brought to offer. It was still there.

Bodies formed a colored carpet that roared like an ocean shoreline, flowing across the ground. Circling about the relic with the grand height of the cathedral, each piece of the fabric offered prayers, attempting to touch heaven's doors somehow—some kneeling, some prostate, other cross-legged. Each unique. A raw and real awe was all he could feel in the moment, making him want to fall to his knees right then and there. But he resisted.

Instead, he decided to take it all in and strolled the room slowly, hearing prayers of hope, hurt, and love. One struck his heart, a young child crying out to God for his mother to be returned to him, her life to be brought forth from the grave. Would this be the prayers he would have to utter for his sister? *God forbid.*

He tried to move closer, but there was little room to budge. The strange man, having followed him, stepped near and whispered, "I heard the only way to get a miracle is for you to go down to the Holy hole."

Whispering back, Owen said, "Is that so?"

He glanced at the side of the man's head and quickly noted his dark eyes desperately scanning the entire sanctuary. What was the man's business here exactly? Who was this man looking for? Owen hadn't seen him even move his lips with prayer. It didn't even seem that the man was moved by the experience. Instead, the man was wild-eyed and ludicrously searching for his lost maiden. It was odd indeed. Owen took mental note of it but then felt a twinge of guilt. *Who am I to really judge. We all deal with grief and despair differently,* he thought.

God knows Owen would want to help someone find their loved one, if he could. But at what cost? Would Owen give up searching for his own sister to assist this man in finding the person he came here for?

No.

Owen caught sight of a deep scar on the man's lower lip. *Hmm.* The man was a fighter by the looks of it. Owen did a quick scan of the man's physique, noting scars and old wounds on his arms, hands, and neck. He was a rough one. *Interesting.*

"And where, my good fellow, would the Holy hole be among this great throng of people?"

"There." The man pointed. "It leads underneath St. Swithun's relic and is said to be the closest place to the Holy relic in order to receive a miracle." The man smirked. "I've also heard that St. Swithun wanted to be buried outside the cathedral to allow pilgrims to tread over his bones. This was to ensure they'd still receive his miraculous healing powers after he was dead. But, because they moved his bones inside the cathedral by King Edgar in 964, it rains for forty days and forty nights upon the site every year." The man leaned even closer. "And ever since, no one has had a true miracle."

How could he say such a thing and dash a person's hope? Here of all places? Owen's jaw slacked, but his fingers squeezed into a fist, ready to hit the man and give him another scar to remember his mistake by.

Owen sucked in a breath. Then another and clenched his teeth while releasing his fists.

"You hear many things. I daresay this isn't the place to breed foolishness, nor trample on a man's prayers." Owen swept his arm over the people sprawled out in the room. "But seeing as though there's no room to approach the relic itself, I will try below." He forced a grin. "Good day."

Owen couldn't move fast enough away from the man. He wouldn't let this stranger's lies quench Owen's only quest to find a miracle. Not now. Not ever. Not after coming this far.

He would dig until he hit the very relic itself, if it meant getting his sister back.

Disappointed, Prince Owen wiggled his way out of the Holy hole. After a few hours of heartfelt cries and dirt-stained tears, his prayers were still unanswered. No feeling of confirmation entered his soul. No signs. No visions.

Nothing.

He came with nothing and left with nothing. Kicking the dirt from the sole of his leather shoes, he made his way out of the Cathedral after giving his gold to retrieve Absolam.

"Here's your horse, sir." The lad handed him his reins.

"Thank you. Was he much trouble for you?" Owen attempted to

smile and patted the mane of his horse. The poor boy didn't need to feel the brunt of his burdens. Besides, it was comforting to think the small lad was taking care of Absolam. Always faithful to him, he could count on Absolam, not like the stories of St. Swithun. He tried not to scowl.

"Yes, sir, the best horse of the bunch. Though there was a fellow here, not long before you came, and was in quite a hurry. He even wanted to buy your horse from me. I didn't let him, sir!" The young lad jutted out his chin in pride.

Owen pursed his lip. "Did he have a scar?"

"Yes. I believe he did." The boy beamed.

Perhaps it was the strange man looking for the black-haired girl. I wonder why he was in such a hurry, Owen thought.

A monk beside the boy nudged him, gently directing his countenance towards the lad, "We do not want to let pride overtakes us, now do we, young one? That is not the way in which humility stands tallest." The monk made eye contact with Owen. "He's still learning. Of course we would not have sold your horse. We take care of all"— the monk's hand swept the vicinity of the manger— "with the same kindness of one's heart. Isn't that right, Luca?" He patted the boy on the head and turned again to the cinnamon-colored horse he was brushing.

Innocent eyes looked up at Owen.

Owen beamed down at Luca. "I see an honest, well-raised lad here who's making fine judgments, I daresay. Thank thee for that." Smiling, Owen continued. "Even though—as this fine monk says—you would have done it for anyone." Owen winked at the boy.

"Where's your pilgrimage taking you, sir?" Luca said, his expression lifting.

"Here, actually," Owen hid his discouragement while straightening the white tunic bearing the iconic red cross.

"And you are leaving already? Do you need any assistance? I—"

His head spun to the monk beside him. Then, his small voice dropped to a whisper. "I can help you, sir."

Longing eyes gazed back into Owen's. He marveled—such a familiar spirit was in the boy as if he were his own son. A boy yearning for adventure like he did as a child.

Owen bent down. "You've been enough help. Taking care of a man's best horse is a lot to be grateful for." Owen rolled his shoulders back and stood to his full height. He swung up on Absolam. "I won't forget that, and should you need anything, you write to me."

Owen squinted as he looked toward heaven. He might not have a miracle today, but in this one boy, he could at least be the instrument of one, should he need it.

"You write to Prince Owen Williamus of Wealas, and you shall have whatever you need, Luca." Owen smiled at the boy. "I promise."

Luca's eyes grew wide. "Yes, Your Highness. I shall."

"Luca has all he needs." The monk turned and glared at Owen. "The Lord tends to that." Pulling Luca toward him, the monk handed Luca a brush for the horses. "Good day, sir."

Owen jabbed Absolam into a trot. He looked back at the cathedral. What a fool he had made of himself, believing in miracles…

On his return home, Owen pondered what words he could possibly say to his father. *The money spent for pilgrimage and the miracle I hoped for is gone forever…* His father would remind Owen that '*A man is not fit to rule if he can't tend to his own house.*' Wasn't that what he heard the bishop say? He wasn't good enough to find his sister, nor rule an entire kingdom if he did not have the blessing of God on his side.

While he trotted along, Owen watched townspeople, monks, and other pilgrims meandering toward the cathedral. Pain intensified behind his eyes, threatening to spill rivers of destruction and defeat over his mind.

I am no good to my father's kingdom as a broken man. I have nothing to offer but self-pity. He pinched back the tears. *I will not give into defeat. I shall be like David; I'll encourage myself in the Lord.* But how?

Even if he could encourage himself, what kind of King Apparent was he? If he couldn't find his sister, he would be forced to return to his kingdom empty-handed and made to marry. He wasn't ready to face his father, especially now.

Halting his horse, he stared at the path before him. He couldn't go home yet. Pivoting, he veered down the narrow path to his left. Determining in himself to find peace—a refuge in the only place he knew had found it before—at Brother Obadiah's. A man content with his lot in life.

Kicking his horse into a gallop, Owen faced forward. He would confront his father and the disappointments of his people when the time came.

But tonight, he will find rest.

Sixteen

STOPPING TO LET ABSOLAM GRAZE, OWEN PULLED OUT A hooded cap. The wind had picked up and seemed to be racing down the pathway, sending a shiver down his spine. He would have to pick up speed to reach Brother Obadiah's by nightfall.

"You stay here, boy." Owen tied the reins of his horse to a nearby branch. "Eat and get a bit of rest. We won't be stopping again for some time." He patted his horse and went to relieve himself.

When he returned, he took a swig of Adam's ale and poured some over the palms of his hands, rinsing them. "It's cold, ol' boy." He shivered again.

A faint melody wound its way through the wind. He splashed some of the water on himself and rubbed his face clean.

"Do you hear that, Absolam? Or am I dreaming?" He smiled at his horse. Absolam kept tearing away at the grass, ignoring his master's comments. Not even a flicker in his ear. "All right, I must be dreaming." He laughed.

Suddenly a scream echoed through the forest, stealing the wind. Sending another kind of shiver up his spine. *Sister?*

Owen's blood shot to his brain. Out of sheer adrenaline, he pulled the sword from his sheath on Absolam's back and dashed toward the cry. Rounding the bend, he saw a hooded man holding a woman's black hair in his tight fist, the other clutching a knife above her.

Owen slowed his pace, not wanting to give himself away to the man. Ready to move at the slightest inclination the man might attempt to kill her, Owen attempted to listen carefully, catching some of their conversation.

"You thought you could run away, did you? That the queen wouldn't find you? Ha! Well, that was before they sent *me* to come and get you."

"No one was supposed to be in the forest. I thought it was safe!"

Owen watched as the man's face nearly touched the woman's. "Weren't you wrong." He pulled her hair hard, and she let out another scream. "Your huntsman will be dead by now, and you—" He ground his teeth at her. "You filthy wench will have no heart by the time she gets you. It pains me that I can't kill you right now."

Owen's fist clenched on his sword. He was almost close enough to make a move, but the man lowered his sword away from her neck.

"Let me go." She tried to scream again, but her words were muffled.

"I can't. You see, I need you to stay alive for proof." He pulled her up with her hair, and she screamed again. "Proof, so the queen can see for herself you're indeed still alive!"

The man growled, yanking the girl's head toward his horse. Owen used the noise to creep closer. The wind, the girl's legs scrambling to walk, and her muffled cries stifled any sound he was making. Positioning himself behind the man, Owen realized who he was—the creepy man from the cathedral! This must be the girl he was looking for.

"If I were you, I would be quiet." The man brought his knife close to the damsel's chest, and Owen's whole body responded. He burst forth from the forest, but the man's horse neighed and kicked up at him.

The man threw the damsel on the ground and turned to face Owen.

"You!" The man laughed. "You couldn't find your precious miracle and had to come meddle with mine. Prithee, what do you intend to do with that sword?"

The man's mocking, murky laugh drew vile from Owen's gut. Owen's eyes shot to the damsel on the ground. A blade swung at Owen's chest.

"Don't get any ideas, pilgrim. She's mine."

"The only idea I have is rescuing a poor maiden."

Owen parried the close blow. Lunging with his sword, Owen jumped back and thwarted the man's advance. The clang of the metal rang through his arm and brought his body to life. This is what he was made for—to defend. To protect.

He swung the blade and blocked another jab. He lifted his sword high and took a step forward. Aiming for the man's chest, Owen's sword came down hard. Swerving, the man spun and kicked Owen from behind.

Falling forward, he almost rammed into the girl whimpering on the ground.

"Run!" Owen whispered to her.

Heaving for air, he stood and lifted his sword again. He turned to face the man, but the man was gone. Owen scanned the area and saw the man's body ducking through the heavy forest, running from them.

Quickly turning back to the girl, he realized she was no longer on the ground. She must have run into the forest like he said. Looking through the thick forest, he could see her black hair flinging under some branches.

Another scream pierced the air. The man must have run after the girl. Had he reached her already? Pumping his legs, Owen swatted away branches desperately following the path where he last saw her raven locks. His footing gave way, and Owen slipped, landing on loose pebbles. He lay still for a moment, catching his breath. A branch cracked to his far left. Owen lurched forward. Hopping first on one leg to let the sting out of his ankle, he then pounced at full speed. He leaped over a dead tree limb like a deer. Why would this man want to harm such a beautiful woman? She was incredibly captivating. Another scream stilled his thoughts, and all effort poured into his stride. He wouldn't let another helpless girl slip away from his grasp.

Seventeen

EIRA

EIRA'S HEART WAS POUNDING SO FAST SHE COULD BARELY HEAR A thing. Was he still behind her? Did he hear her scream when she fell? She looked down at where the rock had scraped her arm. She was bleeding, and now there was a blood trail left, leading her assailant to exactly where she was.

Still, she tore off a slip of her dress with her teeth. She needed somewhere to hide and stop the bleeding. Seeing a large brush, thick with leaves, she dove into it and tried to still her panting breath.

Gently, she wrapped her arm and tied the cloth tight. A snap of wood brought her senses to attention. He was close. She slowly turned her head to see where the noise had come from. It was not her assailant, but the man who tried to save her.

Not wanting to give herself away, she froze and watched as the man knelt to the ground and lifted something to his nose. He rubbed it between his fingers and eyed the landscape slowly. She watched him. He knew someone was close by. The man who saved her crouched to the ground staying completely still. They both waited for someone to show their face first.

They waited and waited.

Thinking her assailant had gone, she whispered through the thick brush, "Sir?"

The man quickly sprang forward, sword ready. Eira studied his face as he searched for where the voice came from. He was handsome, well-built, and tall.

"Is it safe?" she whispered. "Shall I come forth?"

He looked to the right. "I believe it is only us now." His voice was low and sweet, like her father's. "Are you injured?"

Eira wiggled out of the brush, dusting herself off. "It appears I am." She walked forward, presenting her arm.

His eyes popped open and held to where she was bleeding through the cloth. "You're bleeding badly. The wound is deep." His eyes found hers, and for a moment, she felt safe.

"We should leave immediately, before he comes looking for you," he whispered.

"Thank you." Her head spun. "For what you did. That was very noble of you—" Eira lost her balance. "I am feeling—feeling faint." She reached out to him and felt his arms around her before her world spun to a painful black.

EIRA'S HEAD bounced to the rhythm of horse hooves. Where was she? Peeking up to the rider holding her in his strong arms with ease, she was relieved to see it was the handsome man who had saved her.

"Rest. I am taking you somewhere secure until you heal." He looked down at her. "Then I will bring you back to your home."

Home?

She wanted to burst into tears. Could she ever return home?

"I have somewhere safe to go already, and there is a doctor there." As soon as she spoke, the horse halted.

"Are you well enough to tell me which way to go?" Tenderness and reservation slipped through every word he said.

"If I slowly get up, I think I should be fine to sit and assist with the directions." She went to move, and his arm steadied her.

"Don't move. Which way? North, south?"

Too weak to argue, she obeyed. "They live northeast."

"Good." He kicked the horse to move again. "That is the direction we were going already." He smiled at her.

"How long have we been riding for?" Eira took note of the way the sun streamed through the trees, setting in the east. She shivered, and his arm tightened immediately.

"An hours' time has not yet passed. But it will be dark soon."

She could feel the words rumble through his chest, bringing a sense of warmth and comfort. She wanted to revel in it and close her eyes, but a small speck of white caught her eye. It floated softly and landed on her arm.

Snow.

Fall was gone. Another season had begun. One that marked the passing of her birthday. How strange to be at an age where life was not in order, arranged carefully to hide her. Yet, here she was exposed, being hunted by a cold-blooded murderer.

She should have stayed at the Men of Ore's instead of wandering out to find some berries. But how could she have known that thanking her new friends for their hospitality by picking berries for a pie would result in an attack? She had been assured by Doc that the men swept the area early that morning for any intruders. Truly, she thought it was safe.

Desperately clinging onto another strange man in need of protection—yet again—safety was a word she felt further and further from. But maybe it was her fault. Perhaps she had wondered off too far, leaving too much of a trail to find her. Or perhaps she would never genuinely be safe any longer and it was futile to try.

Slipping her hand into her bubble-bow pocket, she patted the book of psalms and grasped her father's signet ring between her fingers. How could she take the place of her father or stand up to the women seeking her death now? She would go to any lengths to find her.

Eira was not strong enough. She would never be strong enough for the queen. The Men of Ore could not fight off an army if they found Eira at their home. Yes, they were good with axes, and perhaps bows, but not compared to the skill of her papa's army.

Pain seized her thoughts as her arm throbbed with intensity. Sucking in a breath, she dug the ring into her palm harder. They were getting close to the Men of Ore's cottage. She hadn't wandered that far away.

A darkness settled into her heart. Would they come searching for her again? Were they being followed? Were the Men of Ore in danger? Her hand released her father's ring and caressed the psalter once more.

Dear Heavenly Father, please guide us to safety. Bless this man for his bravery and kindness. I am forever indebted to you for sending him and the huntsman when you did. Thank you.

She watched as another flake landed on her nose. Memories of her mother breezed through her mind. The arm around her tightened again. Could he sense her sadness? The cold air made her shake uncontrollably in his grasp. Like a blacksmith's hammer, she could hear her teeth chatter.

His arms weren't for comforting her, only to warm her. Regardless, she would enjoy the embrace of a man. A kind man. She peeked up, studying him, taking note of his jawline, stubbled cheeks, and dark wavy hair. She wondered if he had any scars under the stubble on his cheeks like her father had.

Following the line of his jaw, her eyes outlined his lips. They were full and had a slight turn at the edges, almost as if he was perpetually grinning. She smiled and watched his eyes holding fast to the path ahead of them. They had hints of brown, like the hue of tree bark—strong and protective—but were mostly green like a bright emerald.

Creases formed, crinkling his eyes as if he knew she had been gazing at him. Quickly, she averted her focus to the mane of his horse. Could he see the heat rush to her cheekbones? If he had, he did not shame her. His eyes held the path ahead, and he hadn't released his grip on her.

Whatever the reason their paths met, she was grateful for his warm arms. Besides her father, she was never this close to a man in Whiteshire. Now, it seemed as if she were surrounded by men: Mason, the huntsman, the Men of Ore, and now this handsome and brave pilgrim.

Was it providence or mere chance that he happened on the same trail as her attacker? Whatever the reason, she was thankful it had been perfect timing. She could have died.

Thoughts of the man's dagger ran an icy chill down her spine again. She swallowed deep, daring another glance at the man who embraced her. His white tunic blended into the snow that had started to fall around them. Perhaps it was wishful thinking, but the one desire that hung from her mind like a tantalizing fruit on the vine was … perchance he was meant to be there with her at this time in life, to help her, be strong on behalf of her … to be the white prince from her dreams as a child. And the queen wasn't around to tell her how foolish her dreams were today.

She squeezed the man's arms.

Despite her fuzzy head, today her dreams felt more real than ever before.

Eighteen

EIRA

"Eira!" Fredrick stormed up to the horse. "Where have you been? We told you not to go out on your own—" Fredrick halted when he saw blood on Eira's arm. "Well, now you went off and hurt yourself. Did *he* do this to you?"

Eira saw rage flood Fredrick's eyes. "No, Fredrick. This kind soul has helped me. Please, run and fetch Doc for me."

Through the darkened sky, she could see Mathew and Hugo chopping wood. They ran over to help carry Eira down from the arms of the pilgrim.

"Thank you," she said, her teeth still chattering. "No need to carry me, I am well enough to walk."

The pilgrim slid off his horse. "Keep her steady, she may faint. She has lost a lot of blood."

"Your Majesty, let me help you." Matthew held her good arm steadily so she could stand.

Eira smiled at his sweet nature, always wanting to help. Then, she frowned. "I'm sorry I wasn't here to make dinner for you." Her shoulders slumped in defeat. "And I was going to make a dessert for you all. A surprise that has not ended well. You must be awfully hungry."

"Never mind about us. We've taken care of ourselves long before you showed up. It's you we are worried about."

Her weakened legs hobbled toward the front door of the cottage as he continued. "You had us worried sick. We swore to protect you, and now you're wounded." His head hung low. "We promised, m'lady."

As he mumbled something under his breath, Eira rested her hand on Mathew's arm. "Thank you, Hugo. I appreciate your concern. Such a nobleman, you are." She patted his arm.

Eira looked at the man behind her. "God sent sufficient help. But you are right, I should not have gone out today, and for that"—sweat beaded on her head, and she couldn't wipe it away as both arms were being held to keep her steady— "I am deeply sorry."

Doc was ready for them at the front door. "Exactly right, m'lady. From now on you should not leave our home. We thought you would not be found here. We even did a sweep this morning and last night. But they must have followed you somehow. Nevertheless, you should have known better. Leaving when there was no one here to help you— how could you?" The look of betrayal on Doc's face turned her heart into a puddle of mud. She knew he meant well, but Eira didn't like being scolded, not even from her papa.

"I am sorry, Doc. I thought it was safe and wanted to do some-thing special for you all. I didn't mean to disappoint you. But I see my error now and it won't happen again."

"Come in, and I'll see to your wounds." He turned to Matthew. "Take the pilgrim over to the well and fetch some water for his horse and for Eira. Return quickly."

"Yes, Doc." Mathew nodded at the pilgrim, who followed him, while Doc and Hugo helped Eira inside.

Ben was rushing to meet her, his face beaming as bright as the sun, when Hugo almost knocked the man's feet from under him. "Not so fast, Benjamin, she's hurt. Go get some pillows and make a bed for her by the fire."

Ben's face dropped as he caught sight of the bloody cloth wrapped around her arm. "Right." Ben's head bobbled as he rushed down a corridor, bouncing off the wooden walls to find pillows.

"Sit here until we can lay you down to rest." Doc pulled a chair close to the fire and helped her sit down on it.

She swiped at the sweat now gliding down her temples, and Doc immediately started to fuss over her. Trying to clench her jaw and minimize the chatter, she said, "I'll be fine, Doc. Don't worry."

Soon she would be warmed by the fire, and everything would be alright.

GENTLE FINGERS BRUSHED Eira's hair off her cheek.

"Wake up."

A soft voice spoke near her ear, so close it prickled the back of her neck. Attempting to prop herself up into a sitting position, she moaned as pain surged through her arm.

"Here, let me help you," the voice said.

Hands scooped under her back and eased her into a sitting position against the stone hearth. Pressing against her back, the cold radiated into her flesh and bones. Shivering, she pulled the blanket up, clutching it under her chin.

"You need to eat." Hands pulled the covers from her fingers. She resisted, but it was futile; her fingers held no strength. A cup pressed into her palms, and her fingers curled around it, reacting to the warmth. The weight was too heavy in her hands, and the person knew that. They held it while she took a sip. Then, the warmth was gone from her fingers.

Feeling the blanket being tucked under her chin again, she tried to speak, lift open her eyelids, and thank whoever it was. She couldn't quite make out if it was Christopher or Mathew. But they stayed shut. The cold seemed to seep straight into her veins. Her teeth wouldn't stop chattering, and no words came from her lips.

"The soup will help. You need to build your strength back up," the tender voice said. As tender as the man who saved her.

Perhaps her prince had stayed? Her eyes attempted to open, and the man who rescued her was kneeling in front of her, the fire illuminating his face. He was much more handsome now than she noticed before. His skin was creamy white but had a sunset hue from the embers in the fire.

Emerald eyes flickered back to hers, and she was smitten by them. They were so sincere and held her for some time. She could see the fire reflecting in his eyes and wondered if they could ever spark with a flame for her. A longing panged in her heart. A longing she never knew she yearned for—the love of another, the love of a man.

Papa had given her the love of a father, and it filled her days with joy. But seeing all the heartbreak her papa went through; she was uncertain of love and marriage. Memories of her mother and the love between the two of them seemed to keep any bit of hopelessness at bay.

All throughout her childhood, the thought of a husband for her was nothing but a dream. Fanciful wishes that certainly did not involve the handsome man before her, staring down at her with those wonderful eyes, easily stealing her heart if she was not careful.

The burning she felt was merely the fire and not the affection for a stranger. Eira had to be on guard. One person was already after her heart, and she didn't need another taking it captive, making her vulnerable when she had everything to lose.

They broke eye contact, and she tried to smile, but he shook his head. "Save your energy."

Nodding, she marveled in his comfort. Such warmth and tenderness.

Stay alert, Eira, he's a stranger.

Her head felt heavy, and she tried to keep it up. His eyes met hers again. Something exchanged between them. Was it electricity? She tried to lean forward, breaking eye contact. *No.* She couldn't be distracted from her purpose. She was to continue east.

As much as she wanted to welcome it, love was not on the horizon. On the contrary, death clouded over her wherever she went, waiting to pour out its dreary, merciless rain. Eira was being hunted. Soon, the huntsman would be back to protect her, providing the much-needed shelter on her journey east and far away from the warmth of Sir Emerald Eyes.

Her head bobbed, and she let it roll to one side as her body started shaking. Queen Amara would learn of Eira's whereabouts, and there was no doubt in Eira's mind that the queen would come after her once notified. But did the queen know she had Papa's ring? That Papa gave her the right to rule now?

Papa? Had he truly been killed? Was he okay?

Shivers ran all over her body, breaking her thoughts. A hand pressed again her forehead.

"Doc, she's burning up again."

Like a snowstorm, thoughts of her father blurred her mind, and she couldn't see. Nothing would stop the vile wickedness of Queen Amara. Eira had seen her wrath firsthand.

Hands moved her body away from the fire. Was that Doc? Or Laurentius?

She wanted to claw herself back to its warmth. Her arms failed to do as she commanded. She was so weak, shivering uncontrollably. Doc grabbed Eira's arm and pulled something back. It was numb, but she stared at it, blinking. Was that a bandage? What was on her arm, and what was that awful smell?

The room spun, and a memory swirled with it. One sweet maid came into view as the room around her darkened. The picture of a smiling girl bringing toys to Eira sharpened. Even at the early age of seven, Eira knew the girl had taken a risk by being her friend. One day, she snuck into her bedchamber, wanting to bring Eira to the Royal Garden and play a game. Eira refused at first, but curiosity compelled her to go. So, she went.

For the first time in a long time, she had a friend playing games and frolicking among the flowers and budding vines. It all seemed so magical, until they were in the middle of hide-and-seek and Eira came to a stop on the paved stones, screaming.

There, on the stone path by the white roses her father loved so dearly, lay the girl. Dead. Blood was pooling from her head, her eyes blank and staring at nothing. Looming over the maid's unmoving body was the queen.

She spoke slowly. "I guess you won the game, Eira." Queen Amara laughed. Then she stepped forward, her face twisted. "You were not supposed to leave."

Eira could feel the air freeze around her, suffocating her. Was it a dream or a memory only? No, it was real. Queen Amara was going to kill her this time. The queen lifted her hand to Eira's neck, nails digging into her throat. She was so close, so real—

Screaming, Eira grasped at the floor, at the hands grabbing her, restraining her. Had the queen gotten to her? Had she found her already? Was she about to have the same fate as the maid?

Eira was going to die. She screamed and clawed at the hands on her throat. Why couldn't she fight back? What was wrong with her?

Hot pain ran up her arm like a lightning bolt. Tears slipped down her cheek as the vision and memory turned into inky darkness. Taking her slowly down into a bottomless pit. She let herself go, giving in to her fate.

Death.

Nineteen

OWEN

"I SEE THE NARROW ROAD HAS NOT LED YOU DOWN AN EASY path, my brother," Obadiah hollered from the little cosh.

Owen trotted closer and Obadiah laughed. "You look very rough."

"I've had better days." Owen dismounted and handed Absolam's reins to the monk. "I am in desperate need of rest. May I stay for a few more nights?"

"Of course." They started to walk toward the manger that housed the monk's animals when Obadiah turned to him. "Something is weighing heavily on you. I can tell. Did you find your miracle?"

As if his day couldn't get any worse, now he'd have to admit defeat to this kind, God-fearing man. Running his hand down his face, he said, "Sadly, no." Owen kicked at the dirt on the small path. "It appears I've come all this way for nothing."

The monk stopped. "Truly? You believe it was for naught?"

Owen scratched at the back of his neck and kept his eyes forward. "Perhaps…" He squeezed his neck and released the tension. "Yes, I do believe so. I've come a long way, Obadiah, and have nothing to bring back with me. No answers. No miracles. No sister."

"Miracles take time. Some are not always instantaneous as one would hope. Besides, brother, God knows what you need before you even ask."

Despite the kindness that exuded with every word the monk uttered, Owen felt pure anger. He bit his lip, but the response came anyway. "*Does* God know already? Then why make me ask for it and not answer when I obey? Have I not done everything He commands me to do? Am I not good enough? Does He fancy games?" Bitterness came out in the form of a laugh.

"What makes you think He won't answer you? Are not good things worth waiting for?"

Obadiah's sincerity was evident, but Owen started to walk. He was hoping for rest, not a lecture.

"Perhaps they are…" Turning his face toward Obadiah, he studied his profile. Obadiah was so sure. So confident. He stared at the cosh. "…worth the wait, that is. And perhaps some answers are needed quicker than others. I need an answer soon. It's imperative. One of life and death. But to bear honesty as one naked before you…" Owen faced Obadiah. "The more time that lapses, the more I lose hope that she is indeed alive, and—" Owen eyed the dirt. "And results in one losing faith in God who knows where she is and where she has been all along."

"Losing faith?" Obadiah smiled. "That is impossible. Even a mustard seed of it can move mountains. You even admitted to having faith that God knows where she is right now. Faith is exactly what you've experienced. It is hope for the unseen." Obadiah paused long enough for his comment to sink in. "One can lose hope, and perhaps you've lost that, but from my perspective, you are living out your faith."

Obadiah looked at the sky, and Owen followed his gaze. It was bright and radiant.

"I have learned over the years, which may or may not bring you comfort." Obadiah dropped his chin and placed his hands behind his back. "Living out one's faith is the most difficult of tasks." He brought his chin up, and the reflection of the sun flickered off the top of his bald head. "However, it is the one way to sift a person and find if they truly had any in the first place."

"Any what?" Owen scrunched up his nose, trying to follow the conversation.

"Faith. If they had any faith at all. Because it is impossible to please God without it." Obadiah gently patted him on the back. "Faith, my dear brother."

Slowing his pace, Owen let the monk pass. His words struck me like no other had. Was that the emptiness he felt—the thing he was missing all this time? Perhaps hope was indeed faith.

Faith?

Had he come all this way without it? Never once did Owen think God wouldn't do a miracle for him. Was Owen not a man willing to follow God all the way to St. Swithun's Cathedral from Wealas, even if God chose not to answer his prayers? Would Owen still serve Him from his heart with unanswered prayers? Did he not hope? Was that not faith?

Owen pinched the bridge of his nose and looked back at the welkin above him. He didn't want to think about this. He wanted to rest and go home. Facing his father almost seemed better than facing the thoughts invading his mind.

He looked at the back of Obadiah heading to the manger. Had his pilgrimage been about his sister, or was it about himself—his failures, the mistakes he had to make better, his faith, and salvation?

Shame broke his reserve. How could he only think of himself when his sister needed him? Pushing out his thoughts, he continued walking and caught up to Obadiah. After brushing, feeding, and bedding down Absolam, they returned to the little cosh. By the fire, they enjoyed a bowl of barley and stewed meat.

Owen stared into the fire.

"You have barely eaten." Obadiah stood staring at the half-eaten food and took Owen's bowl. "Are you unwell?"

"Sorry, Obadiah. Your meal was fine. I have been … thinking … about everything…" His voice trailed as Obadiah cleaned up from dinner and then sat down next to Owen by the fire.

"Thinking about what, exactly?"

"I am thinking about my father, my journey home, and—and a girl."

"Ahh." Obadiah lifted a cup of tea. "I see now why worry lines are cast upon your face. They are not the shadows dancing from the flames." Obadiah laughed. "Maidens can do that to a brother. Is she back at home? Do you long to see her again?"

Yes, he would love to see her again, but he couldn't tell Obadiah that. Her beauty was so rare and yet so sweet. He barely wanted to leave her side. But he did.

"She is not back at home. She was in danger on my way here, and I assisted in helping the lass, that is all." Owen stood. "Is there more tea?"

"I will get it. Sit. Rest." Obadiah got up to serve him the tea. "So, she is here … in Whiteshire?"

Owen sipped the tea and thought of how his eyes had held hers. Did she feel the electricity between the two of them?

"She is not far from here. Do you know of the Men of Ore? She is healing there." He investigated his cup.

"I do know of them. Honorable and hard-working men. They seek gold in the mountains, and we have purchased some for the scriptorium at the monastery." Obadiah took a long sip from his tea before continuing. "By the looks of your face, I would gather there's more to this damsel than you're telling me … you're quite troubled."

Owen glanced at him and smiled. "Yes, I'm concerned for her safety. She was injured." Owen smirked, then chuckled. "Has anyone told you you are a wise man and very observant? Perhaps too observant!"

"Indeed! Some say that, but I would hope my wisdom comes from prayer and God alone."

"Yes, well"—Owen swallowed— "a deep wound penetrated her arm. Doc was knowledgeable in medicine and tended to her wound. It was going putrid." Owen sighed a little too loudly. "She seems to be in capable hands now."

"How did she get the wound?" Obadiah asked.

"I happened upon her in the forest trail going back home from Winchester Cathedral, when I heard someone being attacked. A man who had spoken to me earlier was attempting to capture her. I overheard his conversation, and his intention was to kill her. She was wounded trying to run from the man. After I rescued her, the wretched assailant fled. Then I brought her to the Men of Ore. While the girl slept, I spoke with the men who knew her. Supposedly the man was sent by the queen to have her killed. I can't fathom why a maiden such as her could find any ill favor with the queen, or why she would want her dead."

Owen's questioning eyes searched Obadiah's as if he held the answers. Obadiah's face turned toward the fire and twisted in contemplation. Finally, he spoke.

"You may not have gotten your miracle today..." Obadiah's gaze focused on Owen's. "But, my dear brother, *you* were the miracle sent for another."

Owen leaned back, gulping down the last of his hot tea in one swig. "The damsel?" he choked out.

Obadiah nodded, got up, and retreated to his humble chambers without saying another word. Picking up his cup, Owen washed it before placing it back on the wooden shelf.

He tried getting comfortable and listening to the Gregorian chants like before, but everywhere he looked, he saw her dove-like eyes. So many things were uncertain about his future. Now, he couldn't shake this girl from his thoughts. Adding more questions to his already-frustrating list. Should he stay and see to her safety? Should he use his nobility to aid in her protection? What was the moral thing to do?

Despite the maddening questions, Owen was certain of one thing. Though he came to Obadiah's for rest, he knew tonight he wouldn't find any.

Twenty

EMPRESS AMARA

"Matilda, might I say you look—"

Queen Amara's arm flung out as fast as a cobra would pounce upon its prey. The smack of her palm across Justin's face sounded like a leather whip on a horse's back.

"If I ever hear you use my Christian name again, I'll have you hung by your thumbs. I'm Empress Amara of Whiteshire. Do I make myself clear?" Empress Amara waited until Justin nodded his pathetic head and stepped beside Herrick.

"What news do you bring me, Justin?" The words were forced, but soothing. One mess-up shouldn't ruin any good news he came to share. Unlike Herrick. Glaring in his direction, she added, "Herrick has been rather useless of late, so don't disappoint me."

"Your Majesty, I've brought proof of reasonable doubt. Herrick was right to worry. The girl's still alive."

"It can't be true!" Empress Amara pinched her eyes before the room swirled. "Show me the proof!"

Jason reached for something in his tunic, his breathing heavy. "Here. See for yourself. I know she is alive."

"Alive?" Forcing her body to move, she stalked toward Justin. "Show me!" she demanded.

A threadbare piece of ribbon tied with raven-colored hair lay in the cloth napkin in the bed of his hand. Her eyes bulged, and she snatched it from him. *Could it be?*

"You lie!" She thrust it at Justin.

Motionless, his crooked smile never left his wretched face. Glancing down, she watched the inky hair disburse on the floor while the silky ribbon floated to the base of Justin's feet.

"You're a fool!" Her nerves were coming back to life. "It could be any feather-headed maiden with similarly colored hair." She picked up a thread of hair and rolled it between her thumb and index finger. She sniffed it, looking into Justin's eyes, studying him.

"Perhaps this was soaked in blackened walnuts to reflect the same shade. Do you take me as a simpleton? You want recognition"— Empress Amara smirked and released the thread of hair— "you'll have it." She spun to face Herrick. "Kill this man, and make sure all are there to see his hanging."

The smile on Justin's face faltered. She was finally pleased.

"And what of this?" Justin pulled out a tattered piece of fabric. One that was most definitely Eira's. Empress Amara eyed the piece of cloth. Then, she peered back at Justin, laughing.

Numbness spread from her heart to the tips of her fingers. Watching her hand flinch, she saw, rather than felt, her own fist smashing the Looking Glass into the wall. If there was blood dripping from her palm, she wouldn't have known had her eyes not captured it.

To describe the utter pain engulfing her with rage would be deafening. Her ears were already ringing because she knew what her father would say. Regardless, it was pain she must've felt, but the deadening feeling alone was immeasurable and left her with nothing, like her father's distant words.

"You play a game you shall not win. If you found her dead, you could've simply cut a piece of her clothing off." She walked around Justin slowly, and put forth her hand, palm up. Blood was still seeping from the small wound where a shard must have nicked her flesh. "What is it that you want, hmm?" She took a step to his left. "Gold?" Walking around to his back, she leaned near his ear. "Position? Honor?" She continued to his front. "Everyone wants something, Justin. What is it that you want?"

Empress Amara waited until Justin stood tall and stared just below her eyes. "I want to win your favor. I want Eira dead just as much as you." Glancing at Herrick, he continued. "And ... yes. I want a position. I want Herrick's position."

Immediately, Herrick advanced on Justin, probably to kill him. She wouldn't have minded watching them fight, but before Herrick had his hands on the pathetic soul, he squeaked out, "I know where the girl is. I can get you to her. I swear!"

Empress Amara pulled out her dagger and snatched Herrick's arm. "Kill him and you die, Herrick." Shoving Herrick out of the way, she approached Justin, nose to nose. "You want my favor?" she asked.

Justin nodded, smart enough not to speak.

"Herrick. Bring me Seilda." She faced Justin again, and once Herrick left the room, she spoke slowly. "You bring Seilda to the girl and watch her die. If she is dead, when you return, you will have my favor." Pressing her long nails into his chest, she added, "But if you return and I find what you say isn't true..." She let the nail point dig deeper into his flesh. "I will eat your heart instead."

"Yes, m'lady." The crooked smile reappeared.

She pushed him back and paced the suddenly small room until Seilda entered. When Herrick followed behind Seilda, Empress Amara spun to Seilda. "This man claims Eira is alive and that he knows where the pathetic girl is hiding. Go with him in disguise and kill her. If he indeed speaks truth, he will stay with the girl and make sure she's dead before returning. Is that understood?"

"Of course. My pleasure, Empress." Seilda slowly backed out of the room.

"Seilda," the queen hollered. Seilda peeked her head back into the room. "A quick death. Understand?"

Seilda smiled, and the queen walked to the window. This ordeal needed to be over and done as soon as possible. Her coronation was dependent on it.

"Leave us, Justin." She flicked her hand at him. "Herrick." Her eyes looked out toward Whiteshire through the windowpane.

"Yes."

"Come closer." She swept her fingers and remembered the blood in her palm. "And bring me a rag."

Pathetic people were mingling about. Some appeared frantic. Word was beginning to spread that the king was dead.

"My Queen." Herrick stood by her, the rag near her shoulder. Taking it, she rubbed off the deep red bits of her humanity from her hand.

"What is the word from the Barons?" In the reflection of the window, she could see Herrick trembling. He was a weak man ... maybe Justin would be better suited by her side.

"They are torn, m'lady."

"Torn. To pay homage to their queen, their empress? Well, that means war, does it not?" She looked back at the townsfolk gathering near the market. So much for an easy entry to the throne. She would make them suffer for not paying homage to their empress. She was their rightful ruler. No one would take that away from her. She planned to announce it officially with a town crier, which would lead to anarchy, but she didn't care.

Ungrateful people. I will rip everything they own from them if they don't!

"Send word to my uncle, the King of Scotland, and to my cousin, the Earl of Gloucester. Let him know I'll need reinforcements." She tapped her nails on the glass. "Also, send the town crier to all Whiteshire with word of the king's death. Let us make this official so they can stop squabbling." She turned to face Herrick and handed him her filthy rag. "If anyone seems to doubt their empress's rule"—her eyes penetrated his— "they shall be killed immediately. Let them learn from another's mistakes. A disloyal individual will not be tolerated in this kingdom." Watching him a moment longer, she added, "Including those in this castle, Herrick." She side-eyed him.

Holding his gaze as if in challenge, Empress Amara waited until he squirmed, then gathered her skirts and walked out of the room, leaving him to wither by the window. She made a mental note to kill him eventually. For now, he proved himself worthy to live another day.

Seeing a maid in the hallway, she stopped. "Prepare for me a bath in my bedchamber."

The maid scurried away like a frightened mouse.

Just the way she liked it.

Twenty-One

EIRA

"She's sanded, Christopher." Mathew gawked at Eira.

"You talk as if I'm not in the room—indeed alive." Eira tried to smile, but it didn't reach her eyes. She felt like she had died. "I am surely not dead if I can talk, Mathew. Besides, Doc has fixed me up well."

Locking her eyes on the arm lying beside her, she realized it was still weak, but not the awful state it had been in. Even a scar was starting to form. This was a good sign, she told herself. The wound was healing well.

"I don't mean that. I merely meant … well, that is, you look— tired. You're still the most beautiful—"

Fredrick interrupted Mathew with a blow to the back of the head.

"We should let her rest then." Christopher stood. "Fredrick, may I speak with you outside?"

Eira could see the frustration on Christopher's face. Being the reverent Christian leader he was, he wouldn't scold his fellow brother in front of a maiden.

Fredrick mumbled something incoherent as he stomped out of the room toward the hallway leading to the front door.

"I am sure he meant well." Eira turned to Doc.

"It is never meant well when you hit a brother."

Supposing Doc was right, she nodded.

"I need to sharpen some of our tools. Will you be alright here? Hugo, Laurentius, and Benjamin can tend to anything you may need before we all must go into the mountain." Doc's gentle eyes were outlined with concern.

"I am quite capable of getting up and about myself now. You've taken good care of me."

Eira could tell Doc didn't want to leave her today and go off into the mountains, but the men needed to work and provide for themselves. There was no other choice. Already, they'd sacrificed two days to fret over her, and she wouldn't hold them back another day.

"Prithee, go get the men ready to be off. I will be fine."

"If you say so." Doc left, and the men started to gather their things.

Christopher came up to Mathew with Fredrick dawdling behind.

"Alright, Fredrick. Go ahead," Christopher said.

Fredrick growled and gritted his teeth. "Fredrick. Don't act like a child in front of the princess. Own up to your mistake like a man."

The whole scene reminded Eira of her papa when she would get into trouble as a young girl.

Fredrick's eyes darted past Eira to Christopher. "I'm-sorry-I-hit-you." His words were as quick as a horse's whip.

"And…" Christopher prompted.

"And…" Fredrick exaggerated the word, mimicking Christopher. "I-wasn't-acting-like-a-brother-in-Christ." Fredrick finished by rolling his eyes. "Happy? Can I go now?"

With a buoyant and beaming smile, Mathew replied, "I forgive you."

Such brave and yet such childish men. She loved them. Everything in her wanted to squeeze and pinch their cheeks as if they were children. Fearing their pride, she held back.

Fredrick stomped off to get ready while Christopher glanced at Mathew.

"Well, that went better than I expected." He smiled. "Probably because you were here." Christopher's eyes met her. "But nonetheless, it was a success."

Eira sat forward in her chair. "I would say a *great* success." She laughed.

Christopher chuckled.

"What joy it brings to my ears hearing you laugh, m'lady," Hugo said as he entered the room. "The men are almost ready to go, Christopher. Doc said you should grab your things now."

"Thank you, Hugo." Christopher made a slight bow.

Out of all the Men of Ore, Hugo spent the most time on his appearance, his clothes, and his room. Clean, neat, and tidy was the way he liked it. His beard was dark and trimmed neatly. His dark, wavy hair was combed to one side. and his broad smile made him quite handsome, even if he was slightly smaller than his peers.

"Not only do you carry yourself as a prince, but you also speak as one too." Eira smiled.

Hugo's grin spread across his jaw line as he threw his pickax over his shoulder. "I will take that as the highest of compliments ever given to me, m'lady." Taking a reverent bow, he swung the axe over his chest.

"Don't believe him. That *is* the highest compliment he's ever received." Christopher laughed and patted Hugo hard on the back, dislodging the axe from his hand and dropping it to the floor.

Eira gasped. The axe nearly missed Benjamin's feet. Shocked, Benjamin fell backward.

Suddenly, Laurentius came charging into the room.

"What are you fopdoodles making all the ruckus for? We're going to be late. It's simply woodness, and I won't have it!"

Before anyone could answer, Benjamin was attempting to stand upright but fell again, directly into Laurentius' arms. Laurentius growled.

"There's no time to play like children trying to impress a girl, we've got a darg to finish." Shaking his head, he dropped Ben to the ground and left as quickly as he came.

Ben jumped up to his feet and approached Eira, apologizing profusely.

"Benjamin, you did no wrong. You merely entered a room. No one can shame you for that." She patted the back of his hand tenderly. "Have a wonderful day and be safe in the caves." She looked up into his sweet eyes. If she could have a brother, Ben would be the one she would choose.

"You too, m'lady." He rethought his words. "I meant to say, I hope you are well and safe. Here ... not in the caves..."

She watched as both of Ben's cheeks flared into the pigment of red matching her lips. But before she could put his mind at ease, Doc was beckoning the men to leave, herding them out of her room like a shepherd.

Making his way to her, Doc asked again, "Are you sure you are all right to stay here by yourself? I wonder if we should be more vigilant. Perhaps hire someone to watch over you? I can go into town—"

"It is alright, Doc. Go and work."

"You should not speak to anyone," he insisted. "And lock the door when we leave. There is a latch at the top of the door. Slide it over and that should do the trick."

"I will be fine. No need to worry."

"You should not open the door to strangers." Doc continued. "Only us. Perhaps we should have a secret code to say for you to let us in." His hand scratched at his chin. "What about, 'Fool's gold'?"

"If that makes you feel better. Fool's gold, it is! But who would come for me here, Doc? You are far from the nearest market, and at least a day's journey on horseback from Whiteshire. I will be fine— now go."

"There is soup left on the coals by the fire. It should stay hot until we return home in the evening."

"Thank you for everything. You've been more than kind."

"It is my duty." Doc backed away, then left down the hallway.

Waiting until she heard the door close before getting up, she stretched and organized some small knick-knacks. It felt good to move around again. After pitter-patting about, she was tired.

Sitting near the fire, the sound of the crackling seemed too loud for her ears only. She sighed, hating each moment alone. Hearing tiny footprints, she perked up. But, besides the rodents looking for food, there was no one around but her.

She was alone.

But at least she was safe, she thought, propping her feet up close to the fire. No longer under the influence of Doc's sleeping medicine, Eira was able to take in more detail. The house was quaint. Not too pretty. Surrounded by necessity and not overly complicated, like her life. She had no say in her room, but she wondered how she would decorate it had it been hers.

Eira stood and stretched again. Taking in the room, she spotted some carding tools for wool. She might as well make herself useful. She started to work the wool, wishing the day would pass quickly, as her thoughts ebbed and flowed on an ocean faraway with princes and knights in shining armor.

Twenty-Two

"NICE THINGS, LOVELY THINGS TO SELL. BARLEY FOR YOUR bread. Cheap, cheap!" A woman's high-pitched voice woke Eira up from her nap. Was she dreaming?

"Lovely things to sell. Barley and good things. Pretty things," came the voice again. Then, a thud at the door.

Eira stood and approached the door.

"Hello." She cautiously said.

"Hello! I have barley for the Men of Ore. Usually they come to greet me. May I come in."

"Forgive me." Eira tried to raise her voice and make sure the woman could hear her through the door. "I am strictly forbidden to allow anyone to enter."

"Oh, but they always buy my barley and I have walked all this way. I am very old you see. Could you be a dear and let me in?"

Eira hesitated. Perhaps she was telling the truth. What if she turned away the lady and the men had no food for the coming weeks for her? Eira briskly walked over to the cupboard and opened it.

Peering in, she didn't recognize what could be barley or not. She pinched her nose. What should she do?

"Miss?" She could hear the women faintly through the door.

She strolled back to the door, trying to think of what she should do. When she reached it, she cleared her throat and said, "Perhaps you could pass it to me through the windowsill?"

"I guess that could do."

Eira .walked to the windowsill near the front of the house. There, in the yard, was an old woman hunched over and frail, carrying a black bag over her shoulder. Her face was dark, as if the sun had taken its toll over the years, and she was clothed in a cloak of bright colors.

There was a familiarity with her, but Eira couldn't place it. It certainly wasn't the queen. It must be past the noon-hour now. Most likely, the woman was on her way back home from the market, hoping to make a few sales—the Men of Ore supposedly one of them. Eira gathered from her frail fingers and body that the woman was completely harmless.

Eira leaned on the window and called out, "Good day, tis' nice to see a friendly face."

"Ahh. It is. More than barley, I have pretty laces of all different colors. Would you like to see?" the woman asked and pulled out a bright yellow ribbon woven in quality silk. The old woman's chin pointed up, and her teeth glinted with a strange contrast to her skin as she smiled at Eira. *Odd.* Where had she seen a chin like that before? The laces, caught in the light, were very beautiful and stole her attention.

Eira tapped her lips. "One moment."

Near the fire, her bag sat filled with the coin her papa had given her before she fled the castle. She rummaged through it and felt a piece of paper. She stopped and slowly pulled it out. With everything going on, she had forgotten to look for it in her sack. Unraveling its folded edges, she took in what she hoped it was—a map to the Eastern Kingdom.

To her delight, it was indeed a map with her Papa's own written words etched onto its outline. She smiled at the thought of a piece of him being with her. Reviewing the map closely creased her forehead with lines like a weaver's loom. Never having studied maps, she had no idea how to distinguish what things meant. She understood the trees to be the forest. But where she was now in comparison to Whiteshire, and how to determine the right path towards the East, she wasn't entirely sure.

The women called out and Eira quickly stuffed the map back into her bag, resolute to investigate it further once the woman leaves. She plucked out one small coin, then another, before heading back to the window.

"I have two coins. Would that be sufficient?" Eira said, approaching the window.

"Yes, it shall." The woman greedily pointed at the door.

"You want me to open the door?" Eira asked eagerly looking towards her bag with the map inside and then back at the woman.

"Child, you look like you'll need assistance tying up these pretty laces. I can lace you up properly if I am to enter."

Eira winced, conflicted with herself. Half of her desperately wanted to grab the goods and send the woman on her way, so Eira could go back to understanding the map. The other half wouldn't mind the assistance in lacing her dress up and a bit of womanly companionship, something she has greatly lacked.

She wasn't sure when she would get a new dress being on the run, and the silk ribbon was beautiful. Besides, the Men of Ore certainly couldn't—shouldn't—help her dress and tie up her laces. This woman was elderly, yet eager to help her. Should she not take up her offer? Eira walked to the front door. Hesitating at the latch, Eira slowly unlocked it and opened the door.

The woman gingerly breezed by her, entering. The old woman clasped her gnarly fingers around the coins and placed them into her bag. Untying her own laces and setting them aside, Eira stood before the woman and allowed herself to be laced. The old woman had quick hands and got to work right away.

"Thank you for offering to help me. I fear it would've been very difficult for me to do this on my own. New laces aren't something I've had in some time."

Eira kept her arms up and out of the way while admiring the way the silk shone as if it were the sun itself. How pretty she would look when the men returned, she thought. The woman didn't respond and Eira noticed how rash she was being with the fine silk.

"If you could be a little gentler, I would greatly appreciate it."

The old woman ignored Eira's request and pinched even harder on the lace, tightening up the dress much more than Eira was used to. Suddenly her breath was taken.

"Oh, I must say"—Eira puffed out— "that should be tight enough, my dear woman."

Eira felt lightheaded, and an eerie feeling lifted her skin. The laces were compressing her like that of the torture chambers in Whiteshire's dungeons. Claustrophobia stifled her breath, and she felt imprisoned.

"Dear woman, you may stop now and loosen the laces," Eira panted.

But the woman cinched the laces even harder. So hard, Eira could hardly speak. She attempted to pull away from the old woman, but the woman tugged her back into place, and Eira could not fight back.

"Almost finished," the woman cackled.

Did the woman's voice change? The hair on Eira's arms stood at attention and rippled up her spine.

She wheezed out, "Woman, that is enough!"

But the old woman tightened again, and Eira's ribs squeezed into her organs, no longer able to breathe at all. Dizzy, she fell to the floor.

Angled, her vision could only see the worn slippers of the old woman. The skin above them was hairy and wrinkled. Her skirt hem fluttered about until the face of the old woman was looking directly into hers. The woman was smiling at what she had done.

Lying on the ground, Eira gasped for any ounce of air, fighting her eyes to stay open.

"Fool!" the woman said. "With you dead, the queen will rule forever. She'll be the most beautiful and most powerful."

A sinister laugh followed the sound of worn soles padding on the floor, away from her. Eira blinked back a tear. The old woman was right. She was alone and had trusted a stranger when she knew she should have listened to Doc. She was a fool to believe the old woman. A fool to think she would be safe.

The queen found her. She would always find Eira. Everything in her wanted to just give up, give in to her obvious fate—dying as a fool.

Alone.

A tear slid from her temple into her black hair. She scanned the floor with her blurry vision, trying to look for any sharp object that could cut away at the laces. But what was the use? She could barely breathe. Life was being sucked out of her. Any extra effort would only speed up that process.

The thought of the Men of Ore coming home to her dead body made her want to fight and squirm her way out of the hold she was in, but she was too weak. Trying to call out, she merely gulped for air like a fish out of water, her voice completely soundless with no breath left. Unable to scream. Unable to move. Left for dead.

Death was inevitable for anyone. But more so for Eira White. Caught like prey spun in the queen's web. Body weak and eyes closing, her world darkened.

Twenty-Three

OWEN

ABSOLAM REARED AS AN OLD WOMAN TOOK UP THE WHOLE ROAD, passing Prince Owen and Obadiah on horseback.

"Wooooah! Calm down, ol' boy." Obadiah's horse shimmied to the right and allowed her a bit of room.

"Good day," Obadiah said to the old woman.

The woman only snarled at them and continued to gallop off. Owen looked at Obadiah, thinking that something didn't seem right. Did Obadiah have the same feeling as he did? A sinister-looking woman such as herself was never up to any good. Lawlessness has been entering the towns in growing numbers of late. Watching the old woman for a few more seconds, he pulled Absalom toward the path and moved forward again.

"I am no one to judge, but I suspect she's up to no good. There has been an uptick in thefts throughout the kingdom and abroad with the news of King Henry and Geoffrey's death."

Owen nodded. "I would have to agree. But we have no time to pursue it." Owen whistled at his horse. "We are almost at the Men of Ore's home."

"I am not certain." Obadiah seemed to follow his train of thought. "With her particular cloak, something tells me that the old woman might have been a—"

"A witch. Or perhaps a woman of the night in disguise," Owen interrupted. "It doesn't matter. If she is coming from the direction of the men's house, whether or not she is up to no good, we need to check on the maiden."

A sudden urgency took over. Immediately, he kicked Absolam into a cantor, and Obadiah followed, as if sensing the danger as well.

"There's the cottage." Owen pointed a few moments later.

"You see if the maiden is alright. I will tend to the horses," Obadiah said.

Owen dismounted in one quick movement, then headed for the door in a sprint. If she was all right, he didn't want to frighten her with his haste. But if she wasn't all right—he picked up speed anyway. Owen slid to a stop at the front door. There, on the ground, the beautiful woman once again was lying as if dead.

"Obadiah! Come quick!" he cried.

Was she dead?

He rushed to her side and leaned over, pressing his cheek to her mouth. He could feel no heat, no moisture or air escaping her lungs.

"Quick, Obadiah!" he yelled again. "Come quickly!"

He examined the awkward way she lay. Had she broken a bone?

"Forgive me," he whispered before skimming his hand over her legs, her arms, her back, and shoulders.

Nothing appeared out of line or broken. Frantically, he scanned her body once more. There was no blood, no puncture wounds, no sign of struggle. His brows crunched together. He watched her chest. Was there a slight movement there? Or was she already dead?

His eyes fell to her waist. Had she always been so morbidly skinny? A petite woman, he remembered, but average, he thought. Not grotesquely slim! She appeared emaciated from when he left her last. Had she been so ill and weak that she shriveled away to naught?

No…

His eyes bulged as he noticed a brightly colored ribbon wound incredibly tight about her back. Pulling out his dagger, he heard Obadiah's feet pounding into the room behind him. Owen carefully thrusted the dagger between the yellow ribbon and the girl's back, then pulled it toward him. He tore the fabric all the way down, instantly releasing her body from the clutches of the suffocating clothes. He could hear her lungs fill. But she went incredibly limp in his hands. Time slowed, willing, wishing, and praying she would breathe again on her own.

Lord God, I pray. Do a miracle…

Obadiah knelt beside him and laid his hands over the girl. Soft prayers lifted to the ceiling, giving him a tiny bit of hope. If she had taken a breath, it was weak and not noticeable. He leaned down to her blueish-purple lips again. Perhaps she was breathing?

Her skin was so soft, and he wanted to caress her cheeks, kiss her lips, and wake her from the grip of death. But he held back. Instead, he breathed in her sweet, rose scent.

How long had she been there without air? He laid her gently back down and examined the yellow lace in his hands. The color reminded him of the old woman riding away only moments ago. Slipping his dagger into his sheath, he spun the lace between his fingertips and silently prayed. Suddenly, an unearthly sound came out of the girl, instantly filling her lungs to their fullest capacity.

Letting out his own breath, he watched as she coughed, wincing in pain, holding her stomach. Looking up at Obadiah, relief filled his eyes with tears, and they both smiled, thanking God they were able to help her in time.

"Bring her by the fire and stay by her side." Obadiah motioned to the chair by the fire. "I'll go and fetch the men in the mountains."

Owen put his arms under the girl and lifted her up. She was shivering as if cold. Or perhaps from fear of being only moments away from escaping death itself. When he reached her chair, he lowered her down gently and stoked the fire. She was moaning in pain, and he wanted to sit by her side to comfort her.

"I will be right back." He rested his hand on her shoulder instead.

When he got back, he determined within himself to not leave her side until certain she was safe this time.

Twenty-Four

EIRA

"SHE MEANS WELL," BENJAMIN PIPED UP. "I KNOW SHE DOES. A heart of gold she has!"

Eira could overhear the men talking around her while lying on her makeshift bed by the fire. They thought she was asleep, but sleep wasn't coming with the low voices of the men hushing about and filling the room with the edge of frustration. She peeked through her eyelashes. They all sat at the table near the kitchen.

"Means well? She almost got herself killed. She didn't listen again." She watched as Fredrick clenched his jaw and ground his teeth before continuing. "Not to mention, she led those wicked people here. To our home. What will they do to us now? It is already getting harder and harder to trust folks in town. Seems like everyone is a thief these days. How will we survive?"

Though it hurt her, she couldn't help but think Fredrick was right. Her decisions had brought danger to these fine men and herself. Though she was grateful for their hospitality, she was careless and selfish to think she should stay and risk their lives any longer.

Deep bruising was around her ribs, and she knew she would not be able to move well or travel. She would be vulnerable and an easy prey of any man or woman. Her escape seemed to be for naught if she kept getting caught by her hunter.

Was that how her papa intended her flight to be—for naught? Thoughts weighed like bricks on her heart. Papa had his own reasons to make her leave, and she would have to trust him.

"She didn't lead them here, Fredrick," Mathew said, breaking her musings. "She was merely seeking refuge by coming here. They sought to kill her, not us. Otherwise, they would have surrounded the house and fought us all. They wanted her when she was alone. She must have been followed. Perhaps even watched to make sure she was completely alone before confronting her."

The kind gentlemen who saved her—yet again—piped up from the side of the room. "There was a man who attacked her. We thought he ran off in retreat when I helped her escape him. Perhaps he followed us here to report her whereabouts to the queen instead. It is the only conclusion I can draw from the events."

"Either way, we made an oath to her." Christopher pinned his eyes on Fredrick. "And it is with our own lives—our own safety—we pay homage to her. To the king. Whether it be here in our home or in the queen's presence, we've given our word to keep her safe."

Mathew's hand slammed against the table and Eira jumped, immediately regretting the sudden movement. She bit back the intense pain pulsing in her ribs. "We all agree, but—"

"Homage?" the kind gentlemen queried.

Silence filled the room, and the Men of Ore glanced at the kind gentlemen.

"You don't know who she is?" Hugo asked.

"Enlighten me." The gentlemen laughed, eyes looking at each man.

"She's Princess Eira White of Whiteshire Castle, daughter to the High King of England. Heir to the throne…"

They all stared at him as if he were a child.

"Heir?"

Before he could speak again, a taller man entered the room with a small boy in the same monk attire beside him. She watched as he held his chin in one hand and a letter in another.

"The bishop has given us sad news by way of this fine messenger." He patted the boy's head and smiled down at him. Then, his face became somber. "News of which we should all be mindful of with our next decisions." He cleared his threat and slowly spoke words that pierced Eira's heart. "I've received word by way of the bishop that King Geoffrey of Whiteshire has died on his return home from Normandy."

A gasp rang through the whole room.

"Long live the king," Ben said. The men looked at Ben as if he were an intruder.

Fredrick hit Ben on the back of the head. "You don't say long live the king once he has died. He is dead, you fool!"

Christopher glared across the table at both men. This time, no laughter filled her heart with their banter, only utter sadness. She couldn't have heard correctly! But something in her confirmed he spoke the truth. Her papa was really gone.

Blood pulsed in her ears. Her *papa* ... dead?

She was now an orphan. Tears seeped out of her closed eyes. Everything she feared as a child was coming to fruition. She was now all alone. No wonder she was locked away all her childhood. It was better that way. Every person she loved, favored, or cared for had likely died because of her.

Her mother died from complications after giving birth to Eira. If her mother hadn't died, her papa wouldn't have died at Eira's stepmother's hand. The girl she played with as a child died because of her foolishness ... everyone. Everyone she loved was dead, and it was all her fault.

Pain shot through her stomach when she tried to move. Biting her bottom lip, she attempted not to make a sound, but noise came out of her despite her efforts. Tears stung like bees and poured from her eyes, slipping down her cheeks onto the wimple resting behind her neck.

Looking again at the men willing to risk their lives for her, she felt guilt spread across her chest. How could she risk their lives? She stared at each of them. Bruised or not, she didn't want them to suffer for her. Leaving would mean they got to move on with their lives. Something she desperately wished she could do.

"Upon the death of a king, immediately the heir is made king or queen. A coronation would soon follow with those in council paying homage along with the barons, nobles, and princes in the kingdoms throughout..." He paused. Eira watched his adam's apple bob. "With all due respect, we've never seen a queen rule in all of Normandy or England. A regent, yes. I assume Queen Amara has taken over duties in her husband's stead. But not a queen in her own right. If what you say is true, and if the young maiden is of age, as she appears, that would make" —he pointed at Eira without looking in her direction— "her High Queen of Whiteshire. Am I correct?"

When the gentlemen turned to look at the monk's face, the monk nodded affirmatively in response.

"I see."

When the gentleman suddenly sprang his eyes toward her, Eira shut hers, pretending to be asleep. She felt the floor thud as all the men went to one knee in unison.

"Long live the queen," she heard them say quietly.

When she could no longer feel eyes on her, she peeked up, catching Laurentius waving his hands, animating his words which he was attempting to keep quiet.

"You bunch of fopdoodles! Why else would the vecke come to kill a bellibone lass and leave her sanded, hmm? She's a threat to the gleedy eyethurl, and the wallydraigle wants nothing more than her fair head and crown, I daresay." Sitting back down, Laurentius crossed his arms over his chest. "We must protect the princess—I mean the queen—

from the awful wind-sucker, Queen Amara. We're all the bellibone's got left."

"I agree. We need to protect her," the monk said.

She watched as the monk folded the letter that bore news of her papa's death. Eira wanted to curl up and wither on the dirt floor. *Bury me here*, she pleaded to herself. These men were full of goodness; how could she just abandon them? Yet, they said it to themselves. The queen wanted *her*. If she removed herself from them, they would be safe.

The monk paced the room and spoke as if speaking to himself instead of the group of men. "If the maiden is not of age, the queen would be regent and reign on her behalf, but if the queen could convince the people the princess is dead, Queen Amara would be crowned in her stead."

Eira wanted to tell them she was of age, but what good would it do? She was not fit to be queen.

"I, Prince Owen Williamus from Wealas, have not heard of her. Ever. Nor seen any likeness of her in any Royal Ball, or noble masquerade, or in any court being held. Who else would know of her in the surrounding kingdoms?"

Did he say he was a prince? Prince of Wales?

She had been held in the arms of a real—handsome—prince?

Prince Owen continued, "If she were hidden all this time from the outer realms, barons, and nobleman, surely no one would question the queen's authority to take the throne immediately. But if they knew she was indeed alive—"

"Some know she's alive," Mathew said cautiously. "There are whispers of it in the market and with the townspeople. If they had confirmation that she was alive and the queen had taken the throne, truly there would be anarchy in the streets, I fear even in all Whiteshire."

"You are correct." The monk dropped his hand from his chin. "However, I know of a man who would challenge the queen, a cousin in line to the throne, Henry of Blois. I may be able to get word to him through the bishop." The monk placed his hands behind his back.

Doc walked over to the monk. "I know you had plans to head to Winchester for work. Can you go straight away to Winchester Cathedral and inquire with the bishop there?"

The monk nodded. "I think that is a good idea."

"Who's to say this *cousin* wouldn't challenge the princess for the throne?" Christopher questioned.

"A fair question, dear brother. I believe him to be a kind and just man who would fight for Princess Eira to be queen if she were the rightful heir. When I am there, I will search the archives of the church scriptorium and library to help with the proof of her birth before sending for him. Perchance I can find record of her birth and prove its authenticity," the monk stated while sitting down in a chair by Fredrick.

"In the meantime, we must make sure the princess—or queen—is safe," Hugo demanded.

"Yes," Doc answered. "I believe she would be in better hands with the prince."

The men slightly bowed their heads at the word *prince* in the way they did for her before Doc continued. "He's skilled in battle and would bring better safety than here, alone in our home while we are off at work. She's vulnerable during the day to the queen's tactics." Doc paused and stared at Prince Owen. "What do you say, Prince Owen Williamus of Wealas? Will you stay here for now before returning to your kingdom to protect the princess from her enemies?"

Eira was silent, waiting for his response as if she wanted him to say yes, but did she? The men talked as if she weren't even in the room, making decisions on her behalf as if she were a child and not the queen, they said her to be. If they honored her as queen, why didn't they seek council *with* her, not for her?

A flash back of Lance-man, the dark-haired man, and the old

woman made Eira shiver. If she were honest, Eira hadn't been the wisest person of late. Dropping her chin to her chest, Eira's cheeks flushed, and she became rapidly nauseous.

How could I have been so naïve? What kind of queen would allow herself to be in such danger? Not only her, but she had also put the lives of others at risk and exhausted their resources all because of her own carelessness and blind trust in strangers.

Papa was such a good leader. Her eyes welled and her vision blurred only for a minute. She could never live up to his legacy and rule. Her mind went to the ring in her pocket. *Why did he think I could hold such power? Did he believe in me? Did he think I could offer wisdom and not be naïve?* These men sure didn't think so by their actions. Eira tugged at her clothes, feeling uncomfortable in her own skin.

She pondered her father's reign. *What made him so good at being King?* Eira's chin trembled as she reimagined her Papa's stories; him sitting in all his regalia with his council during court, scratching his scruffy beard while seeking guidance of religious leaders during dinners, and his warm, big hands reaching out to shake the locals during the Great Hall feasts to get their perspective on matters.

Suddenly, realization struck her. Being a queen isn't about making all the decisions solely on oneself but also letting wise and trustworthy people help assist you in them. If she were to lead and be respected, being left out on the discussion was not the way. Yet would she fight it? *Could* she fight it? Did she have enough strength?

A strange darkness had been threatening to settle in her mind, starting to find a home there—one of fear, nightmares, worry, and helplessness. More than she had ever felt in the past. They stole every ounce of bravery she had left.

The letter, now behind the monk's back, was just as vivid to her as if he held it in front of her very eyes. Did her papa know he was going to die when he shoved her from his bedchamber into the secret passageway? Is that why he gave her his ring? And did he want her to be brave, to fight the queen for the kingdom? Most likely, but every question she had for him would be left unanswered.

He was gone.

Forever.

Never would he hold her again, rub his garlicky fingers onto her cheeks, tell her fairytale stories before bed, tap his finger on her nose like the snowflakes falling on her mother's. She would never hear his voice, feel his love, or the safety and security he brought.

The only thing she had to remember was the last words he'd said. And she would hold on tight to the sound of his voice against her ear, hoping it would never leave her memories, forever etched into her mind. Because he was right. It was a 'forever' goodbye when he held her last. He knew he would never see her again.

Tear after tear slipped down her cheek, and her body began to shake uncontrollably. She was suddenly cold and couldn't even stop her lips from trembling. A hole was being ripped in her heart. A hole no one could ever replace. How could she live without her father?

She looked at the prince, who seemed to be in agony over the question presented to him. An agony she understood. Why would anyone want to fight her cause?

With every attempt on her life, she started to fear death less and less. When dead, she would be with the Lord and her father and mother again. Tears continued to flow as she wept in silence. They slipped down her lips and chin, falling onto her hands. It was a foolish wish, but she wanted death in that moment.

Twisting the ring between her fingers, she knew her papa had chosen her to be queen. He had chosen her despite her foolishness and her weaknesses. How could she not fulfill his last desire?

An ache filled her soul. *What would you have me do, Papa?*

Slipping on her papa's signet ring, she waited for the prince's response. *Say no. Say no. Say no, and I will run away for good.*

Pinching her eyes shut, she released the stinging sensation and held back her hushed cries. A coward. She was a coward. No prince would want to protect a coward even if a king chose her.

"I will." Prince Owen grunted. "I will fight for the princess!" He stood, clenching his fists. "I will protect Princess Eira of Whiteshire, even if it means forfeiting my life, my plans, and my future. I'm with you till the end, men!"

As if in celebration, the men cheered and clanked nearby glasses together. A jig and song broke out, filling the air with laughter and joy, but Eira slumped into the darkness. Desperate to be unseen. Dreadful nightmares took over her thoughts and held her captive.

His declaration meant she would have to stay longer, and she wasn't prepared to run from him, from a handsome prince, but she would now be forced to. What would he do after realizing she was not worth saving, that he gave up his plans, his future, for someone not worthy to fight for after all? Would he, too, be ashamed of her like the queen was? Like she was of herself?

She covered her face and hid in the dark corner of the room, wishing for morning to come.

Twenty-Five

EMPRESS AMARA

"Looking Glass, Looking Glass on the wall, who is the fairest of them all?"

The queen smeared fucus on her lips and looked at Herrick, squirming in his chair. The bright red color contrasted beautifully with her white skin. The little worm of a man kept moving in the reflection of her mirror.

"Go on, Herrick. Let us play our little game..." She smiled and turned to face him. "Why do you insist that I prompt you every time? I must say, it is getting dull." Her eyes lowered at him.

Seilda had returned with the most wonderful news late last night. Why did Herrick have to insist on souring her day? Everything was as perfect as it should be. Eira was finally dead. What more did he want?

As she stared at Herrick, her left eyebrow lifted, and she twisted her hands. Why was the pathetic fool so skittish? The townspeople knew she would be crowned empress in all of Whiteshire in only a few days. Besides, the King of Scotland was on her side, and the Earl of Gloucester was on his way to pay homage along with the other nobles. Everything was in order.

"Herrick?" she snapped, her patience weaning.

"I've word from Justin, My Queen. It is of great importance and takes precedence over our—your—game."

"Justin?" Her face fell with disgust. "What does he have to do with our little game?"

"Nothing, m'lady. He has word about the princess." He quivered like a small child; she hated small children.

"You torment me, Herrick!" Queen Amara let out a puff of anger. Even in the girl's death, Herrick found a way to ransack her with great annoyance. "Go on."

"When Justin returned this morning—shortly after Seilda—he came to me immediately and said that, while waiting for the girl to die, a man on horseback came to her aid. He took out his knife and saved the girl from the laces that Seilda had wrapped her in to suffocate her." Herrick swallowed. "I am sorry, Your Majesty ... the princess—"

"Don't," Queen Amara demanded, trying to catch her breath. "Don't you dare speak her name."

It can't be! Little Snow White was back from the dead and haunted her as Empress Amara's own father had through the years.

Her nails dug into her knees. Once she felt the pain of skin breaking, she released.

Shaky hands tried to put the fucus back on the stand near her mirror, but it slipped and fell to the floor. The sound of the small metal container hitting the stone floor echoed in the room. Sweat beaded her hairline, making the white powder cake along her forehead and on the top of her upper lip.

"Is he certain? Did he see her breathing?"

Herrick nodded frantically.

Blood rushed to her heart, but it was fear that pumped through her organ's chambers. A fear she'd not felt in a long time. Her father's face looked back through the mirror into hers. With eyes like her own, like a ghost stealing her soul, he was disappointed with her again.

"*Little Snow White* will die this time. Even if I shall die myself in the attempt!"

"I think we should send more men this time. She has been crafty every attempt to her life. She is cunning and seems to have people around her that will assist in her escape."

"Have you not forgotten, Herrick, that she is of royal blood?" The queen glared at Herrick for his ignorance. "You want me to risk the people's good faith by showing up with a small army of men to kill the girl. When they find out she is the heir and know that I have bade it, there will no doubt be a revolt for my throne. There is already unrest with the king's death. No! I will go disguising myself and kill her in secrecy."

"I will not let anything happen to you. I will go—" Herrick took a step forward.

"You have done nothing for me." Her voice rose to an octave she had never heard before. "Nothing!" she screamed. "You will stay here, and I will take *Justin* to accompany me." She used his name as a curse word, and it worked—Herrick jolted back and sat in his chair, defeated. "*You* may go and get him for me."

Empress Amara flicked her wrist at him. She allowed the trembling to take over her body and fell to the floor. Hot tears smeared her makeup, streaking down her face and uncovering the wall of perfection once again. She was exposed, vulnerable, and weak. All the things she despised. But today, she would allow the tears to fall—tears of anger, tears of envy, tears of revenge. She would allow them one day to manifest themselves and then vindicate every single one of them.

Nobody made her cry. Not without paying for it.

Memories of her father swinging at her made her wince. Instantly, her body pulled in on itself like she was a child again. The only way to get rid of the horrible memories was to be the tormentor.

And she would be.

Queen Amara wiped at her face. She needed to clear her mind and think of a plan. It was her father's will that she would be queen. An empress in her own rite. She would honor that.

Pulling herself up off the floor, Queen Amara stormed toward the entry. Hands still shaking, she held fast to the wood.

"Get me Seilda!" Her voice quivered and echoed down the hallway. She turned to where an urn sat on a small table and threw up in it.

Wiping her lips with the back of her hand, she concocted something extraordinary. So deceptive, even the princess would have no idea what hit her. That is, until she was dead. Laughter bubbled out of her. Going back to the mirror, she sat down on the chair.

I will be the most beautiful one again. I will have the kingdom, not Eira. Everything shall fall into place, and Eira will be no more.

Reaching down to the floor, she picked up the small metal container that had fallen. Lifting the white powder up with one hand, she smiled at the mirror, but it never reached her eyes. Applying the makeup blindly, she pushed thoughts that would threaten her plans to kill Eira out of her mind. She wouldn't be weak like her father said she was.

She would be ruthless.

Twenty-Six

EIRA

EIRA REACHED FOR THE CUP ON THE STAND NEAR HER. SHE winced and instantly pulled back her arm. Her ribs were still too bruised. Leaning back in her bed, she groaned. Doc was certain that she hadn't broken anything, which was a relief, but insisted she rest until there was no sign of internal bleeding.

"I thought you were sleeping," Prince Owen said near her.

"Sorry. I didn't mean to wake you," she whispered.

Watching his hands, he picked up the cup for her and handed it to her.

"Thank you." She took it.

The pad of his fingers brushed hers. They were a little rough. Probably from his travels. Her glance caught his white tunic lying on the floor next to him, then bounced to the thinner tunic clinging to his body. She averted her eyes from his sturdy chest.

"Were you keeping guard?"

"I was trying but must have fallen asleep." His hand ran down his face, and she noticed dark circles under his eyes. He smiled while his eyes closed, and he tilted his head back on the wooden wall. With his eyes closed, she studied his face and drank Adam's ale.

Cool and refreshing water slipped down her dry throat. Swallowing, she noticed his chin had a slight line in the center of it. The shadows and the glint of light in the fire caught the fine lines starting to creep around his eyes. Surely the prince wasn't that old, probably a few years older than her—but clearly, he had lived enough life to bear the lines of age.

When people inherited them, Papa said it meant they smiled a lot. Thinking of her papa caused a heaviness to wash over her, and she drank the last of the water. Leaning over, she held back a groan and put the cup back on the table beside her makeshift bed near the fire.

The prince's eyes popped open, and he went to do it for her.

A firmness came through her whisper. "No, sir. I'll do it myself."

"Of course." Concern flooded his eyes. "Shall I get you anything else?"

"Nothing at the moment, I thank thee." She propped herself on one arm and pivoted her body, facing him. "So." She bit her lip when a sharp pain ran along her side. "I hear you're a prince. Where are you from?"

"Wealas." Putting his forearms on his knees, he tilted his head. "But some townspeople like to call it Wales. I am not sure which title I like better myself."

"I have never been. I hear it is beautiful there. My name originates from Wealas. My mother loved it. Or so I have heard. I can only assume it has been a long journey for you to come to Whiteshire." She dropped her chin for a moment, eyes staring at the strewn hay underneath her. She missed her bed.

"Do you know what your name means?" Prince Owen's eyes locked onto hers.

"Nay. Pray-tell. What does my name mean?" Eira said a little too eagerly.

"Snow." He smiled. "In my language, it means snow."

"Really?" She closed her eyes. "My mother must have known that. I wish she had told me herself. She said she always wanted a child as white as snow."

"I heard of your childhood. There were stories that came to Wealas filling the halls about a young princess hidden for years from a wicked queen. I had no idea it was real. We all thought it make-believe—a fable. It was a terrible thing done to you. For that, I am truly sorry."

"You? Sorry?" When she looked back up at him, there was no pity, only kindness. "You don't need to be sorry for me. I had a good Papa. He loved me." Because all she ever wanted was to be loved. Even if it was by a wicked queen.

She bit her lips hard to avoid tearing up. *Focus, Eira … don't cry. He will think you are weaker than you already are.*

"I've met him before." The prince coughed, probably trying to distract her. "Your father, that is."

Her insides came alive. *He knew Papa.*

"King Geoffrey was one of the most distinguished and kindest men I had the privilege to meet. A man of great honor. You should be proud of him."

She almost burst into tears. She was proud of him. He was a man of great valor. Everyone who met him knew that. He didn't deserve to die. A tear slid down her cheek, and she discreetly swiped it away.

"I've even been to Whiteshire…" he continued. "With my father, the King of Wealas."

"In Whiteshire? Truthfully?" She wanted to sit up further, but the pain prevented her. "You don't jest?"

"Nay." His laughter was hearty and made her chest swim with warmth. "I don't jest with a queen."

She wanted to argue the last bit of his comment, but let it go.

Whiteshire? To her castle? Why had she not seen him before? When royalty was announced at the gate, she would sneak out of her chambers and peer down from the walls as they arrived. She had not recalled any boys coming from other regions. She would have noticed a boy.

"Pray-tell, what was your visit about? Was it for business?"

Clearing his throat, Prince Owen rubbed his hands along his legs for a brief second before replying. "It was to strengthen our alliance with one another. Or rather, with Wealas and all of England." He swallowed loudly.

"Alliance?" She really wished she had been taught more in these moments. "What alliance?" What kind of 'queen' didn't know what the word alliance was? "Do you perhaps mean trades? Military? Or farming?"

Her question lingered in the air. The silence grew between them, and with every passing second, heat tingled in her cheeks. She felt even more foolish for having asked at all.

The prince sprang to his feet, and she was startled, sucking in a breath through her teeth as a sharp pain dug into her side.

"I don't want to bore you, m'lady. Would you like more water?"

"You do not bore me, Prince Owen. This is the most interaction I have had in many years with one person."

Reaching for the adam's ale, the prince knocked the jug completely, making it teeter on its side. Prince Owen's hands grabbed hold of the jug, and he marched over to pour more water into her cup.

Looking down, he held her stare. His eyes were etched in confusion. Was he frustrated with her childish questions? He was surely making her feel foolish enough as it was. Why did he insist on dragging it out?

An irritation rose within her.

She couldn't quite pin the emotion stirring behind his emerald eyes, but one thing was certain, he was uncomfortable speaking of this 'alliance' with her papa.

"Thank you for your conversation. I understand if you wish not to speak of the matter. However, I do insist on you *not* pouring water all over my bed and blankets." She pointed to her cup.

"Oh, dear." Prince Owen rushed to clean up the water he'd spilled. "Forgive me. Honestly, I'm embarrassed to tell you." He looked at her and huffed out a puff of frustration, then continued. "My father had me come to Whiteshire to see if there were any *eligible* women…" His cheeks turned as red as her lips. "To wed."

Perhaps it wasn't merely the idea of being married that made him uncomfortable … maybe the prince was distraught over the thought of an alliance in the form of a marriage to someone in Whiteshire. To someone like her.

"I see," she said softly. Lifting her regard to his emerald eyes again, she became vividly aware of the brown lines outlining them. His pupils seemed large, as if taking her all in. She couldn't help but gaze down at his full and defined lips. She quickly looked away.

"And you left Whiteshire because there was no potential wife to be found or wed…" Dropping her stare to the floor, she continued. "…or so you were told."

The annoying thing in her chest flooded with a kind of sadness she'd not experienced. It pounded against her chest with uncertainty. And want.

"Yes." His answer was curt.

Why did Papa not speak of him before? Was the prince told she never existed? Forgotten throughout the entire kingdom. Was she that invisible? Or did her papa keep her a secret for her own protection? Did Papa fear what the queen would do to Eira as she grew older and more desirable to become queen?

Something strange skimmed over the prince's face. So lightly, she almost wondered if she saw it at all. Was it guilt? Remorse? A sudden dread hollowed out her gut. Was it disappointment—in her?

Eira lay back and stared at the wood trestles above her, wanting nothing more than to disappear—again. Despite his painful look of dissatisfaction or disappointment—if indeed that was what she had seen, Eira was determined to enjoy his conversation. She glanced at his chiseled chin. Being in his company was nice.

"I've never been outside the castle walls until now." She turned to face him. "What would've happened had your father found an eligible woman in Whiteshire? Would there've been dancing, or perhaps a Royal Ball? I heard they are quite dazzling."

Thoughts of her papa swayed through her mind. Her hands in his, her tiny, leather feet on top of his shiny shoes, swinging around like an innocent child while music filled the room. She looked up into her papa's face and saw Prince Owen smiling back at her.

Jolted, she focused on reality, staring at her. The vision of Papa quickly vanished. She pushed back the tears building behind her eyes and continued. "I always wanted to dance. I did once, only briefly as a child, but never really learned the complete art."

"Yes, there would be lots of dancing at the ball. Like you said, it's dazzling." He smiled. "Eligible women bring their families for one evening of divine elegance. Everyone's dressed in their finest, and the food is delightful. And the laughter ... well, simply splendid. All in all, it would be a fine event. You would've enjoyed it immensely, I am certain."

"You make it sound heavenly. I think I would've loved to have been invited." Her smile faltered. Keeping her eyes above her, she asked, "How does a prince know, after searching of course, that he's found his bride?"

The prince repositioned himself. "Well. I wouldn't know firsthand, as I haven't found a bride yet, but from what I gather, it can be rather —well, it is complicated."

"Complicated. How could it possibly be complicated?"

In her peripheral vision, she saw his eyebrows lower, and his smile grew weary. He stared at his hands as if mourning a great loss.

"My father has been gracious with me, I must admit. He has not forced me to marry through a betrothal. This is something I greatly respect. However, that deal won't last forever. In the meantime, he has kept himself busy putting on all these balls where women would take turns dancing with me, the eligible—and heir to the throne—prince, of course." He puffed out a deep sigh. "It can be quite exhausting, actually."

Her eyebrows pinched, and she shook her head. "It doesn't sound tiresome in the least. It sounds lovely." Her smile was genuine, and she tried to ignore the heat creeping up her cheeks.

"The thing is, as you dance with each partner, you must examine if you are…" He shifted in his spot and put his hands on his knees. "You see if you're compatible. Or if there is—"

"Love," she whispered.

"Yes." He quickly averted his gaze back to his hands. "*If* there is any love, as you say, or passion between the two while you danced."

A moment of silence passed before she felt he was watching her from the corner of his eye. Electricity between the two of them divided the small space between them. Did he feel the sparks too?

"Did you ever find someone to love?"

"No." She could hear shame wriggle its way out in his deep whisper. "There were many beautiful ladies. But none that I could love and spend the rest of my life with … or see sharing a kingdom with." He laughed. "My father says I am chasing a dream. You see, not all marital unions share true love. Most marry for position and wealth rather than based on love. But that is not what I want."

"I know that." Eira slumped back down.

"You do? You understand?" His head perked up.

"My papa married Queen Amara." She let her hands smooth out the crinkles of the blanket. "That should say enough."

Their eyes caught for a moment.

"I don't believe they had any passion for one another." She blushed and found herself staring at the blanket again. "If hatred was considered a passion, they definitely shared that … but it was never love."

"Exactly." Prince Owen's hands became animated. "My parents were fortunate. They learned to love one another, and their union was made strong because of that. Over time, they fell in love. But I want my marriage to be different. I want to marry for something." He paused. "For something more." Standing up, Prince Owen stretched his legs. "And thus! I'm still unwed at my father's disapproval." He shook his head.

"Why would your father disapprove of you if you do not wed?"

"Because if I can't find my sister, I will be king." Prince Owen walked over to the water and poured a glass for himself and then her. He sat back down before continuing. "And when I return home, I will be forced to marry right away. My father believes that a great king is only made by having a wife. Besides, it is tradition." He sighed. "My father is sick and dying. There will be no time left to choose a wife for myself. He will choose for me, and that will be the end of it. My dream … gone."

Eira's nose tickled, and she sneezed, unable to stop the moan that came out with it.

"Are you all right? Did I cause you pain?" He touched her shoulder. "I'm sorry, Eira."

She wanted to speak, but the electricity that suddenly shot through her paralyzed any words that begged to come out. Peering up through her lashes, she wondered if he felt the same way too.

As if he touched fire, Owen pulled his hand back and stood.

"I will fetch fire for the wood. I mean—" His right hand sprang to cover his eyes. He squeezed the bridge of his nose in frustration. "I mean, I will fetch wood for the fire."

Grunting something she couldn't quite make out, he spun in one spot, unaware of his surroundings, and finally picked up his white outer tunic before bolting out the door.

Her heart was pounding too fast for her to concentrate on anything but the door for a few moments. When the beating rhythm finally slowed, she remembered the map in her sack and her plan to escape. Despite how this prince made her feel, Eira would find a way to escape for his own good and, perhaps, for hers. He was too good of a man for Eira to have protecting her alone when the queen had an army. It would be his death. By morning, perhaps she would already be gone, and he could forget about her.

Twenty-Seven

Eira snuck another glance at Prince Owen's profile before slipping down the hallway and out the door. After attempting to study the map all night, she finally had a faint idea as to where she was amongst the squiggly lines and diagrams. She was semi-confident that she may know the way to the Eastern Kingdom. She was surprised that she was able to get as far as she had. Most of the men had snored loud enough to cover the sound of her leaving. After getting Absolam ready in the barn, she walked him out. Her eyes lingered around the edges of the Men of Ore's home. She would miss them.

Palms slick, she gripped the reins and awkwardly maneuvered herself onto the horse, trying not to grimace in agony. Coughing from the sharp, cold air in her lungs, Eira tried to stifle a whimper as a searing pain shot through her ribs, she was sure the old lady had broken one or two of them.

Gently, Eira tugged the reins and veered the horse away from the little house. Tightening her legs around its ribs, she began a slow trot. A pang of guilt ran through her chest, tightening it. *Leaving is for the best. That's all this is … protection for those you care about. You can do this.*

Though she hadn't gone far, she was beginning to miss the men's company already. They were similar, whether they wanted to be or not. Through chance encounters, she felt tied to them in such a unique way.

Her mind quickly went to Prince Owen. Both were handed kingdoms and roles they felt gravely unprepared for. The Men of Ore were hard-working, and yet quirky and fun. They all had a strong sense of honor and valor that made her feel as if she were once again in the presence of her papa. And the monk brought wisdom and clarity to her soul, as if her guiding light.

Eira sighed heavily. *Lord, why is every decision I try to make on my own so hard?*

Keeping an eye on the path in front of her, Eira's one hand slipped into her bubble-bow, delicate fingers wrapped around her papa's ring. How odd—his whole kingdom in the palm of her fragile hand. Poised that his signet ring meant he chose her to rule after him. But if she was missing from her kingdom, like Owen's sister, another would have to rule instead, would they not? In her case, it would be Queen Amara. Perhaps she was better suited to rule than Eira.

Thinking back to Papa's last words, Eira recalled him saying, *"Remember, Eira, remember what your mother told you…"* It was the story about her mother that Papa used to tell her before bed. It was some kind of fairytale about purpose. She wished she could remember what the story was or its purpose. But the details were foggy like it was a dream, a make-believe story that felt familiar and nostalgic but completely lost in childhood.

Despite their subtle similarities, the prince was stronger and more knowledgeable than she was. Eira was weak. Her body would agree. If only they'd met under better circumstances. Maybe things would be different.

Eira ducked under a branch, and the dew brushed her hair. She pulled her hood up over her head. With one hand still gripping the reins, she rolled the edges of the large hood piece back so she could still see in her peripheral vision.

Destiny was already set before them like the path in front of Eira. It seemed like nothing could be done about it. She huffed out another sigh. Perhaps the prince couldn't do anything about finding his sister, but she could do something. She could make sure he got back to his life, to his family, to being free from helping Eira so he could find his sister. Her eyes scanned the forest. Eira pulled out the map and re-examined it. She questioned her ability to read it but felt determined to stay on the path ahead of her.

Eira leaned into the thin leather saddle to relieve the pain in her ribs. Her sides were still tender from being tied up so tightly. She deflected her pain with thoughts, simpering in the moment when she felt the heat of Prince Owen's body near hers, making each nerve dance with anticipation.

Why did the image of Prince Owen have to keep popping up in her mind? To think of the prince's companionship now would be of no use. But her thoughts betrayed her. They lingered on Prince Owen's scent, his strength, his kindness, his sudden friendship.

Eira chided herself for lingering on a boy. She didn't have time to worry about such frivolous things. Getting as far away as possible from Whiteshire, as Papa had said to, was her top priority. That is what he had wanted for her, and she must obey. East was her destination.

She repositioned herself more securely on the horse and then leaned down.

"You don't happen to know where east is, do you?" Eira whispered to the horse, then chuckled and patted Absolam's mane.

Noticing the fragile leaves crushing in her path on the ground, Eira stopped to catch her breath. One small leaf fluttered into her hand. Its color was dull, yet beautiful. Somehow the delicate leaf brought her comfort. She could somewhat relate to the poor little foliage, cut off from its branches—its home, its roots, its very essence of life, and what made the leaf who it was. Now, it was weathered, waiting to be crushed by the soles of men. Destined for the wind to carry its remains away. So fragile, yet so beautiful.

Closing her fist, she let the dry leaf crumble in her hand.

Eira urged Absalom on. Pushing branches away from hitting her face, she kept vigilant, watching for any large logs to avoid. As she carved out a path further away from Prince Owen, she noticed the trees getting wider. The thick, gnarly roots of the frost-laden floor mesmerized her. Vines crept up the trunks and covered the branches hanging from the trees. In the cooler spots of the forest floor, ice sparkled and glistened. A shiny bit of moss made her stop.

They were the same emerald color as Prince Owen's eyes. It even had the same golden-colored flecks underneath the vibrant green as he had. Lingering in its enchantment for far too long, she scorned herself and kept moving.

Why did she feel so guilty for leaving him? Had her papa felt the same way when he pushed her out of the kingdom, leaving her? She shivered and watched snow start to fall. Soon, it began blanketing the ground in a thinly veiled layer.

Suddenly, a fearful thought came to her. Could someone follow her trail now? Spinning back, she groaned. A small line in the snow behind her sketched out a clear path where horse hooves marked her direction. *No!*

Eira wouldn't be able to go back and remove all her markings. She must move quickly. Although she didn't anticipate being captured by evil men again, she was alert and always paying attention to her surroundings, feeling at ease with the dagger her papa gave her being in her sack. If she had to use it, Eira would. She only hoped the snow would melt and not give her whereabouts away before she was far enough away.

The canopy above her let in more light. Eira was finally breaking through the trees and noticed an open roadway darting toward what she hoped the map said was east. She breathed in a sigh of relief. Assuming it was used for merchants entering the towns, Eira stopped and listened before fully exposing herself.

Except for a few chirps from birds above her in the trees, nothing made a sound. Once on the path, she picked up speed.

She was free.

Twenty-Eight

EMPRESS AMARA

EMPRESS AMARA AND JASON RODE ALL NIGHT OVER THE SEVEN hills to the dwelling place of the Men of Ore. But after storming the place, she realized the miserable whifling had already left.

"How do you intend for me to kill the girl?"

"I have my ways. You will not lay a hand on her."

"You, m'lady? But I could slit her throat and be done with this charade. You will know then and there she is dead once and for all, Your Majesty. There would be no mistaking that."

"Yes, I am sure that seems right to you. But unlike you I have thought this through. You see, the marketplace is not far from here and what if you or I were seen doing such a thing, and her origins were found out. What then? I have my plans, and I need you only to follow my lead."

Veering west, they rounded a bend of an old path that would lead them into the depths of the forest. Queen Amara almost shrieked with joy when they happened upon the miserable wench hobbling down the path toward them...

Alone.

The fool. Empress Amara smiled.

Eira wouldn't have to be hunted after all. The pathetic girl walked into her own web and now was trapped. Empress Amara could almost squeal with happiness but suppressed the laugh wanting to burst out of her. *It is all going so perfectly.* Queen Amara's left eyebrow cinched up like a battle tent. *Perhaps even better than planned.*

She watched the girl's eyes go wild as Justin bound his horse toward the frightened little thing and circled around her, not allowing the girl any chance of escaping from the path or darting back into the forest. It would make the chase harder for them among trees and branches and logs on horseback. Not that they wouldn't find her.

Empress Amara slowly dismounted and pulled a bag of apples from her horse. She took her time and approached the girl, who now had her hands up, trembling and crying like the pathetic fool she was.

"Get away from me! I don't want to have anything to do with you. I demand you to let me be!" Eira's small, timid voice was like nails digging into Empress Amara's face.

Demand?

She was stupid, wasn't she?

Empress Amara held her face still. She couldn't give away her distaste ... not yet. *Everything had to go as planned.* Soon, she would hear no demand uttered out from the ruby lips. Eira, daughter of the king and heir to the throne, would die after today.

But first, Empress Amara would play a little game and make the foolish girl believe she could demand anything from the empress of England.

Empress Amara forced her eyes to be gentle. "Hush, child." Managing to make the request sound as sweet as honey, she continued. "I've been on such a long journey searching for you. Alas, as providence has seen to it ... *you* have found us."

"I know you are searching for me! You're hunting me down. Get away!" Eira screeched the words out like a small mouse, frantically looking up at Jason and then back at Empress Amara.

The Empress watched as Eira's shaky hands pointed at Jason.

"He said you wanted to kill me, wanted my—my heart." Her hand fluttered to her heart as if on its own accord, knowing Empress Amara wanted it torn and ripped from her chest.

Good. Empress Amara smiled on the inside. *She's afraid.* Fear was a great tool to use. But this time, fear wasn't her tactic.

She lowered her face, pinching her brows together and pouting her lips to appear sad. Queen Amara pleaded with her eyes and peered up at the pathetic fool. "Eira. I would do no such thing. You see that man was only ordered to bring you *back* to me. To our home. We were all so worried about you and had no idea what happened to you. Truly, we thought you were already dead. But look, you are alive and well." A snarl wanted to creep up onto her upper lip, but she held it still.

When Eira turned her questioning eyes toward Justin, Empress Amara winked at him. *Play along*, she mouthed. He nodded his head in response.

"Does she speak truth?" Eira's voice was raspy and weak.

"Of course. I only had orders to bring you to the queen and…" He paused. Marginally too long to make it sound believable. "I confess, I lied to you. It was a trick, and none of the queen's doing at all. I said words to scare you into listening to me. I feared you would not heed my voice if I wasn't stern with you." He met the Empress's eyes. "Forgive me, Your *Highness*."

Good recovery, Justin, Empress Amara thought.

Nodding toward Justin, she wanted Eira to notice her acceptance of his apology. "Now, all is forgiven." The queen lifted her face into the best smile she could summon. "Alas! You have found her safe. This was all I asked. So, thank you, honorable servant."

"I don't understand. Why come in search of me? What do you want?" Eira's eyes widened. "Are you still going to kill me? Like you did Marie when you found her? Or like you did to—" she hesitated, then spat the last words out. "—my papa?"

Empress Amara's tongue threatened to spew out the word *Yes!* with all the fury of a dragon's breath, but she held still. Instead, she forced herself to appear sullen and utterly sad.

"My poor child. I am truly sorry I was not the one to tell you in person. It should have been me, your Queen Mother, giving you the news of the king—your father's—untimely death. He had been getting sicker and sicker."

She couldn't hold the pathetically long face any longer. Lifting the bag of apples, she stepped closer to Eira. "I've searched high and low to find you." Empress Amara paused and held the bag up in the air before lowering it to eye level again. "Now that I have, I wish to pay homage to you—" The Empress's eyelids pinched shut, and her lips pressed into a firm line, not wanting to call Eira anything but worthless. After an intense second, she pulled herself together and lowered herself into a curtsy before continuing. "Your Majesty."

Empress Amara kept her head so low the girl couldn't see the disgust smearing all over her face. She would play this game right. Deception was an art, and she would master it, even if it killed her to do so. Empress Amara stayed lowered, as any subject to a royal should, until Eira spoke.

"Homage?" the girl whispered. "Why would you come to pay *me* homage?"

Empress Amara rose. "Are you not the sole heir of King Geoffrey?"

"Yes, of course. But I don't understand. You are—you're being kind to me?" Eira looked to her left and right as if, at any moment, someone would come out and attack her from behind.

Silly, feeble creature... However stupid, the girl was correct in being cautious. After all, Eira would die—one way or another. And it was true; she was set up. She just didn't know it.

Let it be up to Eira to decide if she'd take the easy way—

Empress Amara lifted the bag once more to Eira—or the hard way. Giving a quick slant of her eye to Justin, she put her arm into the bag and questioned the girl again. "Will you not take my offer of homage?"

Eira's eyes swept the forest, then held Empress Amara's like a challenge. "An apple? Is that all?"

"I've come to pay you homage regardless of the fruit. These apples are merely gifts for you! You can take them or leave them. It means no difference to me." She laid the bag on the ground and placed one bright red apple full of poison on the very top.

The apple reflected the same color of red fucus Empress Amara applied to her lips daily. A delightful contrast to the dusting of snow falling on the ground. But it also mirrored that of Eira's own lip color. A pain twisted in her gut. One of envy, hatred, and something else. Even after attempting to kill the foolish girl, she still was the most beautiful. Rage wanted to tear out of her, but she silenced it. She had to be patient.

Hatred often resembled the look of love, so the Empress pinned eyes full of hatred on Eira. It was the same scowl she gave Geoffrey. And by the looks of it, her plans were working. Confusion was setting in the creases of the girl's brow.

Soon Eira would die, and Empress Amara would be the most beautiful once and for all. Her lips pressed into a genuine smile while Eira's face changed into an odd appearance. Queen Amara's smile hung in the cold winter air.

What flashed over Eira's countenance?

A creepy and unsettling feeling came over Empress Amara. Was that kindness? Kindness penetrated Empress Amara's eyes from the pupils of Eira. It was genuine. Real.

Empress Amara shook her head. It couldn't be.

Queen Amara tried to scatter the feelings away from the girl by picking her fingertips. It was working. She started to dig her nails into the palm of her hands. What should it matter to Queen Amara what the whifling cared about? Eira was nothing.

Her thoughts were jarred when Eira got off her horse and stepped toward Empress Amara. The girl winced and knelt in front of her. Empress Amara fought the urge to stumble away from her or even slap Eira. Anything to get the awful feeling to leave her body, but Eira reached out and touched Empress Amara's hand. It was with such gentleness that it made Empress Amara want to alleviate all contents of her stomach. Her heart beat faster. *Don't flinch. Keep the smile plastered on your face, and whatever you do, don't flick Eira's hand away.*

Queen Amara slowly sucked in a rattling breath.

Stay calm.

Keep with the deception.

Don't speak…

Sweat beaded on her forehead. Empress Amara watched the girl closely. She was so close. Too close. Empress Amara remembered the dagger in her pocket. She could easily kill the girl now. But if she were seen, or if found out, she could lose her chance of convincing the bishop, nobles, and barons to crown her queen. She could rid the world of the girl's beauty forever. Right now, even…

Empress Amara's hand twitched, which startled Eira. She let out a small laugh and attempted to speak in a nice manner. "I am so very honored. I will take your gesture as acceptance to my homage."

"I am honored you would even offer it." Tears started to fall from the girl, dripping onto the queen's hands. "After all these years—" Eira continued. "All I have ever wanted, ever longed for, has finally happened." Her pitiful eyes looked up at Queen Amara. "I have waited for this moment since the day you came into my life. All I wanted was to be accepted by you. And now you're here, bowing before me in humility and sincerity, and"—Eira almost choked out her words—"love!"

Eira whimpered uncontrollably, wiping at her nose, which made Queen Amara's skin crawl, but she held her face without a response.

"I've have been praying. I know now that God answers prayers. It's true, and all these years, I never thought it was possible. Never thought that you could ... that one's heart could change from the blackest of blacks to the purest of whites..."

The way Eira spoke and how her eyes clung to Empress Amara's with such love and innocence suddenly brought fear into her bones. She wanted to shut her up, make her stop, prevent her from speaking ever again ... but then her act of deception would not be believable, so she listened.

"...and all this time, I thought you never loved me, never cared to be good, to be..." Eira's voice sounded strangled. "...to be my mother."

Something sticky ran from the nails digging into her palm. It was Queen Amara's blood. *Eira thinks this whole deception was really love. Ha! Won't she be sorely disappointed?* Queen Amara never loved anyone besides one person, her very own father, and he never returned it. Nor deserved it. And neither will Eira. Ever.

Only a fool would seek the love of another. She made that mistake once. Never again. Love made people weak. And what was this nonsense of God seeking *her*, the Empress of England, to change her black heart? Empress Amara wanted to burst out in laughter. Such a ridiculous notion. Why would she need a change of heart?

For a mere second, an ache so deep clouded her judgment, mixing with an awful storm growing in her stomach, revealing the answer she had kept hidden all these years.

Avoiding the pain, Empress Amara remembered why she needed to come in person to the girl. Her eyes quickly dipped to the girl's hand. Then, she abruptly stood, wiping the hand smothered in Eira's tears on her skirt.

"Did you need an escort back to your castle, m'lady?" Empress Amara abruptly stated.

Eira swiped at the tears still hanging from her chin and shook her head, 'no.'

"Prithee, how will you get home?"

"I know of someone not too far away. He can escort me." As if to confirm her words, horse's hooves sounded in the distance.

Maneuvering her glance quickly to Justin, Empress Amara marched back to her horse before turning to face Eira again. "Very well. I shall keep your things in order till your return, m'lady." As Empress Amara reached for her horse's reigns with her left hand, she quipped a hard stare over at Eira before adding, "Oh!" She wagged her pointed one in the air at Eira and then snapped her fingers. "There was one more thing I forgot to mention...when your father's body returned. There was something missing." Empress Amara paused, staring directly into Eira's eye. "Your father's signet ring. Do you happen to know where it is?"

Eira faltered slightly. Then slowly shook her head.

"I see." Empress Amara knew she was lying. Her eyes screamed it. "Very well then." Empress Amara feigned a smile back at the girl and started to mount her horse watching Eira carefully.

Eira picked up the bag of offerings and held the brightest apple sitting on the very top in her hands. Staring at it, Empress Amara's greedy eyes waited until the girl finally took a bite. A true smile lifted the edges of her lips into a crescent shape. The queen fixated on the jaw of the girl, grinding through the poisonous bite until she swallowed. Then, Empress Amara breathed a sigh of relief.

Finally.

Justin left his post and came near the Empress's horse. Leaning down, he asked, "Do you not wish to stay and watch her die first?"

Holding up the reins, Empress Amara turned in time to see Eira scratching at her throat. "I've seen enough. Even if someone comes to her rescue now, nothing could be done. Small shards of glass will make sure the poison gets into her blood. By the looks of it, it's already begun a fine job. Let someone try and stop it!"

Kicking her horse into a gallop, Queen Amara refused to look back.

Soon the pathetic girl's body would be a carcass. Empress Amara would be the most beautiful, and Eira would not be the heir any longer. Once dead, she will send men to find the signet ring. In the meantime, the uprising that had begun in the streets upon the king's death would simmer to nothing, and the girl would soon be forgotten.

The notion of a lost heir would drift away as merely a fantasy, and the barons would move on with Queen Amara as their empress. She alone would have the right to rule over Whiteshire and be the High Queen and Royal Empress of England.

The wind blew her black cap in the air, sending a whipping tail behind her. Leaning forward, her heartbeat quickened, and she kicked her horse into a full gallop. She would be empress, and nothing could stop her now from getting that crown.

Twenty-Nine

OWEN

Prince Owen jumped from Obadiah's horse and ran to Eira, who was falling to the ground. He slid to his knees and caught her in his arms before she hit the hard dirt. Her fragile hands were clawing at her neck. He could hear her attempts to speak but couldn't make out what she was saying.

"What happened?" His hand cupped her cheek. "Why did you leave?"

Tears trickled down her face.

"Don't cry. It'll be all right." His fingers caressed her face.

She swung her head back and forth as if to say, "No."

"I don't understand."

More tears streamed down her face as her body started to shake in his embrace, her hands still on her throat. Something was clearly very wrong.

"Are your injuries still bad? Can you breathe? What's wrong?"

She kept weeping. Looking up, Owen saw horses galloping away.

"Did those people do something to you?"

Her head bobbed up and down as a "yes" response, and her eyes started to droop heavily. He held her close, glaring at the two cowards retreating. Anger rose from his bowels.

"It's going to be okay," he whispered in her hair, but his voice was strangled. He should never have left her side last night. Even for a minute.

Fighting the urge to run after them, making them pay for hurting her, his face instead fell to hers. Her head rocked back and forth, and she was gasping for air. Suddenly, her eyes went wild before rolling into the back of her head.

No.

"Stay with me, Eira."

Was she dying? What had they done to her? Shifting his vision to her body, he did a quick sweep. Nothing seemed to be injured. Why couldn't she breathe?

"Stay with me, Eira."

He laid her on the ground. Her bloodshot eyes tried to focus on Owen again.

"That's it, Eira. Everything will be alright. Doc will help you feel better. I'm sorry. I shouldn't have gone to sleep. It is my fault. Forgive me."

She mouthed the words "sorry" before her eyes closed and her body went limp in his arms.

"Eira!" He shook her. "Wake up. Just wake up and wait for Doc."

He rubbed the sweat from his hands onto his tunic and tried to steady his shaking arms.

"Eira?" He touched her cheek, but she wouldn't move.

Panicking, he ran his hand through his hair and looked around. Absolam was rummaging through a bag of apples. He glanced down again at Eira, scanning her face and body. He had no idea how to help her, but he did know how to fight for her. Adrenaline like he never felt pumped through his veins as he ran for his horse and mounted him in one sweep of a motion. He heeled Absolam hard, and they sprang into a full gallop. His horse was trained. A kick like that meant battle, and he was ready.

As Prince Owen got closer, the cowards sped faster away from him. There was no way he would let them get away with what they did. Examining the road ahead and the trees flanking them, he planned his attack. Owen made the woman his first target.

Bringing his horse to the rear of the woman's, he veered Absolam, forcing her horse off the road. Reaching down, he retrieved his sword. Raising it, he waited a moment to get even closer. Swinging to his right, he brought the sword down hard and barely missed her. The woman's horse struggled to keep its speed in the gulley between the roadway and the forest wall. Its hooves hit rocks and tree branches too large to avoid, keeping them off balance. He had her where he wanted her.

His peripheral vision picked up on the horsemen turning around up ahead. His fingers dug deeper into the leather straps guiding his horse while the other hand clung to his sword, ready for any move the man would make. Returning his focus to the woman frantically grabbing at her weapon, he swung again. This time, his blade met flesh, slicing her cheek clean. She growled and yelled, "Justin!"

Eyes of fire met him for a moment. Owen froze. It was Queen Amara.

A roar came out of Prince Owen. One he had never heard before. "What have you done to her?"

Before his sword rammed into her wicked heart, an arrow buzzed past Owen's ear, making his whiskers stand at attention. Pivoting his horse at Justin, Owen's jaw clenched, and he kicked his horse. Suddenly, the glint of a sword glistening near him caught his attention. His face turned in time to see the edge of Queen Amara's sword aimed at Absolam's flank. A clang of metal rang in his ear as he knocked the sword out of the queen's hands.

"Trying to kill my horse too! You senseless woman," Owen growled.

Queen Amara's lips smiled in response. Blood from her wound filled her teeth. They were as vile and bloodthirsty as her heart. Veering Absolam harder onto the shoulder of the roadway, Owen pushed her horse enough that it started to stumble. *Good*, he thought. Though he didn't want to harm her horse, he had to get her to stop running and fight him. Wretched screams pierced the violent air as she fell with her horse.

Lurching forward, he pulled his sword up over his shoulder and charged toward Justin. He was ready to end this till his death if he had to. As relentless as Queen Amara was in killing Eira, he was just as relentless in avenging her innocence.

With grit in his teeth, he aimed his sight at Justin. The clang of metal on metal rang through his ears before dirt stung his eyes. He was on the ground, knocked off his horse. The ground and sky met in a handshake while his head spun before he caught sight of Justin's dark robe and legs standing above him. The tip of Justin's sword pointed straight down at his face, ready to plunge directly into his head.

Quickly, Owen maneuvered and kicked Justin's legs out from under him. Gaining distance between the two, Owen scanned the ground for his sword. He blinked back dirt encrusting around his vision and tried again.

Queen Amara grunted from behind him as she heaved his heavy sword above her head. "Looking for this?" she cackled, holding the reins of Absolam in one hand and Owen's sword in another.

Trying to run, he was hit in the back of the head with something hard.

"Ugh!"

Falling to his knees, Owen slumped forward and braced his fall on the palm of his hands. Moving in a quick motion, he pushed himself off the ground and turned in time to face Justin.

Reaching down, Owen pulled the dagger out of its hiding spot under his trousers but didn't quite get it out before he had to dodge a strike from Justin and spun to Justin's left. Owen's vision blurred, but he hit Justin hard in the ribs with the point of his elbow, hearing a distinct cracking sound. His rib, most likely. Turning, he knocked Justin's sword out of his hand.

"Let's fight man-to-man!" Justin yelled, wild-eyed and teetering back.

Taking his challenge, Owen avoided his dagger again and lifted his fists instead. "You don't give me much of a choice, do you?"

Prince Owen shifted his sight to the queen holding his sword and Absolam. His fists almost fell from their position. What he saw made him sick. Smiling, the queen lifted her sword and plunged the blade into Absolam's side.

"No!" Owen cried.

"A blow for a blow!" she screeched.

Everything in him wanted to run and protect his horse, but he knew if he turned his back on Justin, he, too, would be dead. Absolam reared, then dropped to his knees, neighing in an unbearable pitch. Owen felt captive. He may have already lost Eira. Now Absolam.

Clenching his fists until they became numb, he determined they would pay for their crimes! Throwing wild punches at Justin, the world went dark until he could feel the sticky blood on his skin, and soon, they were both struggling on the ground. Emotions flooded Owen's heart, and tears bit into his eyes. Owen's face became stained with tears while growling and grappling at Justin.

Owen swung and clocked Justin on the side of the head, giving him enough time to stand.

"You'll never get away with this, so help me!" The words cut through clenched teeth.

The darkness faded as Owen felt the skull of Justin's head smash into the sharp rock beside him. A sick vibration from bone on bone jarred up his spine. Justin went limp.

Picking up Justin's sword, Owen pivoted toward Queen Amara and charged her like a wild bear. Determined to wipe the wicked smile off her face, he let out his warrior cry. The cry you call on the battlefield. This was his battlefield today. And he would shed the queen's blood if he had to.

Tings of metal rang through the forest as the queen parried his blow like a man of war. In a moment of weakness, she glanced behind him, exposing the side of her body. He advanced, taking her wrist and twisting it awkwardly until he heard her scream. The sword dropped out of her hand.

Hearing footsteps, he spun himself behind the queen and faced Justin.

"I thought perhaps you were dead. Should have made sure of that, I guess!"

One hand still holding onto her wrist, Prince Owen's other was now holding the sword to the queen's neck. Justin's hands flung up, palms fanned out in retreat.

"Be careful of your next move," Justin said, his own smile creeping up the scars on his face.

"Careful?" Prince Owen's breath was heavy as he laughed. "You should be careful. First, you attempt to murder the rightful Queen of Whiteshire, and then you plunge a knife into my horse, trying to kill him." Owen's eyes targeted the man with a challenge. "You, sir, are guilty of treason, and therefore must die along with Queen Amara."

"We did not *attempt* to kill the girl." Justin's own laugh echoed in the forest. "We have successfully killed her!"

Owen almost stumbled backward at the realization that Eira could be dead. Justin advanced in his moment of weakness, but Owen pressed the tip of his sword into the queen's neck. "Don't make another move."

"You can't kill me! I am the empress," she shrieked.

"You are no empress to me. I have every right to kill you." Owen pressed harder until the layer of skin was pierced and blood slid down the woman's neck.

"I am with child," Queen Amara screamed. "No honorable man would dare kill a woman with child."

The words hit him like a brick. Was this another one of her lies? His eyes darted to Justin, and then back to Absolam and Eira. Was it a deception to prevent him from plunging the sword into her heart? If she spoke the truth, this would be Eira's sibling and worse, another heir to the throne.

The queen slammed the back of her head into Owen's jaw, splitting his lower lip. Justin suddenly advanced. Owen dodged the sloppy blow while still holding the queen's wrist. Prince Owen swung at Justin with his sword, and with a clean slice, cut into his bicep. Blood splattered back at him, and Owen tasted the familiar metallic tang of battle.

Embracing the sight of Justin moaning in anguish, he again pressed his dagger to the queen's throat. "Tell me what you did to Eira!"

"It doesn't matter. The girl is dead." The queen smirked.

"If it doesn't matter, then tell me anyway."

The queen was silent for a bit, then said, "It was poison."

Prince Owen tightened his grip on his knife. He looked over at Absolam and then thought of Eira's helpless eyes peering up at him. Chest constricting, he shoved the queen to the ground. Something inside of him knew Eira wouldn't want the queen dead. And if he killed her—a peer and noble woman—would he not be just as guilty of treason before God as the queen would be by taking Eira's life? His father's voice reverberated through him from a particular day during court.

"You see these men arguing over lands, you are made for so much more than squabbles, frivolous fights, and conquests, my son. You are made to be

my son. You are of royal blood. Destined to be distinguished as a gentle-man, fit for honor and integrity. You will one day rule alongside your sister and hold this court to that standard."

How could killing a regent royal honor his father's legacy, the standard of his kingdom, and the calling set before Owen? The temptation to finish off this ridiculous feud was alive and thriving within Owen's veins, but unlike the queen, he wasn't bloodthirsty. Did he want vengeance for Eira and Absalom—yes! But at what cost?

He was just starting to feel closer to God. He didn't want to lose that connection. The story of King David came to the forefront of his thoughts. Just like King David, who could have taken Saul's life after he sought to kill the boy repeatedly, chose only to cut the fabric of his tunic. Owen wouldn't stoop to the queen's level at any cost. Just like the man after God's heart, he would also choose life over the death of an ordained royal.

"You're a disgrace as a queen and a wretched evil vecke, deserving nothing but death! But I am nothing like you." His voice was a ragged whisper in her ear. "God is your judge, and I leave you to His justice. He will take vengeance on you!" Owen spat at the ground, both from utter disgust at the woman before him and to try and rid his mouth from the taste of Justin's blood. "I know God is just and will hold your deeds accountable. You won't be able to run from Him like you did from me."

Prince Owen picked up his sword, stepping backward, ready for any sudden moves. Once far enough away, he approached Absalom. Kneeling he brushed his horse one last time.

"I am sorry boy. Thank you for protecting me, being brave in every battle we faced, journeying with me, listening to me, and most importantly being my friend. You will be greatly missed."

He wished he could feel Absalom breathing under his fingertips, but Owen couldn't. He was gone.

"Goodbye my friend."

He stood and ran with all his might toward Eira.
To where she lay … also possibly dead.

Thirty

"Eira?"

Was she dead? Prince Owen fell to his knees beside her lifeless body. His fingers smoothed over her left cheek and caressed it. He thumbed her soft chin while his eyes searched for any sign of life left. There was none.

"You're so beautiful. So, kind..."

His throat was constricted. His palms ran down her raven locks. He couldn't help but bring his face closer to hers. Breathe in her smell and speak prayers over her body.

"This wasn't how it was supposed to be." He leaned closer. "I wish I knew how to help you. I wish it was me that they hurt and not you. If I could, I would've taken your place, protected you..." He surveyed her closed eyes. "Speak to me, Eira. Wake up." He shook her, but she did not move.

One hot tear fell from his chin onto her pale face. She didn't even flinch. *Think, think.* Fists clenched, he leaned back on his heels and lifted his face toward heaven. Though weeping and wanting to scream at the top of his lungs, not one noise came from his lips. His heart spoke for him.

"God, I was beginning to believe she may be the one. The one I would dance with … her alone. After all I've been through, how could you let her be taken from me? Am I not worthy enough to save—" He couldn't finish the words. As if an arrow suddenly shot through his heart, a realization struck him.

Like the smoke from a fire stinging his eyes and stealing his breath away, words burned from within his heart. Even if she couldn't hear him, Eira needed to know, and he needed to tell her. He continued with shaky, yet audible words.

"From the moment I saw you, my heart found a new rhythm to dance to. *To dance with.* I fear I am in love with you, Eira."

But … it's too late.

Nothing mattered if she was dead. For his whole journey, all he wanted was a miracle. But love found him first, and now she lay dead in his arms.

With the back of his hand, he wiped away dirt and the salty liquid flooding his vision. The smell of blood lingered on his hand and mixed with his tears—

Wait a minute.

Blood?

From his peripheral vision, he caught sight of the bag of apples Absolam had been eating from when he first found Eira falling to the ground. If she were poisoned, there may still be time to save her life.

With Eira in his arms, he walked toward Obadiah's horse and lifted Eira and himself onto the animal. He held her lifeless body tight and kicked the horse toward the Men of Ore's cottage. Even though brother Obadiah's cosh was closer, he veered in his direction of the Men of Ore's instead. If there was any chance to save Eira, he would have to try, and Doc was more knowledgeable in medicine. He would come back to get Absolam when he knew Eira was safe.

WHEN OWEN ARRIVED, most of the men were just washing up from their day of work in the mountains.

"Doc! Where are you?" Owen stumbled into the doorway, Eira in his arms. Between catching his breath, Owen yelled again, "Doc, I need you. Come quick!"

Doc was wiping his beard when he came to the door, but after seeing Owen's face, he went white as a ghost.

"Eira! Quick. Bring her in here." Doc frantically gestured with his arms.

Owen followed Doc to his room and gently laid her in his bed. Painfully, Owen watched as Doc desperately checked Eira for life.

"She's becoming cool to the touch, perhaps she needs a warm clothe…" Owen's voiced trailed as he rubbed his left arm. He didn't know what else he could say or do to help.

"She'll need more than that." Doc mumbled.

The room was silent. Finally, after hovering over Eira's face for some time, Doc gave a curt nod. A sigh of relief escaped his lugs. She was alive. But the look in Doc's eyes made him want to fall to his knees. Not only had he failed Eira in protecting her, but he had disappointed and failed these fine men. All of whom loved her and were willing to die protecting her. He was to find her and return her home safely. Not like this.

Owen's palm ran down his face. His fingers and his legs were completely numb. The moment conjured defeat. Deeper than he ever experienced, it pierced him through like a thousand needles. Owen noticed the men all gathering at the door.

"Laurentius, get me my medicine supplies," Doc snapped.

Without question, Laurentius did as commanded. He understood time was at stake and would most likely ask questions later.

"What do you suppose happened?" Mathew asked at the door.

"The queen said she poisoned her."

"The queen?" Hugo blurted, "of Whiteshire? You saw her!"

"Yes. The queen attacked her, and I tried—"

"What did she poison her with?" Doc interjected while grabbing some medicine from the bag Laurentius handed him.

"I don't know, but Absalom was sniffing around a bag of apples before—" Owen couldn't finish the sentence. The thought of Absalom alone and dead on the roadway seized his heart for a moment before he could continue. "I will go fetch them and see what we can learn."

"Yes, you do that. Christopher, go and grab me a blanket and some warm water."

"Do you think she will die, Doc?" Benjamin asked sheepishly, holding back tears.

"I don't know. Right now, we need to find out what she was poisoned with first." His eyes swept Eira's body. "I am afraid we don't have much time. Perhaps hours…perchance, with the Lord's blessing, a few days if we are lucky."

Soft whimpers filled the room as Owen left to get the apples. After grabbing them from Obadiah's horse, he had a thought. *The Men of Ore's is no longer safe for Eira.* Once back in Doc's room he went to assist with putting a warm cloth on Eira's forehead.

"I was thinking…" He glanced up at Doc. "…perchance it is not wise for us to keep Princess Eira here any longer. Maybe she would find peace and comfort at brother Obadiah's house."

The mortar in Doc's hand seized grinding his concoction. "Do you not think we can keep her safe?"

"Nay—it's not that." His head swung low as he rung out his cloth in the warm water and reapplied it to Eira's soft skin. Even in her illness, she was more lovely than any other woman he had ever seen. "I just think…" His thumb traced her forehead. "…that once she is stable enough, she would heal faster in peace and quiet there. I, too, found much healing in brother Obadiah's home once. Besides, they knew that she was here. Should they come back, they would not seek her there."

"Very well." Doc nodded, paying particular attention to Owen's thumb. "Once she is stable, we will transport her to brother Obadiah's cosh. I can see that this means a great deal to you."

A few hours later the men built a platform of wood, to lay Eira on and carry her in an open wagon to brother Obadiah's cosh. The wagon itself was hitched to brother Obadiah's horse. Eira's health had not changed, and they all felt it was time to take her there.

The men marched behind the carriage while Owen sat on brother Obadiah's horse. Every so often, as they walked, Owen could see one of the men sneaking a peak of Princess Eira and sending a nod or a hand gesture his way for reassurance. Though he appreciated the sign that she was doing alright, it still didn't put him at ease.

It wasn't long before brother Obadiah opened the door to see Owen carrying Eira in his arms. Brother Obadiah immediately rushed to a small back room and cleared the bed of equipment and writing tools. Owen and the men followed closely behind. Then, brother Obadiah flew to the kitchen to grab items for Eira.

Owen wasn't sure if he'd ever seen a man move as fast. Especially a monk. They seemed to always be in a state of peace and slow movement when together. Never had brother Obadiah been one to rush. But today was different.

"Thank you," Prince Owen hollered out to the kitchen. Owen pulled the bedding and blankets over Eira. "Doc will stay here as well, to check on her and offer remedies. We still haven't found the cause yet. But we are working on it."

Brother Obadiah stepped back into the small room, squeezing past Owen, and placed a cold cloth on Eira's forehead. "I do not know what has happened. I am sure I will learn about it in time. However, may peace and help come from our Lord today."

Prince Owen clasped Brother Obadiah's hand and gave a firm squeeze. "I thought, if she were to die—" His throat caught, and he choked. He tried again. "If she were to die—at least she would be peaceful here."

The men of Ore were solemn, and the room was dim with grief.

Brother Obadiah smiled. "Take heart my dear brothers. She is not dead but sleeping. Let us wait on the Lord for His perfect timing and His miracle."

Owen knew brother Obadiah meant well. But the word 'miracle' stung deeper than he would ever know.

"Prithee, take care of her, dear friend." Owen's eyes burned when they fell to her still body.

Owen desperately wished she would wake up gasping and say everything was alright. He would fold her up in his arms and never let her go. But she wasn't moving. Owen fought the abrupt pain that bubbled up in the form of an accusation. He wanted to blame someone and the thought of blaming her for running away was too easy. But how could he? Whatever her reasons, there was no motive enough to be angry at her. It was not her fault for being hunted by a wicked queen. That was the queen's doing.

Lord, what am I to do now? I thought I was doing everything you asked. Am I to leave the woman captivating my heart and return home brutally empty handed? Is this your plan?

As if brother Obadiah heard Owen's silent, but desperate cry to the Lord, he said. "Have faith, my brother. She is in God's hands. Let us both do our part in His plan. Go pray for her health and strength to be brought back like He did for Lazarus."

Brother Obadiah nudged Owen out of the small room. Owen grudgingly obeyed, not knowing the next time he saw Eira, whether she would be alive or dead.

Thirty-One

EMPRESS AMARA

"QUICKLY, SEILDA, MY CORONATION IS ALMOST UNDERWAY." Queen Amara ruffled her dress and pulled out her small Looking Glass. "Where is Herrick? He was supposed to be here now. The barons better have assembled as I requested."

"Yes, ma'am. I am sure he's on his way. This concoction should seal your wounds and conceal them enough. It has at least stopped bleeding. We will also make sure your hair is covering it ... like so." Seilda tried to smile as she maneuvered some hair, but her words made Empress Amara flinch.

She was imperfect.

Flawed.

Just like her father had said she'd end up being. A disgrace to him. Nothing Seilda could do could cover up such a gash in her flesh like the one she had. Everyone would see it plainly. And if they didn't see that, they would see her limping from the horrible fall she had with the horse. It wouldn't be good enough.

"Go see what's taking Herrick so long." She slapped Seilda's hand away, ignoring the instant frown she gave in return.

Everything was coming together—Eria was dead, she was going to be crowned queen and empress just as she had planned—so why wasn't she happy?

She tapped the long nail of her index finger on the wooden chair. What was taking Herrick so long?

Herrick bound through the door. "My Queen."

"Finally. I have been waiting long enough. Is everything ready for my coronation?"

Herrick fidgeted.

Queen Amara's brows lowered. "Herrick? I don't like the look of you. Tell me what's the matter."

Herrick wrung his cap in both of his hands as he paced in front of her. "The barons are split, My Queen. Some do not wish you to be queen. They say no woman can rule in her own right. That no Normander, nor English queen, has ever taken the throne, and they will not have it. Others claim—" Herrick paused and finally looked directly into her eyes. "They give their full support, m'lady. However, they say they will pay you homage if you harken and listen to their advice."

"Whether they like it or not, I will be empress and rule. It is my rite and duty. They will be my subjects just as any king would have it. Besides, on my father's death bed, we had sworn men to his wishes that I would be queen. My husband is now dead, and serve me, they will!" Queen Amara pushed past Herrick. "Come along. You look worse than a dog with its tail between its legs."

She would not let the quiver in his voice take away from such a momentous day. She had everything planned. Yet something strange started niggling at the pit of her stomach.

Herrick followed behind, mumbling something about everything going to anarchy.

"Silence, you fool!" She had to think without his nonsense.

She approached Westminster Hall with her head held high and

shoulders pulled back. Her eyes danced around the room, taking a mental note of all those in attendance. Her half-brother, Robert Earl of Gloucester, was there. She dipped her head in greeting. He exchanged the same gesture.

She scrutinized all the barons huddled in two separate groups about the hall. When she saw the King of Scotland, her uncle, the taut skin around her thin lips stretched into a smile. Keeping the grin in place, she shifted her eyes to the corners of the room, where there were many merchants from London mingling about.

Everything seemed perfect. Except it clearly wasn't.

The hall became still and silent the closer she got to the center of the room.

"Gentlemen." She approached the throne. "Where is the archbishop?"

No one spoke.

A shout rang from the far end. "No woman has ever become queen. Why should you receive the throne and not a male from the royal bloodline?"

Noise erupted around her. Voices pulled her attention from every corner of the room.

"You're not our queen! Where is the heir?"

"If there is any woman to rule, it should be Eira White, daughter of King Geoffrey, as our queen."

"The throne should go to Stephan, your cousin. He would be the next male in line."

"Stephan of Blois is the only male heir that should be appointed king," another confirmed.

"We want Stephan of Blois as our king," more shouted.

"It should be Eira White!" came from a noble.

"Enough!" Queen Amara stood by the throne, slamming her foot down, demanding silence. "Your king is dead." Her voice was clear, loud, and resounding. "Eira White is dead." She placed her hands regally in front of her. "And Stephan would not dare contest the throne. He's currently being held captive under my rule for treason. Would you, my subjects, dare to further disgrace your empress on the day of her coronation?"

"Empress?" The King of Scotland stood up. A nervous laugh stuttered out along with his words. "Dear child, you surely don't intend to be called empress. Do you?" His eyes half-scanned hers and half-embraced the soon-to-be rioting crowd. The king's eyes pleaded with her. "Tell them, Amara. Tell them you only intend on being called queen." A weak smile and big eyes peered around the room.

But she would not bow. Not even to him. A rage so fiercely came over her that she smacked the King of Scotland across his face with the back of her hand. She would not be fooled in front of her subjects. "Yes! I intend on being empress. Don't be such a coward and never disgrace me in front of my people again."

She measured her stare until he and his men left the hall. Let them cower, walk away from her throne in disappointment and shame to ever have known her. She didn't care.

"Anyone else want to challenge me and my intentions? Speak now." She waited until the room was silent. "Get me the archbishop! My coronation will be today."

"Perhaps you should speak kinder, My Queen. The Londoners mentioned they wished you to be modest and gentle after the manner of your kind ought to be." His fake encouraging smile was over-exaggerated. "People warned of anarchy, and this is not a way to win them over, My Queen—I mean Empress."

Murmurings echoed louder and louder in the great hall. Like a mountain awake from slumber and ready to erupt in volcanic rock, suffocating anything in its path, including Empress Amara. An earthquake of voices erupted in the room.

"We say Stephan of Blois should be king!"

"We want Eira to be queen!"

Sweat clung to the skin of the bishop as he arrived, eyes wild with something she couldn't put her finger on. He stood before her and the barons in all his regalia.

Good, he must be afraid of the crowd with his beads shaking like that. He will act accordingly and announce me as queen of all. Once and for all.

Empress Amara did not kneel when the bishop motioned her to do so. She stood.Her chin held high before her subjects. After all, she was their empress.

The bishop cleared his throat, and the crowd stilled.

"On this day, the day of our Lord, Matilda Amara of Whiteshire, Queen of Germany and Italy, through the witness of God and the peerage, now hold you accountable to honor and encompass always and wholly, the title of..." He paused, and his voice cracked before continuing. "...Lady of the English."

Lady of the English. Those words echoed through her mind as if she hadn't heard it the first time. His resounding voice pitched before registering in Empress Amara's ears.

"I beg your pardon?" She pinned her gaze on the bishop. Did she hear his words correctly? Indeed, it was difficult to hear over the noisy crowd. The crown shook in his pathetic hands like a leaf in the wind. Why was it not already on her head? And why hadn't he named her Empress Amara of Whiteshire, Germany, Italy, and the sovereign over the Duchy of Normandy?

"My apologies. It was discussed by the council and nobles that we could not honor your father's request as you are a woman. You were to only be named, Lady of the English, and not deemed Empress as you wished."

"My father made the men around him on his death bed swear their allegiance and claim me as his rightful heir. With the sole kingdom of Whiteshire under my command, as well as my father's kingdom, England, and my late husband's recent concurring of

Normandy, I *am* an Empress!" She demanded, her voice raising an octave.

The bishop licked his lips. "Since you are a woman—m'lady—no female has been given the crown in the history of England."

"It must be more than that." She eyed the bishop.

"It—" He choked. "It has been mentioned that you were not at your father's bedside. That your relationship was strained and your father's request done of ill-will. Had you been there to show alliance with your father and claim loyalties of his men, it may have convinced them. But since, those men have faltered and wavered in their fidelity, recounting their allegiance and giving it to his next male successor."

"My cousin? And you—you have blessed this?" She shrieked.

"I had no choice." His shaky hand wiped the sweat from his brow. "And there is the issue with Eira…" The bishop's voice trailed.

"What issue? People have heard now that the girl is dead. Her father too. I am the rightful regent to take over as queen of Whiteshire. This is the law."

"The people are undecided on Eira being dead. The council too. They have not seen her and think…well, that she may still be alive. Even if she is dead, some of the nobles want the next male successor in line for the throne, Stephen of Blois. They have stated he will be a better ruler over you. They are very much divided."

"Then me?" She scoffed. Then, darting her eyes at the bishop, Queen Amara asked. "In what meetings have they said such hearsays and treasons?"

The bishop stilled. His eyes bulged.

"You will regret this day, Bishop, for the rest of your short life," she breathed, her words venom to his soul.

The mung having erupted in both anger and increasing excitement, was too loud for her to know if the bishop heard her words, but he would know them soon enough. He would always remember this day. She would be sure of it.

The barons and knights pulled back from the hall. Half of the peerage exposed their weapons, and the crowd pressed in around them. Her empire was literally splitting before her very own eyes, and she was falling in the crack it left.

The hall broke into a vicious war. Fists and blades went flying. Blood and screams filled the cathedral walls. It was a reverberating echo, one that made history.

Robert of Gloucester leaped from the mung towards her.

Herrick grabbed her arm. "Come, My Queen. We must get you to safety."

"No!" She tried to pull from his pathetic grasp, but something inside her resisted, and reluctantly she followed his lead behind Robert.

One thing was certain: Empress Amara would not rest until she found all those who had dared to betray her as an empress. She would kill them and make their families suffer for taking away her perfect day.

Those in contempt of their queen, whether she held the crown, would be judged for it with death. She intended to raise an army so large; nobody would dare to stand in her way of being empress again. Empress Amara would have her crown...

...in one bloodshed or another.

Thirty-Two

OWEN

"Is she still breathing? Has she awakened at all?" Owen paced in front of the fire as Doc came out of Eira's room.

"Yes, still breathing." Doc slumped into the chair by the fire and looked over at Owen with eyes that could pull a hillside down, they were so heavy. "But not even a stir."

"You have worked all through the night, Doc. Go home and get some rest. Come back in the morning. I can administer any of the remedies you have left for her."

Owen stooped to the level of the embers and stoked the fire. When Doc didn't reply, Owen conjured enough courage to ask what had been weighing on his heart since carrying Eira the day before.

"Do you think she will live?"

"I'm not sure. Her pulse was barely there in the beginning. So terribly faint that if it wasn't for her skin being slightly warm, I would have thought her dead."

"I am sorry, Doc." Owen stoked the fire again. "I shouldn't have left with her."

He stoked too hard, and hot embers spat out of the hearth with vengeance. One, still sizzling and popping, landed on his arm and burned it. Served him right. He hissed with the sensation and flicked the ember back into the fire. He stood, putting the iron rod back against the stone wall. "Seems I can't do anything right."

He could hear Doc slide off the rocking chair and stand beside him. Doc's small hand reached up and grabbed his arm. "Listen to me carefully. You did everything you could. You're not to blame for another's sins. They hurt her, not you. Their bad choices are not a load you were ever fit to carry. Jesus did that alone. Now, pull yourself together. Rest. She will still need your strength if she will ever be well again."

Owen pinched the bridge of his nose. "You're right. I thank thee."

"I know I am right." Doc laughed.

Owen couldn't help but guffaw. "So much for polite conversation…" He was still chuckling as he sat down near the fire. "It feels good. To laugh, despite what has happened." After a pause, he asked, "How did you know what poisoned Eira?"

"There are many things that can poison a person. If it were a variety of mushrooms, she would have hallucinated and been mad before falling to the ground." Doc sat near the fire with Owen. "Cyanide is the most popular to use and tastes like almonds. It is so easily hidden, but she would have complained of stomach pain, and most likely would have tasted the difference in the apples. Her skin would also be red, not paler in color. Her breath also would have the scent of almonds, which it did not." Doc wiped his hands with a cloth and slung it over his chair. "By deduction, I would submit, it was another more dangerous kind. Strytoxifer, I call it. It causes a person to be temporarily paralyzed." Doc put out his hands and hovered them above the flames. "Enough of it can cause certain death."

Owen heaved a heavy sigh. "How do we know she hadn't had enough of it?"

"We don't know." Doc's shoulders sagged slightly, and he sat back in his chair. "But we do know that we saved her as quickly as possible, and I must say, you did a fine job of helping in that area."

Doc's furry cheeks spread into a mischievous grin, and Owen could see his perfectly white teeth glistening by the firelight. Heat crept up his neck, and Owen pulled at his tunic.

"Just to be clear, you were the one who told me to do that. I have never in my life experienced the practice of medicine like that before, but I was willing to try and help—that is all."

"Now, now. No need to get embarrassed, Prince Owen. I know you're a gentleman, and I did ask you to help push air into her lungs by way of mouth-on-mouth. Though unconventional, it was necessary in saving her life with this particular poison." Doc paused and rubbed his chin long enough for Owen to play back the moment his lips touched hers. His whole body came alive while Eira was at death's door and her body as if paralyzed.

"She needs oxygen in her limbs," Doc had said. "Breathe for her," he had said. "Place your mouth on hers and give her breath."

So, he did. But her lips were—

"Thank you for your quick aid." Doc smiled. "Perchance you didn't have to linger on the girl's lips as long you did. Especially when we heard the young lass' lungs working again, hmm?" Doc looked at him with one eyebrow quirked up.

Was he being scorned or ridiculed? Doc's gut-roaring laughter filled the small cosh and lifted Owen's spirits. "That part was all on you, dear friend. All on you."

The front door quickly burst open, and a cool breeze brushed his cheeks, cooling them down.

"Brother Obadiah," Owen said, slightly shouting. Happy for an interruption and break in conversation with Doc, Owen added, "Were you able to get all of the items on Doc's list?"

"Fresh meat, berries as requested, and barley. Has she awakened yet?"

"Nay." They said in unison.

Brother Obadiah arranged the items in the kitchen and covered the meat. "I see." He put water in a kettle and placed it on the fire to heat.

Once seated by the fire, Brother Obadiah began to tell them of his journey to Winchester and the market. "I bring more bad news, I am afraid. There was an uprising at the cathedral today. My brothers are heartbroken. They will need my prayers, and I will return in the morning to assist them in the clean-up. There was—"

"What has happened?" Doc interrupted.

"The queen attempted coronation. The place was divided. People were calling out for Eira or Stephan as their Monarch."

"Was she crowned?" Owen spat the question out as if it were moldy bread.

"No. Only titled as Lady of the English."

"Who is Stephan?" Doc asked.

"He is the next male heir after Eira from her father's side. A cousin that has a claim to the throne." Brother Obadiah sighed. "This is now making more sense to me. I believe I understand why Eira has been hunted. Not only did she come of age to take the crown of Whiteshire and the Duchy of Normandy that our king established, but Queen Amara's father ruled over England, Germany and Italy, and has recently died. Queen Amara was attempting to become an empress over all territories in her own rite. Her father named her heir. The only problem is that there has never been a female heir in all of Normandy or England, and the nobles and barons are torn on who they want to be crowned."

"So, will Eira, being female, have a chance to be queen?" Prince Owen queried.

There was a heaviness in the room as Obadiah continued. "As I said, they are torn. The Londoners who would benefit from him named Stephan of Blois as their king. They say he is the next in the royal line to be crowned. Others want Eira. Few are loyal to Queen Amara."

"I know of Stephan's family. We hunted together before. Maybe we can send word to him about Eira's health. Perhaps he would fight alongside her?" Prince Owen tried to add an inflection of hope to his last words.

Obadiah shook his head. "I am not sure it will be as easy as you hope. The barons are wary of putting a woman on the throne. As it is, half are refusing to swear an oath to Queen Amara simply because she is a woman, and to my knowledge, Stephen is imprisoned."

Prince Owen stood and paced before the hearth. "I see. This will be challenging indeed. No doubt, the queen's charms have won over the peerage in doubting a woman's royal ascent to the throne. But Eira is the rightful heir, and we have made an oath." His eyes darted to Doc's. Doc nodded. "So, that is final. I shall go and speak with Stephan of Blois, to seek his intentions on the matter. If he pledges an oath to Eira, and if she has his support, the Londoners will listen. I doubt he has lost influence due to his capture. If anything, he might have more allies."

"Agreed," Doc said.

"It's settled, then," Obadiah said, standing.

Owen's eyes caught a cross on the wall behind brother Obadiah. His mind darted to his sister. If he takes on this quest, there is no guarantee he will find his sister in time. He promised to be back before Spring.

Owen had no idea how long this attempt to help Eira would take or how long until she recovered before he could return home or continue seeking his sister. Owen sighed. But if he didn't help Eira, what kind of man was he? When he was finished aiding Eira, he would continue the search for his sister. But what were the chances he had found a wife on his own?

Brother Obadiah's voice interrupted his thoughts. "In the meantime, I'll care for Eira here and keep her safe until she regains strength. Doc, you said she must eat red meat and berries only?" Obadiah inquired.

"Yes. Her muscles need to be rebuilt and strengthened. This will be a slow process. But she will recover. She will need to walk and exercise, so do not be afraid to give her chores." Doc was gentle with his words. "It will be for her own good and will keep her mind from wandering and seeking to go out of doors."

"I will need plenty of meat, then. I doubt the queen will grant us permission to hunt on her lands, and the monastery will only give to us on occasion, as it is not for me. Do we know of anyone that can help with providing more?" Obadiah's eyes searched each man before it dawned on Owen.

"Yes. Once, Eira spoke of a huntsman that helped save her. I don't mind paying for the meat, but since I will be away to speak with Stephan, I will try and send word to find the huntsman and ask if he can assist in providing meat for her."

"Very well." Doc looked pleased as he stood and went to check on Eira.

"Thank you, Brother Obadiah, for opening your home once again." Owen patted his arm.

"It is not my custom to allow ladies to stay here alone, but she is, after all, the Queen of Whiteshire. I feel peace about it. God will take care of the rest."

"Brother Obadiah?" Owen rubbed his forehead.

"Yes."

"Don't let her die." Owen pinched tears from his sight.

"Prince Owen, I cannot prevent death. Death is in the hands of the Lord. But I will do whatever I can to help her. To alleviate her pain. That, I can give my word on." Obadiah rose and left Owen by the fire.

Prince Owen stayed there, staring at the orange and yellow flickering lights. He needed to pray. Pray for forgiveness. Pray for healing. Pray for God to do a miracle. Even if it meant losing the miracle he'd hoped to find when he first came.

He would give it all up if it meant Eira could live.

Thirty-Three

EIRA

THE EBB AND FLOW OF MELODIC HYMNS WOVE THROUGH HER consciousness, waking her. Blinking, Eira's eyes opened. Blinking again, she tried to take in the room. No one was there. She attempted to lift her head, but it felt like a mighty stone. Where was she?

Following the line of a small window frame above her, she caught sight of a ledge full of wooden cylinder buckets and long, thin brushes. A distinct smell filled the room with earth, spices, and metal. Eira didn't care where she was as long as she was safe. Eira sucked in a deep breath. She was breathing. Her hand fluttered to her chest. She gulped in another deep breath.

She was alive.

The smell of smoke from a fire brought her senses to life. The rumble of men's deep voices echoed from somewhere in the house, bringing her comfort. Perhaps it was the Men of Ore. She felt strange, yet at peace in this small room. She tried to get up but noticed her feet didn't respond. *How odd.*

Trying to swallow made her wince. Eira's throat both itched and throbbed with pain. Her eyes stung in response to trying to swallow again, while memories sliced through her skull in its own kind of ache. Eira remembered taking the apple, a sign of a truce between her and the queen and then eating it. How naïve could she be? A tear slipped from her eye. Her stepmother betrayed her kindness and tried to kill her—yet again. And she almost succeeded. Eira shivered. She was—once more—naïve. The queen would never give in to Eira's love for her.

Never mind the poison, the look on Prince Owen's face as she started to fall almost killed her on the spot. It was the look of betrayal and regret and … and perhaps that of love and passion.

She had been so foolish to believe someone could change. How foolish she was to think that by leaving, she could protect these kind men. Why did she leave him? He was only trying to help, and by taking away his decision to help her, she was taking away her respect for him to choose on his own. Who was she to step in the way of another's will for their life?

Eira remembered how he held her in his arms. She was helpless but felt the strength in his embrace. She felt his compassion, and perchance something more than that. He'd stared at her with a tenderness that was authentic. It was genuine. He wanted to protect her. Not run away from her like she did to him.

How could she leave him there? She was such a coward. Everything she'd dreamed of as a child—the handsome prince—had held her in his arms, and all she did was push him away.

Was she scared of him rejecting her as the queen had done so many times before? Perhaps she was tainted—not good enough to be loved? Too damaged? Or was he simply too good to be true? Perhaps it was only pity that he felt when he looked at her. Perhaps she will never know.

The sound of hymns suddenly turned into prayers, filling every wall with hope. She must try and think about good things…

Papa.

Oh, how she loved her papa and missed him. There was no doubt in her mind that his intentions were to protect Eira, because he left himself vulnerable and died to keep her hidden. Would she do the same for Owen? For the Men of Ore?

A flood of bottled-up tears fell, and Eira didn't bother wiping them away. Her entire body felt like heavy water was over her. Drowning her. Stopping her from moving. She needed someone to help her up. Someone—

Who was it that she heard praying? Whose house was she in? It wasn't the Men of Ore's. Perhaps she should pray to the Lord, as her host was so beautifully doing, and thank Him for letting her live again. At least she had that—life. That alone was something to be grateful for.

Closing her eyes, she tried to pray. As she lifted silent prayers of her own, thoughts of Papa invaded her, invoking a small bit of strength. His voice rumbled with words almost entirely forgotten. *"Remember, Eira, remember what your mother told you..."*

Trying to remember his ancient words and stories calmed her mind and her heart until she fell silently asleep.

"Ah, I see you've awakened."

The shadow of a tall man loomed over Eira.

"You must sip on this broth and try to eat some berries until your stomach can handle stronger meats." He placed two wee bowls and cup of water beside her bed on a quaint wooden table covered in stains of many different colors.

"Thank you," Eira said as he helped lift her into a seated position on the makeshift bed.

"There. That is better. Now, if you need anything, I'll be in to check on you soon. I've some work to tend to." He went to leave.

"Sir?" Her voice cracked and she grimaced in agony.

"Please. Rest my child." He urged.

"Nay. I must know what has happened."

"As you wish." Brother Obadiah crossed his hand gently in front of him.

She shivered with confusion. "I think I remember you. You were at the Men of Ore's home. Forgive me. I can't remember your name."

"Call me Brother Obadiah." He smiled.

She smiled in return. "I thank you for all you've done to help me. How long have I been here?"

"You have been here for three days and four nights now."

She shook her head, and the room spun. "I don't deserve it. Your kindness, that is."

"No one deserves anything, dear child. Besides, 'tis no trouble. As God wills, I follow and serve. You should get some rest and eat. Soon, you shall start moving and building up your strength."

"You know Prince Owen. Is he here? May I see him?"

"He is gone, Princess Eira. He went to find Stephan of Blois and fight the queen on your behalf, m'lady."

If Eira could faint, she would have. She took a sip from the cup to ease her throat and get her bearings on what she had just heard. She placed the cup back down again.

"Fight?" She shook her head. "On my behalf! I don't understand, what for?"

Had she not seen him run off to kill Queen Amara before everything went black? Dread filled her bowels, and she tensed, waiting for Brother Obadiah's reply. So much had happened. Was he wounded?

"Many people thought you to be dead, and the queen attempted her coronation as empress over Whiteshire." Brother Obadiah sat on a small chair in the corner, the back of his head almost hitting the shelf full of buckets above him while his eyes evaluated her. "There's much to tell. Do you feel up to it? Or should I allow you to get rest before I go on?"

"Prithee, do tell!" She was weak. But if there was going to be a battle, if there was a chance she could lose Prince Owen, she had to know. Besides, she was happy for the respite in speaking and took another sip of water to cool her throat.

Brother Obadiah examined her before proceeding. "As you wish." His hands fell to his lap. "The queen set her coronation to be held immediately upon returning from your death. A select few were assembled, because she had been planning this for some time, but word came to the streets, and the Londoners attended. They were very much in opposition to the queen."

He looked around his room before continuing. "All the barons were there, of course, along with Robert of Gloucster and King David of Scotland. Nobles and merchants were also in attendance. But the peerage was split from the beginning. Some were loyal to the queen, others loyal to Stephan of Blois. Some were confused about your mere existence, but many knew of you. When Queen Amara was not crowned as empress as she wished to be called, but titled Lady of the English—when that happened—the place went into an utter uproar. Death, fighting, and pure anarchy spilled into the streets. People were killed, and the townsfolk were in a rage. Buildings and tents were damaged. Everyone feels betrayed. It was a bloody day, and sadly, our bishop has perished at the hand of the queen as well."

"I am so, so very sorry. I am sorry for your loss. For the loss of our peace and the loss of lives gone." After a moment of silence, taking in everything Brother Obadiah had said, Eira asked, "And what of the queen? Where is she now?"

"She is with Robert of Gloucester, assembling an army of her own. Everyone is devastated and taking sides. I feel as though this will not end easily."

"I see." Eira reached up and rested her forehead on the palm of her hand. "That is terrible news indeed."

"You must rest, Princess Eira, if you're going to win the battle against the queen, for I believe she will not rest until you are dead."

"Yes. That has been made very clear to me. I will not fall for her charm again." Eira swept over the food. "Must I eat that?"

"You'll need a regular diet of red meats and berries to gain muscle strength. It's an order by Doc." Brother Obadiah stood up. "Now, eat and sleep."

Eira picked up the broth slowly. Brother Obadiah was right. Her muscles were weak. She tried to wriggle her toes, and they did not budge.

"Very well, I will proceed on my journey of strength." Despite the raw feeling on her tongue and throat, Eira tipped her bowl and began to drink down the hot liquid.

"Oh, I forgot to mention," Obadiah said while she slurped away at the broth. "When you are feeling better, Mason would like to come pay you a visit. Prince Owen has managed to get word to him, and he is staying with the Men of Ore until you are ready to see him."

"Mason! Yes, yes. That would be splendid."

"Very well. I'm only a whisper away should you need anything, m'lady."

Nodding as he left, Eira finished off her broth. She replaced the bowl with a saucer of berries and began nibbling at them. Her stomach knotted, but she didn't care. She would eat all that was required to get better.

A lot of events had transpired while she slept, and it appeared war was coming whether she liked it or not. Reservations aside, she was done with running and couldn't wait a single day longer to face Queen Amara.

Eira was ready to finally reclaim Papa's kingdom forever.

Thirty-Four

OWEN

"Stephan!" Owen grappled for his dagger. "Behind you!"

He plunged the blunt knife into the back of the man attacking Stephan. His body instantly went limp and slumped to the ground. Mouth agape, Stephan nodded his thanks and kept swinging his sword at another man in front of him.

Owen nodded back and reviewed their plan of escape.

After seeking Stephan for a few days, Owen finally ran into his wife, Matilda. There, he became appraised that Queen Amara had Stephan secretly locked away in a nearby castle. With Matilda's aide, they planned an attack to free Stephan. And up until that point, it had worked.

Owen and three of Stephan's men secretly breeched the small castle, took out the prison guards and rescued Stephan. But now, they needed to get out of the castle walls before they were locked in and surrounded. The men posted to guard him were filing in one after another making every chance of escape difficult.

Angry grunts and the sound of blade striking blade clanged all around him. Any words Stephan tried to say otherwise would have been useless. Stephan and he fought well side by side, picking up the non-verbal cues amid battle.

They seemed to be a good team and became allies instantly after speaking to Stephan about Eira and what had happened. It was a bond much like a brother, and Stephan made an oath right then and there, vowing to bring justice to Eira. It pleased them both so much that they plotted their tactics of war on Queen Matilda for that very night.

Owen parried another blow, spun, and sliced through the middle of one of the guards. Another man approached him, and he ducked before the glint of the blade reached his neck. He pushed another man and ran up a small hill. Finding Stephan's eye, he gave a quick gesture of his head. Stephan nodded. Owen evaluated the men around him and the thick of the battle at large. They were gaining momentum.

"You there! Grab this rope and help me pull open the gates." Owen looked at another of Stephan's men. "You, cover my back!" He put away his sword and pulled the rope hand over hand, opening the gates.

Arrows rang out and hit men farther out from him. He could feel the press of someone trying to attack him from behind, but Stephan's man, who came to assist Owen, assailed him. Prince Owen pulled harder, and the gate rose farther. He tied off the rope and left the gate half open. Stephan was now free and ready to make war for Whiteshire's throne.

A FEW HOURS LATER, word that Queen Amara was hiding at Robert of Gloucester's castle made its way to Prince Owen and Stephan. Whether or not it was true or hearsay, they adjusted their plans and had gone to take ground in their territory.

It didn't take long before it was a success.

Owen smiled, and his gaze swept over the battlefield, catching sight of their victory. The castle was now surrounded, and Stephan's men followed their lead, pressing into the fight near the gate. It wasn't easy, but Prince Owen was thankful they had made it this far.

Prince Owen retrieved his sword from his belt. Coming alongside Stephan, they penetrated the castle gate. Robert of Gloucester stood victoriously upon the steps as if challenging them with their presence. Had he not noticed they were winning?

Stephan lifted his sword and led the army in the final attack. Prince Owen raised his voice in a roar and went for the first man in front of him. Swinging low, Owen caught him off guard and knocked the man's balance off. Quickly, he plunged the tip of his sword deep through the man's armor. It sank into the chain's weakest point. The man fell forward.

Something constricted Owen's chest. As if he could feel the man's pain when dying. As if a part of him died with each man he killed. He hated that part of the battle. He had been on a pilgrimage for too long and had forgotten the feeling.

Owen turned to his right in time to see Stephan surrounded by Robert of Gloucester's men. He angled his view to where Robert stood gallantly. To his left, Stephan's men were charging in.

If you catch the dominant wolf, his pack will flee, Owen thought. Stephan would have to wait for Owen's help later.

Bounding the stairs of the castle, Owen attempted to follow Robert. Footsteps on stone slapped as if someone were running through the open corridors. He followed the sound. It led him to a darker walkway. He slowed his pace and cautiously proceeded.

The space was open, with tall ceilings and candles alone lighting the path. It would be very easy to get ambushed here. His ears tuned with every minuscule sound that echoed off its walls. Slowly, he rolled his feet over the cold marble floors, padding each footstep to be silent. The slapping sound faded. He hit his fist against his thigh and barraged himself quietly. He had lost whoever he was following.

Suddenly, a figure stepped out of the darkness from the far-right corner of the corridor.

"Looking for someone?"

"Come to think of it"—Owen wiped the sweat off his brow— "I am." He smiled.

"You're fighting a losing battle." Robert scoffed and spat at the ground in front of Owen.

"Am I?" Owen shifted his eyes over his shoulder. "From where I'm standing, you're at a disadvantage."

"You can't force the kingdom out of a royal's hand." Robert took a step forward, his blade shining in the dull light around them.

"I could say the same to you! King Geoffrey had a daughter, and she's the one who is royal here. You are forcing the kingdom out of her innocent hands."

Robert laughed. "So, you fight for ghosts, then." He stepped even closer. "Because I hear she is dead."

Robert grunted as he lifted his sword.

Owen's veins shot into motion, pumping the adrenaline to each muscle and parrying Robert's blow. "I fight for the living!"

Prince Owen growled and split some of Robert's chain mail open. Stepping back, he held his sword between the two of them and allowed Robert to realize his armor had been compromised. It was a failed attempt to try and reason some sense into the man. Prince Owen circled around him.

"You're the one that's serving a madwoman. She's pure evil. She's no queen, and only thinks of herself, not the people. Not you!" Prince Owen evaded another hit. "By aiding her, you're forcing the kingdom into anarchy instead of unity."

"Stephan of Blois is throwing the kingdom into anarchy!" Robert snarled as he brought his sword down on Owen.

Owen tried to catch his breath before swinging again. The jar from the hit sent a shock wave to his toes. Pressing in, Owen struck, hitting close. Finally, he was able to knock Robert's sword from his hand. It went flying into the dark. The tip of Owen's sword was at Robert's throat.

"Robert of Gloucester, you are hereby my prisoner. Now, move!" He motioned, letting the point of his blade direct Robert back down the corridor.

"Unhand him at once."

The shriek of that woman's voice could kill a bird mid-flight. Out of the corner of Owen's eye, he could see the robe of Queen Amara, but it was too dark to tell if it was her or a decoy. That is, until Herrick stood beside her. It was most definitely Queen Amara.

"I will not." Owen stood firm.

"Herrick," she said with no emotion. "Kill the man."

"Ye-yes, My Queen." Herrick nodded viciously.

This is going to be easy, Owen thought. That is, if he could keep Robert and the queen at bay. They were both skilled with a weapon, and it was hard to tell if either of them had any more weapons at their disposal. Herrick, however, was not a great swordsman, and sadly, not best suited for war.

Before he could figure out the queen's motive for sending a novice to fight him, Herrick was swinging a wild blade in his direction.

So be it. Let's play a little catch-the-mouse game, shall we?

The tip of Owen's sword slipped from the neck of Robert, and Robert pounced at his chance to fight back. Punching Robert hard in the ribs, Owen's hand went slack for a mere second before tightening again on his weapon.

It was now two-on-one. Repositioning himself to see both Robert and Herrick, he felt ready for any sudden move. Robert ducked behind Owen while Herrick advanced him to the front. With one swipe of his blade, Owen thwarted Herrick's move and advanced Robert. Coming down hard with the sharpest edge of his blade, Robert's quick move avoided the blow. *Lucky.*

He could hear Herrick's next move behind him. Swinging in time to parry another of Herrick's weak strikes, he was taken off guard by a strike in the back from Robert. Falling to his knees, his sword clattered to the ground.

Robert's hand swooped up Owen's sword before he could get back onto his feet. Shaking his head, Owen repositioned himself. Robert backed away, still gripping Owen's sword.

"Alright, Herrick, you got this one." Robert smiled and ran to where Queen Amara stood laughing and clapping her hands like this was indeed a real game. They turned in unison and started stalking away into the darkness of the corridor.

"My queen!" Herrick hollered.

"What?" She bit back, annoyed.

"Where are you going? I cannot face him alone."

"I would not tell you in front of him." She pat. "And yes! You will face him alone. You shall fight for me, Herrick. And you will die for me so we can get away. That is all you are of use for me now." With that, Queen Amara sauntered in the dark hallway. Her laughter lingering, as if taunting Herrick.

"But I am no knight, I am your administrator." Herrick mumbled to himself.

Owen faced Herrick. "You know they left you to die, right?"

Herrick's sword stayed in front of him, gripped with both hands, and his forehead glistened with sweat. Owen observed his fragile eyes flickering in confusion from the darkness surrounding him and the man he was left to fight alone—Owen.

"Drop the sword and I will go after the Queen, Herrick. Keep it up and I will be forced to fight you to get to her."

With a blank face, Herrick wildly charged at Owen. It didn't take long before Owen had Herrick's weapon, and Herrick lay motionless on the ground before Owen's feet. He wanted to throw up. There was no joy in the victory over Herrick. The poor man didn't even know he was being betrayed by the woman he devoted his life to.

Owen could barely lay his eyes on the man motionless at his feet. A sad soul, though loyal. Herrick would've fought till his death, and Owen didn't take pleasure in besting him. Kneeling, Owen closed Herrick's eyes gently.

Rest in peace. Praying over his body, he vowed that if they won the fight, Herrick would receive a proper burial. Until then, Owen let his fist grip his sword tighter. It was time to finish the foolish game once and for all.

Beating his legs as hard as they could go, he ran after Robert and Queen Amara.

Thirty-Five

EIRA

A RAP CAME AT THE DOOR.

Eira slowly made her way to it. She was regaining strength, thanks to the extra work and care Brother Obadiah had given her. Brother Obadiah halted her before she could reach the door.

"We must be cautious, m'lady." He'd insisted he be the one to walk to the door. Before he could announce who was at the door or if it were safe, a small, red-cheeked boy, with his blond hair stuck to his forehead with perspiration, bounced into the threshold eagerly.

"Well, hello," she said, smiling at the wee lad. He was awfully sweet to look upon.

"Good day." His eyes were full of wonder as she stepped back into the cosh. "I've brought something for brother Obadiah." he continued.

"Of course, come in." Eira gingerly made her way back into the living area where Brother Obadiah had set up his new workstation.

"Obadiah? Prithee, who is this wee boy?" Eira asked as she went into the kitchen and started the kettle for tea.

She overheard the boy mumbling, "I am a man, not a boy. And my name is Luca."

Eira held back a giggle. *He is absolutely adorable. What a pleasure to have such a tender lil' lad visit us.*

"I came to give you this," he said, shoving his hand toward Brother Obadiah.

Obadiah accepted it graciously and pulled out a letter with a seal on it from the small velvet bag. "I thank you, young brother. I can tell you've come a long way to give me this, and that is dually noted." As he attempted to break the seal, Brother Obadiah inquired, "May I ask who this is from?"

The boy's grin filled her heart with a joy she hadn't felt in a long time, perhaps ever. She'd never seen someone smile so wide. His little toothy grin caused her to smile in return.

"'Tis from Prince Owen." The boy's tone was of pure reverence.

Suddenly, the kettle slipped from Eira's hand as she was lifting it to the hang in the fire. "Prince Owen?" The words sounded more desperate than she'd hoped.

The boy turned to look at her, and his smile faded. "Yes." He glanced at Brother Obadiah as if he were in trouble. "Did I say something wrong?"

"No," she quickly blurted, then laughed, more nervously than genuine. "You have done well indeed. It's wonderful to hear we've received a letter from Prince Owen. Does it say he's well?"

It had been weeks since she had heard any news of the battle? She waited with her hands clasped in front, but her foot deceived her and started to tap on the ground underneath her skirts. She wished for more bodily strength to assist the men.

Crinkling paper caught her attention, and the snap of wax from the parchment as the seal broke echoed through her mind. Had Owen been injured? God forbid. *He indeed sealed the letter in Obadiah's hands, so he must be well, right?*

Obadiah cleared his throat. The sound of fire crackled, and her foot intensified with every beat on the wooden floor. Eira eagerly smiled up at Brother Obadiah, though he wasn't looking. The silence took over her senses. Finally, she heard the low tone of Brother Obadiah's voice.

"Brother Obadiah and my dear Princess Eira, I am sending word of our battle at Gloucester Castle. We were in advance and took victory after victory. We had penetrated the castle walls but, in the end — Princess Eira, do you wish me to continue?" Brother Obadiah cleared his throat and looked up with worry outlining his sincere face.

"Let me sit. But aye, I wish you to continue." She maneuvered the chair near the fire and braced the sides. What if he was injured, or worse, dying? She lifted her chin and bit the sides of her mouth to stop the emotion clamoring at her heart. "I—I'm ready."

Obadiah nodded before continuing. "But in the end, we were forced back. I had almost captured Robert, the Earl of Gloucester, but was ambushed by the queen. Herrick was forced to fight me when the queen and the earl ran off, leaving him to die at my hand. Herrick is now dead, but the queen captured Stephan of Blois. They're holding him at Whiteshire Castle. Soon, we are going to go and rescue him.

"We will wait until it is bitter and cold, swarm the castle, and not allow food or drink to enter. This will guarantee their stores have been used up and give time for me to heal. We will starve them out and get Stephan back. The recent murder of the bishop during the queen's coronation has allowed for Stephan of Blois's brother to be the new Bishop of Winchester. We've heard rumors that he's become an ally to our cause. This is good news…"

Brother Obadiah's eyes fell further down the page. He took a deep breath and sighed, pausing mid-sentence.

"Is—is that all?" Eira asked.

"No, my dear. He goes on." Obadiah's eyes creased with sadness.

"Go on. Is he well?"

"Nay. He says he's been injured in battle trying to save Stephan." Obadiah scanned the letter further.

"Injured." Eira stood. "Was it bad?"

Brother Obadiah folded the paper gently. "There was a wound to his leg, and he's resting near the city. There has been no fever, so that is a good sign. We shall pray for him. Though he does mention he would enjoy some letters while he recovers. I believe he intends those to come from your hand, m'lady, not mine." Brother Obadiah smiled. "Come. Let us pray for his speedy recovery. He's in the Lord's hands."

Bowing their heads, they prayed, but her heart was heavy as they said, "Amen."

She wanted to trust that God would protect Owen, that God would return Stephan to their hand safely, that this would all be over and everything would be set right again ... but more than anything, she wanted to see Prince Owen again. To look into his eyes. Feel the spark he gave her again. And to help him. Help the cause. This was her fight, after all.

Even if she were taught to use a sword, the sight of blood and death falling around her would make her cave. Her stomach protested the scenes and visions already playing through her mind.

Snapping out of her musings, she noticed Luca. His face was particularly sad. Finally, she had something to distract her own desperate thoughts. Eira reached over and laid her hand on the wee lad's shoulder.

"Hello," she said. The boy peeked up at her. "Everything will be okay." Eira squeezed his shoulder and released her hand. Smiling at him, she swung her arm around his shoulders. "I promise."

"I didn't know the bishop was murdered. Who kills a God-fearing man, Princess Eira? He did nothing wrong but pray and read the holy scripts! Now, Prince Owen is hurt, and Stephan is captured. I'm—"

Tears welled in the boy's eyes as if the weight of his world began crushing his spirits. "I'm scared." His thin little lip quivered.

She knelt to his level and settled her eyes evenly on Luca's, both hands now on his shoulders. "You're right. It doesn't make any sense, does it? The bishop was an innocent man and didn't deserve to die. But you don't need to be afraid. His life was all about serving the Lord, and he did that until his last breath. That is something to be proud of. Besides, we are here with you. Nothing will happen. Okay?"

She wished she believed her own words, but that would be lying. What would she do if someone barged in and took them captive? They were no match for the strong men fighting in battle. A weak princess still healing, a monk who was as gentle as a tree bug, and a boy who was brave but innocent.

A distant voice came alive and illuminated her soul.

Remember, Eira … remember what your mother told you…

What were the words her mother used to say? What did Papa tell her she had to remember?

Suddenly, Papa's eyes penetrated her heart as if she were a young little girl all over again. His words rolled in and out of her mind like the chant of the wind, swirling about her until she was completely frozen. Time stood still.

She had thought Papa's voice was completely gone from her memory, fading away like the dust of the earth. But it hadn't, because his throaty rumble was as clear as if he were standing in the flesh next to her, whispering in her ear…

"You're special…"

His voice carried a kind of joy along with it, a tone she'd never heard before, breezing through each syllable. Was it her imagination? Was she conjuring up what she wanted to hear? Or perhaps she'd never noticed it until today? She pried her memory open more, straining for every word from her long-forgotten story. His final words burst through the fog…

"Created for the Lord. Though the world will tempt your heart to become as black as ebony, Christ is able to save you through His crimson blood. Making you, Eira, white as snow!"

In that moment, something happened in her heart. Something

strange took over her. A confidence crept up within her. Her mind shifted, and she knew what she was created for. She did have a purpose. And that purpose felt like hope. She wouldn't settle for the darkening thoughts she so often fell victim to. Eira would focus on the One who made her. Created her.

Eira held comfort in the Book of Prayers she had near her. But if she were honest, her confidence in God was not where it should be. Perhaps even her relationship. When had she last prayed? Last read the scripts? Last trusted Him? Lat sought His will over hers? But the words of her mother made Eira realize that God was all she truly needed.

She didn't have to be as strong physically. Despite her weaknesses, she could be confident and brave because she knew in that moment, God would make up for the rest. God would be the strength for her. She didn't have to be anything else but herself.

Her eyes caught the ease and comfort settled in Luca's. Bringing hope for someone else brought an entirely new meaning to her life. A meaning that was electrifying. Her encouraging words could change someone. That thought alone breathed life into her bones. She would give the wee lad hope because that is what they all needed.

"Tell me you will come visit every day," she said, smiling with wide eyes.

"I will," he promised with a little glow sparking in his own.

After Luca ate and they said their goodbyes, Eira turned to Brother Obadiah as she shut his door. "Tell me more of Jesus. Tell me how He can make me as white as snow. I need to know. I'm—I'm ready to know."

Brother Obadiah's eyes twinkled before he replied, "I would be honored, Princess Eira."

Thirty-Six

OWEN

PRINCE OWEN LEANED BACK AND BIT HIS LIP, DEADENING THE pain searing in his leg. Why was his healing taking so long? It had already been a week and a bit. He'd never been this injured before. A few cuts and nicks, but never a wound so deep he could barely walk. Blood had soaked through his clothing.

Doc had done a great job of healing him up, but time was of the essence, and he needed to be back in the battle before Queen Amara made her victory. His thoughts sprang back to Stephan of Blois and the men surrounding him before Owen chased after Robert of Gloucester. He shouldn't have left Stephan alone. Why did he always let people slip from his grasp?

He groaned and slammed his fist into the wall beside him.

Mason walked in. "Everything alright?"

"No. But yes. When will you tell her you're staying here?" Prince Owen tried to change the subject. He dipped his spoon into some soup and slurped it back.

"Soon."

Prince Owen wasn't convinced. He growled. He needed to get

240

back into the battle, not lie in bed all day. He tossed the blanket off and tried to get up.

"I wouldn't do that if I were you." The right side of Mason's lip lifted into a grin. "On the bright side"—he pointed his spoon at Owen — "if you do, I'll most certainly be entertained. By all means"—his spoon swirled in the air— "go ahead."

"Aren't you supposed to be fetching Eira some meat?" Irritation crawled under Owen's skin. From what exactly, he couldn't tell. If he were to guess, most likely from being motionless. Sliding his left-hand underneath himself, he tried to push off and pull his weight with the edge of the door. He grunted every inch of the way.

"You're going to make yourself sick trying to move so much. I've strict orders to keep an eye on you for a few days until you're ready to fight again. And that there..." His spoon aimed in Owen's direction again. "...will keep you in bed even longer!"

"What do you know?" Owen sputtered with a groan. Suddenly, Owen's hand slipped, and the weight on his leg was unbearable. He fell backward into bed, smashing his head against the wall. The shelving above him, along with its contents, fell all over him.

Mason's obnoxious laugh erupted like a volcano, piercing Owen's head like a sharp blade through his skull. Could he be more annoyed?

"Woah! Woah, now. I told you you'd get sick. But oh no"—Mason's palms went up—"you don't want to listen to me!" Mason cackled and snorted as if he were still a boy.

Swiping at his mouth, Owen placed the bowl on the floor and leaned back, his right arm under his head avoiding the rough edges of the wood. "You find all this amusing, do you? I think it's *your* presence that is making me sick."

Mason either had no idea of the importance of his healing ... or he was simply mad. Eira was in grave danger, and Mason just wanted to joke around. A lot was at stake, and he needed to be there—in battle. For her.

"As a matter of fact, I do find this amusing!" Mason howled.

How could Eira think this man noble?

Owen shook his head and stared at the ceiling. "Well, while I'm here *not* fighting for Eira, I am left with an imbecile who would be better off fighting on my behalf instead of babysitting me."

"Do you know what else is funny?" Mason's face dropped like a ton of bricks. He walked over to Prince Owen's bed and knelt beside him, staring at him before continuing in a low tone. "I find it funny that you've come all this way to fight for a princess that you don't even know." Mason's thick eyebrows and sharp jaw clenched together at the same time. "And instead of protecting her, which I have vowed to do, I'm stuck here"—Mason's lips twisted— "protecting a man who thinks he can be a hero without any pain."

Picking up the bowl Owen had just vomited in, Mason stood. "If you're not willing to die and heal for her, I suggest you leave the fighting for someone else that would."

"And you?" Owen's chin jutted with a challenge. "Would you die for her?"

"Yes." Locking eyes for a moment, Mason spoke slowly, "I would. I would do anything for her."

Turning away, Owen was left staring at the wooden slates above him. His jaw clenched uncontrollably. If only Mason wasn't Eira's friend, he would—he would do what? He was in no place to fight. As much as he hated to admit it, Mason was right. He needed to rest so he could fight and protect her.

Raw and exposed, the man clashed with Owen in a way that no other had before him—challenging him. No one ever spoke to him with such directness. Yet wasn't that what he needed to slap him out of this stupor he was in? Didn't Brother Obadiah say iron sharpens iron? Perhaps this was the iron he needed. It felt raw, sharp, painful. But it was good.

Owen was willing to lose everything, even a limb, for a fight that wasn't his own. If he were honest with himself, this was *his* fight as much as hers because she was in it. Because he needed someone, something, to fight for, and she was that something. He would heed Mason's advice. She needed him, and Owen needed her. That was final. Regardless of any of his failures, his decision was made. He closed his eyes.

Before he could fall asleep, Doc entered the room. "You're stirring up trouble with the guests, I see."

Prince Owen didn't answer; instead, he heaved a heavy sigh.

Doc walked over to his leg and started replacing the bandages, then cleaned the wound. "You should be well in a day or two. But to fight..." He tsked and tilted his head. "Perchance a fortnight still to heal, depending on your strength and God's mercies."

Doc washed his hands in the bowl of clean water by the bed and scrubbed his fingers with soap.

"I want to fight in a few days."

"Will you?"

"Aye." Owen pushed himself into a seated position in the bed and moved some books and bottles away to scoot back into the wall. Leaning his head back, he blew out a puff of air. "If I am able."

Doc dried his hand and swung the cloth over his shoulder before picking up the items scattered around the bed from the knocked shelf. He placed each neatly in the corner. "You can do a lot of damage by getting up too early if you're not careful," Doc said cautiously, staring at the items he gently placed down.

"You asked me if I was willing to protect the princess." Owen squinted at Doc as he summarized his thoughts. "I still am." He breathed out frustration before continuing. "And right now, Stephan is our best chance at getting the kingdom back for her. It will do her no good having him stay as a prisoner. I don't know how long he'll last in that dungeon before he dies, or the rats eat him alive. The queen may even execute him for treason."

Owen pinched the bridge of his nose with his fingertips. "Regardless, we both know once the queen finds out Eira's still alive, she'll stop at nothing to kill her. I must get to the queen before she gets to Eira."

Doc nodded. "Agreed. Let's get some blood flow moving to help the healing process, shall we?" Doc started rubbing Owen's calf on the leg that was wounded. "This should work."

Owen winced and sucked in a breath through his clenched teeth.

When he was done, Doc washed his hands again and moved over to the window. He gazed out into the forest for a moment. "They say the townspeople are fighting in the streets. People are stealing, and there is confusion over what coins are of use now. Stephen of Blois has issued his own and Queen Amara has minted her own. The barons are split over who they'll serve. It is getting worse with each day the battle goes on. I am praying that Eira will not have a hostile throne to sit upon when the time comes."

"One battle at a time, Doc. We will tend to what happens on the throne when it comes."

"I will be in to check on you after I've been to see Eira."

Owen's whole body came alive when he heard her name. "Does she fare well?"

"Yes, I believe so. She has been visited often by the young chap named Luca, which she seems very content with. I hear she's also becoming stronger in her faith, which is a beautiful thing in and of itself."

"Yes…" Owen couldn't help but smile. "Beautiful." How she radiated his thoughts with beauty. "When do you suppose I should go and see her?"

Doc laughed. "Not anytime soon. Mason and I will be paying her a visit tomorrow. We shall know more of her healing at that time and can relay the message in the evening."

"All these feather-heads have cleaned up. Stop your blob-taling,

Doc, and come eat! I'm hungry," Laurentius hollered from the other room.

"Rest, Prince Owen." Doc smiled and left the room.

How could he rest when he just wanted to ride his horse and be with her? Thinking about his horse ushered in a renewed sadness. Owen's father had given him that horse. He deeply cherished him, and no other animal could ever compare. When he rode him, it was as if Absolam knew where and when to move without any guidance from Owen. They were in sync, and now their melody faltered on a sour note.

Even Fredrick, the grumpiest man Owen had ever met, helped bury his horse near the Men of Ore's cottage and cried a few tears as Christopher said a word in prayer. There, Owen staked his white tunic stitched with the pilgrim's crest into the ground and marked where their journey together finally ended.

Owen suppressed a sob aching to leave his chest. Though he hadn't forgotten about his sister, Owen was on another mission now. One that was far more than a selfish miracle.

He wanted to serve God, serve a woman in her need, defend a kingdom against unnecessary evil, and fight for something greater than he ever could be on his own. That day marked him for life and changed his course for good. There was no way he could go back now.

Prince Owen stretched out his legs and got comfortable in his bed. He had to admit; it wasn't the miracle he hoped for—it was better. He'd found Princess Eira. And though he lay wounded, he felt more alive than he had in a very long time. Seeing her face in his mind, he closed his eyes. He could finally be able to rest.

Before slipping away into bliss, Owen suddenly felt a numbing sensation in his leg. His head begun to feel fuzzy and his stomach turned. *Strange.* His eyes sprung open. Looking down he could see a green substance slowly oozing out of his wound. He hollered for Doc before he passed out.

Thirty-Seven

EIRA

"Leave me alone. Get back!" She couldn't breathe. "Get away!" Sticky sweat clung to her linen underdress, suffocating her skin.

"Eira."

A masculine voice entered her ears. She blinked. The queen's distorted face melted away like the snow falling outside her window. Rubbing her eyes, Eira sat up and blinked again. "Brother Obadiah?"

"You were having a nightmare."

"I was?" She looked at the room bathed in candlelight. Items were knocked over, blankets thrown about. "I'm sorry. I—I must have been."

"Hush. Here's a piece of cloth. You're drenched through, and we don't need you catching a cold."

She took the cloth from him and dabbed it on her forehead. "I haven't had a night terror like that since I was a child. I'm so sorry for the mess."

"I am going to go back to bed." He smiled at her reassuringly. "We will clean up in the morning."

Obadiah went to leave the room, but she caught his wrist.

"Before you go, can you pray for me?" She shook her head. It ached in pain. "I haven't had one this bad in a very long time. My father would tell me a story, and it would help me sleep. He called them my fairytales. But he is gone now, and I would like some prayer at least."

She couldn't help but smile at the memory of her papa and how she would plead with her eyes, begging to hear the story over and over again. She fixated her gaze back on Brother Obadiah.

"I will pray, but first, tell me of this story. What was it about?" He sat on the edge of her bed.

"My mother." She beamed. "It was mostly about my mother. She was beautiful. You would've adored her."

"I did adore her." His gentle words sent a thrill through her body.

"What do you mean, you *did*? How—"

"Do you remember anything at all? How she looked?"

Eira shook her head.

"She looked like you. She was every bit as radiant, and when she died, I feared you had died in childbirth along with her. Though she was fearless in spirit, she was never strong in body."

"I am the opposite." She laughed. "I don't die easily, do I?"

His baritone voice sounded like a stringed instrument when he laughed. It made her smile widen. "No, you don't, thankfully. But you are also strong in spirit."

Her eyes sparkled up at his tender ones—like her father.

"Was she kind?"

"Very. Her greatest work was that of the poor. Always trying to tend to them. She worked with the bakers and exchanged a small fee for their day-old bread to be given out to the needy."

"What of her character?"

"She had a stubborn streak to her. But she was known to hold herself with a sense of righteousness, but with a great deal of humility.

247

She truly encompassed the word meek. Yes," he smiled, as if reminiscing, "she was meek."

"Meek, you say." Her shoulders slumped again. "I thought my nightmares were gone for good." Her slender brows pinched with confusion, and she looked up at Brother Obadiah as if he had the answers.

"Now. Now." He took the wet cloth from her hands. "Don't be discouraged. He who is in you is greater than your weaknesses. God has not left you nor forsaken you. You will get better. I promise." He stood and said a prayer over her before leaving the room.

She felt at ease knowing that part of her fairytale was coming true. She was as white as snow. Washed by another's blood. Not even death could stop her from being God's child. Queen Amara could try and kill her, but she could never kill her spirit. That was something worth holding on to.

But facing Queen Amara in battle made shivers crawl down Eira's spine. Was she physically able to fight? She had never been taught. Was she prepared to sit on the throne? To be a queen for the people—a people torn in uproar and unwilling to have any woman be queen, even her? What kind of person could rule a divided people?

Only God knew.

Eira's job was somehow content in that thought. She had to be. She did trust Him for what lay ahead, for she had nowhere else to turn but hope and trust. Because if her nightmares were telling her anything, it was that the future was about to get hostile, and she wasn't sure if she was completely ready for it without something or someone like God on her side.

Dawn was shaking hands with the soft snow pressing against the windowpane when she awoke. Noticing a letter on her nightstand, she opened it. The letter was written entirely in Latin. *Silly Obadiah, trying to teach me how to read…*

Once deciphered, she read that Brother Obadiah had gone for the day already. Getting up, she stretched and started to change her clothes into daywear. A piece of a wooden stick rested beside her bed, along with a cup of water. She drank the water and started to chew on the end of the stick while making her bed.

After the end had been gnawed enough, she used the bristle to clean her teeth. Once satisfied, she broke the end of the piece she had chewed into the fire and laid it down next to her bed again.

"Princess Eira?" A small voice came from outside her door, startling her.

"Luca." She beamed and sat on her bed. "Come in. I was hoping you'd stop by."

Luca came around the corner, and a tall man fell in step behind him.

"Oh—"

The man stooped low in a formal bow. Eira was unaccustomed to such courtesy but knew how to respond appropriately.

"You may rise, sir." Jutting out her chin, she looked into the man's eyes and almost jumped off her bed and into his embrace. "Mason!" she shouted. "You're alive." She reached for his outstretched hand. "Kind sir, how are you?"

He dipped and kissed her hand before replying, "I am well. Been staying at the Men of Ore's and will continue thereafter in the fight for the kingdom, Your Majesty."

She could see worry lines in his eyes, but his demeanor appeared calm. "Mason, please. What is it? Here"—she swept her hand across the small area— "in this room, we're merely friends." She turned to Luca. "Prithee, fetch us some water for tea. I made some cookies yesterday. You'll be pleased about how well they turned out when you return."

She cupped his chin and gave him a little hug. Warmth by way of tiny arms caressed her middle. Nodding vigorously, Luca darted into action.

"He is quite the boy, Princess Eira."

"He is." She motioned to the chair by the fire. "Come, sit with me. So, tell me all. How do you fare?"

"I am well." The rough whiskers on his beard bounced like her father's once had when he smiled.

"It is good to see you." She held back tears. "I was afraid the queen—"

Eira couldn't finish her sentence. She didn't want to think of death any longer.

He patted her arm. "I am fine. There was a close encounter after one of my men was murdered—Charles." She saw his adam's apple leap through the skin on his throat.

"I'm sorry for your loss," Eira said. "He was a good friend?"

"No matter now. What's gone is gone. I tried to come to you earlier, but I was being closely followed for some time."

"Oh." Eira clapped her hands. "I am glad to hear you didn't come here. We've had nothing but trouble. And, I must thank thee for your provisions. Your meat is truly the finest."

A blush crept over his face. "I met and married. I have a wife now. I hope to one day have you two meet, if that is alright with you, m'lady."

"I knew there was someone."

"You did not," he teased.

"As sure as the sun, I did." She smiled. "You had her kerchief on your horse when you rescued me. I noticed it on our way to the Men of Ore's. Do you not remember?"

"Nay. But you did." He shifted in his chair uncomfortably. "Prithee, you have an eye for detail. And you? How have you been?"

"All goes as well as it can." Eira wished Mason would not gaze at her with those brotherly, ever so scolding eyes. "I have tried to stay free from the queen's grasp. But I have been foolish and believed in her sincerity."

His eyes softened, and he examined the fire. "That is no fault of your own. The fault lies in the one who takes advantage of a kind heart, not the one who possesses said heart."

She sat in silence.

"Did you know, where I come from, kindness is bravery? It is harder to not give in to the lesser man in us all."

"That is very thoughtful of you to say. You will be a good husband, Mason, I have no doubt. I would be honored to meet your wife, if all goes well. I meant what I said. I will knight you if we win the kingdom."

Mason shifted uncomfortably. "I do bring news."

The crackle of the fire made his words pop with concern.

"Good news ... or bad?" Eira dipped her head and whispered.

"It is about Owen, m'lady."

Thirty-Eight

"OWEN HAS TAKEN A TURN FOR THE WORSE, I FEAR."

"I don't believe it. Owen will be okay, will he not?" Eira gulped for air.

Luca bounded in through the hall carrying their water. Eira gasped, startled. Luca looked up to Owen; he couldn't know he had fallen much more ill than they originally thought.

"For your tea."

"Thank you, Luca." She tried to smile. "Please set the water there on the table. Grab two cookies. One for me and one for you. Then, go sit by the fire. You must be cold from being outside."

Luca could tell something was wrong but did what she bid him to.

"My dear Princess, let us talk further about that later." Mason nodded toward the boy.

Eira winked in response.

Mason lifted his eyebrows up and down dramatically, emphasizing the word *good* before continuing. "Now, I have other news I would like to share?"

"Ah, yes." Eira cleared her throat. "Please, go on." She gestured with her hand.

"Katherine—or Matilda, as she's otherwise called—the wife of Stephan—captured the Earl of Gloucester and threw him into a secure kidcote with the help of a small army. In exchange for his life, Queen Amara agreed to free Stephan of Blois."

Mason got up, poured the water Luca brought, and placed it over the fire again to warm.

"That is good news." Eira's spirits were lifting.

"Word is that Queen Amara has gone back to Whiteshire Castle. With Stephan being free, the plan is to invade the castle and starve Queen Amara and her men out." Mason stretched out his legs closer to the fire. "Now that it's the dead of winter and snow is covering the earth, food is scarce, and they won't be able to trade. We hope, in short time, they'll surrender, and all will be done and settled."

"I've a feeling it won't be as easy as you say. I know all the nooks and hideaways in that castle. They may attempt an escape. Perhaps a few. The queen is relentless. She won't give in easily."

The plan was faulty at best. If she was such an observer of details, why hadn't she been consulted on this plan? Eira bit her lip and crossed her arms over her chest. She knew that castle better than anyone. She wanted to ask so many questions. Had they started to surround the castle yet? Were the people of Whiteshire still in the castle? Where were they being relocated, if so?

Luca looked back at Eira. Softening her features, she instantly gave him a snuggle. "No need to fret. Brother Obadiah says God can do all things, and He's working out everything for good, right, Luca?"

Swallowing, Luca took a small bite of his cookie, then offered half of a smile. "Right."

"Everything will go according to God's mercy and abundant grace."

"Exactly." Mason's tense smile appeared unnatural as he chewed on his cookie and Eira's comment.

"Luca, why don't you go tend to the horses. They're in need of fresh hay and water. Bring the hood with wool to keep you warm." She gave Luca another squeeze. "Make sure you get Obadiah's coat on too. I can't have your little nose getting too red from the frost." She wiggled her nose against his.

Luca giggled, making her think of her and her papa. Would Luca remember this moment as she remembered the small moments with Papa? She hoped so. Though she wasn't Luca's mother, she wished she was. His sweet, tender eyes stared back at her, almost reading her thoughts before he wrapped his arms around her waist again. The smell of honey mixed with earth invaded her senses. When he spoke, her heart almost burst.

"I love you..." he whispered into her hair. "Princess Eira."

She could pretend he said *Mama* instead.

"I love you too, Luca." She swiped at a tear and sent him off. She wished this time with him would last forever. Tucking Luca into bed, telling him bedtime stories, laughing and playing games like Tric Tac filled her thoughts with joy.

"He's a sweet lad." Mason's voice broke her muse.

"Yes. He has been quite the treasure to me as of late." She smiled. Her hands twisted in her lap with anticipation. "Now." She paused and sat up straight. "Speak truth with me, Mason: How is Owen?"

Mason stood and retrieved the hot water from the fire and made them both tea before responding. Perhaps to be sure the boy was out of earshot or perhaps to settle his own nerves for the news he was about to share. "He received a major wound to his leg on the night Stephan was captured. Doc has been with him ever since."

"Yes. I am aware."

"But the stubborn fool won't rest and heal properly. The wound has begun festering. If he doesn't get better soon, he shall surely die."

Mason put his elbows on his knees and rested his hands on his forehead. His gaze dropped to the floor. "I'm sorry, Princess Eira. I've tried to stay by his side, but he's insufferable and miserable. I don't know how you were ever able to stay in his presence for longer than a day."

"Well, he wasn't wounded when I was with him."

Eira's heart was pounding in her chest. How many times was Owen by her side while she walked the thin line of shadow and death? If he was going to die defending her kingdom, defending her—she owed it to him to be by his side and serve him in his time of need.

"Where is he? I must go to him!"

Mason's head whipped up, and his eyes met hers. "No. You must stay here and rest where it's safe. It is my duty to protect you, m'lady."

"Mason, you've not known me for long. But in this short time, have you known me to be sitting still longer than a few days? I'm going stir-crazy. Besides, I must see him. I *need* to … to … thank him. To tell him I—"

He held up his palms to her. "I know you to be a very willful and yet a tender and timid woman. One of great value and kindness. Even showing mercy to those who don't deserve it." His thumb and forefinger rubbed sharp whiskers on his jaw. "However, I don't want to see you get hurt," he continued. "Prithee, do not take offense, but you can be very naïve, and I need to protect you. I gave my word."

She stood and nodded. "You're right. About everything, all of what you said 'tis true. And I give you my word when I say I do not take offense to your honesty. 'Tis what I like most about you, Mason. But you were correct in that I'm willful when needing to be. So, take me to him." Eira lifted her chin. "I am foolish at times and inexperienced, God knows. However, this is not a request. This is an order." She shrugged her shoulders. "Besides, you *will* protect me because you will accompany me."

"What about the boy?" The worry lines he tried to mask earlier appeared on Mason's face became very evident.

"He should come too." She gathered her skirts. "Is it far?"

"Doc is going to kill me. You know that, don't you?" Mason stood and separated the wood in the fire. He picked up his mug of tea and gulped down some of the hot liquid. The rest he threw on the fire, and the sizzle of dampening wood hissed in her ears. "I really don't like being around Sir Grump-A-Lot," he huffed out. "Besides, you are supposed to be healing as well."

"I am feeling much better all of a sudden." Her smile couldn't have been more genuine at that moment, and Mason embraced it fully with his gaze.

"It's nice to see you smile like that, m'lady." Mason smiled. "I will take you there. It won't be long till we arrive." Mason walked toward the door. "I'll relieve Luca and ready the horses. Gather your things." Bowing, he slowly backed away from her with the words, "My Queen," and left her presence completely.

She admired how authentically devoted, yet honest and reverent he was to her. He was a master of many things, not just hunting. How blessed she was to have him. With all that Mason had sacrificed for Eira, she wished she could do more for him and his wife. But she had nothing in her name—no castle, no army, no bishop, no barons, no extensive wealth besides a ring and bag of coins her papa gave to her when she was forced to leave. She had merely a make-believe title, a claim to the throne, and a world where no one knew she had ever existed.

She could do nothing until the queen was off the throne. Until then, they were just as trapped as she was in a cruel web of blood-thirsty evil, where only God knew who died, who was crowned, and whose vengeance ultimately won in the end.

Please, Lord, let it not be Owen that dies in the end.

Thirty-Nine

OWEN

Stephan paced the small room. "Sit down. You're making me nervous."

Prince Owen weakly spread out the parchment against the wooden stump of a table and put stones on each end, securing it. "Let's go over the attack once more."

Owen tried not to stare at the gaunt look on Stephan's caving cheeks and instead focused on the plan. Queen Amara's men had not been kind to him while he'd been held captive. Remnants of his bruises still lingered under his clothing, flashing out every time Stephan moved.

"I beg your pardon, men." Knocking, Doc walked in. His eyes studiously swept the room, no doubt noticing the few men Stephan brought from battle standing in a half-moon around Owen's bed. "You've company," Doc announced. He acknowledged each one with a nod, then darted his gaze toward Stephan for a second longer before finally landing on Owen's. "Princess Eira is here."

Eira's here? Now?

A wave of astonishment roared through the room, and suddenly he became acutely aware of the rancid sweat that emanated from him. He wished he could blame it on the other men in the room. Sweat slipped down his back, and his leg started to ache even worse than it had in the past few days. This was not the time to have another fever attack.

Biting his cheek, he tried to relax.

But she's here.

"Please. Let her in." Owen glanced at Stephan. "Maybe we should ask your men to leave. As it is, there isn't enough room for us all. We can go over the plans later."

Stephan lifted his chin at the men, and they all filed out one by one. Stephan remained standing. Eira walked into the room, and Owen's breath caught. Even Stephan's mouth fell agape, revealing his high cheekbones. He probably had never seen her before and surely was caught up in her beauty, as Owen was when he first saw her. He didn't want to look away then, nor did he now.

Oh, how he'd missed her.

"Prince Owen." She curtsied. Her lips spread into a gorgeous smile, lifting his spirits. Seeing her brought strength to his bones. By the glint in her eye, he could tell she didn't want to break their gaze, but she turned, dipping her head at the man standing in the far corner. "Hello, sir."

Stephan bowed low. "M'lady. We have not met but are related through Queen Amara. We are cousins. May I introduce myself? I'm Stephan of Blois." He raised his head to her and walked forward. She lifted her hand and met him halfway as he bowed to kiss her hand. "'Tis a pleasure to finally meet you."

Eira's eyes glistened like icicles in the morning sun. "I haven't had the luxury of meeting many family members. And I am sorry it has to be under such..." Her voice caught. "...under such unfortunate circumstances."

Stephan stood to his full height. "You look like her—your mother, I mean. You have many of her attributes. You're truly a lovely memory to gaze upon." Stephan choked back some emotion. "I am honored to serve you, m'lady."

Bowing one final time, he stepped back.

Eira's cheeks flushed, and she grinned. "I thank thee for your kind words, but I'm no fool. Beauty is vain and not trusted. I seek to be beautiful on the inside, more so."

"A fine statement, m'lady."

Though she tried not to broach the subject, heaviness regarding the king's death lingered in the air. No one wanted to be in the situation they were in. Owen couldn't help but wonder if the king hadn't passed away, perhaps he would've found Eira on his own, fallen in love, married her, and taken her back to his kingdom in Wealas. But that was wishful thinking. They were plotting to overthrow Queen Amara's rule. All three of them in the same room for completely different reasons. One thing they shared was battling a queen whose sole purpose was greed and power.

Owen wanted to avenge his past regrets with every blow of his sword while protecting the princess. His initial journey to seek peace didn't turn out as peaceful as he imagined. War did something to him. It was a place to get his frustrations out, to breathe a vengeance that had no other place but in the heat of battle. But this time, it was more than that. It was for Eira.

Stephan's reasons were most likely political, gaining favor with greedy merchants, expanding his wealth, name, and lands—typical for a man of his caliber. No doubt, in Owen's mind, Stephan's reasons were closer to Queen Amara's than he wished to admit.

Would Stephan be a good ruler? I guess it wasn't really up to him to decide. However, Stephan's heart wasn't altogether wicked. He saw that when he fought with the man. He did care for his men and often exuded a kind heart. Owen had seen him refrain from fully punishing a man when wronged. Wealth didn't appeal to him like the people he was standing for—the merchants, but power—that had to be seen still.

An idea sprang from the back of his mind … he would ask Eira to run away to Waelas with him. Let Stephan have the kingdom and save her own life.

Would she say yes to his offer?

Perhaps she would want to stay and rule? Owen pondered if Eira would be a good ruler. He remembered her sweet nature and was assured. Could he stay here for her? Fighting for her was one thing but staying here and never going back to his own kingdom was another. Sweat beaded on his head. He felt a tear rippling through his heart, separating each chamber. There were so many moving parts and decisions to be made. He felt torn.

A kind of guilt he was angry with himself for allowing, crept up on him. He blinked. He hadn't even reflected on what Eira might want. He blinked again, glancing at Eira. Had he ever asked her if she wanted to rule? How could he not even consider her thoughts on the matter?

"I am sorry for your loss," Stephan said, breaking Owen's muse and bringing him back into the conversation. "It was a great loss to all Whiteshire … all of England, rather. Everywhere. Your father was a great leader and friend."

Eira slowly sat on the edge of Owen's bed, as if the memory alone made it difficult for her to stand. His nerve endings stood in rapt attention at the mere proximity of her. Her sweet aroma made waves of emotion run through his body. How could one person make him feel so strong yet so vulnerable with one glance?

His eyes watched as her hand fell to his.

Ignoring Stephan's comment, she said, "How are you doing? I had to come and see that you were well and thank you for all you've done." Before he could answer, she lifted her face to Stephan. "And you. Thank you for fighting so valiantly. You have both risked more than I could ever ask of you."

She squeezed Owen's hand. Like a spring of water pouring in from the depths of the earth, flooding a mighty hole, so sudden emotions filled an empty space in his heart. Eira's gentle words and tender touch saturated every crevice of his empty well. He'd risked everything fighting for her—his quest to save his sister, his remaining funds, his father's blessing if he didn't return home by spring to take over the kingdom. He knew it now more than ever: Eira was worth staying and fighting for.

"I would do anything for you, Eira." Prince Owen squeezed her hand in return.

She shifted in her seat, and it took everything in him from intertwining her fingers with his. An awkward silence surrounded the room. Did she feel as he did?

She focused on Stephan and removed her hand, breaking their connection. "Stephan. May I speak with you alone?" she asked.

Wait. What?

Eira stood and walked out of the room with Stephan, leaving him alone. Both body and mind, wounded. What was she eager to discuss without Owen's presence? Did she not trust him? Perhaps it was for deeper concerns. Owen thought she'd come to see him, but perhaps it was to see Stephan.

A slippery snake named Jealousy wormed its way around Owen's stomach, making him feel sick. He tried to fight back, but its ugly head wouldn't go away.

You're being foolish. Stephan is going to help Eira, not hurt her ... or him.

HOURS HAD PASSED before either of them returned to see Owen. He grinned at each of them, doing his best to shrug off his feelings when they entered. Eira sat at the far end of the room and spoke with

Stephan about the upcoming attack on Whiteshire, until Stephan excused himself to prepare his army for the days to come.

When Owen asked what they'd discussed privately, Eira avoided the conversation.

"I've been learning Latin lately." She beamed brightly. "Brother Obadiah says I am a good student and will begin writing lessons soon. I'll be able to write you a letter. Wouldn't that be nice?"

He wanted to be happy for her. It filled his heart with joy that she was learning Latin, as any princess should, but he couldn't shake the feeling of being slighted. As if she planned something behind his back. He hadn't known Eira or Stephan for that long, if he were honest. Perhaps he couldn't fully trust either of them.

The room suddenly spun. Owen quickly reached for the table to stable himself. Seeing his cup there, he reached out and took a sip of his drink, tasting the distinct bitter herbs Doc concocted to ease his pain. He stared at the cup. Perhaps he just wasn't himself from the medicine. Jealousy was not something he dealt with often. Perhaps he was being overzealous.

"Are you well?" Eira asked, concerned.

Ignoring her question as she had done, he continued the conversation. "How come you didn't learn it as a child?" The question came out more accusatory than he anticipated, and he saw her wince.

"I—I was forbidden. I was never allowed to learn matters of the court or combat and war or much about politics, besides what I could glean from conversations." When Owen didn't give a response, she continued. "I've kept busy with house chores. Cooking. Cleaning." She laughed. "Who would have thought a princess would enjoy such mundane tasks as tidying up a room. And little Luca has been a darling. Helping me and keeping me company."

"Your papa never helped you learn Latin?"

She quipped a darted look at him, he assumed for pushing the matter. "He was too busy. Besides, he went with what Queen Amara said. You know, mothers know best and all." Eira akwardly laughed. There was a pause between them. An obdurate and painful one. "It's —" She sighed. "It's always nice getting a letter from you."

Owen nodded but found it hard to speak. He stared out the small window on the far side of the room. Everything in him wanted to wrap her in his arms, but she was holding something from him. He could tell. Perhaps a secret of her own. It was as if the secret were a cleaver, cutting the room in two, separating them. He couldn't focus on her. His mind flicked to the war that he needed to be in. Then to her. Then to his family.

Despite what Doc thought, he was sure he'd be well within the week. He was already getting up and practicing sword maneuvers, gaining strength and muscle. If it weren't for the pesky infection and fevers, he would be back in battle on this very day.

Frustration made him hold his breath.

She was the one worth fighting for, and yet, here she was, uncomfortable in his presence. He puffed out his breath and looked over at her. Perhaps he was uncomfortable in *her* presence. Another snake, fitly named Insecurity, weaved its way around his heart and choked out any words from his throat.

Would she run from him as his sister once did? Would she keep secrets from him like his sister had, not able to trust Owen? Not allowing him to help her?

"I better be going," she whispered. "You probably need your rest."

No.

He wanted to take her hand in his, tell her how he felt, kiss her rose-petal lips softly, and let her see he'd do anything for her if he could. Instead, he nodded, and she left, leaving him with unanswered questions and a nagging reminder of his past of distrust.

THE FEVER WAS WORSE this time. Owen's body kept shaking. He shouldn't have pushed himself so hard to get better. He grunted, not hearing the faint footsteps enter the room.

"Good day," the voice of an angel said. Eira must have stayed overnight.

He went to speak, but his lips chattered. Doc entered behind Eira.

"Save your teeth and don't speak," Doc muttered. "I've got a concoction for you. It's very strong, and you may sleep for a few days."

Owen tried to interject, but it was useless. He moved his arms, but they, too, refused to cooperate. He could only nod his head.

"I thought you'd say that."

Doc called for Hugo, and when he entered, they lifted him up enough so he could sip the concoction. Choking back a cough, the liquid burned down his throat and hit his stomach with a burning sensation. Already he could feel the medicine taking hold of his conscious mind.

What choice did he have but to let go and hope for the best? He couldn't lie to himself; his leg reeked and was putrid. If he was lucky, he might heal. But he'd seen other men in battle lose their legs to better situations than the one he was in.

Feeling a soft hand wrap around his, Owen let go, and his body fell limp. Eira's endearing, kind eyes were the image he took with him to darkness.

Forty

EIRA

EIRA SPENT DAYS STAYING BY OWEN'S SIDE, BUT HE DIDN'T WAKE up. She cleaned and dressed Owen's wound, applying the right medicines, until finally, Doc told her to go home and rest for fear she would grow ill from weariness. Reluctantly, she left with the promise that they would inform her of any changes.

No word had come.

Eira was wandering around the house aimlessly until something caught her eye. It was a pot of colored paint. *Ah, yes. The secret project Brother Obadiah's been working on for the cathedral.* She had all but forgotten his hidden passion of late. Busy at the scriptorium all day, he would sometimes come home just to squirrel himself away again. He would come out and check on Eira from time to time, then he would duck back into the small room, hiding himself away. What could be so secretive that he couldn't let her see it? Should she investigate?

She stepped toward the small door, holding her hands together, contemplating whether she should take one small peek inside. *It wouldn't hurt to take a small glance.* Besides, it would help distract her from riding over to the Men of Ore's home to check on Prince Owen.

She had promised not to do it. But … she didn't say anything about not peeking into Brother Obadiah's room.

She tucked a strand of hair behind her ear and looked back toward the front door. He shouldn't be home for some time. Taking another step closer, her fingers found the latch. Gently opening the door, she analyzed the inside.

To her amazement, a beautiful sheet of paper laden with colors of rich blues, reds, and golds lay on a post before her. Shelves lined the walls with brushes, tools, and pots. Some were full of powders, and some held liquid colors. One was pure gold. It was majestic. As if God had splattered the room and filled it with creativity.

Her feet couldn't help but bring her to the sheet in the middle of the room. Words in Latin filled the page. Drawings of great art bordered each word. And the light from the window hit the gold in such a way, making it pop right off the page. She had never seen anything like it.

Her fingers reached for the gold patterns and swirls, wanting to stroke each one.

"Princess. What are you doing in my study?" Brother Obadiah's hung in the air evenly, but sternly.

"Brother Obadiah." She swallowed. "I am so sorry. I—I…" She had no words. No excuses.

He came in and touched her hand. "I forgive you."

She turned to look at the page again, reading the Latin words easily. "Initium sopientiae timor Domin. Oh!" Her eyes lit up. "I know this one… The fear of the Lord is the beginning of wisdom."

"Said beautifully." Brother Obadiah grinned from ear to ear. They both admired his workmanship. "You're a good student, Eira."

"Why haven't you told me about this?" She pointed at the sheet.

His smile brightened his eyes. "It was supposed to be a secret." His lips pursed, and he rocked on his heels, a sign she knew he was about to say something serious. "This will continue to be a secret. Do I make myself clear?"

"Very." She glanced around the room, taking in the collection of clay, canisters, and material. "But what is all of this for?"

He sighed and walked over to the shelves on the one wall. "'Tis a page from the Bible. A few select people have been chosen to scribe the first illustrated Bible. We are calling it the Winchester." He lifted some tools up humbly, like a child when his father says he is proud of him. "We've come up with some beautiful techniques to bring Scripture to life on the pages."

"The colors are so vivid. Is this gold?" she asked.

Brother Obadiah nodded and placed the tools down. "That is how I know of the Men of Ore. I buy gold from them. This tint is lead, red, and white." His index finger pointed to each hue. "Some colors I make from plants like this one."

"And the drawings. Did you make those?"

Brother Obadiah nodded again.

"Can I make a page?"

He smiled. "You may practice on a sheet. I will show you how. But the final decision is not up to me. I'll present any work to the other contributors, and they'll scrutinize it before approval. Once approved, it can then be added."

Obadiah brought a stool over, and they both sat down to a new sheet of parchment each. He started to explain details regarding the different pigments, the drawings, and the Latin scriptures he was working on next.

Eira inched her stool closer and watched every move Brother Obadiah made, imitating him, dipping the small tools in the colors and delicately pressing the tip on the page. "I can see why you would want to keep this to yourself. It's as if working under the hand of God. He is the painter, and you are the brush. I feel as if God is pleased with this work, Brother Obadiah. Thank you for sharing it with me."

"I have done only what He has asked. But it must be kept a secret. No one is to get credit but God."

"You have my word."

With that, Brother Obadiah's voice filled the room with hymns, and Eira's imagination filled the page with peaceful swirls, elaborate designs, and interesting imageries beside God's living Word.

Not once did Owen enter her thoughts.

Forty-One

"Luca!" Eira beamed with pride.

"Princess Eira." Luca bowed with such maturity.

"Wow. You've sure grown this past week. Has it been so long since I've seen you last?" Eira placed her brush down on the table and stood. "I'd say you're even a finger-width taller."

"I've brought a letter from Prince Owen, m'lady." His head dipped while blindly holding the letter out to her.

Eira slipped the parchment from his gentle grasp. "Thank you, kind sir." She grinned. Butterflies erupting in her stomach. "You may lift your head now."

He popped up like a fish jumping from the water. Then waved at Obadiah who was busy working at his station.

"Now come give me a hug before I open it." She laughed. In one swoop of her arms, she held him close and breathed in his earthy, sweet, innocent smell. Her heart soared with such tenderness when he was around. In these brief moments, she wished he never went away, never had to run errands. She would simply bask in his childish heart

269

forever. If it weren't for the position she was in, she'd perhaps request that the bishop adopt him immediately.

"Now. Tell me honestly." She pulled him back and looked him in the eye. "Have you been good to the Men of Ore?"

His fragile shoulders drooped in her hands, like cheese hanging from a soggy cloth, as he let out a heavy sigh. "Fredrick is always so grumpy. I can never do anything to please him. And … and Laurentius is constantly mumbling to me, or himself—I'm not sure." Luca's hands became animated, and she let go of his shoulders. "Just today, I was helping Mathew tend to Prince Owen when Benjamin came bursting into the room, knocking over all of Doc's supplies." Luca gave her a look. "You know Benjamin."

"Yes, I do." She laughed.

"All of a sudden, Fredrick came in yelling at me. But I didn't do anything wrong! He insisted I had to leave anyway. When Laurentius tried to help clean up the mess, he kept hollering and bluttering about 'whiflings' and how 'everyone was teenful' or why he needed to 'shab all of those fopdoodles.' He wasn't making any sense at all. But I tried to be kind in return. I promise. I just—"

Eira's right hand quickly shot up to cover her lips, concealing her laughter. Even Brother Obadiah, who was all too familiar with the Men of Ore, was trying desperately to keep his lips turned down and not sneak out any laughter.

The poor boy was obviously upset and pouring out his disturbed soul. To let any giggle slip would be cruel. However, the sound of mad chaos brought joy to her soul. She couldn't help but miss Benjamin, Fredrick, Laurentius, and all the Men of Ore's company deeply.

"They can be cantankerous, can't they?"

Luca's eyes smiled before he continued. "Christopher tried cheering me up. Even prayed for me." His little shoulders visibly inched their way back to normalcy. "Hugo was waiting at the door with Prince Owen when I went to leave. He handed me the letter, patted me on the head, and told me to deliver it to you." His eyes became misty. "They both left for battle."

"Come. Sit down, Luca. You're looking very upset." She offered Luca a chair, and when he sat, he burst into tears.

"Prince Owen is trained to fight, but he's sick, m'lady. I saw his wound! It's still festering. And—and Hugo is the same size as me. He looks like a boy. What if he got hurt? One swipe of a sword, and he wouldn't recover like Prince Owen. He might d—" Luca's hand made a slashing motion instead of finishing the word.

"Perhaps his size *is* his advantage." Brother Obadiah turned to face Luca. "Perhaps no one will even notice Hugo, assuming he's what you say—merely a boy. He can be well disguised. Even forgotten. You know how unnoticed you can become with no one paying attention."

Kneeling, Brother Obadiah met Luca at his own level. "When adventure strikes a man's soul, no one can merely stamp it out. You must let them discover life for themselves. If you don't, he'll go find it regardless. Am I not right, Luca? I remember a wee lad wanting to be close to adventure. I seem to recall pulling a few strings to have him assist us here." His eyebrows waggled at the boy.

Luca craved adventure. Eira knew that about the boy from the start. He always wanted to follow Prince Owen on his valiant and noble escapades. You could tell even by the way Luca talked about the prince, his face would light up and his jaw would jut out with pride. He wanted to be like him. But it was at Prince Owen's own request that the bishop finally said yes. And now the sweet boy was stealing her heart.

Understanding flooded Luca's teary eyes. "You're right, Brother Obadiah. He must go on his own adventure. I'm just scared. I don't want to lose them."

"Ah … but loss is a part of life, and the one to fear is God alone. Besides, God says the fear of the Lord is the beginning of wisdom. It is not wise to fear war or what man can do. But pray for them. Pray they'll leave legacies and follow true wisdom; despite any evil they must face." Brother Obadiah stood and continued to the kitchen to prepare for supper.

"Brother Obadiah?" Luca called before he left the room completely.

"Yes?"

"Are you an adventurer? Will you leave a legacy?"

Brother Obadiah's gaze swept over to the pot of red lead used on the secret project, then slipped back to the boys. "I am. Perhaps not in the way you'd expect, but yes, I'm an adventurer. And if the Lord wills, it will be His legacy that I leave for many people to remember."

Eira sat next to Luca and patted his knee. "He's right. Now, let's find out what these adventurers are up to, shall we?"

Cracking the prince's wax seal, Eira slid her finger between the paper edges and opened the letter. Her eyes clung to Owen's penmanship. Knowing he wrote them made her insides swell with longing and comfort. His lines were deliberately made, pressed deeply on the paper, but his strokes for the letters 'o' and 'e' were fluid and open in style. She could see his character even through his writing. Strong, determined, and loving.

"Dearest Queen Eira of Whiteshire,

I apologize for not writing sooner. As you know, I was very ill. Thank you for staying by my side for the days when I was in a mad sweat. I'm sure that was not a pleasant sight to see. But I am grateful for you. Truly. My journey to health has been slow, but I am improving daily.

I am doing all I can and helping to prepare the men to camp near Whiteshire Castle. Hopefully, I will join them soon. *The snow is heavy and blanketing the ground. Food sources have been completely cut off from the castle for weeks. It shouldn't be long before Queen Amara surrenders.*

I must inform you; it appears people are having a change of heart. They're looking forward to having a queen after all, and the nobles are sending word to Stephan that they're in support. If trades stay steady for the merchants, all should be well. I must believe God is on our side. Nightfall is coming, so I better be off. I promise to send word as quickly as I can.

~~Eira. I wish I had said I to...~~

I wish I had said more when you were at the Men of Ore's. For that, I'm deeply sorry. I can be such a coward when it comes to gentlewomen. I will leave my bravery on the floor of war before speaking from the depths of my bowels. That makes me a fool—I know.

When all is finally over, perhaps I shall tell you all that is weighing on my heart. Until then, I shall leave you with this...

Gratias ago mice, semper et pro semper.
Prince Owen Williamus of Wealas."

Eira blinked and spoke the words aloud that he wrote in Latin. "Thank you, my friend, always and forever."

She wanted to hold the letter to her chest. Let the ink bleed on her like it bled on her heart. Was she only a friend to him? Her mind raced to know the secrets of his heart. Even a glimpse would have been better than nothing. Would it reveal he was leaving, going back to his own kingdom when the war was complete? Would it reveal he had found his sister and would go to her immediately?

Regardless, her thoughts pumped with adrenaline because she wanted to tell him what was weighing on her own heart. She loved him and wanted him to be with her forever. Would this brave adventurer make it through the war?

Sensing Luca's eyes, Eira carefully folded the letter and laid it on her lap. While Luca distracted himself and fiddled with some pottery on the shelf, Eira picked up a sheet of parchment paper. She turned to the small writing desk and dipped her quill in the ink.

Dearest Prince Owen of Wealas,

Thank you for your kind words. It fills me with great joy to know you are well enough to go into battle. It was my pleasure and honor to serve you. The news you bring is wonderful.

I have been learning many new things here under Brother Obadiah's teaching. One thing is the Word of God. Did you know it is alive? Every word seems to be filled with hope and the breath of God. There is such peace in the cosh. Thank you for bringing me here.

I must admit, you have my curiosity piqued. And 'tis not true what you said of yourself. I believe you to be braver than you give yourself credit for. It is I who is weak. I wish I could stand up to the queen myself and prevent further bloodshed.

I may never understand why she has chosen to hate me so. But in these last days, I have learned that King David in the Bible had such an enemy, and I plan to do to her as he did—a man after God's own heart.

Speaking of hearts, mine is heavy. I want to bear all of it on this paper. But I fear you will be frightened by the words. Because of that, I shall keep silent like you, until we see each other again.

I do ask one thing of you upon your return...

If we are victorious, I intend to celebrate with a ball, and I need you to promise me something of great importance. Would you save me one dance? Perhaps two?

Credunt. Deus spes nostra. Dominus Vobiscum ago amice.

> *Have faith. God is our hope.*
> *The Lord be with you, my friend.*
> *Princess Eira of Whiteshire.*

Eira poured the wax of a burning candle onto the creased paper. Pulling out her father's ring from her bubble-bow, Eira held it close and stared at it. For a mere moment, she allowed the memories of her papa and everything that happened since her birthday to wash over her —Papa's tearful goodbye, his strong hands shoving her out of the kingdom, Mason the huntsman in the forest helping her escape the queen's first attempt at killing her, and every attempt the queen had taken after that to hunt her down.

She particularly embraced Prince Owen's appearance to rescue her, the Men of Ore's vow to defend her, and Brother Obadiah's hymns and kindness and wisdom ... those moments made her heart broken before God in quiet prayers.

She looked over at Luca, and her heart melted before pressing her papa's ring firmly into the hardening wax. The letter was sealed, along with her memories. Forever marking and searing her mind. Regardless of how weak she felt at times, she was here for a reason, and she would muster everything within her to make herself strong, to think of what was next. Her future. Her family.

Eira's mind came to a crashing halt.

Perhaps she wasn't the one needing saving anymore. Perhaps it was the prince who needed her. He had lost a close family member at a heavy price and felt inadequate for his role to become king. In so many ways, they were both alike. She might not have his physical strength, but she had a strength that no one would think was a weapon—love and kindness.

Eira started to mentally form a plan to face the queen. Tired of the games, fears, and constant reminders of the queen's senseless hatred for her, strategies formulated vividly. Like the queen's attempt at murdering Eira, it was potent and came with a fire deep within her. It burned with fierce energy and passion. In the past, she'd been easy prey, letting the hunter rule the game, but not this time. She was about to change the rules.

No poison could shrivel what God was sealing in her heart. This was the moment she was made for. To be the queen her people needed her to be and rely on something greater—God. Stronger than all men combined, He was a Mighty King ready for anything her enemies could bring her. And just like King David, she would be a woman after God's own heart.

Eira would make one final move in the hunt and lay her trap—

Herself.

Forty-Two

Eira picked up the quill, dipped it in the ink pot, and wrote a second letter.

Dearest Prince Owen of Wealas,

Give me word instantly if circumstances change. I have a plan and will see you shortly.

Dues caritas set et amor regnans. Semper.

> *God is love, and love prevails. Always.*
> *Princess Eira of Whiteshire*
> *and future queen over Normandy and Italy.*

Sealing the letter with her father's ring, she handed both letters to Luca. "Go and give these to Prince Owen as fast as you can, my dear boy. Be quick."

Without question, Luca obeyed in haste, leaving the house as quickly as he'd come.

Forty-Three

EMPRESS AMARA

"I've had enough!"

Empress Amara paced the room. Stephan's and Owen's men had surrounded the castle long enough, she thought. Outnumbered, it would be foolish to risk venturing outside. However, there must be another way, and she was determined to find it.

Think, think, think.

"You must rest. We need to keep our strength." Robert, the Earl of Gloucester, grabbed her shoulder and eased her into the nearby chair.

She sat for a moment in silence. Elbows on the table, chin propped in her hand, tapping her lip for a single beat. Restless legs won, and she stood again. "You do what you must." She began pacing the small area again. "But I'm not staying in this—" She swung her arms out and raised her voice. "We are living in a tombstone, and I won't have another minute of it."

"Where will you go?" Robert laughed, taunting her like she was a child again. The sound was familiar. Like her father's.

Her lips curled, and Empress Amara stood, glaring at him—more like challenging him. "Think about it. Pray tell, how will you leave?"

Robert's arms fanned out from his sides like a crow's wings, his palms facing up. He was right. She was not as free as the bird taunting her mind. She was trapped in a stone-wall cage. Barred inside by the people who supported Eira, not her, in hopes she would die.

She had to think of a way out.

"Our enemies have encamped around us," he continued.

She pinched her eyes shut. Why did he insist on telling her things she already knew?

Ignoring her obvious annoyance, he went on. "Can you not see? The castle's surrounded, and every attempt at escape has been useless this far. We are down to merely a few strong men and knights. The rest are weaker than children. If they attacked now, I fear we would be jelly to their knives."

She watched the crease in his mouth bend. "Or dust to their wind?" She raised her voice. Even to her own ears, it was a screeching cry. "I can clearly see what we're up against, you idiot! The rations have dwindled to limp soup, or shall I say wash water. Regardless if they attack us or not, one of the maids reported we only have but three days of rations left. You know as well as I how war goes. It's their tactic—one that has given our armies victory before. They shall have us die of starvation or surrender and I—"

Looking down at the finger pointing toward his chest, she noticed how small it appeared, and her voice weakened. "I will not surrender. Something must be done. Already I'm looking…" Catching a glimpse of her reflection in the candle-lit window, she shivered. "…I'm looking gaunt and—and—"

The words *ugly* bit at her chest, and her hands wrung, pressing bone into skin. Her lips quivered. She was breaking. Her perfect visage was cracking.

"Leave me," she yelled and turned to see Robert's scowl. Disgust was written all over his face. She knew she was cowardly and weak, just as she was when they were young, but she couldn't stop it.

Robert spat out the last words like he was ashamed to be her family member. "I'll be in the hall, *m'lady*." His face was that of her father's.

Empress Amara flung herself onto the bed. She would've cried if she had any tears left. Bitterness had dried them up years ago.

Everything Empress Amara had ever wanted was slipping from her grasp. As much as she tried to win the game, she was losing her beauty and the crown to a mere girl, all her dreams taken away.

Funny, she had never feared death before, and blood never turned her stomach like it did other weak girls, but recently, the constant battles were warring on her soul. Draining everything she had left to give. She swiped at her tearless face. Even her child was suffering. The baby barely moved anymore. Was it dying too?

Hunger pains rumbled, and her hand went to her belly. She felt a little kick. Suddenly, a strange emotion, one she'd never experienced before, overwhelmed her. A sudden urge of protection, pity, and something she couldn't quite grasp flooded her heart for the child she was carrying.

Never had she thought of the baby as anything but a plan, or a means to an end. Another kick on her palm made her jump. She sat up. It was as if the baby was trying to speak to her, begging her to listen, *"Hey, what about me, Mama? I am here too."*

Weak and practically helpless, Empress Amara couldn't give up and die now. Pushing out her father's baritone voice telling her she was a failure, ugly, useless, she should just give up and accept defeat because she was never going to amount to anything in her life, she braced her fragile arms on the bed and pushed with every bit of energy she could muster. Rolling off the bed, Empress Amara stood, catching her breath before she stormed out into the hall.

"Bring me my things. Now! We're leaving."

Forty-Four

EIRA

BROTHER OBADIAH LOOKED PLEASED, PRACTICALLY GLOWING with excitement. "Do you think the bishop will like it?"

"Of course." Eira grinned. Her fingertips outlined the drawings, rich with color. The sparkle of gold caught her attention and aligned her focus on the top left of the page. Its design pivoted your eye to run down the swirl and land where the Word of God began.

"It is a work of art, Brother Obadiah. I think the bishop will be pleased once you bring it to the scriptorium."

Eira groaned.

"Is everything alright?"

"Prithee, Brother Obadiah. I must ask you a question." She watched Brother Obadiah roll up the sheet and place it in a leather bag.

"Yes, m'lady ... anything." He nodded to her and reached for his brown overcoat.

Twirling her right index and thumb together, she tried to look him in the eye. "May I take your horse for a ride today? I haven't been out in so long. Though you've been an incredible host and very kind to me, I wish to feel the air of freedom once again."

Brother Obadiah cleared his throat. "M'lady, I am in no place to tell you what to do. However, I'm humbled that you would consider my opinion of great value. If I have your favor, I'll permit you to take my horse." He bowed slightly. "But I only ask one request in return." His hands fell into a gentle hold in front of him.

"What, perchance, would that be?"

"Wait for me to accompany you. I shouldn't be long, and I vowed my word to care for you. When I return, we can travel anywhere you want to go." He smiled. "Does that seem fair?"

"I suppose that is the wisest response." She held back the tight knot of frustration and forced a smile.

And I suppose I'll wait until he's gone before borrowing his horse. Perhaps his horse decides to wander off the property a fair distance before she can get help.

Letting out the hot air she'd been holding, her smile became genuine. "Thank you for giving me permission to ride your horse." Her eyes twitched, looking back at him, and she averted the topic. "I pray all goes well for *your* journey."

Grabbing the small leather bag she'd filled earlier with cheese and dried meats from the kitchen table, she handed it to Brother Obadiah. "Here. I've made a traveling picnic for you."

Appearing genuinely touched by her small gesture, Brother Obadiah presented a small smile at the corners of his lips. *What a sweet man,* she thought. She would miss him terribly if something were to go wrong with her plan.

"Thank you, Princess Eira. 'Tis very kind of you." He took the bag and walked to the door. "Take good care and be sure to stay indoors unless to feed the animals."

"Have a safe trip." Her voice cracked and she looked away. How could she lie to a man like Brother Obadiah?

She observed Brother Obadiah mounting his horse from the window and waited a few moments before gathering her own things. Despite the guilt eating at her heart, she planned to leave with or without his blessing. Facing the queen was what she must do to stop the chaos spilling into the streets and end this war, once and for all.

Owen was too weak to fight this on his own and she was tired of not being the one to make decisions about her own life. She had thought about this for some time. Eira had a plan: her route was marked out through the map her Papa gave her, she prepared food for her journey, which was ready in her sack, along with the knife Papa gave her. She even drew a plan to enter the castle unseen. This time she wasn't naïve. This was her decision, and she was ready for it.

The queen wanted her, and that's what the queen would get.

Eira White.

Heir to the throne of Whiteshire.

Whether death met her, or God granted her victory...

She must go.

Forty-Five

EMPRESS AMARA

Empress Amara ran the corridor along the edge of the castle leading to the garderobe at the northwest end, facing the forest.

"What are you doing bringing us here? This is no place to be with a lady."

"Be quiet, or you'll alert someone," Empress Amara hissed, looking back at Robert. Her legs moved down the corridor to the last privy at the far end. "Are the three knights bringing what I requested?"

"Yes, My Queen." His tone was low to appease her, but Queen Amara could detect annoyance in his voice. As if realizing where he was for the first time, he continued. "Why are you wasting my time? There's no way of escape from here, at the top of the north tower. Are you mad with a fever? This is the highest place in the entire castle. How do you expect us to leave? Jump?"

Tired of his whining, Empress Amara spun and almost knocked her fist into him. She jutted her chin and cocked her eyebrow. "Listen. I know what I am doing."

He was as useless to her as Herrick was. She marched to the end of the hall and pulled him into the last chamber of the garderobe. The whitewashed walls gave an open, airy feeling to the room. One long window reflected pleasantly off the walls, filling the room with light brilliantly. It was enough space for both of them. Plus, perhaps, another man or two could easily fit in snugly.

Lifting the top of the wooden privy bench, she cringed. No matter how cheery this place could ever appear to be, it was still the privy. Despite the best efforts of the lavender rushes littered on the floor, the smell lingered in the air.

"I will *not* stand here as one of your chamber maids, My Queen. This is madness." Robert went to leave in utter disgust, but Empress Amara snatched his arm.

"You will do as I say. I need your strength. You're not going anywhere until I have escaped."

"There is nowhere *to* escape. Look at these windows! A child might be able to squeeze through it. Not us."

"Yes. You can't escape by the window there, you fool! But look. The privy expels refuse from the hole down below," She pointed at the hole where two iron bars were sitting in the stone bench, "It leads to the moat surrounding the castle."

Just then, movement caught her eye. "Get down," she whispered. "Someone is near the forest edge. I don't want to be seen up here. It's not a well-used area of the castle, and I don't want to raise any suspicions."

As they crouched, Empress Amara turned and faced Robert, the Earl of Gloucester, again. "You will need to remove the metal bars and slowly drop me down through the hole and into the moat. Some or all the water should be solid enough to stand on at this time of year. If not, I'll swim to the edge and escape on foot through the snow."

"Okay, I'll admit, you could probably fit through there if you remove the iron bars. But they will see you. This is a reckless plan, and I'll have none of it." He went to stand, and Queen Amara's nails dug into his flesh.

"I am your empress, and you will do as I say. Now fetch me the knights and bring me the white cloth I ordered. When you return, you'll remove the iron from the seat and lower me down. I require you to go with me for protection. Do you understand?"

She could see his face morph in disbelief as he nodded his head and crept out of the room. Finally, things were starting to go as planned, and she may have some kind of victory in the end after all.

EMPRESS AMARA SHIVERED ALONE in the cold breeze. The window and the privy hole let the freezing air easily seep in. It was useful when using the garderobe to allow sour smells to escape, but not when trying to keep warm.

The cold, mixed with the pungent smell of human refuse, reminded her of the days as a child. It was the same smell as the dungeon her father used to throw her in when being naughty. Her father would laugh and tease her while she cried. Empress Amara never thought his callous humor was funny.

Distracting from her inner thoughts, she focused on her escape and played the scene repeatedly. It kept her on task and successfully pushed away her memories. Her father had long since been dead, and those days couldn't hurt her any longer, or so she tried to tell herself.

The grunts of men padding the steps from the corridor perked her ears up. Her knights were close, and soon, she would be gone from the castle trying to consume her very flesh. She'd no longer be a prisoner in her own home. Soon she'd return as the rightful queen she deserved to be. And once she quenched all their rebellion, she would make them pay for the pain they caused her.

The men rounded the corner, and one by one, bowed as they entered the room. With four bodies in the cramped space, it brought some warmth to her, physically and emotionally.

"We have what you've asked for," Robert whispered.

Each pulled a variety of white woolen linen out of their tunics and put it in a pile, laying each strip gently down on the knotted rushes lining the floor. They calculated how to tie the large pieces together and form a cover or blanket wide enough to wrap around her. The other shorter pieces would be used to make a rope that would guide her down the side of the castle through the privy hole.

One of the knights cleared his throat. "May I ask how you intend for us to make your escape, My Queen?"

She quickly noted his facial features and size. *With Jason dead, he might be of use one day.*

"Yes, well, this rope will lead me down as one or two of you hold the other end in the garderobe. I'll wrap the white blanket over me and blend in with the snow on the ground. Because it's dark, no one should notice me if they're far enough away. This should give a clear escape on the ice to safety before anyone is alerted to my departure. There, I'll wait for the Earl of Gloucester, and we'll follow the Thames to the nearest village."

"This is an unusual plan, m'lady. Normally there's earth below the privy shoots, and men come to clean away the refuse. Why did you choose the highest tower that escapes to freezing water?"

These men made her feel proud of her half-brother, Robert. He chose them well, and they asked meaningful questions. A smile almost made it to her lips before she spoke.

"I remembered that these garderobes were custom-made to directly allow refuse right into the moat. Their iron bars are crafted to come out unlike others. This is a fighting advantage as archers can easily hit targets entering the moat without fearing attack. It works in our favor now as the water is frozen and it will lead us to Wallingford Castle. We will take refuge there and seek aid. Otherwise, we would have to go straight through the enemy's camp and risk being caught."

"I see. That is wise, My Queen. I have one more question, if I may?" He ripped a piece of linen and tied it without looking into her eyes directly. Suspicion grew in the pit of her stomach. She glanced at Robert, who continued working with his hands, also avoiding her stare. She wasn't sure if the knight's avoidance was a sign of loyalty and respect for her as queen or an aversion to his next question.

"Proceed."

"What of us, m'lady? Shall we escape with you this night also?" His voice was like a dog's whimper.

I was wrong. He is useless, just like the others.

"You will await our return." Annoyance crept into her voice. "Once secured in a nearby town, we will send messengers to seek help from Scotland and will forthwith bring an army to rescue the others."

She didn't make eye contact as she spoke. She knew they would all be dead when she returned. No one could survive the number of days it would take to bring an army big enough back without food.

"Scotland?" the knight to his right asked, his voice squeaky.

"Aye. Scotland." Empress Amara's eyes rolled. She pivoted, stood to check the window, then knelt again. "It looks as if it's all clear. The watchmen must have left for the night. Snow is beginning to fall heavily. We should hurry before another comes to replace the guard."

Helping the men finish the rope, she listened as the wind howled through the window slits in the stone wall above them. Empress Amara studied Robert as he pried the bars out of the stone wall, anchoring each one, scraping the mineral away meticulously. Finally, there was a large enough exit to go through. She breathed a sigh of relief. The day was finally here, and she was about to get her revenge.

It was time to escape.

Empress Amara's eyebrows furrowed. Something was wrong, and she couldn't quite bring herself to celebrate in any sort of way. Something foreign was niggling its way through her. Was guilt gnawing in the pit of her stomach? She looked back at the four men willing, at all costs, to save her and her child, the future king or queen, without thought to themselves…

No, I can't think like a weak woman! Father would never allow it. She flinched, remembering his frequent beatings. Rolling her shoulders back, she dared to look each man in the eye. What would her last departing words be to them—to these few men that had stuck with her till the end? *Goodbye, hope the pain of starvation numbs death for all of you. Thank you for serving your empress to your last dying breath, forfeiting family, children, and life. You have made me proud and given the empire honor.*

Would that be enough to quench the guilt invading her emotions and stealing her happiness? The feeling was so intense she darted her eyes away from the men.

What was happening to her?

She turned to Robert but kept her eyes low. "Do not refuse them but let the men try to escape with us this eve. There may not be enough cloth to hide their whereabouts in the snow, as I need it for myself. Have them leave at half past the hour just in case they get caught and give away our escape. We'll at least have had a head start."

Something between shock and disbelief washed over Robert's face before he nodded and replied simply, "As you wish."

Her father would not be proud of her at that moment, but this time, she couldn't say no to the guilt quenching every ounce of her. It would not be silent. The guilt unveiled a gaping hole in her heart. Before she could dwell on it, the men stood gathering the white material into a coiled pile at their feet.

"Are you ready, m'lady?"

She looked out at the storm and didn't want to leave the room. She was finally feeling warm from all their bodies huddling around her. What if the water wasn't frozen solid, and she fell through? She would surely die from fever. Perhaps her baby too. But what if she didn't try and escape? Death was on all sides regardless. It was now or never.

"Cover me with the sheet," she demanded.

One knight positioned the material so she could still see, wrapping it around her head, neck, and shoulders as if she were royalty from India. There was enough space to see and breathe adequately. The rest draped over her like a blanket of snow covering the castle grounds. She was confident the disguise would be successful.

Patiently, she waited as another knight tied the end of the rope to her ankle. She looped a piece of the running fabric around her waist, giving it some slack, then spun the loose end around her right arm. She would be secure enough to be led down the castle wall like a bail to the bottom of the well.

All three knights lifted her to the hole's entrance while Robert held the rope. They slowly eased her down. She held her body as close as possible to the side of the castle. The thought of touching old refuse caked on the edges of the stone wall made her want to throw up. If she had any contents in her stomach to purge, that is.

A tight pull on the rope made her bite her lip in fear she would cry out. She wanted to glare at them and yell, but she had to keep quiet. A mix of jagged and weathered stones snagged the linen and dug into her flesh as she passed through the opening.

A snapping sound startled her as the rope strained in each knot as she was lowered further and further down. Once exposed, the frigid wind seeped into her bones. Icy flakes of snow clung to her thin body, and her teeth started to chatter. This was going to be a long journey to safety.

Finally, she was hanging in the air. She glanced up at the men above her. They smiled, which gave her instant satisfaction that perhaps the plan would have no hiccups. The rope twisted, and she spun slightly. Biting down hard on her lip, she kept her mind from spinning and feeling woozy along with it.

The rope pinched her hand, making it bleed, but she wasn't

concerned. She caught a view of the enemy's camp, and from her position, mid-way down the tower, they would clearly miss her escape.

She closed her eyes for a brief second. Hope beckoned to appear in her heart, and she allowed it. Cold, bitter air stung as her frail body hit the hard water. It was slushy on the top layer, but secure enough to stand on. She waited for any cracking noises of ice breaking beneath before unwinding her hand from the rope and releasing her ankle from the throbbing pain of bearing the brunt of her weight.

Glancing up one last time, she nodded to the men.

She was free at last.

Forty-Six

OWEN

PRINCE OWEN STIRRED IN HIS TENT. HE GOT UP AND stretched. "Brrr." His teeth chattered without warning. Perhaps it was the storm that woke him or the sheer cold that swept in overnight. He peeked out of his tent, and the chill quickly stole his breath.

"Go to sleep and leave me to rest in warmth," Stephan moaned as he rolled onto his side, obviously feeling the cold draft too.

"I can't sleep." Owen padded his way around the tent, lit a single lamp, and began putting layers of clothing on. The snow outside increased the light in the tent, but not by much. "I can't shake the feeling something's amiss. As if I've had a lapse of mind and have forgotten something important." He thought for a moment. "I hope Eira is all right."

"Go back to bed. Nothing is wrong. We haven't heard a word from the queen or her men. They'll all be dead soon." Stephan turned to look at Owen. "It's merely a waiting game now. But you'll surely be dead from fever if you go out in this cold air. In a few days from now, you'll be heading toward Princess Eira, and everything will fall into place. You'll see. Now, go back to bed and turn off that light!"

"I'm just going to do a quick check of the parameters. Then I'll be able to rest."

Stephan's head hit his pillow with a thud. "Do as you like. I am staying here."

"Of course." He picked up the last letter from Eira and stuffed it in his pocket. At least her written words would be close to him, warming his heart on such a bone-chilling night. Owen continued to layer clothing on and wrapped his winter cloak over his shoulders.

Another moan came from Stephan's side of the tent. "You've given me no choice but to go with you," he growled. "I wish you would've just gone back to bed." Stephan yawned and stood, shivering. "You know, you can be extremely stubborn at times. There must be an incredible reason we're waking in the dead of night to freeze to death, I'm sure of it!" The scowl Stephan gave Owen was playful.

"Thank you. Truly I can go alone. You don't need to attend. I'm a big boy, you know." Owen whipped his pillow at Stephan, laughing. Then, reaching for his lamp, he smiled. "Truth be told, I wouldn't mind the company."

"Be quiet, you fool, or you'll wake the others." The subtle smile in Stephan's response was evident. "Give me a moment, and I will meet you by the north end of camp. I'll be sure to alert one of the watchmen we're doing a parameter sweep. You should grab your sword and dagger—"

Owen sheathed his sword. "Already got it."

"Go grab some food for us. I don't know about you, but I'm getting hungry, and if you don't break my fast, who knows what I'll be capable of." Stephan pulled some of his clothing on and began getting dressed, layering on clothing as Owen did.

"See you at the north end." He smiled.

Owen untied the tent and flung the door panel back, stepping into the icy weather. The blustery wind burned his eyes. It didn't take long before they adjusted. Flurries of snowflakes painted the sky an eerie dull gray.

Continually scanning the entire camp, Owen walked past tents with snoring men. He tried to step quickly and not wake them as he moved forward. His feet crunched on the snow, and his leather boots absorbed the cold without hesitation. Why did it have to be this night, the coldest night of the battle, that he was unable to sleep?

Nothing appeared out of the ordinary as he made his way to the food storage. He couldn't negate the awful feeling that something was terribly wrong even if he wanted to.

Searching the gray skies for any stars biding him a good morning, his mind sparked back to him as a mere pilgrim seeking refuge at Brother Obadiah's cottage. So much had transpired since the day he found true peace. He hadn't found his sister yet, but through this journey, he found something more.

Real love.

Eira had to stay safe so he could return and—

Thoughts fell away. What if she didn't want him? What if she didn't feel the same way as he did? Eira's letter was near his chest, warming his heart. It brought comfort knowing she was with Brother Obadiah, becoming the woman of God she was meant to be. But what if this whole journey all ended there?

If she wouldn't be his one day, he felt proud to have served her— the future Queen of Whiteshire. At least his father would have gained an alliance like he always wanted between the two kingdoms.

Owen sacrificed finding his sister to serve Eira, which meant he would one day be king of Wealas. Though he had to be fair to himself, they had no idea what happened to his sister. Whether or not she ran away on her own and never wanted the kingdom for herself, or if she was taken against her will. That is why it was so unsettling in Owen's heart. And one day, he would try again to find his sister. But where his life had led him to search for her was to this moment. Should he have to be king, he would—and he would use that army and that privilege for good.

It was clear to him—more than ever before—that he would use his kingdom to serve others instead of himself. He saw firsthand the cruelties of selfish ambition in Queen Amara and didn't want to be that kind of ruler. He wanted to be brave and valiant, but humble and a servant to his people. Thinking of their needs before his own. Until then—

A man snored and turned in his sleep in a tent nearby, breaking Owen's revere.

He needed to focus on the task at hand. Find out what woke him up.

God, where are you leading me to?

I know you're wanting me to go somewhere, but where? Guide my feet, my eyes, and show me the path I need to take tonight.

Forty-Seven

EMPRESS AMARA

EMPRESS AMARA LURCHED FORWARD, STEPPING OVER HARD ICE toward freedom. Once near the tree line, she would wait and allow the other men to make their escape. Her eyes pinched together as a flood of emotion stung them.

Her father would have called her weak and useless. She should have only thought of herself and the bloodline for the kingdom's sake. That *was* all that mattered, wasn't it? She shook her head and blinked back tears.

Heaving heavily, her hand found the bump forming on her stomach. She had to make sure her baby was okay. The thought of becoming a mother put an icy chill in her veins. This was her flesh. She shivered. Would she be like her father?

Spinning back to when she was an innocent child, her father consumed Queen Amara's every move—said what she could do, who she could be, play with, talk with, marry. He controlled her every move, and she resented him for that. Now she was the one in control. She tried to smile and stand taller, but she was far too weak. Her legs shook from standing in the cold for too long.

What was taking them so long? Her eyes adjusted, and she could see Robert hit the ground and move toward her. Relief flooded her, but the bile scratched up her throat along with another disturbing thought. Eira was her unborn child's half-sister. Empress Amara thought about her brothers. She was never allowed to be close to them. Perhaps she could change that. Blaming the starvation for her recent delusions, Empress Amara refused to allow the thought to hold any merit. She paced. Waiting.

"What's taking you so long?" Her voice was scratchy.

"There was movement in the camp. We thought it could be a change of the watchmen. So, we had to wait." He shivered and rubbed his hands together, breathing into them.

"Stop that, you fool. They'll see the steam puffing out from your breath into the air!"

They both cocked their ears and turned to face a sudden sound.

Queen Amara leaned into Robert and whispered, "I'm not waiting any longer. I need to start moving before they're alerted to our escape."

Queen Amara walked along the thick, icy waterway. Its path led farther away from the living tomb she desperately wanted to leave behind. Robert was in her peripheral vision. "I'm glad to see they found you some white attire also."

"I am the only one to have a camouflage. But one of the knights made it down. He headed toward the trees to avert any trails away from the river."

"Good." At least she had to give them credit for that. They would most likely follow along through the forest's edge.

They walked in silence before Robert spun around and noted another knight had made it out of the privy hole. Queen Amara stayed focused on the path ahead.

"M'lady?" Robert's voice sounded reserved and almost childlike.

"What is it?" She slowed down and took a break.

He watched the castle and warmed his hands by rubbing the palms together and breathing into them.

"Are you okay? Do you feel well enough to take the journey? I mean…" He paused, rubbing his hands a little too roughly, and then continued. "I mean, if you need me to carry you—"

He let the question hang in the air like moisture from his breath, suspended in the cold. It was as if his kind gesture became icy crystals down her throat. She tried to swallow. Was it the cold that made her throat dry, or was it because she hadn't eaten anything and had walked miles in wintery elements? Or perhaps she was truly tired and so desperately wanted his help but was afraid to accept it.

She blinked back the emotions keeping her from speaking, refusing to give in.

"Yes, well…" She cleared her throat, finally able to swallow. "I shall manage."

"What of the child? Will it be all right?" He coughed and looked at the frozen water beneath them. His words, though merely a question, almost completely broke her. She attempted to conform the foul emotions into rage or hatred, just as she had done in the past, but they wouldn't change. Tears pooled instead, releasing over her frozen cheeks.

"Please. I can't bear to speak of it," she choked out.

Suddenly, a shout reached them from the castle.

"Run!" Robert grabbed her bony elbow and guided her across the ice. The looming image of her castle prison faded completely in the distance. The white snow concealed their escape.

Forty-Eight

OWEN

"Found one!" Prince Owen screamed at Stephan behind him.

"And where do you think you're going?" A scuffle broke out, and Owen had the man on the ground, pinned. The knight kept quiet. "Where did you escape from?" Owen's eyes interrogated the area where he saw the man running from but couldn't see anything obvious.

The knight spat in Owen's face.

"Fine. We'll get it out of you the hard way, then." He dug his elbow into the man's chest a little harder for that. Owen heaved him up and let Stephan bind the knight's arms and legs. Swiping to clean his face off, he grimaced. Realizing the commotion, men from the camp came to assist, bringing torches blazing through the night sky.

Once they arrived, Owen handed the bound knight over to them. "He was found on the west side of the castle. Make sure he talks. Do whatever it takes. We need to know if others have escaped with him, where they escaped from, and if the queen's still in the castle or gone."

Stephan added, "And if this one doesn't talk by mid-morning, penetrate the castle and kill the queen. We'll continue to search the area for any signs of others that may have fled."

Stephan paused and pointed at two of his knights. "You and you. Go get your horses and meet us by the forest. Bring mine and Prince Owen's horses with you. If we can't find anything, you will escort us in searching through the forest till daybreak."

Kneeling at the moat's edge, Owen spotted marks appearing almost from nothing. They went from the center of the waterway out to where he'd seen the man running toward the forest. It was hard to tell if some of the impressions were only from him or others. Perhaps deer or another animal? But it was fresh. That he was sure of.

"Such a mystery, don't you think?" Owen rubbed his chin, glancing at Stephan. He stood, his knees cracking into place. He rubbed his hands, wanting to also rub out the frosty air stealing his warmth, but it was futile.

"Sure is." Stephan pointed to the moat. "Looks safe enough. Should we investigate?"

"I don't see why not. We're already freezing to death out here." As if on cue, Owen's teeth chattered.

"What's a wee bit of frozen water going to do?" Stephan slowly walked onto the thick ice.

No cracking noises. All was good. Stephan drew closer to where the markings appeared.

"Well, I wouldn't say it was merely water. These moats are usually filled with—"

"Keep it to yourself. I don't want to think about it…" Owen tried staying alert. Who knew if more men escaped and were laid in wait.

"Suit yourself." Stephan chuckled. "You know, I'm beginning to wonder if someone came from the forest edge and stood here, hiding." He spun around. "There doesn't seem to be many other clues, and it's difficult to see in the darkening sky. Perhaps we should wait till morning light. Perchance the dawn should lead us better than the blind bats we are now."

Following the line of the bricks, Owen glanced up, examining each crevice of the castle's exterior wall. "What is that?" Owen scrunched up his face and squinted his eyes, pointing to the guard rope above him. "Does that appear normal?"

"It's hard to tell, but there does seem to be something amiss." Stephan swept his gaze at Owen. "Perhaps your gut was right all along. It appears the bars are missing from the privy seat above us. Someone must have lowered the knight down."

"We should have an extra man watching this area before we leave, in case any more try to escape," Owen muttered. His eyes were still maneuvering over the wall.

Stephan whistled at the men lingering about. Their glowing embers made their way to Stephan. "We will seize the castle and note those missing. Meanwhile, you and I will advance the forest and see if we can find anyone else." Stephan quickly left the moat and stood on solid ground. "Ah, much better. Are you coming?"

"If I were the queen, I would have been long gone by now." His eyes followed the moat to the river attached to it. No movement caught his eye. "But where?"

"It would be too risky to seek flight on partially frozen ground, Owen. A woman in her condition would not risk it. She would have left for the forest like the others," Stephan insisted, but something still wasn't sitting right in the pit of Owen's stomach.

"All right. I am right behind you."

Forty-Nine

EIRA

CROUCHING LOW BEHIND A WALL OF TREES, EIRA LEANED DOWN
and patted Obadiah's horse. Her hood wasn't rolled back for two
reasons. One, to keep the wind from hitting her face and regaining as
much heat as possible, and two, to conceal her face.

She was almost halfway to Winchester already and hadn't been
noticed by anyone that may recognize her or be on the lookout for her.
If the Men of Ore or Obadiah realized she had gone, they, too, would
scour every place in search of her.

She stayed vigilant.

Eira's face was near the horse's mane. She breathed in the distinct
smell of horsehair and sweat and peeked out from under her hood.
People were passing by. She waited until most had cleared until she felt
safe enough to stop for a well-needed break.

Eria's stomach grumbled. She had already eaten all the contents of the
food she had brought. Noticing a woman selling bread by a small
makeshift hut, she veered the horse near and slid down his flank. Holding
the reins, she stepped slowly and approached the woman, eyes down.

"Do you have any bread to sell?" She tried to make her voice sound older and less like her own.

"For ye, lass?" The old woman's eyes crinkled as she smiled. Her teeth were perfectly straight and white.

"Aye." Eira's breath hung in the air, suspended by the cold.

Turning to her side, the old woman reached into a linen bag and pulled out a large loaf of barley bread. Eira salivated.

"How much do I owe you?" Finding the small bag in her bubble-bow, Eira's hand wrangled out a small coin, unsure of how much it was. "Will this do?"

The woman's eyes popped out. "I haven't seen a chinker like that since—"

Eira looked down at the coin. Her mother's appearance was embossed on the coin. "Oh!" She fumbled to put it back and present another coin. "This one will surely do." Her voice wavered, and she suddenly felt nervous. Her papa must have given her one of their old coins in memory. His words fluttered through her mind. *"Remember, Eira..."*

The old woman kept staring at her. Examining her.

"Will this do? I must be on my way."

She held up the money. "You must be heading to Whiteshire." The woman's eyes hardened. "There is only death there. I wouldn't waste your time." The woman snatched the coin from her hand, shoved the barley loaf at her, and spun away from Eira as if she were stricken with a plague.

"Ah, thank you," she said to the back of the woman's head.

Lifting herself up onto her horse, she broke off a piece of bread and savored it. But the taste became sour when she saw the woman dart over to a group of men standing near a fire.

She kicked her horse into a steady pace. Fast enough to leave, but slow enough to not warrant suspicion. One thing was clear: she needed to get to the kingdom sooner rather than later and restore some peace with the people.

She could still feel the woman's cold shoulder as she ate her bread.

Fifty

EMPRESS AMARA

EMPRESS AMARA WAS GROWING TOO WEAK TO KEEP MOVING. They had to choose. They decided to enter the forest, deflecting the course off the waterway. It was a risky move because they could be easily seen in the forest compared to blending into the snowy embankments. But she had to take it, or risk dying on the waterway from sheer exhaustion.

Robert approached a monk toting a small child while she kept out of view. They exchanged some words, and soon they walked together to purchase wood from a local man. Binding the wood together, Robert threw the planks over his shoulder, and all three of them made their way to where she was hiding. She could finally hear them talking.

"Where is the deceased you would like me to recite the Word of God over?" the monk inquired.

"Just a bit closer. We're almost there." Robert dropped the wood with a loud clank as planks and narrow beams clapped against one another. Robert wisely discarded his white cloth earlier to blend into the mingling people, but it was difficult to camouflage his noble attire.

She almost gasped as he took off his hood. He looked even more gaunt and tired than she.

Empress Amara thought she had slipped out her astonishment, but it was the small boy's gasp that she heard.

The monk gripped the boy's hand and said, "We must be heading back now. I'm afraid I cannot fulfill your request, sir."

The monk gave him a knowing stare before he turned to leave, but Robert was no fool. He pulled out his dagger and quickly snatched the boy from the monk's hand. The blade pressed against the small boy's neck.

"Leave, and the child dies," Robert growled. "I swear!" His eyes were frantic. "One small move and he will meet God."

"We do not fear death. Nevertheless, you have my word. I shall not leave. Prithee, take the sword away from the child, and I will help you."

The monk stood motionless as he spoke. As if he feared no man. She noted how the boy didn't cry as Robert lowered the tip of the blade away from him.

"Good." Robert sheathed his dagger while still holding on tight to the boy's wrist. With his other hand and his teeth, Robert began tearing off long strips of white cloth from his discarded garments. Once satisfied with the amount, he yanked the boy's arm, bringing the child over to the monk. "You two, grab those long wooden planks. First, we will build something to carry the dead on."

Robert lifted one of the longer wooden planks and laid it on the ground. The thud was a muted sound that she felt, even on the frozen ground. She couldn't help but appreciate all that Robert was doing to protect her. But his noble station was noticeable. Even the monk knew. She saw the look in his eyes when he had stared at Robert.

What if others discovered who he was and caused a stir? Queen Amara couldn't think like that. She had to keep her mind on escaping and getting her army back together to defeat the princess.

"There," Robert continued. "We shall wrap the corpse as I command, and then you will march with me in short progression until we are out of Winchester. Is my direction clear? Or shall I persuade you further?"

Empress Amara understood the subtle threat and wondered if the monk did as well.

"Crystal clear, m'lord."

For a mere second, they shared a hard glare. Robert broke eye contact first. Their hands continued to build Empress Amara's momentary bed of death. Obvious to her, the monk knew who Robert was and was willing—for the safety of the child, no less—to keep it a secret. But for how long would the real question be?

At last, the wooden pieces were tied together tightly using the ripped sheets of fabric. The form of a pauper coffin was finally in place. All three of them stood. Robert grabbed the boy again.

"For collateral, he comes with me to get the dead." Robert jerked the boy, and he winced.

"Understood." The monk placed his hands gently in front of him, his face calm like the eye of a storm, ready to rage at any given moment.

In a strange way, the monk brought Empress Amara comfort, yet she feared him. Something about him was unsettling. She never feared any man. Perhaps the fear was respect. Regardless, she couldn't dwell on that, as Robert was walking toward her. She emerged from her hiding and started to approach them.

"Good day." Empress Amara unwrapped her face.

The boy started to scream. Robert's hand clapped over his small mouth.

"Quiet, boy!" he snorted.

The monk took a few steps towards them and reassured the lad she was not a ghost. He instead placed a hand on the boy's shoulder and dipped his head in a gesture of reverence. The monk knew who she was before Empress Amara tugged the final piece of white cloth away from her face.

"My dear child, you are standing before royalty. This is Queen Amara," he said, squeezing the boy's shoulder.

Hearing the boy's sharp squeal didn't register any alarm. Yet, the sound of the monk's gentle tone soothed her. Almost as if a father's tender voice to his child. Not her *own* father. He would never speak to her with such love, such kindness. *No.* It was the voice of a father she longed for all her life. Her eyes met the monks, and something tugged in her heart. A burning sensation flooded her eyes.

"Thank you." She could barely speak. "For your respect." It was as if she didn't even know who she was anymore. Her eyes caught Robert's. A strange and uneasy feeling came over her as Robert's face was aghast. He looked at her as if she were foreign. An unearthly being. And perhaps she was. Perhaps she even looked like a beast. Her skin was blackening. She was thin and gaunt. It was any wonder the monk recognized her at all. She couldn't even recognize herself these last few days.

"Please. Would you help us? I need to appear as if I were dead." She quickly wiped at her tears forming.

The boy cried out in earnest. "NO! You can't. Brother—"

But the gentle index finger of the monk pressed into his shoulder slightly and silenced the wee lad. "We are called to do as God wishes. This is a great lesson for you, my boy. We are to love and to show compassion, are we not?"

The monk's eyes found Empress Amara's and made an awful mess of her gut. This time, she couldn't hold back her tears. As he spoke to the child, his eyes never left Empress Amara's. "If our enemy asks us for water to drink, we shall give it." The monk turned to Robert. "There is no need to pay for our services today. We shall gladly give it without complaint."

Seeing the boy shaking his head in silent tears somehow moved her. She questioned what her little child would look like one day ... that is, if it survived. It felt as lifeless as she had been the past few days. Perhaps it was being with child that was changing her? Perhaps it was starving in the castle? Perhaps it was the constant fighting?

A sudden urgency came over her, and she turned to Robert. "Bind me and place me in the makeshift coffin. Hurry."

"Wait," the monk said. "May I approach you?"

She hesitated and nodded. "You may."

Out of the corner of her eye, she watched Robert place his hand near his dagger. The monk pulled out something wrapped in burlap from the sack at his waist. Her mouth watered, and her eyes stared at the beeswaxed parchment. Greedily, she licked her lips.

"You must eat something. Here." He gently placed the wrapped food in her hands. "Eat."

She glanced at Robert and pulled back the paper, unearthing the smell of freshly baked bread, making her mouth water. A small loaf of bread and five pieces of cheese were revealed. Pulling further, two long bits of dried meat were revealed. She glanced again toward Robert and handed him the meat. Their eyes met, and it filled her with gratefulness.

Empress Amara broke the bread in half, handing Robert a piece and a larger portion of cheese. He would be carrying her body all the way through town and would need more strength than her. Before she was about to take a bite, the monk interrupted.

"Now, may I offer a blessing over your food and a prayer to God for your safety?"

The only words that fully registered in her mind were *a prayer to God.*

God?

She hadn't thought about Him in so long. Completely cut the idea of God out of her life. Wasn't He manipulative, cruel, and controlling like her father? Didn't He always point out her flaws, waiting to pounce on any mistake she made, like when she was an adolescent?

As Empress Amara stared at the tall, gentle man before her, glancing at the food that her bony hands held, she realized her version of what God might have been may have been false. The version the monk portrayed and acted on behalf of were two different things.

She was forced to give credit to the person, or being, or whatever God was, whom this monk served. He was giving her food and being kind despite knowing who she was, her wicked deeds, and what she had become. A monster.

A bit of awe struck her mind.

Should she also obey Him? He reigned over the heavens and the earth. After all, she was trying to reign over His earth. But what if He didn't want her to? Out of all the monks that could have been walking by at her time of need, this one showed up. Was it just a coincidence? Or did his God send him for her?

So many conflicting thoughts piled onto each other, one after another, wrestling with her instincts, logic, and black, tainted heart. Who was she becoming? She could easily dismiss his request and sink her teeth into the bread tantalizing all her senses in one mouthful. Selfishly indulging in the moment like she always had. But she wasn't.

What was holding her back? What suddenly changed inside of her that she would even contemplate things she abhorred before? Perhaps she was just too hungry to think?

Before a clear answer came to her, she responded with a curt, "Proceed."

Fifty-One

EIRA

Eira White was beginning to grow tired. The road was widening the closer she got to Whiteshire Castle. Servants, paupers, bakers, and merchants alike started to litter the streets since the break of dawn. They brought their goods in the hope of making a sale or trade at the daily Market.

Another half day's journey, and she would be at Whiteshire Castle. She imagined what it would be like to see Prince Owen again. During their time apart, she had grown stronger as a woman and closer to God.

Would he see that in her now? Would he find her favorable, worthy of a queen? Some men preferred a woman humbler and meeker in character. Would he be the type of man to find her new courage a challenge to his own masculinity? Eira hoped he'd love her for who she was, and as they grew, who she became. That was, of course, *if* they were to continue their lives together.

When he found out the reason for her visit to the castle, he may not be so happy to see her or to honor her decision. But he didn't have a choice in the matter. It was something she had to do alone.

Seeing a patch of open grass, she dismounted. Only time would tell how he'd react. For now, she needed a break from riding. She stretched her legs and rubbed the sores out of her back while letting Obadiah's horse graze the frozen grass. She made herself comfortable on an old log. Looking around, she realized this was the spot where she had stopped with her huntsman, Mason.

A smile crept along her lips. She was grateful for that day in more ways than one. He led her to safety ... to friends—the Men of Ore's, and finally to Prince Owen. She let out a little laugh and, out of her pocket, took some raisins to nibble on. She popped a few in her mouth and chewed, enjoying the sweet and tart flavors. Brother Obadiah's horse came over to her and huffed his nostrils. He nudged her with his nose, sniffing at her raisins.

"Oh, so you want some of these, do you?" She patted the velvety skin and kissed the top of his head. "Here."

She let him eat the rest of the raisins. His soft, padded lips tickled the palm of her hand as he picked each dainty one up. *What a sweet horse.* Seemingly naïve to the world and the dangers around it, just like she was not that long ago.

The horse's ears perked up, but she continued to muse about the day she met Mason. He turned out to be an honorable man, and she was thrilled with the news of his marriage. Obadiah's horse lifted its head, looking back behind itself. Her eyes followed him.

"What is it, boy? Are you ready to go already?" Picking up a small, dainty twig, she started to chew the end of it. "Now that I have no more treats, you're going to ignore me." She giggled. "So be it. Relax and eat some more grass. You'll need your energy to make Whiteshire by evening."

Once moistened and frayed, she polished her teeth with the end of the stick. Finishing, she threw the stick into the bush and heard a cracking sound in the opposite direction. It had a ring to it as it rippled low through the tree trunks. She noticed it was the direction the horse had stared at earlier. She stood, and the horse's ears twitched.

"What is it, boy?"

Quickly, she mounted her horse. An eerie feeling made the hair on her arms rapt with attention. People walked through these forests all the time. She figured it was normal to hear sticks snapping, people conversing, and feet padding the earth, but something felt wrong.

Eira maneuvered herself to a thick of trees nearby while still being able to view the pathway unseen. Listening, she could hear birds chatter and squirrels darting and chirping to one another across the forest floor. Finally, she caught what Obadiah's horse had been hearing all along. A subtle Gregorian chant slowly weaved its way through the forest into her ears. The song was familiar to her. Floating with each long note, heavy steps compressed snow and dirt as the sound of marching inched toward her.

"Someone's coming." The face of Obadiah's horse swung back at her, and he blinked his beautiful lashes as if to say *yes*.

"It shouldn't be of too much concern. Eat your grass so we can leave quickly." She patted his broad side, brushing him with her hands as if to reassure him. Or her. She wasn't sure. Perhaps she was being paranoid. It was the place that would have marked where her bones lay had Mason followed through with the queen's order. Most likely her heart would've been carried off to Whiteshire, assuming that's where she would have wanted her heart to live on forever. Little did anyone know it wasn't.

She would've wanted her heart to be buried where she met Prince Owen. Or perhaps at the home of the Men of Ore's, among her friends.

The sound was getting closer. Her eyes skimmed the snow-covered ground with blades of grass standing upright throughout the area. She would have been buried under the cold, hard ground, completely forgotten.

Lifting her eyes up through the branches, she breathed in the fresh air. She was thankful God had other plans for her. Born for a purpose, she would remember what her mother had told her. She held fast to the snow-covered branches.

She was to be as white … as snow.

She pulled her hood over her head and rolled back the edges to see from her peripheral vision. The chanting grew louder and louder. The crushing of leaves and twigs beneath people's feet became clear. They were almost all nearby.

"Don't worry," she whispered to convince the horse. "It's probably just some men on their way to Winchester Cathedral. I saw it close to us on the map."

She pushed away the nagging thought that people wouldn't be coming in the direction of Whiteshire since they had surrounded the castle and were allowing them to die of starvation. Her heart was broken thinking about people starving. Whoever was trudging through the forest from Whiteshire may also be hungry.

She instantly wished she had saved her barley loaf. But then a nasty thought came just as quickly. Perhaps these people were part of the anarchy. Ruthless and full of thievery. Her body tensed. Like the men who chased her into the forest when she escaped the castle.

The chanting swelled, swaying to the branches above her and easing her mind a little. One of them surely was peaceable to sing such melodies as they neared her. Even still, she would stay guarded.

She grabbed the horse's reins and wanted to mount the horse. To leave immediately, but she would have to pass them regardless. It made no sense to draw attention to herself. Here, she could stay tucked in the cove and avoid them. She shifted her eyes to Obadiah's horse standing at attention, rapt with anticipation. He could tell something was not right, couldn't he?

She ducked her head and rolled the sides of her hood down to cover her face as much as possible. Whether these people were safe or not, she would soon find out.

Fifty-Two

MUCH LIKE THE HORSE BESIDE HER, EIRA WAS ALERT. FINALLY, she could see the distinct brown robe of a monk and his hooded head coming through the bush. He swayed back and forth with each step, like a moving tree trunk through the forest. Her eyes were strained. She couldn't say for certain, but it appeared he was with another man, perhaps shorter than he.

Eira drew closer to the horse, almost hiding behind him. Her face was still in the shadows of the thick hood. Though it didn't allow her to see a whole lot, it helped keep her identity a secret. With the clothing she wore of late, no one would be the wiser that a princess was parading through the forest unaccompanied. Not that anyone would truly know she was a princess. No one knew who she was besides Stephan, Prince Owen, the Men of Ore, and a few people from Whiteshire Castle—if they were still alive—and, of course, the queen.

Patting Brother Obadiah's horse, she pulled her spine up and straightened. She grabbed the reins tighter and went to mount the horse. Swinging up on the horse, he shimmied to one side preventing her from getting on.

"Whoa…" She ended up sliding off the horse. "What's the matter, boy?"

Acutely aware of the forest suddenly, she noticed it became silent around her. Had the people not passed already? Standing still, she realized the singing had completely halted.

"Who goes there?" a heavy voice barked from the bush to her right.

Clearing her throat, she tried to disguise it like she had to the old woman. "A fellow traveler. You've room to pass. Proceed."

She could hear some whispering, and finally, a response echoed. "We thank thee."

Footsteps crushed the snowy floor. Brown material whooshed around the last bush. Perhaps all monks looked familiar? She couldn't help but compare the likeness of this man to Brother Obadiah. They were the same height. They had the same crescent-shaped hair that didn't quite round at the nape of their necks. It was too peculiar for her liking.

He kept staring at the floor below him, which made Eira uneasy. He was acting more like a slave than a monk. Perhaps the man wasn't Brother Obadiah like she could've sworn he was. He wouldn't be hanging his head so low. He would be standing erect. Noble, even.

Behind him, she noticed he was carrying a long coffin-like box. Most likely a corpse was in there. She shivered. That must be why they were coming from Whiteshire. Perhaps this man was merely sad at whoever died and couldn't bear to lift his head. Visions of starving people invaded her mind. She needed to leave and do something before more died.

The idea of death brought her thoughts back to her papa. How she wished she could have been there when he left for eternity. She would've wanted to follow his funeral progression and mourn for him like any great king. Anger for the queen and all she took from her rose within her.

No. She couldn't let bitterness blacken her heart. Not now, not ever. She made a promise.

Following the line of the casket, another man came into view carrying the rear. He was in black; his body was strong like a knight. Shielded by his hood, his face was focused on the ground also.

Nobody made eye contact with her.

Typically, there'd be mourners proceeding with a funeral. Not a singing monk. Her brows furrowed. Scrutinizing the casket, her eye caught the top of a boy's hood bobbing along the side of it. Perhaps the deceased was a mere pauper who couldn't afford to have a proper burial. Regardless, she found it strange that the boy was dressed like a monk too.

Luca came to mind. If something were to happen to her, who would take care of the boy? He would be sad to know she had left without saying goodbye. Any decision she made would likely hurt someone, but it pained her deeply to think her actions could hurt Luca in any way.

Focusing on the lad with these men reminded her of Luca so much her heart almost burst. Perhaps it was the bobbing motion that resembled him so much. She studied the boy. It was hard to tell on the opposite side of the casket whether this boy, too, had a slight limp in his gait. But the resemblance was uncanny.

She scorned herself for missing Brother Obadiah and Luca so much that she'd seen them in these strangers. She wanted to laugh at herself. Surely it couldn't be. They were at home, probably wondering where she had gone. Guilt festered like a wound in her, but she couldn't dwell on it because her horse let out a snort and walked forward as if to follow them.

"No," she whispered, clenching her reins tight.

As she did, the boy peeked over the makeshift casket, and their eyes met. Ice ran through her as her feet practically froze to the snow beneath her.

"Luca," she whispered. Her mouth slacked, drooping and agape. Was she seeing a ghost?

A flash of fear swept over his curious gaze, and instantly his eyes widened. He quickly averted her stare and snapped his head forward.

"Wait," she yelled. "Stop."

The monk leading the front slowly turned to look at her.

"Brother Obadiah. Is that you?" Her head spun. Was she seeing things?

The monk didn't respond. But the look of guilt and fear crossing over his face spoke for him.

"What are you doing here?" *What was he so afraid of?*

Silence settled around them like the quiet snow falling from the sky.

It was so silent.

Why wouldn't he answer her? Wasn't he going to the scriptorium? Had he lied to her? Suddenly, the man at the rear took two large sweeping steps toward her and snatched her up like a mouse caught in a trap. She screamed, and the horse reared up, his hooves coming down on the man's shoulder, releasing his grip on Eira. She ran toward Brother Obadiah. Confusion sucked the strength out of her bones as Obadiah pushed her shoulders away from him.

"Run!" he whispered, eyes wild. "As far as you can away from here."

"Nay."

Eira's eyes searched for answers in each of his irises as if she had heard him wrong. Disappointment outlined his eyes. Was he upset she left without his approval? Probably. Her gut twisted. She would never make the mistake of leaving him again.

"Nay!" she repeated.

Her eyes turned back and pinned to the man, now groaning on the ground before Brother Obadiah's horse. Why had the man tried to snatch Eira like that? When he looked up at her, she immediately knew.

Robert of Gloucester. The queen's ally. How could she be so blind? What was Brother Obadiah doing with him? Why was he leaving Whiteshire?

Her eyes rounded, and the air was stolen from her breath. *He's escaping.*

Was Brother Obadiah a prisoner? Whipping her head to him, she saw the rope bound around his wrists. She looked at Luca. His eyes were full of tears. Pulling out a small dagger, she stood as tall as she could and faced the man. Robert got up after moaning on the ground.

"You?" He laughed. "And here I thought you a peasant. Never in my wildest dreams"—he stood to his full height, looming over Eira—"did I imagine I would be able to kill Princess *Eira White* with my own hands."

A rustling came from where the dead body lay, and it took everything in Eira not to look, keeping her opposition directly in plain view. He was quick, and he was large enough to snuff her out like a small wick. She prayed for strength—God's strength. She wanted to face the queen, but she would fight here if it meant protecting Brother Obadiah and Luca.

Robert's face was pure mockery, but she didn't let it bother her. He laughed again. "I think this whole thing is providence, you see—"

She pivoted as he took a step toward the casket. "I'm warning you. Don't take another step!"

"Or what?" he jeered. "You'll kill me? You? Who's never hurt even a butterfly?" He stalked toward her and her body shook. With everything in her, she jutted out her chin in defiance. He continued to taunt her. "You couldn't hurt a grown man who's killed men with his bare hands. You won't hurt me even if you wanted to—"

"No. But I will fight with everything I have!" Eira gripped her knife and lunged forward.

The man jumped back and started laughing. "You think you are strong and brave, do you? We'll see about that!"

Robert came running at full speed. Gasping, Eira twirled out of his blade's path, tripping. Her legs—having awkwardly flung out from under her in the fall—must have protruded enough to make Robert tumble. Or perhaps it was his momentum from running that caused it. Eira wasn't quite sure, and it happened so quickly. Robert went barreling onto the ground.

"You think you can make a fool out of me?" A growl came out of the man before he attempted to get up. Eira scurried away, fear gripping her.

A voice came from the trail behind them. "No, but I will!"

She could recognize that voice anywhere. It was Prince Owen. A renewed strength held her bones from quaking. Stephan came from behind Owen. He rushed over and tied Robert while he was still on the ground with ropes. Eira moved like lightning and cut away the ropes holding Luca's hands together. She kissed them.

"There, there. I'm sorry this has frightened you."

"I'm scared," Luca cried.

"I am too. Hushhh now. We are safe." Eira hugged him tightly.

A noise startled her, and she let go of Luca. It came from the casket. Before she could react, the lid of the casket fell to the ground, and an arm wrapped around Eira's neck. She felt the tip of a knife at her throat. The smell of death strangled Eira's nostrils so much so she found it hard to breathe.

Brother Obadiah fell to his knees in prayer. Owen's arrow was pulled back and pointing at Eira—or the person holding her. But it certainly felt like it was aimed at her. She had been through this before, and God had favored her before. She prayed He would again.

Stephan's sword was now unsheathed from his leather belt. What was going on? Who was in the casket holding her? She still had her dagger in her hand. But what could she do? The person was angled above her. Had she been held from behind, she could position the blade toward her back and stab their gut.

She was held like a noose with nowhere to turn. Her eyes found Owen's. She pleaded with him. *Shoot. Shoot the person holding her.* But he wouldn't. Eira's head was too close to the person holding her captive. It was a dangerous shot to make. Even she knew that.

"I've been waiting so long for this moment."

The breath of death spoke in a whisper near her ear. Such a foul odor emanated from the woman. The words spilled from her lips like black tar, and Eira realized who held her—Queen Amara.

Eira smiled. This was exactly what she wanted. Where she was meant to be. God had brought the battle to her. Finally, she could do what she planned and lay her life down for the ones she loved. She smiled at Prince Owen and released her dagger, letting it fall to the ground. Eira's fingertips reached up and gently wrapped her fingers around the thin arm. The arm tightened around her neck in response to her touch. But Eira could feel her tremble. The queen was weak and feeble. Most likely Eira could have overpowered her if she attempted it. Compassion moved something in her heart.

Eira had set out to give the queen what she wanted—herself. In a small way, she wondered if she would literally have to fight for her life with her stepmother and pondered what would happen upon meeting her again. She knew by giving what the queen wanted, it would end the war. But perhaps it was more than that. Perhaps Eira wanted her stepmother to know that she cared for her, despite her hating Eira. Even now, she loved her in some small way still.

Just like Jesus had surrendered himself to death, setting everyone He loved free, Eira was finally ready to make that same sacrifice. If her death meant that her people would be free from war, her stepmother would be free from starvation, and her kingdom free from anarchy, she would do it.

"I'm not going to fight you, Queen Amara," Eira spoke softly.

The woman jerked her neck back, and Eira winced.

"Shut up!" the queen growled.

Eira saw Prince Owen take a step forward. The thin snake of an arm around her neck responded and squeezed tighter, making it difficult to breathe.

"Don't you dare take another step, or she's dead," Queen Amara screeched.

"I won't fight you, Queen Amara. You have my life in your hands. I give you my permission to take it. Do what you must."

A somber silence fell around them like snow.

"What are you saying?" The queen's voice rose to an unbearable octave. "Are you surrendering yourself to me?"

She sounded betrayed, as if the question hurt her.

"Aye. That is what I am saying. Do to me as you wish for the sake of my people. For the sake of their suffering and to bring unity, I'll allow it." Eira swallowed down the intensifying pain in her throat. "I can't bear it any longer. I was coming to Whiteshire to surrender." She fixated on Robert, bound on the ground to her right. "This is providence. I am at your will, My Queen."

Prince Owen's arrow dropped, revealing his full face plainly. He was so handsome, but his face was smashed with confusion. Or perhaps remorse? She had hoped it was respect, but it didn't matter. This would probably be the last time she saw him. Though a pain at the way she left him started to worm its way through her stomach, she had to do what she was called to.

Aching cries filled the air. This time, her heart broke, and her strength wavered for a moment. Luca's cry filled her with regret. She didn't want to leave him; he was like a son to her. But what choice did she have? She was resolved in her purpose. She hoped he would come to the realization too.

Eira braced for the pain of death once again. Eira smiled as she felt the tip of the knife dig deeper into her flesh. Her destiny was being etched into the stars. A calm engulfed her. She knew she would be all right somehow. Whether in this life or the next.

A single snowflake landed on her nose, and she smiled, allowing it to fill her face. The blade started to pierce her skin.

I remembered, Papa. I remembered what Mother told me. I was made for this moment; to be white as snow, to overcome the evil of this world with the good that is within me—that is my strength.

No one could take away the strength and the beauty that was within Eira. All she ever wanted was love from her mother and father. But she was loved. Loved by her friends and, most of all, loved by God.

Jesus truly did make her heart white like snow, and more precious than any stone or kingdom could be worth. She had no anger, no bitterness, only love in that moment for her enemy. Like Jesus, her blood would spill, and she hoped her mother and papa would greet her in heaven, ready to wrap her up in a warm embrace.

Breathing out, she closed her eyes.

"Go ahead, My Queen. Kill me. I forgive you."

Fifty-Three

EMPRESS AMARA

QUEEN AMARA DUG THE TIP OF THE KNIFE INTO EIRA'S THROAT.

This was it. This is what she was waiting for.

So why did it feel so wrong?

Eira was just handing herself over. There was no malice. No hatred. Empress Amara didn't understand. Her father would be so proud of her becoming the victor. But the cries of the boy and the act of selflessness from Eira were creating such turmoil within her soul, it was unbearable. Why was she being so weak?

The thought of her own child growing in her womb weighed her down even further. Would her son love her like this boy obviously loved Eira? She hadn't been a good queen mother to Eira. Empress Amara's hand trembled.

She was about to kill the only child she ever had. She pushed away those thoughts and gritted her teeth, trying to plunge the dagger into Eira's flesh. But her hand stopped. What was wrong with her? This was what she wanted, wasn't it?

The child's cries haunted her like her past. Like when she was a child. She would cry, screaming for her mother while her father beat her until she was black and blue.

"Tell him to stop crying!" Empress Amara cried, starting to sweat.

Empress Amara gripped the dagger tighter. Grinding her teeth, she went to push the dagger in once more. But the wails pierced the forest, and the boy ran toward them, falling to Eira's feet, embracing her legs, and throwing Empress Amara off balance.

"Please don't kill my Eira. Don't kill my momma!" She watched as Owen went to console the boy.

"Tell the boy to stop," she stuttered.

Tears dropped onto her arm. They were Eira's. Why, when she had her enemy in her hands, couldn't she follow through with killing her? Empress Amara was her father, wasn't she? Isn't that what he wanted? He would be so proud of her. But was that what she wanted?

Pinching her eyes shut, Empress Amara pushed Eira out of her hands.

Empress Amara was not like him.

She never wanted to be him!

Teetering back into the casket, she looked at her hands. Blood was on the point of the blade in her hand. Following the line of the handle, she took in the awful sight of her arms. She was no longer beautiful, but somehow it didn't eat away at her as it had done in the past. Her tears matched the boys, and she curled into a ball on the frozen wooden planks.

She heard the shuffle of snow near where she lay. But she didn't care. Let them kill her. She was practically dead already. But instead of an arrow piercing her heart, it was Eira's voice.

"No! Don't. Can't you see her hurting… Leave her to the Lord."

It was only then that Empress Amara felt the warmth of Eira's body covering hers. Protecting her from the revenge of death from the hand of Stephan's men. Owen yelled at the men to, 'stand down.'

Eira saved her.

Empress Amara's eyes burned even more when she opened them, barely able to see the girl covering her. "Why would you do such a thing? I deserve to die."

"We all do. But you're all the family I have left. I don't wish you to die."

The kindness Eira gave to her obliterated something in Amara's heart once and for all. A part of her did die. It was the words of her father—her past. And she was finally glad it died.

"Thank you." She held onto Eira and hugged her for the very first time. She pulled back and looked at Eira's, almost with new eyes. "I see why you're the fairest. Your beauty is not only on the outside, as I thought it was. But it is within."

Eira smiled and touched Queen Amara's face. The warmth sent foreign feelings to her heart. "Thank you, Queen Mother."

The monk came to her. He picked up Luca, who was still crying, and brought him over to Prince Owen, exchanging words with him. Making his way back to them, he looked Empress Amara in the eye and reached out his hand toward her. "M'lady?"

Grabbing it, he helped her out of her deathbed.

Robert indignantly piped up. "So, who shall be queen, then?"

Empress Amara's hand slipped to her belly, and she opened her mouth. "Eira White of Whiteshire will be queen, and her sibling to follow."

Eira leaned over and kissed the queen's hands. Dipping low, she bowed slightly before meeting her eyes. Eira stood, and Empress Amara felt like the young woman truly was becoming the woman she was called to be.

Eira smiled with a glint in her eye. "I am honored to be named queen." She looked over at Owen. "But my heart is leading me somewhere else. I am not called to be Queen of Whiteshire." She paused and looked at the crowd. "I name Stephan of Blois as king. Only if he swears the child in the womb of Queen Mother will rule after him. I abdicate the thrown and hand it over to my cousin." Turning to Stephan, she bowed and then rose again. "What say you?"

A shock resounded as destiny laid its course, and Empress Amara's respect for Eira grew from nothing to something.

Stephan accepted the offer.

Eira's voice rose. "Long live the king."

Everyone repeated her, even Amara. Prince Owen ran to Eira and embraced her, pulling her slightly away from the queen.

Amara still didn't understand why Eira didn't let them kill her. As if sensing her question, Eira turned to her, her tears falling to the ground and melting into the snow.

"I've learned that God is more than the scripts alone. He loved me so much that while I was His enemy, He died for me... Truly knowing that made my heart go from darkness to light. I didn't deserve it, but He did it anyway."

"I see." A tiny crevice of a smile escaped the sides of her lips. Amara looked down, avoiding Eira's eyes. Eyes she had once violently hated.

Stephan announced his intent on making his heir apparent official in the court and with the council that week. He also assured Queen Amara that she was safe to return with them, leaving her his own horse and provisions. "I would very much like to go to Normandy and live in the castle my husband fought for, there."

With a curt nod of acceptance, Stephan and his men turned to leave.

As Amara watched Eira depart cleaving onto Prince Owen and the small child, Whiteshire's new king Stephan leading the way, and their prisoner Robert, who would be placed in prison by Stephan once they got back to the castle, she whispered to Brother Obadiah, who was still standing near her. "I would like to know God as Eira knows Him. Will you show me?"

A smile spread on his lips. "That would be my pleasure, m'lady."

Epilogue

"WHAT IS IT, LUCAS?" A PARCHMENT NOTE SLIPPED INTO THE palm of Eira's hand, sealed with the queen mother's signet. "Oh! Thank you."

Eira hesitated. It had been a few months now but their relationship, though growing, was not always great since Eira abdicated the throne. However, it was on the mend, and that alone was worth hearing from her. Slowly, Eira broke the seal and began to read.

Dearest beloved daughter,

I am doing well here at the monastery. Brother Obadiah has been so kind to me. Though I'm saddened I cannot come in person to your wedding due to the baby nearing its time, I know you're in good hands. My spirit is there with you also, and I pray your future is wonderful with Prince Owen.

I've asked for special arrangements with regard to your

escort to his home and have already begun plans to visit you in Waelas after the wee babe is born. I will use that time to do work for the glory of God as well. But I look forward to our time together as if it were already here.

You mean more to me than you know. You're truly radiant and have touched many lives with the love of Christ. Mine included. I know you've forgiven me for what I've done, which I will never deserve. And I know we will continue to build trust and love as best as we can. The purest of love has me captive now, and there's nothing I can do to be set free from it. I am forever indebted to you.

Love,
Your Queen Mother

A flood of tears stole her heartbeat before she whisked them away and smiled down at Lucas. "Thank you, my sweet boy. Now go get your sash on!" She swatted at him with the letter. "You'll be late."

"You look radiant, My King!" Stephan came to her and dipped in a slight bow.

"And you look like the beauty of the sun," Stephan said while giving the nook of his arm to her. "Are you ready?"

She lifted her chin. "I am."

In her papa's place, Stephan had agreed to walk her down the aisle. He guided her down the great hall while the pipes, harps, dulcimers, and trumpets engulfed the place with the beauty of sound. She walked slowly, one step in front of the other. Her eyelet dress cascaded down behind her. Eyes met her with eagerness and excitement.

Though the kingdom was still in unrest, with small wars breaking out in town and people were divided on who should rule had continued, the wedding had the community coming together in merriment, joy and unity. Even if it was just for a moment, Eira would take pleasure in that.

Spotting the Men of Ore, Eira's soul lifted. She tucked her arm into Mason's, and he smiled down at her, patting her arm with his hand. As promised, Stephan knighted Mason, and he was given permission to walk her down the aisle in full regalia with Stephan. One on each arm. Seeing Brother Obadiah in front of her made butterflies soar in her stomach. She was almost there.

Prince Owen stood next to Brother Obadiah's left, dressed in all white, waiting for her. Luca was by Owen's side in an identical suit. It was his day, too; they were adopting Luca as their own, and her heart was bursting with gladness at seeing both her handsome men waiting for her.

She no longer feared death or being unloved.

She was deeply loved and alive. She blinked back tears.

Stephan leaned over and kissed her cheek as they approached Prince Owen. She slipped her hand out from the crook of his elbow and then Mason's before standing beside the prince. As Eira grabbed hold of Prince Owen's hands, peace settled in her heart.

Her thoughts soared back to when she was a child with her papa. Her dreams of Prince Charming came to life right before her very eyes. The fairytale had a perfect ending after all.

His emerald eyes held hers with such endearment. He stepped closer to her, and she could feel his warmth. His left arm went around her waist. He tucked her in close to his chest, and she could smell his savory scent of lavender and leather.

She didn't care who was watching as she lifted her chin up to his. Owen's hand caressed her cheek before she could feel his breath on her lips. She closed her eyes. Sparks ignited as they tenderly kissed her for the first time, sealing their marriage and unity as one.

She wanted to fall into his arms and stay in the moment forever. It was as if all the darkness she had ever felt melted away. Like a bird freed from its cage, her heart took flight. She was no longer hunted. No longer bound to the crown. Finally, she was happy and free to do as she pleased.

She didn't want to come down from the euphoria she was soaring on, but when their kiss ended and he pulled away, she remembered there was something still left unfinished. As they were saying their goodbyes and getting their horses ready for their long journey, she tapped Owen's shoulder. Plucking one single red rose from the bunch in her hands, she said, "I need to do one last thing before we leave for Wealas."

Picking up her dress, Eira ran to where Papa was buried. She knelt in the dirt and pressed her hand against the tombstone marking his resting place. "I wish you were here, Papa."

Tears sprang to her eyes once again. She blinked them away, and her finger traced the words outlining his name. His legacy.

"You'll forever be my hero, Papa." She choked back more tears. "I did as you asked. I remembered. I remembered what Mother told me." Her sobs took over, and she pressed her palm into the dirt. "Thank you for protecting me. For loving me the way you knew how."

She laid the red rose on the thawing ground. Spring was breaking forth like the new beginning she was entering into.

Prince Owen knelt beside her, clasping her hand. They knelt in silence. In memorial. They basked in the moment until, finally, Owen pressed her hand gently. "Have I told you how beautiful you are to me? On the inside..." His hands caressed her cheek and hair. "... and on the outside?" His eyes fell to Eira's lips. "Thank you for saying yes to being my wife. I feel like the luckiest man alive." His smile took over his eyes while a mist covered them. "I am thankful to have found someone I can share true love with..." His lips fell on Eira's. He leaned his forehead on hers. "...someone I can share passion with."

The taste of their kiss was sweet and salty from her tears. His smell flooded her mind, reminding her of the first time she met him. She knew she loved him from the very beginning.

"Now." He pulled away and zapped all the intensity building, cupping her face in his hands. Emerald eyes sparkled like the bright green grass around them. "Let me take you home and dance with you." He kissed the top of her nose.

"Only you."

THE END

Acknowledgments

A special thank you to my favorite author, Melanie Dickerson, who sprung in me the love for medieval fairytales. This book literally would not have been made without her perseverance as an author to not give up and seek publication for The Healer's Apprentice—and continue to create beautiful stories that display the love of Christ. You are truly my inspiration.

I want to thank Chautona Havig for originally giving me the inspiration I needed to write my first novel. A long time ago, she dared to read the first draft of my novice book via an email I sent her. That book only ended up in the hands of a few people and never really saw the light of day, but that's okay. What made a mark was her kind gesture to take time out for me and say I had something worth writing about. It was the courage I needed to start as an author and it has kept me going ever since.

I particularly want to thank my editors Olivia Smit and Caitlin Miller. Their efforts to go over my painstaking mistakes takes courage. They are what make my book sparkle! Without them I would be lost in the world of purple prose, misconstrued sentences, and grammar misfortunes. Their critique and honesty have been a light to my path. Thank you to Emilie E. Hendyrx or Emily Haney, as well as Nick K for making my book stand out!

Thank you to my family for helping when I needed to focus on my writing. For giving up Saturdays for an entire year while I was working so I could dive into this medieval world. Their sacrifices have not gone unnoticed.

I also want to give a shout out for my BookTube Besties—the OG's of Christian BookTube—you know who you are! Though I have been busy writing this book, you ladies are the glue that holds me together. I love you more than words can say.

Lastly, I want to thank you, my reader, for being a part of the journey. For taking a chance and picking up this book, and for joining me on this beautiful, creative adventure! You make all of this worthwhile!

Author Notes

"FINDING HISTORY IN A FAIRYTALE"

Imputing aspects of the classic fairytale was very important for me to add in my Snow-White retelling. For reference, I used the story, Little Snow White, from Canterbury Classics Copyright 2011 in the book titled, Grimm's Complete Fairy Tales by The Brothers Grimm.

Though I took creative freedoms, I've integrated historical tidbits and nuggets into my story. When I was researching an evil queen for my Snow-White retelling, I stumbled upon Empress Matilda of the 12th century and was so impressed by her history. She seemed to fit my tale like a glove.

I did my best to bring some of her iconic moments and others to life, while maintaining a resemblance of accuracy. For example, King Henry was really nicknamed Le Bel. Empress Matilda really was said to have slapped the King of Scotland across the face during the coronation, she had a beautiful cross made for her, like the one I mentioned, that is still in existence and embedded in a much larger cross, and she secretly escaped the castle undetected that she was held in through snow.

Albeit timelines are not the same as her real records state, and of course, I took liberties with character, castles, land areas, and names, etc. However, I was mesmerized by her story and had to tell just enough of it to bring you intrigue. Perhaps you'll do your own research on the woman who literally changed the world upside down. Her incredible story was filled with failed marriages, family drama, political intrigue, betrayal and royal upheaval, as well as positions of great power and wealth. But what I loved most was there was a redemptive arc in her story that I wanted to dive deeper into and pursue.

She and Stephan of Blois are literally what brought anarchy to that era. Empress Matilda had the weight of the world on her shoulders and fought ruthlessly to maintain her father's wishes. She was known to have repeatedly battled back and forth with Stephan but yet, showed great piety; both parties displaying random kindness toward each other during war. This was very intriguing to me. In the end, she surrendered her life for the works of God and even built churches.

I also wanted to bring in some of the historical elements of the first printed bibles. Illuminated bibles began around this timeframe. They had elaborate drawings made using gold and other precious elements. As an artist myself, I could see the beauty and how they brought forth such stunning pieces of the written word of God. That, I had to honor. Often these men went unnoticed for their creativity and exquisite works of art within the holy written pages. They spent years perfecting them, and I wanted to highlight their contribution to our history as well.

My desire is that you learn a little bit of incredible history while indulging in the nostalgia of classical fairytales full of hope, love, and most of all—faith.

MEDIEVAL WORDS & SLANG WORDS

Mung – crowd or lightly formed body of people

Cosh – small abode

Pray-tell – Used as a phrase, 'tell me please'

Prithee – Maybe or please

Wealas – Wales

Bubble-bow – Pocket in a dress

Whifling – Small, less-than person

Wurp – a sour side eye

Chinkers – Money or Coins

Feather-head – not very bright or a person who is air-headed

Crier and Blutter – A phrase referring to the action a person does when calling out wrong being done

Adam's Ale – water

Killbuck – a person who is rowdy and arrogant

Tric Tac or **Trick Tac** – The game Tic Tac Toe

Fopdoodle – goofy or dumb person who makes mistakes often

Fucus – concoction used for makeup

Pulse - Purse

Gleedy – greedy and obnoxiously proud of it

Eyethurl – evil person

Wallydraigle – someone who wastes your time

Fairhead – beautiful person or lady

Windsucker – a person who takes the fun out of something or kills the energy

Blobtalling – gossiping or gossiper

Welkin – Sky or the heavens

Darg – job or work

Woodness – Silliness or dense in humor

Sanded – tired or exhausted

Vecke – Wench
Bellibone – beautiful face or beautiful woman
Garderobe – Bathroom or toiletry room in the castle
Shab – unkept, unkind person
Bluttering – spilling out words or someone who talks too much
Teenful – a naïve person or naïve behavior

Discussion Questions

1. In what ways did Eira feel unimportant and unloved by her stepmother and by her Papa? Were there any moments you could relate to in your childhood? Did that experience affect your trust in people and relationships?

2. Why do you think Eira chose to run instead of facing her fears? Was there a time when you chose to run from your problems instead of giving them to the Lord or facing them by relying on His strength?

3. Prince Owen struggled to find his miracle. Has there been areas in your life that you have sought God and not received an answer? Did this strengthen your relationship with Him or make you dig deeper into areas where you may be struggling with your faith? Were you able to grow from that?

4. Eira couldn't remember the words of her mother when she was a child. Why do you suspect that is? Have you ever experienced something like this? Is there a distinct memory of a family member that you hold dear?

5. Like the classic story, there were many attempts to take Eira's life, and she fell naively into each one. Do you feel that this is because she is a people-pleaser, why or why not? Do you feel that the scripture verse about the wolf in sheep's clothing applies here? How do you think Eira could have avoided these mistakes?

6. Eira was able to forgive her stepmother and show kindness for her wickedness and evil doings. Do you feel that displayed strength? Or weakness? If you were in her position, would you be able to do the same?

7. Who do you think Queen Amara truly was vengeful or angry at? Eira White? Or her father? Was there ever a time the truth about a loved one was difficult to face? Did you confront it or direct your anger to someone or something else?

8. Prince Owen has his own breakthrough moment where he decides he will fight for someone he loves and face the consequences head on. Have you ever had a breakthrough moment that changed the course of your life—where that single event directed you onto a path that couldn't have happened without that moment occurring?

9. Brother Obadiah was a key player of wisdom for both Eira and Owen. Certain people can come into our lives and speak a sense of peace and clarity over us when we need it most. Have you experienced this before? How did it help direct your actions?

10. In the end, Eira didn't accept a prominent position. Why do you think that was? Do you feel that was a sense of her giving into her thoughts and feelings of weakness, or a sign of strength in her character? Why or why not?

11. Queen Amara had a redemptive story arc. Do you think people can change from their wicked ways? What makes

you determine they can, or cannot? And in what ways do you feel Queen Amara had her biggest changes?

12. In the end, the story states that Queen Amara and Eira were in the process of mending their relationship. They had space between the two and Eira mentions it had not been easy, but hat they were making progress in their relationship. Have you ever had to deal delicately or manage a broken relationship? What boundaries were important to keep while maintaining the relationship to stay safe and build trust?

About the Author

AURORA BELLE resides in Canada amid piled cups of tea, lush leaves, rocky mountains and organic living. This novel won her Runner Up with the Word Guild for their In the Beginning Award. She writes YA, Middle Grade, and Children's 12th century adventure books that breath life into the fairytales you know and love while saturating the pages with God's unchanging hope. At the heart of Aurora's fairytales and message is a passion for fealess living, embracing one's talents despite weakness or failings, and drawing readers closer to Jesus. Most days you can find her sneaking in a quick read beneath forest trees or revelling in research to find true adventures for her heroines to illuminate within pages of her stories.

SIGN UP FOR AURORA'S NEWSLETTER

Keep up to date with Aurora's latest news on book releases and events by signing up for her email list found by visiting Aurora's website.

www.aurorabelle.com

FOLLOW AURORA ON SOCIAL MEDIA!

Facebook Aurora Belle

Instagram @aurora_belle.author

www.ingramcontent.com/pod-product-compliance
Lightning Source LLC
Chambersburg PA
CBHW030516120726
47904CB00005B/1486